Florien Giauque

A Manual for Guardians and Trustees of Minors

insane persons, imbeciles, idiots, drunkards, and for guardians ad litem, resident

and non-resident, affected by the laws of Ohio

Florien Giauque

A Manual for Guardians and Trustees of Minors
insane persons, imbeciles, idiots, drunkards, and for guardians ad litem, resident and non-resident, affected by the laws of Ohio

ISBN/EAN: 9783337367701

Printed in Europe, USA, Canada, Australia, Japan

Cover: Foto ©Andreas Hilbeck / pixelio.de

More available books at **www.hansebooks.com**

A MANUAL

FOR

GUARDIANS AND TRUSTEES

OF

MINORS, INSANE PERSONS, IMBECILES, IDIOTS, DRUNK-
ARDS, AND FOR GUARDIANS AD LITEM, RESI
DENT AND NON-RESIDENT,

AFFECTED BY THE

LAWS OF OHIO.

WITH

Forms, Notes of Decisions, and Practical Suggestions.

BY

FLORIEN GIAUQUE,

Editor of Raff's "Guide to Executors and Administrators," "The Laws of
Elections in Ohio," etc.

CINCINNATI:
ROBERT CLARKE & CO.
1881.

PREFACE.

Law books upon special subjects of importance, if so prepared as to be clear and trustworthy, into which are gathered within a small com pass and convenient form the widely scattered statutory provisions and at least the more important general principles of unenacted law and notes of decisions pertaining to the subject, with suitable references to the authorities relied on, are a great convenience to even the most experienced attorneys and officers of courts having access to the best of libraries, to say nothing of the less favored and less experienced, nor of other persons directly interested who can not have an attorney constantly within reach for consultation.

To prepare such a work on the subject of guardianship in Ohio, with suitable forms, practical suggestions, index, etc., has been the aim of the writer since this volume was begun and announced. For this purpose, it has been necessary to examine, with care, the standard works on Trusts, Trustees, Domestic Relations, and other subjects in which guardianship is considered directly or indirectly, as well as a great many cases decided by the courts of our different states and of England, and to glean, condense, and arrange from these authorities such matter as would likely be most useful, and yet not to make the book a large or expensive one. The time devoted to it being chiefly outside of usual office hours, its progress was not as rapid as was hoped at first and when almost ready for the press, it, with considerable other manuscript, was totally destroyed by fire. Its data had, therefore, to be again all collected as at first, and its writing done a second time. These are the causes of its delay.

The writer is under obligations in various ways relating to this volume, to Justice Stanley Matthews, Hons. Wm. Lawrence, W. M. Bateman, Rufus King, S. J. Thompson, Judge Isaac B. Matson and Deputy Daniel Herider, of the Hamilton county Probate Court, M W Myers, librarian of the Cincinnati Law Library, and others, which are thankfully acknowledged. He should also state, that for the sake of the forms in F. J. Matthews' Guardian's Guide, its copyright was purchased, and that many of these forms, with or without modifications will be found herein.

F. G

Cincinnati, *May,* 1881.

CONTENTS.

CHAPTER 9.

CHAPTER 10.

CHAPTER 11.

CHAPTER 12.

CHAPTER 13.

CHAPTER 14.

CHAPTER 15.

CHAPTER 16.

CHAPTER 17.

CHAPTER 18.

CHAPTER 19.

CHAPTER 20.

CHAPTER 21.

CHAPTER 22.

CHAPTER 23.

CHAPTER 24.

CHAPTER 25.

APPENDIX.

GUARDIANS AND TRUSTEES.

CHAPTER 1.

PRELIMINARY—INCLUDING CERTAIN DEFINITIONS, AND A BRIEF
REVIEW OF ENGLISH, CIVIL LAW. AND OHIO GUARDIANSHIPS.

1. *Who are minors?*—All male persons of the age of twenty-one years and upwards, and all female persons of the age of eighteen years and upwards are, by the laws of Ohio, held and considered to be of full age, to all intents and purposes. any law or custom to the contrary notwithstanding.[1] It therefore follows that all male persons who are not twenty-one years old, and all female persons who are not eighteen years old are not of full age.[2] Such persons are called *minors* in the ordinary language of practical life, and *infants* or *minors* in the technical language of the law, these two words being used as having the same meaning.[3]

---

[1] § 3136.

[2] Previous to the year 1834, a female was not of full age until she was twenty one years old. McClintick *v.* Chamberlain, W. 547.

By the laws of England persons of either sex become of full age when twenty-one years old. 1 Blackstone's Com. 463, Tyler Inf. & Cov. 34. This is the case also in probably most of the United States.

[3] See 3 Redf. on Wills, 438, note 9.

2. *Ward.*—A minor placed by authority of law under the care of a guardian is called a *ward*.

3. *On what day full age attained.*—It appears from the authorities that a male person is of full age the day before the twenty-first anniversary of his birth;[1] and it follows that, in Ohio, a female person is of full age on the day before the eighteenth anniversary of her birth.

4. *Guardians generally.*—A *guardian* is one who legally has the care and management of the person, or estate, or both, of a person who is incompetent to manage his own affairs. Such incompetency may be the result of incapacity imposed by nature or by law. Hence there are guardians of minors, of lunatics, of idiots, of drunkards, of spendthrifts. etc.

5. *Guardians of minors.*- Of these, the most important, because the most common, are the guardians of minors. Concerning them it is well said that " The relation of guardian and ward is nearly allied to that of parent and child. It applies to children during their minority, and may exist during the lives of the parents; but usually takes place on the death of the father, and the guardian is intended to take his place. If an infant have property and no guardian, neither the parent nor any other person can act for him in relation to such property."[2]

6. *Brief view of various English guardianships.*—As our law concerning guardian and ward is chiefly of English origin, it will assist in better understanding certain matters connected

---

[1] Blackstone's Com., page 463; Sharswood's note thereto, same page, (citing State *v.* Clarke, 3 Harring. 557; Hamlin *v.* Stevenson, 4 Dana, 597.)

If he is born on the 16th of February, 1808, he is of age to do any legal act on the morning of the 15th of February, 1829, though he may not have lived twenty-one years by nearly forty-eight hours. The reason assigned is, that in law there is no fraction of a day; and if the birth were on the last second of one day, and the act were on the last second of the preceding day twenty-one years after, then twenty-one years would be complete; and in the law it is the same whether a thing is close upon one moment of the day or on another. Christian's note to same, same page: (citing 1 Sid, 162; 1 Keb. 589; 1 Salk. 44; Raym. 84.)

See also, to same effect, Schouler's Dom. Rel. 518, 519; Tyler on Inf. and Cov. 34; Jarman on Wills, Am: Ed., 30.

[2] 2 Kent's Com. 220; Swan's Treatise, 587. See par. 8, below.

with our statutory provisions, and others not there mentioned, to take a brief view of the different kinds of guardians known to English law.

7. *Guardians by nature.*—The guardian by nature is the father, and in case of his death, the mother, and at her death, the next of kin. It extends only to the person, and not to the estate, and continues till the ward is twenty-one years of age. It extends only to the oldest son, as he is the heir-apparent by the English law, and inherits all his father's estate. Such guardian is subject to the court of chancery, which might, for a just cause, interpose and control his authority.[1]

8. *As to natural guardian in U. S.*—In this country the father is the guardian by nature, not of his oldest son only, but of all his children, and in case of his death, the mother is their natural guardian, during their minority.[2] But such guardianship gives to neither of them any right to manage the estate or otherwise meddle with the property of the child, and extends only to the custody and control of the person of the infant, and to his maintenance, support, and education.[3]

9. On principle, it would seem that the mother becomes the

---

[1] Coke Litt. 88; 2 Kent's Com. 220, 221; Reeve's Dom. Rel. 314, 315; Bouv. Law Dic., Art. "Guardian"; 1 Black. Com. 461, Hargrave's note.

[2] 2 Kent's Com. 220; Reeve's Dom. Rel. 315; Bouv. Law Dic. "Guardian;" Schouler's Dom. Rel. 406; 3 Redfield on Wills, 435; Tyler on Inf. and Cov., § 166, p. 242.

Mr. Francis Hargrave, the learned annotator of Co. Litt., holds that the term natural guardian or guardian by nature, when not applied to an heir-apparent, signifies only that nature points out the parent as the proper guardian where positive law is silent. Stephen's note to 1 Black. Com. 461.

The mother is the natural guardian of her illegitimate child. Reeve's Dom. Rel. 315, note 1; Bouv. Law Dic., "Guardian."

[3] 2 Kent's Com. 220, 22; 3 Red. on Wills, 436; Schoul. Dom. Rel. 333–4, 391, 392; Bouv. Law Dic., "Guardian;" par. 5, this chap.; par. 14, chap. 3. Also, Williams v. Storrs, 6 Johns (N. Y.) Ch. 353; Miles v. Boyden, 3 Pick. (Mass.) 213; Dagley v. Talferry, 1 P. Wms. 285; Ross v. Cobb, 9 Yerg. (Tenn.) 463; Anderson v. Darley, 1 Mott & McC. 369; Miles v. Kaigler, 10 Yerg.(Tenn.) 10; May v. Calder, 2 Mass. 55; Gerrett v. Tallmadge, 1 Johns. (N. Y.) 3; Combs v. Jackson, 2 Wend. (N. Y.) 153; Hyde v. Stone. 7 do.

guardian by nature of the children whose custody is awarded to her because of her husband's personal unfitness.[1]

10. *Guardian by nurture and in chivalry.*—The guardian by nature occupied much the same relations to his (or her) younger children that he did to the heir-apparent, and was called their guardian by nurture.

11. As property has always descended here to all the children, instead of to the eldest son, this species of guardianship has never been in existence here.[2] Nor has that in chivalry, which has long been abolished even in England, and therefore needs no description now.[3]

12. *These two included in guardianship of person.* To what extent these technical guardianships "by nature" and "by nurture" ever existed in this State need not be discussed here. Our guardianship "of the person" includes all the powers of both, as far as they could be in force under our laws and institutions.[4]

13. *Guardian by socage.*—Such a guardian has custody of the infant's lands as well as of his person. It applies only to lands which the infant acquires by descent. The common law gave this guardianship to the next of blood to the child, to whom the inheritance could not *possibly* descend. Such guardianship ceases when the child arrives at the age of fourteen years, if he then chooses another guardian, which he has the right to do; and in that case the guardian in socage must account to the ward for the rents and profits of his estate.[5]

14. The question as to whether this species of guardianship exists in Ohio[6] has been raised in some of our courts, but not de-

---

354; Fonda v. Van Horne, 15 do. 631; Kline v. Beebe, 6 Com. 494; Kendall v. Miller, 9 Cal. 591; McGruder v. Peter, 4 Gill & J. (Md.), 323.

But see Wilson v. Bayer, 1 Har. & S. (Md.) 297; par. 56, Appendix.

The surviving parent is the natural guardian of a minor child. McKinley v. Noble, 37 Tex. 731.

[1] Schouler's Dom. Rel. 406; same, 338, 339, 391.

[2] 2 Kent's Com. 222; Reeve's Dom. Rel., 315; Tyler on Inf. and Cov., §167; Bouv. Law Dic., "Guardian," and American cases there cited.

[3] Reeve's Dom. Rel. 311.

[4] See chapter 5.

[5] 2 Black. Com. 87, 88; 2 Kent's Com. 221–223; Bouv. Law. Dic., "Guardian."

[6] Wirt v. Turner (Lorain Dist. Court, 1858), 1 W. L. M. 94.

cided. In New York, since the adoption of the Revised Statutes, a father may be guardian in socage in that State.[1]

15. *Testamentary guardians.*—This species of guardianship was instituted by a statute[2] passed in the reign of Charles II. It provided that any father, whether of full age or not, might, by deed or by last will, dispose of the custody and tuition of his child, born or unborn, to any person or persons in possession or remainder, other than popish recusants; such custody to last till the child attained the age of twenty-one years, whether he marry or not, or for a less time. It gave the guardian the entire management of the ward's estate, both real and personal. All religious disabilities, and the power of an infant father to appoint, have since been removed.[3] But a mother can not appoint, nor can a putative father, nor a person *in loco parentis.*[4]

16. The statutes of Ohio provide for the appointment of testamentary guardians[5] by *will* but not by *deed.* Though these statutes use the word "appoint," yet, strictly speaking, the parent can, with us, only *nominate* a guardian, whom it is the duty of the court to *appoint*, if, in the opinion of the court, he be a suitable person.

17. *Chancery guardians.*—The chancery courts of England, chiefly since the settlement of the United States by the colonies of that country, have assumed and now exercise the right of supervision, control and removal of all guardians, and of appointing them when such appointment is not otherwise provided for; and in these respects, and in providing suitable maintenance for infants, in awarding custody of their person, and in superintending the management and disposition of their estates, these courts wield large powers for the benefit of the young and helpless, and adapt themselves far more readily to the various grades of society, the different varieties of property, and the needs of the minors themselves, than can be done by all other kinds of guardianships combined. Chancery guardians are, in general,

---

[1] Fonda *v.* Van Horne, 15 Wend. (N. Y.), 631.

[2] 12 Car. II., c. 24.

[3] 31 Geo. III., c. 32; 1 Vic., c. 26.

[4] 2 Kent's Com. 224; Reeve's Dom. Rel., 328; Bouv. Law Dic., "Guardian;" Schouler's Dom. Rel. 394; and the cases there cited.

[5] See par. 25, page 26.

only appointed where there is property, as such a step can scarcely be necessary otherwise; but the court compels them to give security to invest under its direction, and to keep regular accounts.[1]

18. *Guardianship under the civil law.*—The laws of guardianship, as is true of other laws both of England and the United States, are not without the strong impress of the laws of the Roman Empire, the fountain of the civil law as in force in France, Spain and other nations of Europe, through which channels it has come to be in force in our French and Mexican acquisitions of Louisiana, Texas, etc. By that law a *tutor* had charge of the maintenance and education of the minor, while a *curator* had the care of his fortune.[2]

19. We readily recognize the similarity between these and our own *guardian of the person* and *guardian of the person and estate*, though the likeness is not complete.

---

[1] Schouler's Dom. Rel. 396, 397; 2 Kent's Com. 163 and notes; Reeve's Dom. Rel. 317.

The jurisdiction of a court of chancery extends to the care of the person of the infant so far as is necessary for his protection and education, and to the care of his property, for its management and preservation and proper application for his maintenance. It is upon the former ground that the court interferes with the ordinary rights of parents as guardians by nature or by nurture; for whenever a father is guilty of gross ill-treatment of or cruelty to his children, or is in constant habits of drunkenness or blasphemy, or low and gross debauchery, or professes atheistical or irreligious principles, or his domestic associations are such as tend to the corruption and contamination of his children, the court will interfere and deprive him of the custody of the infants, appointing at the same time a suitable person to act as guardian and superintend their education. And this interference may be obtained on the petition of the infant himself, or of any of his friends or relatives: nay, a mere stranger may at any time set the machinery of the courts in motion. 1 Black. Com. 162, part of Kerr's note.

[2] 1 Black. Com. 460.

CHAPTER 2.

POWERS AND DUTIES OF PROBATE COURTS, AS AFFECTING GUARD-IANSHIP.

PAR.

1. Their jurisdiction generally.
2-5. Exclusive jurisdiction.
6. Concurrent jurisdiction.
7. Oaths to accounts, petitions, etc.
8-14. What books are kept.
15. Probate judge must make all entries, records, etc., omitted by his predecessor.
16. How paid.
17. No probate judge or his clerk can prepare any papers, etc., for guardian.

PAR.

18. Guardianship, etc., when the probate judge is interested, etc.
19. Questions arising in probate court—how determined.
20. Depositions may be used in probate court trials.
21. Sheriffs, constables, etc., must serve in probate court.
22. Fees of witnesses, officers, etc., in such court.
23-24. General duties of probate judges.

1. *Their jurisdiction generally.* The constitution of this state[1] provides that the probate court shall have jurisdiction in probate and testamentary matters, the appointment of guardians, the settlement of their accounts, the sale of land by guardians, and such other jurisdiction, in any county or counties, as may be provided by law.[2]

---

[1] Art. iv, § 8.

[2] The probate courts of this state are, in the fullest sense, courts of record; they belong to the class whose records import absolute verity, that are competent to decide on their own jurisdiction, and to exercise it to final judgment, without setting forth the facts and evidence on which it is rendered Shroyer v. Richmond, 16 O. S. 455.

The act of January 9, 1871 (68 v. 6), conferring jurisdiction upon courts of common pleas to appoint guardians of the property of persons incapable of taking care of and preserving their property, by reason of intemperance and habitual drunkenness, is not in conflict with the provisions of this section defining the jurisdiction of probate courts. Hagany v. Cohnen, 29 O. S. 82.

This jurisdiction may be extended to all the counties in the state by a general enactment. "The words, 'in any county or counties,' were prob-

2. *Exclusive jurisdiction.* The statutes provide that the probate court has exclusive jurisdiction in certain matters, among which are the following:

3. To appoint and remove guardians,[1] to direct and control their conduct, and to settle their accounts;

---

ably used rather as enabling than restrictive language, and were designed to permit the general assembly—notwithstanding the provisions of the twenty-sixth section of the second article, requiring all laws of a general nature to have uniform operation throughout the state—in its discretion, to confer upon the probate court more extended powers in some counties than in others. Upon the opposite construction, a power to confer the jurisdiction in one county by a local enactment, is a power to confer it in all the counties in the same manner; which brings us to the absurd conclusion that the legislature is competent to do by ninety laws what it is incompetent to do by one." Giesy v. C., W. & Z. R. R. Co., 4 O. S. 308–320—Ranney, J.

" A jurisdiction may be given to the probate court in one county which is not conferred in another; but this express exception relates only to the extent of the jurisdiction of the probate court. The whole object of the section is to define the limits of its jurisdiction; it treats of nothing else, and does not once name the courts of common pleas. Nor does it follow as a necessary conclusion that because the jurisdiction of the probate court may be more extensive in one county than in another, the jurisdiction of the courts of common pleas must also differ in extent. The latter may be uniform and the former not. The probate court may, in some counties, possess a jurisdiction concurrent with the common pleas, which is denied to it in others." Kelley v. State, 6 O. S. 269–273—Scott, J.; and see Art. 2, § 26, note 1.

[1] *Children of divorced parents, appointment of guardians for, powers of probate and higher courts as to.* From an examination of the case of Hoffman v. Hoffman,[2] it appears that in 1859 the court of common pleas of Lucas county granted to Mary Hoffman a divorce from her husband, John Hoffman, and also the "custody, care and control" of certain minor children of the parties. In 1861, John Hoffman filed his petition in the probate court of said county, and procured to be issued thereon a writ of *habeas corpus* for said minors, by the probate judge, alleging in said petition that said Mary has not the means to support the children, and that she is a person of temper and habits unsuitable to have the care and nurture of them; that she is profane and vulgar, and keeps, and allows the children to keep immoral company and associations; that, on the other hand, he has the means to support the children, and is, in all respects, a suitable and proper person to have their care and custody. Upon the hearing of the case, he also filed a motion that he be appointed "guardian of

---

(2) 15 O. S. 427.

4. To make inquests respecting lunatics, insane persons, idi-

---

the said children, for the reasons stated in the petition for *habeas corpus* on file."

In opposition to the claims of the father, the mother set up the decree of the court of common pleas, claiming, among other things, "that said judgment and decree were final, and forever binding upon the parties thereto, and that in and by it were determined and settled the several matters and things sought to be investigated by the said John Hoffman in this proceeding, and that the same facts which did exist at the time of rendering said judgment and decree, and upon and in accordance with which the same were rendered and given by said court, still exist, and no new fact or facts have since transpired or arisen which authorize, or give any right or power to any one whomsoever, in any way to interfere with or call in question any of the rights or powers given to this respondent by said judgment or decree;" and moved the probate court to "dismiss and discharge the proceedings, for reason that the judgment and decree set up . . . is final and conclusive, and can not be impeached or inquired into in this case."

The probate court proceeded to judgment, and found "from testimony relating solely to facts transpiring since the decree of divorce . . . set forth (no other testimony having been offered by the parties, nor admitted by the court), that the respondent, Mary Hoffman, is an unsuitable person to have the care, custody and tuition of said children now before the court by the writ of *habeas corpus*, and that the relator, John Hoffman, is a suitable person to have the care, custody and tuition of said children," and that the interest and welfare of the children required that the said John Hoffman should have the custody of them, and that therefore the children are unlawfully detained by the mother. Therefore the probate court appointed said John guardian of the children, and ordered the sheriff to deliver them into his custody, there to remain.

The case was taken up to the district court of Lucas county, which affirmed the judgment and order of the probate court. It was then taken to the supreme court, which decided, in 1864, that where a court of common pleas, on rendering a decree of divorce, further decree the "custody, care and control" of the minor children of the marriage to one of the parties, a probate court, while such decree remains in force, can not, as between the parties to the decree, legally interfere with the custody so decreed, either by *habeas corpus* or letters of guardianship; and that the jurisdiction of the court of common pleas over the subject of the custody of children in divorce cases is a continuing jurisdiction; and that such common pleas court may, on proper application, be invoked to modify orders originally made in respect to the custody of children, whenever the character and circumstances of the case or of the parties require it.

There seems to be nothing in this case that could be construed to prevent

ots, and deaf and dumb persons, subject by law to guardianship;[1]

5. The jurisdiction acquired by any probate court over a matter or proceeding, is exclusive of that of any other probate court, except where otherwise provided by law.[2]

6. *Concurrent jurisdiction.* The probate court has concurrent jurisdiction in the sale of lands on petition of executors, administrators and guardians, and the assignment of dower in such cases of sale.[3]

7. *Oaths to accounts, petitions, etc.* Probate judges may administer oaths in all cases where oaths are authorized by law;[4] and their deputy clerks are authorized to administer oaths in all cases in which it is necessary in the discharge of his duties as such deputy clerk.[5]

8. *What books are kept.* The probate court must keep, among others, the following books:[6]

9. A guardians' docket, showing the name of each ward (and if an infant, his age, and the name of his father), the amount of bond and names of sureties therein, containing a minute of the time of filing every paper, and brief note of every order or proceeding relating to the estate, with reference to the journal or record in which the order or proceeding is found.[6]

10. A civil docket, in which must be noted the names of parties to all actions and proceedings: it must also contain a minute of the time of the commencement of such actions and proceedings, and filing the papers relating thereto, and also a brief note of all orders made in such action, proceeding, or matter, and the time of entering the same.[6]

11. A journal, in which must be kept minutes of all official business transacted in the probate court or by the judge, in all civil actions and proceedings.[6]

12. A final record, which must contain a complete record in each cause or matter of all petitions, answers, demurrers, motions, returns, reports, verdicts, awards, orders, and judgments; which record must be made up and completed within ninety days after the final order or judgment has been made in any of said matters;

---

the probate court from appointing a guardian *of the estate only* of such children, as this would not interfere with their custody.

[1] §524.   [2] §527.   [3] §525.   [4] §526.   [5] §533.   [6] §528.

and he must also, within thirty days after the return of the same, record all inventories, sale bills, and allowances to widows, in a book provided for that purpose.[1]

13. A record of accounts, which must contain an entry of the appointment of executors, administrators, and guardians, and all partial and final accounts of the same, and the orders and proceedings of the courts thereon, within sixty days after the filing and approval thereof.[1]

14. A record of bonds, in which must be recorded all bonds of executors, administrators, guardians, trustees, and assignees which have been taken and approved by him.[1]

15. *Probate judge must make all entries, records, etc.. omitted by his predecessor.* When a probate judge, whether elected or appointed, enters upon the discharge of his duties, he must make all proper and necessary entries, indexes, and records of the business, or any portion thereof, transacted in the court, during the continuance in office of any former judge thereof, which had not been made, as required by law, by the probate judge whose duty it was to make such entries or records; and when so made, they will have the same validity. force, and effect, as though they had been made at the proper time, as prescribed by law, and by the officer whose duty it was to make them ; and such probate judge must sign all entries and records made by him, as aforesaid, as though such entries, proceedings, and records had been commenced, prosecuted, determined. and made before him.[2]

16. *How paid.* The county treasurer, and not the guardian, must pay for the services mentioned in the preceding paragraph, if they have already been once paid for.[3]

17. *No probate judge or his clerk can prepare any papers, etc.. for guardian.* No judge of a probate court, or any deputy clerk employed by him, or who is engaged in the business of such court as clerk thereof, is permitted, during the term of his office, or employment, to practice law, or to be associated with another as partner in the practice of law, in any of the courts or other tribunals of this state ; neither can such judge or clerk prepare any petition or answer, or make out any account which any ex-

---

[1] § 528.   [2] § 530.   [3] § 532.

ecutor, administrator, guardian, or other person is required to present for the settlement of the estate committed to his care and management; nor can such judge or deputy clerk make a record of any paper, receipt, or voucher, produced to verify any charge or credit in the account, filed or presented for settlement as aforesaid, unless the recording thereof is requested in writing by the party making such settlement; but nothing contained in this paragraph will be so construed as to prevent any probate judge or deputy clerk, aforesaid, from finishing any business by him commenced before his election or appointment, not connected with his official business.[1]

18. *Guardianship, etc., when the probate judge is interested, etc.* Letters of guardianship can not be issued to any person after his election to the office of probate judge and before the expiration of his term of office; and if a probate judge is interested, as heir, legatee, devisee, or in any other manner in any estate which would otherwise be settled in the probate court of the county where he resides, such estate, and all accounts of guardians in which the probate judge is interested, must be settled by the court of common pleas of such county; and in all such matters and cases in which the probate judge is interested, the original papers must be by him forthwith certified to the court of common pleas; and in all other matters and proceedings, pending in any probate court, which would properly be disposed of or decided therein, but in which the probate judge thereof is interested in any manner whatever, as attorney or otherwise, or in which he is required to be a witness to a will, such probate judge must, upon the motion of a party interested in such proceeding, or upon his own motion, certify the matters and proceedings to the court of common pleas, and he must forthwith file with the clerk of the court of common pleas, all original papers connected with the proceedings, and the same must be proceeded in and heard and determined by the court of common pleas, at chambers, by any judge thereof, or in open court, in the same manner as though that court had original jurisdiction of the subject matter thereof, and upon the final decision of the questions involved in such proceedings, or on the final settlement of

---

[1] §531, 77 O. S. 183.

the estate in which the judge is interested as guardian, by the court of common pleas, or whenever the interest of the probate judge therein ceases, the clerk must deliver all the original papers back to the probate court, from which they came; and the clerk must, also, make out an authenticated transcript of the orders, judgments, and proceedings of the court therein, and must file the same in the probate court, from which the papers came, and the judge thereof must record the same in the ordinary records of similar business.[1]

19. *Questions arising in probate court; how determined.* In proceedings in probate courts, all questions, except those arising in criminal actions and proceedings, unless otherwise provided by law, must be determined by the probate judge, unless, in his discretion, he shall order the same to be tried by a jury, or referred, as provided for references in the court of common pleas.[2]

20. *Depositions may be used in probate court trials.* Depositions taken according to the provisions of law for taking depositions to be used on the trial of civil causes, may be taken and used on the trial of any question before the probate court, where such testimony may be proper.[3]

21. *Sheriffs, constables, etc., must serve in probate court.* Sheriffs, deputy sheriffs, coroners, and constables must, when required by the probate judge, attend his court, and must serve and return all processes directed to them by the judge.[4]

22. *Fees of witnesses, officers, etc., in such court.* The fees of witnesses, jurors, sheriffs, coroners, and constables, for all services rendered in the probate court, or by order of the probate judge, are the same as is provided by law, for like services in the court of common pleas.[5]

23. *General duties of probate judge.* It is one of the peculiar provinces of the probate judge to watch over the persons and estates of minors. The minor, in law and in fact, is wholly incapable of transacting his own business, or of rearing and educating himself; his experience is nothing, and his judgment immature and unreliable; therefore, a guardian is appointed for

---

[1] ₹ 535.

[2] ₹ 6400. For law governing such references, see ₹₹ 5210–5218.

[3] ₹ 6404. [4] ₹ 540. [5] ₹ 6405.

him. But experience has proved that men, either from inherent dishonesty, doubtful notions of right and wrong, or from incapacity or immoral conduct, are not always to be trusted with the sole management of another's business. Therefore, in this State, the duty of protecting and vigilantly guarding the interests of minors, and of scrutinizing the doings, and enforcing the duties of the guardian, with a view to compelling, if necessary, the faithful discharge of the trust reposed in him, with power to call him to account, and to remove him if he be faithless to that trust or incompetent to discharge it, has been specially confided to the probate court.

24. It is, therefore, clearly the duty of that court to keep a close eye upon all the guardians of its appointment, and to call them to account whenever any wavering from the strict line of their fiduciary duties is perceived; and this, too, without waiting for a formal complaint being made by a third person.

CHAPTER 3.

APPOINTMENT OF GUARDIANS.

1. *Probate court appoints.*—It is the imperative duty of the probate court in each county to appoint, when necessary, guardians of minors resident in such county.[1]

---

[1] § 3136. The courts of common pleas formerly exercised this jurisdiction (S. & C., 1212, § 2), but since July 1, 1853, the probate court has been " vested with full and exclusive jurisdiction in this matter, and that jurisdiction

RESIDENCE.

2. *Why minor's residence must be correctly determined.*—As the only court empowered to appoint a guardian for a minor, except as specified in the next paragraph, is the probate court of the county in which the minor has his actual or constructive residence at the time of such appointment, and as the attempted exercise of such power by any other court, and all the acts of any guardian elsewhere appointed would be null and void,[1] the rules for determining such residence are therefore of great importance.

3. *As to infant non-resident land-owner.*—If, however, the minor's residence is out of this state, and he owns lands in this state, the court of the county where such lands, or where any portion of them, are situate, may appoint a guardian of the estate of such minor. If such foreign minor own lands in more than one county in this state, the court of the county where any part of such lands lies, which first made the appointment, would obtain the jurisdiction in preference to all others.[2]

4. *How minor's residence determined.*—Generally, the minor's

---

attaches whenever application is duly made for its exercise." Shroyer *v.* Richmond, 16 O. S. 455.

Proceedings for the appointment of a guardian are proceedings *in rem*, not *inter partes* or adversary in their character. The order of appointment, made in the exercise of jurisdiction, binds the world. The actual presence of the ward is not necessary, unless by reason of his right to choose a guardian, or for other cause, the statute so require. *Ib.*

The question as to the jurisdiction of the court making the appointment of a guardian is open to inquiry. But when the record alleges the facts conferring jurisdiction, quære, 1843. Maxsom *v.* Sawyer, 12 O. 195.

See also note 1, next page.

A guardian appointed by the probate court has no power to act or control the property of his ward, until he has given bond with surety approved by the court. Letters of guardianship issued to him before he has given bond confer no power and have no effect whatever. State *v.* Sloane, 20 O. 327.

The guardian derives his power from the appointment and giving bond, and letters of guardianship need not, in fact, issue. Maxsom *v.* Sawyer, 12 O. 195.

[1] Maxsom *v.* Sawyer, 12 O. 195. (See pars. 1, 11–14, this chapter), Schouler's Dom. Rel. 412, 413, Dorman *v.* Ogbourne, 16 Ala. 759.

[2] § 6290.

residence is that of his his father, if both parents are living, or of the surviving parent, if either of them dies, and it will continue so during minority, in spite of the minor's temporary absence at school or elsewhere. His residence may be changed by his father during the latter's life, and after that by his surviving mother, at least till her re-marriage, and no doubt afterward by the step-father, if he takes the minor into his family as a member thereof. The guardian of the person, or of the person and estate, can also change his ward's residence. But all such changes must be made in good faith, and not to change the nature of the inheritance. The minor can not of himself change his domicile.[1]

----

[1] See next ten paragraphs of text; also, Schouler's Dom. Rel. 312, 412, 452; 2 Kent's Com. 226, 227, especially notes (d) and (b) respectively; Story Conf. Laws, §§ 45, 46, and cases cited by these writers. Also, denying guardian's right, Daniel r. Hill, 52 Ala. (1875), 430.

The place where its parents lived and died, and where its property remains, is presumed to be the proper place for the court to make the appointment of a minor's guardian. Doe r. Litherberry, 4 McLean, 412 (U. S. Circuit Court, 7th Circuit.)

Parol proof, after a lapse of twenty-three years, not admissible to show that the minors were residents of Clermont county [Ohio], and not of Hamilton. *Ib.*

Temporary absence from the county does not affect the jurisdiction of the court in the appointment of a guardian. *Ib.*

The domicil of the infant is always presumed to be that of its mother. *Ib.*

The last preceding paragraph appears to be in conflict with the authorities cited above; but an examination of the case shows that it is not, as the father of the minors, in that case, was dead, and they were in the custody of their step-mother. The following is the language of the judge, upon which the foregoing is based: "No one will contend that the minors must, in fact, be within the county where the appointment was made. They may have been absent on a visit; their mother was not living, and they were left in charge of their step-mother. Her home would be their domicil, and by the law, she was entitled to occupy the mansion house one year from the death of her husband. What is to fix the domicil of infants? The home of these infants was in Hamilton county. Their property was there, and it was there only that a guardian could be properly appointed. If they had not, at the time, an actual residence in Hamilton county, they had constructively. It was the place of their birth, where their father and mother had lived and died, and where all their property was to be found. They had left the county, at most, only a few months before this appointment was made. There is no suggestion of fraud or unfairness in the appointment.

"If it were proper now, after the lapse of twenty-three years, to inquire into these facts, how are we to ascertain that the court had not evidence

5. *Statutory rules for determining residence.*—The statutory rules for determining the residence of a person offering to vote in this state may, in so far as they are applicable, assist in determining the residence of the minor's parents. These rules are as follows: *First.* That place shall be considered the residence of a person in which his habitation is fixed, and to which, whenever he is absent, he has the intention of returning. *Second.* A person shall not be considered to have lost his residence who leaves his home, and goes into another state, or county of this state, for temporary purposes merely, with the intention of returning. *Third.* A person shall not be considered to have gained a residence in any county of this state, into which he comes for temporary purposes merely, without the intention of making such county his home. *Fourth.* The place where the family of a married man resides shall be considered and held to be his place of residence, except where the husband and wife have separated and live apart, then the place where they resided at the time of the separation shall be considered and held to be his place of residence, unless he afterward, and during the time of such separation, remove from such place, in which case the county, township, city, or village in which he resides the length of time required by the provisions of this section to entitle a person to vote, shall be considered and held to be his place of residence. *Fifth.* If a person remove to another state, with an intention to make it his permanent residence, he shall be considered to have lost his residence in this state. *Sixth.* If a person remove to another state, with an intention of remaining there an indefinite time, and as a place of present residence, he shall be considered to

before it, that the absence of the minors from the county was only temporary, and did not affect their domicil? If this question were open, we would incline to say that the residence of the infants with their grandparents, for a few months only, in Clermont county, is not evidence of a change of domicil, under the circumstances, so as to affect the jurisdiction of the court."

A father, residing in Morgan county, dies there, leaving minor children; soon afterward, the mother dies, leaving the minors in the same county. The grandfather, residing in Jasper county, took the minors home, to Jasper county, to reside with him. *Held*, that the ordinary of Jasper county, and he only, had jurisdiction to appoint a guardian over the minors. Darden v. Wyatt, 15 Ga. 414.

The rule seems to be that the residence of an illegitimate child is that of its mother. Schouler's Dom. Rel. 384.

have lost his residence in this state, notwithstanding he may entertain an intention to return at some future period. *Seventh.* The mere intention to acquire a new residence, without the fact of removal, shall avail nothing; neither shall the fact of removal without the intention. *Eighth.* If a person go into another state, and while there exercise the right of a citizen by voting, he shall be considered to have lost his residence in this state.[1]

6. *When courts have awarded custody of minors.*—When a court of competent jurisdiction has awarded the custody of children to either parent, as in the case of divorced parents, for instance, the residence of such children, without doubt, follows that of the parent or other person to whose custody they are entrusted.[2]

7. *Actual place of residence of parent custodian determines minor's residence.*—In the case of Maxsom *v.* Sawyer, already referred to in the notes, a difficult question of constructive residence was passed upon by the supreme court of this state. Although the appointment of guardians was then vested in the court of common pleas, instead of in the probate court, the application of the principles is the same.

8. In this case, the matter in controversy was the title to a tract of land derived through a guardian's sale, and the validity of the title hinged very largely upon the residence of one Maxsom, a minor, designated throughout the case as "plaintiff's lessor."

9. The essential facts, as far as they affect the matter, are these: The father of plaintiff's lessor died in Geauga county, Ohio, his place of legal settlement, when the plaintiff's lessor was about three years old. His widow, mother of plaintiff's lessor, soon after intermarried with one Seely, also living in Geauga county, and a few months afterwards left him, taking plaintiff's lessor with her. A short time after this, she entered into a written agreement with one Patterson, living in Pennsylvania, that plaintiff's lessor should live with said Patterson, in Pennsylvania, till he should be fourteen years old, which he did do, returning to Ohio but once, and then for one day only, in all that time. After the date of this contract, and about three years after the death of said father, she, undivorced from Seely,

---

[1] § 2946.
[2] See note 1, page 8.

who lived many years after all these events, intermarried with one Niles, in Ashtabula county, Ohio, with whom she resided in said Ashtabula county till after the court of said county, some four years after her last marriage, had appointed said Niles guardian of plaintiff's lessor.   Niles, as said guardian, began proceedings in last named county for sale of lands of plaintiff's lessor, situate in Geauga county, whereby said lands were sold, Sawyer being purchaser.   A report of proceedings was returned to said court, was examined and confirmed, and deed duly executed.

10. The plaintiff, as lessee of this son, brought suit to obtain possession of these Geauga county lands, which suit the lower court sustained, but the supreme court reversed the judgment of the lower court.

11. WOOD, J., in deciding the case, used the following language: ". . . It is also said that Niles was not, in fact, guardian, because the plaintiff's lessor was not, at the time of the appointment, a minor, within the county of Ashtabula; and that the court of common pleas had, therefore, no jurisdiction to make the appointment. This is, perhaps, the most difficult question, and the most important in the case: and if the fact be as supposed, the proceedings in the court of common pleas, and of the guardian under them, are a nullity, and the defendant, consequently, has no title to the land in question. Every court, that its proceedings may be of any validity, must have jurisdiction over the subject-matter; and to have jurisdiction over the subject-matter, in this case, the court of common pleas must also have acquired jurisdiction over the person of the minor for whom the guardian was appointed, at the time the appointment was made, by his being within the county of Ashtabula. And if the plaintiff's lessor was not so within the county, the court had no jurisdiction; and the fact may be shown, and the proceedings impeached in this collateral way.[1]

12. "The statute enacts that the court of common pleas shall have power, whenever they consider it necessary, to appoint a

---

[1] Citing here, Ludlow's Heirs v. McBride, 3 O. 240; Holyoke v. Haskins, 5 Pick. 19; Borden v. Fitch, 15 Johns. 121, 123; Smith v. Rice. 11 Mass. 507; Perry v. Brainard, 11 O. 442; Hall v. Williams, 6 Pick. 232; Latham v. Edgarton, 9 Cowen, 227; Snyder v. Snyder, 6 Binney, 483.

guardian or guardians to all minors within their county, etc.[1] It is therefore essential, at the time of the appointment, that the minor should be within the county, to confer jurisdiction. If the record found the fact, it could not be disproved in a collateral proceeding; but as it does not, it is open to inquiry.

13. "Was the minor, then, in the county at the time of the appointment?

14. "We suppose it to be the law that the legal settlement draws to it the legal settlement of the wife. Peter Seely had his place of legal settlement in Mentor, in Geauga county, in 1830, when his wife, the mother, taking with her the plaintiff's lessor, left him, and went to the county of Ashtabula. She could acquire no legal settlement there, neither by her marriage with her adulterer, nor by her actual residence, because Peter Seely, her lawful husband, is still living in Mentor, and his place of legal settlement is consequently her's. She did, however, actually reside in Ashtabula county for several years, and when this appointment of guardian was made. Did not her actual residence there draw to it the constructive residence of the plaintiff's lessor? We are of the opinion that it did. It is true she had, by her covenant, bound him to Patterson, where his actual residence was. That covenant, however, was of no validity. It was the covenant of a *feme corert*, not sanctioned by the husband, and in which he had not joined. The father is the natural guardian of his minor children. On his death, the mother is, by nature, guardian of those of tender years, and entitled to their custody and control. If she marry, unless the children reside at home, the step-father, as distinct from the mother, has no authority over them. It seems, then, to us, to follow that, as her covenant with Patterson was of no obligation, the mother of the plaintiff's lessor, he being of tender years, had the right, at any moment, to call him to her. Her actual, was his constructive, residence, and he was, therefore, when the guardian was appointed, constructively, with his mother, in the county of Ashtabula. It will hardly be contended that an actual residence is necessary to give the court jurisdiction of the appointment. Such appointment would scarcely be questioned,

---

[1] Swan's Statutes, 430, § 1.

when the actual residence of the minor was in the county, but at the moment of the appointment, he was over the county line for a temporary purpose merely.   He would be considered as constructively within the county, and the appointment would be valid."

15. *Place of actual residence and legal settlement may be different.* It will be observed that, according to the foregoing opinion, the place of *legal settlement* and the place of *actual residence* are not necessarily the same, and that in such case, the court of the place of *actual residence of the parent entitled to the child's custody* is the one empowered to appoint the guardian.

16. *Residence of guardian.*   As a guardian may be removed from his trust if he becomes the citizen of another county,[1] it is evident that he must generally be a resident of the county of the court appointing him.   But guardians appointed by will are not subject to this restriction, as appears from paragraph 26 of this chapter.   It would of course follow that he must be a resident of the state, even in the absence of the provisions of law found in paragraph 12 of chapter 4.

KINDS OF GUARDIANS; HOW CHOSEN, AND FOR HOW LONG, ETC.

17. *Guardian of the estate only.*   A guardian may be appointed to take charge of the estate only of a minor.[2]

18. *Guardian of the person only.*—If a minor has neither father nor mother, or if his father and mother are both unsuitable persons to have the custody and tuition of such minor,[3] or if, from any other cause, in the opinion of the court, the interests of such minor will be promoted thereby, the court may, either at the time of the appointment of a guardian of the estate only, or afterwards, also appoint a guardian to have the custody and provide for the maintenance and education of such minor.[4]

---

[1] §6272. See paragraph 17, chapter 1.

[2] §6255.

[3] When a father, by neglect or abuse, shows himself devoid of paternal affection, a court of chancery may remove his children from his control, and place them in the custody of a proper person to act as guardian, who may be a stranger.   Cowls *v.* Cowls, 8 Ills. 435.

[4] §6255. In the appointment of a guardian, the interests of the minor are the first and most important consideration.   Badenhoof *v.* Johnson, 11

19. *Guardian of the person and estate.*—If the powers of the person appointed guardian be not limited by the order of appointment, the person so appointed will be guardian of both the person and estate of the ward; and the court must in every instance appoint a guardian of both the person and estate of the ward, unless the interests of the minor will, in the opinion of the court, be promoted by the appointment of separate guardians, as already prescribed.[1]

Nev. 87; Succession of Fuqua, 27 La. Ann. 271; Foster *v.* Mott, 3 Brad. (N. Y.) 409; Bennett *v.* Byrne, 2 Barb. (N. Y.) 216; Compton *v.* Compton, 2 Gill, (Md.) 241; Holley *v.* Chamberlain, 1 Redf. (N. Y.) 333.

But not merely his temporary welfare, but the state of the minor's affections, attachments, his training, education, and morals, ought to be taken into consideration. Foster *v.* Mott, and Bennett *v.* Byrne, above.

If children are already in a good home, this is a reason for not disturbing them. 1 McCart. (N. J.), 540.

The declared wishes of a deceased parent are entitled to much weight in the selection of a guardian of its child, and the wish of a dying parent should have a preponderating influence in the selection, other things being equal. Underhill *v.* Dennis, 9 Paige, (N. Y.) 202; Bennett *v.* Byrne, above; Cozine *v.* Horn, 1 Brad. (N. Y.) 143.

But where children had been left many years with their grandparents by their father, who was a widower and sea-faring man, and had, on his death bed, designated an uncle of minors as their guardian, his wishes were disregarded. Foster *v.* Mott, above.

Other things being equal, the mother of a female child, whose father is dead, is the most proper person to be intrusted with her nurture, care, and custody, and should therefore be appointed her guardian. Tyler on Inf. and Cov. § 173; People *v.* Wilcox, 22 Barb. (N. Y.) 178.

But if the mother's manner of life would be likely to exercise an unfavorable influence, she will not be appointed, nor will her wishes have much weight. Albert *v.* Perry; 1 McCart. (N. J.) 540.

Other things being equal, some near relative should be appointed in preference to a stranger. Foster *v.* Mott, above; Moorehouse *v.* Cooke, Hop. (N. Y.) 226.

See Schouler's Dom. Rel. 116–18; Tyler on Inf. and Cov., § 173.

The foregoing notes apply with especial force rather to the appointment of a guardian of the person, or of the person and estate, than of the estate only.—*Ed.*

[1] § 6255.

It is requisite that the person appointed be *sui juris*—"of his own right"—and capable of performing the appointment. He must not have

20. *Guardian chosen by minor; by court.*—Any male infant over the age of fourteen years, or a female infant over the age of twelve years,[1] has the right to select a guardian, who, if a suitable person, must be appointed; but if such minor fails to select a suitable person, an appointment may be made without reference to the wishes of such minor.[2]

21. *Minor can not choose separate guardian, unless.*—A minor has not, in any instance, the right to select one person to be the guardian of his or her estate only, and another person to be guardian of his or her person only, unless the court having the power of appointment is of opinion that the interests of such minor will be promoted by the choice and appointment of such separate guardians, instead of one guardian, both of the pers⋅n and estate.[3]

22. *How long powers of guardian continue.*—When a guardian has been appointed for any minor before he or she has attained the age for making a selection, as fixed in the two last preceding paragraphs, the powers of such guardian will continue until the ward shall arrive at the age of majority,[4] unless such guar-

---

any interest adverse to the interest of his ward, and if he is known to have any such, he will not be appointed. A person under his full age, or a minor, can not, of course, be appointed to take care of another minor: and one under the power of another, although possessing understanding as a married woman, is not qualified for the trust. 1 Bouv. Institute, 42; Tyler on Inf. and Cov. § 173.

[1] The statute coincides with the common law in this respect. "At common law, an infant can elect a guardian at fourteen years of age, if a male; if a female, at the age of twelve years." Reeves Dom. Rel. * p. 240. (Citing Fonbl. 74; Ch. Rep. 55; 1 Eq. Ca. Abr. 282; 1 T. Rep. 618; 2 Vent. 203; 1 Stra. 690.)

[2] § 6257. But the minor can not select, if a guardian has been selected by valid will. See par. 26. below. As to notice to guardian, see p. 58.

[3] § 6257.

[4] Before the enactment of the saving provision, it was held that the guardianship of a minor expired by the limitation of the law, when the ward arrived at the age designated in paragraph 20. It was further held that a guardian appointed for such ward could not, after the ward had reached the age where the statutory right to select a guardian applied, sell the lands of the ward on a petition filed after such time, and that a sale made on an order of the court, under such petition, was void. Perry v. Brainard, 11 O. 442.

Under the old law, it was also held that a guardian for a female under

dian be sooner removed for good cause, or such ward selects another suitable guardian.[1]

23. *Superseded guardian's settlement.*—After such selection is made and approved by the court, and the person so selected is duly appointed and qualified, the powers of the guardian previously appointed cease, and thereupon the final account of such guardian must be filed and settled in the proper court.[1]

24. *If minor fails to select, and when court first appoints, what to do.*—If the minor, after arriving at the proper age for selecting, is satisfied with the guardian already acting, or fails to select another, no action need be taken by the court, as such guardian continues in office till the ward's majority. But the court should, in no case, except in that of a testamentary guardian, appoint a guardian for a minor, of proper age to select for himself, until such minor has had an opportunity to make such selection ; and therefore, before such appointment is made, if the minor does not come himself voluntarily before the court to make the selection, the court should send him a written notice, that unless he appear and make such selection within a reasonable time, or on a day named, the court will appoint a guardian for him ; for until he has had a day in court, he can not be said to have failed to make the selection.[2]

25. *Testamentary guardians—how appointed.*—Any father, or in case the father be dead or have gone to parts unknown, any mother may, by last will in writing, appoint[3] a guardian or guardians, for any of his or her children, whether born at the time of making the will, or afterward, to continue during the minority of the child, or for a less time.[4]

twelve continued only till the ward attained that age. After that, his guardianship expired, and payment of his ward's money could no more be made to him validly than if he had never been appointed. Nor were the acts of the child treating him after that time as guardian, admissible to show authority. 1832. Campbell *v.* English, W. 119.

[1] § 6258. See par. 18, page 58.

[2] See Perry *v.* Brainard, 11 O. 442, 443.

[3] See paragraph 16, chapter 1.

[4] § 6266.

This power of a father to appoint a guardian extends to all his legitimate children who are under age and unmarried at his decease, or who are born afterwards. 2 Bro. C. C. 558.

Where a man having no children, by will appointed his wife and brother,

26. *Testamentary guardian to have preference—his duties, powers, and liabilities.*—When a guardian has been appointed by will, by a father or mother of any child, such guardian will be entitled to preference, in appointment over all others, without reference to his place of residence, or the choice of such minor; but his appointment, duties, powers, and liabilities will in all other respects be governed by the law regulating guardians not appointed by will, except as otherwise specially provided.[1]

27. *Bond of such guardian.*—Such guardian need not, generally, give bond, if excused from so doing by the will.[2]   But this rests

---

or the survivor of them, to the guardianship of all his sons thereafter to be born, it was held that the guardianship extended to all his sons by that or a future marriage.   7 Ves. 318.

A testator, by his will, gave real and personal property *to the children of his nephew*, and appointed their father their guardian, "for the purpose of receiving and managing said property so given.   *Held*, that such testator could not make such appointment, and that the will did not vest an estate in trust in the father for the children.   Brigham *v.* Wheeler, 8 Metc. (Mass.) 127.

A will appointing a guardian must be executed in same manner as other wills, or the appointment will not be valid.   Wardwell *v.* Wardwell, 9 Allen, (Mass.) 518.

Where a testator left the care and custody "of his infant children to his wife so long as she remain his widow, she to be guided by the advice of my executors as to the education of my said children," etc.   *Held*, that the wife was constituted sole testamentary guardian, and that, she having married again, the appointment of a new guardian was necessary.   Corrigan *v.* Kiernan, 1 Bradf. (N. Y.) 208.

An executor was also named in the will as guardian of the minor child of the testator.   He qualified as executor, but never took upon himself the duties of guardian, and renounced the guardianship after six years.   Another person was appointed guardian, who receipted to the executor for his ward's share of the estate.   *Held*, that such appointment was valid, and that the mere naming the executor in the will, as guardian, did not constitute him such, although he may have done some acts appropriate to that character. McAlister *v.* Olmstead, 1 Humph. (Tenn.) 210.

A testamentary guardian can not be appointed by a grandparent of the infant.   Hoyt *v.* Hilton, 2 Edw. (N. Y.) 202; Fullerton *v.* Jackson, 5 Johns. Ch. (N. Y.) 278; Williamson *v.* Jordan, 1 Bush. (N. C.) Eq. 46; Vanartsdalen *v.* Vanartsdalen, 14 Pa. St. 384; Tyler on Inf. and Cov. 253.

[1] § 6267.   See preceding not.

[2] § 6268.

in the discretion of the court, as is more fully stated in paragraph 42 below.

WHO MAY BE GUARDIAN.

28. *Certain administrators and executors are not eligible.*—No person who may have been, or shall be, an administrator on an estate, or executor of a last will and testament, can be appointed a guardian of the person and estate, or of the estate only of any minor who will be interested in the estate administered upon, or who will be entitled to any interest under or by virtue of such last will and testament; but an executor or administrator may be appointed a guardian of the person only of any minor.[1]

29. *Probate judge can not be*—Letters of guardianship can not be issued to any person after his election to the office of probate judge, and before the expiration of his term of office.[2]

30. *Non-resident of state can not be.*—As the statute provides that the removal from the state of any person who has been heretofore or who may be hereafter appointed guardian, shall of itself determine the guardianship of such person,[3] the inference is probably conclusive that a person not a resident of the state can not be appointed guardian. Even if the statutes were silent on this point, the fact that such a person is entirely outside of the jurisdiction and control of the court seems of itself

---

[1] ¿ 6256.

[2] ¿ 535. As to other disabilities of probate judge in matters of guardianship, see chapter 2.

[3] ¿ 6272. See Appendix, par. 71.
"Persons residing out of the jurisdiction will not usually be appointed guardians, although one who was out of the state might yet control from a distance; for, it is said, there must be some one answerable to the court (Logan *v.* Fairlee, Jacob, 193.) But if the sureties on the guardian's bond reside within the jurisdiction and are pecuniarily responsible, is not some one answerable to the court? The cases, however, are rare where such an appointment would be advantageous to the ward for business reasons; and hence, others are usually chosen, both in chancery and probate. In some of the United States, the appointment of non-residents is prohibited by statute; and even without such prohibition the court is justified in withholding letters of guardianship at discretion, where the petitioner is beyond the reach of state process. (Finney *v.* State, 9 Mis. 227.)" Schouler's Dom. Rel. 419.

to be a sufficient reason for refusing to appoint a non-resident to such a trust, even if named for it by will.

31. *Must be resident of the county*—And as it is provided that, if a person who has been appointed guardian removes from the county, it is good cause for removing the guardian from the trust,[1] it would seem that no one should be appointed thereto (except testamentary guardians, mentioned in paragraph 26), unless he resides in the county when the appointment is made.

32. *A minor can not be guardian; nor can idiot, lunatic, etc.*—A minor is entirely incompetent to be appointed or to act as guardian. Nor can an idiot, lunatic, or imbecile; and should any such person be so nominated by will, or become so after the making of the will and before the time for appointment by the court, such appointment should not be made. The power of the court is ample to protect against such a step, or to remove any guardian who may become of unsound mind after appointment.[2]

33. *When father or mother should be appointed.* If the father be living, and is a suitable person to act as guardian of his minor child, the court should appoint him, as being the person first entitled thereto; if the father be dead and the mother be

---

[1] § 6272.

[2] As a statutory power to remove, see § 6272.

It is not believed that the case of Starr *v.* Wright, 20 O. S. 97, in which it was held that a minor could be trustee for certain purposes, authorizes a minor to act as guardian.

". . . These considerations, and others that might be named, render an infant incompetent to exercise the office of trustee." 3 Redfield on Wills, 571.

It is requisite that the person appointed be *sui juris*—"of his own right," and capable of performing the appointment. He must not have any interest adverse to the interest of his ward, and if he is known to have any such, he will not be appointed. A person under full age, or a minor, can not, of course, be appointed to take care of another minor. 1 Bouvier's Institutes, 42; Tyler on Inf. and Cov. 259.

If a person appointed become lunatic or is otherwise incapaciated to execute the trust reposed in him, or if he abuses the trust, the court may either totally remove him and appoint another, or, by obliging him to give security to make good his deficiencies, hinder him from doing any thing prejudicial to the infant. Tyler on Inf. and Cov. 253 (citing Ex parte Salter, 3 Br. Ch. cases, 500; O'Keefe *v.* Carcy, 1 Sch. & Lefroy, 106; Roach *v.* Gowan, 1 Ves. Sen. 160).

living, unmarried, and a suitable person, she should receive the appointment; if both father and mother be dead, or if the father, or in case of his death, the mother, are unsuitable persons, then the court will be authorized to appoint some other proper person as such guardian.[1]

34. *When other relative should be.* If the estate of such child has come by gift from some other relation, as a grandfather, which person is unobjectionable, the court would, in such case, deem it right to give such relative the preference in the appointment. Such has been the rule adopted by courts of chancery, and is undoubtedly a safe rule for the probate court.[1]

35. *May a married woman be appointed guardian?* Whether a married woman is legally competent to act as guardian by appointment of court in this state, except as specified in chapter 19, paragraph 4, is a question that has never been judicially decided. But the generally accepted opinion is that she is not, and the uniform practice of the courts has been in accordance with that opinion.

36. That she can not act in that capacity, unless specially authorized to do so by statute, especially if such appointment would place in her hands the management of the ward's estate, scarcely admits of a doubt. But if there is room for such doubt, the practical difficulties that must attend such management on her part, owing to her general legal incapacity to manage property, etc., and the perplexing, but vitally important questions that would so frequently arise therefrom, as well as her generally existing lack of business training and experience, should be sufficient to prevent the court from making such appointment, and subjecting the ward's property to the risks and entanglements that would arise therefrom.[2]

BOND.

37. *Applicant for appointment must give bond; its amount.* Before any person can be appointed guardian of the person and estate, or of the estate only, of any minor, he must, after filing the statement prescribed in paragraphs 90–99 of this chapter, give bond, with freehold sureties, resident of the state, one of whom must be resident of the county where such guardian is

---

[1] See notes 3 and 4, pp. 23, 24.   [2] See Appendix, p. 297; also, p. 50.

appointed, payable to the state, in double the amount of the personal estate belonging to said minor, and also of the gross amount of rents that will probably be received by the guardian from the real estate of said minor during his or her minority.[1]

38. *Condition of bond.*   The bond must be conditioned for the faithful discharge of the duties of such person, as such guardian, and must be approved by the court making such appointment.[2]

39. *Oath of applicant.*   The person applying for the appointment must also take an oath that he will faithfully and honestly discharge the duties devolving upon him, as such guardian.[3]

40. *Mortgage may be given instead of freehold surety.*   In lieu of the freehold surety required in paragraph 37, above, the applicant may execute to said minor a mortgage upon good and unincumbered real estate, first furnishing to the probate court an abstract of his title thereto, which must, by affidavits duly filed, be shown to be in value, exclusive of all improvements thereon, sufficient to secure said bond to the satisfaction of the probate court; and such mortgage must be duly recorded in the county in which such real estate is situate, and filed with the probate court.[4]

41. *Bond of guardian of person; oath required.*—Before a person is appointed guardian to have the custody, maintenance and tuition of a minor, without the right to take charge of the minor's estate, he must give bond in double the probable expenses of maintaining and educating such minor during one year.   In all other respects his bond must be the same as if he had charge of the estate of the ward; and he must take the same oath prescribed in paragraphs 114–115 below.[5]

42. *When such guardian must give bond, etc.*—Every testamentary guardian must give bond, in like manner and with like conditions, as is required of a guardian appointed by the probate

---

[1] ¶6259. Trust funds should not be paid over to the guardian without security, even though he is the father, and is unable to give security.   Savage *v.* Olmstead, 2 Redf. (N. Y.) 478.   See also par. 8, chap. 1.

[2] ¶6259.

[3] ¶6259.   For form of this oath see pars. 114–115.

[4] ¶6259.   For form of mortgage, see page 35.

[5] ¶6260.

court; but when the testator, in the will appointing the guardian, shall have ordered or requested that such bond should not be given. the bond can not be required, unless, from a change in the situation or circumstances of the guardian, or for other sufficient cause, the court of probate shall think proper to require it.[1]

43. *One bond for two or more wards: and fees in such cases.*— When the same person is appointed guardian of several minors, being children of the same parentage and inheriting from the same estate, separate bonds can not be required; and in such cases only one application can be required; and the letters of guardianship to be issued to such guardian by the court must be in one copy, and not one for each minor; and the court approving and recording such bond, and issuing such letters, must charge such fees as are allowed by law for such services, to bo charged but once, and not once for each ward of such guardian.[2]

44. *Qualification of sureties.*—Sureties must be residents of this state, and worth. in the aggregate, double the sum to be secured. beyond the amount of their debts. and have property liable to execution in this state equal to the sum to be secured.[3]

---

[1] § 6268. See paragraphs 26, 27, this chapter.   [2] § 6263.

[3] § 1953.

The following is the rule of the Probate Court of Hamilton county:

"*By Order of Court.*—On all bonds taken in this court there shall not be less than two sureties, who must be residents of this county; and such sureties on each bond must, in the aggregate, own real estate in this county worth double the amount of the bond, beyond their debts, and have real estate in this county liable to execution, equal to the amount stated in the bond." Journal 65, page 162.

A probate court appointed B. guardian of some of the minor children of W., and he gave bond as required. *Held,* that the court had no power, at a subsequent term, to appoint him guardian of another of said minors, without bond, and simply make an order that the bond executed on behalf of the other children should stand as a bond for the latter also; and that such order was wholly inoperative to constitute the second guardianship. Vanderburg r. Williamson, 52 Miss. 233.

"The bond of a probate guardian renders him and his sureties liable for all estate of the ward which shall come into his possession or knowledge. This includes chattels due from the guardian to the ward at the time of his appointment, or of the execution of the bond, even though the fund be proceeds of land already sold and paid for, and the rent of real estate occupied by the guardian before that time. It embraces chattels and rents and income from every species of property that the guardian actually receives in

45. *The number of sureties.*—The statute does not direct how many sureties shall be required to the bond, but as it uses the plural number, and says that the *sureties* to the bond shall be freeholders, it is evident that the proper course is to require at least two sureties, as in case of executors and administrators ;[1] and the court should look to it carefully that they have a freehold qualification, and are abundantly good for the amount of the bond over and above their debts, liabilities, right of homestead and other exemptions from execution.

46. *Sureties may be examined under oath.*—The law provides that a court or an officer, authorized by law to approve a surety, may require such person to testify, orally or in writing, touching his sufficiency ; but that this shall not, in itself, exonerate the officer in an action for taking insufficient surety.[2]

47. *Oral examination of proposed surety.*—For the purpose of ascertaining the responsibility of each surety, before he is accepted as such, the court may administer an oath to him in the following form :

48. Do you solemnly swear [*or affirm, as the case may be*] that you will true and full answers make to such questions as may be put to you by the court, counsel or parties, touching your property, indebtedness, liabilities or responsibility, and this you will do as you will answer to God [*or if the party affirms, say as you will answer under the pains and penalties of perjury*].

49. The judge may then ask him of what his property consists, the value of his real and personal property, what liens are upon it by mortgage, judgment or otherwise, the general amount of his indebtedness or as to particular debts, what contingent

---

his official capacity, or that he might have received if he had faithfully performed his duties." [Citing Mattoon *v.* Cowing, 13 Gray (Mass.), 387 ; Neill *v.* Neill, 31 Miss. 36 ; Bond *v.* Lockwood, 33 Ill. 212 ; Williams *v.* Morton, 38 Me. 47 ; McClendon *v.* Harlan, 2 Heisk. (Tenn.), 337] Schouler's Dom. Rel. 491.

"The liability of sureties lasts while the responsibilities of the guardianship continue, and it does not terminate by the resignation or death of the guardian. For the ward's estate in the guardian's hands or subject to his control at the time of his death, they continue liable." [Citing Moore *v.* Wallis, 18 Ala. 458 ; State *v.* Thorn, 28 Ind. 306 ; Ashley *v.* Johnston, 23 Ark. 163.]

[1] See par. 37, this chapter ; Raff's Guide, page 60.

[2] § 4952.

3

liabilities as surety or otherwise he has, etc., etc., and whether, if his debts were all paid, he would be worth the amount of the bond.

50. *Affidavit of surety.*—It is customary in many, perhaps in most, of the probate courts of the state, to require each surety to a bond to make an affidavit as to his property qualifications, and to file this affidavit with the bond. This is excellent practice for many reasons, and should be universally adopted. In case this is done, the oral examination just mentioned may be dispensed with or not, in the discretion of the court.

51–4. *The form of* such affidavit should be substantially as follows :

The State of Ohio, —— county, ss.

P. Q., one of the sureties on the bond of A. B., as guardian of the person and estate of [*here name the minor or minors*], being duly sworn, says that he is a resident of —— county, Ohio ; that he is worth, beyond the amount of all his debts, at least —— dollars ; and that he has real estate liable to execution in the State of Ohio amounting, in actual value, at least to the sum of —— dollars beyond the amount of all his debts, legal exemptions and liabilities as surety or otherwise.   [*Signed*]   P. Q.

Sworn to and subscribed before me this —— day of ——, A. D. 18—.   A. C., Probate Judge.

55–62. *The form of guardian's bond,* when freehold surety is given, should be as follows :

Know all men by these presents, That we, A. B., resident of —— county, Ohio, as principal, and P. Q., resident of —— county, O., and R. S., resident of —— county, Ohio, as sureties, [*or, if all parties reside in the same county, give their names and relations to the bond as above, and then add,* all being residents of —— county, Ohio,] are held and firmly bound unto the State of Ohio, in the just and full sum of —— dollars, for the payment whereof well and truly to be made, we hereby jointly and severally bind ourselves, our heirs, executors and administrators, firmly by these presents.

Sealed with our seals, and signed at ——, this —— day of —— A. D. eighteen hundred and ——.

The condition of the above obligation is such, that whereas

the above bound A. B. has this day been appointed by the probate court of —— county, Ohio, guardian of the person and estate (*or estate only, if such be the case*) of C. D., aged —— years, [*and if A. B. is to be guardian of other children of the same parentage and inheriting from the same estate, here name the others also, as*

     G. H., aged —— years ;

     J. K., aged —— years ; etc.,]

child (*or*, children) of E. F., deceased, late of ——, [*or*, now living, *if such be the case*], and which appointment the said A. B. has accepted.

Now if the said A. B. shall faithfully discharge all of his [*or*, her] duties, as such guardian, then the above obligation shall be void ; otherwise it shall be and remain in full force.

Signed, sealed and delivered

   in presence of   A. B. [SEAL.]

                                     P. Q. [SEAL.]

                                     R. S. [SEAL.]

This bond approved in open court, this —— day of —— A. D. 18—.   A. C., Probate Judge, etc.

63–7. *If mortgage security* only is given, the bond should be in form substantially as follows :

Know all men by these presents, that I, A. B., a resident of —— county, Ohio, am held and firmly bound unto the State of Ohio, in the just and full sum of —— dollars, for the payment whereof well and truly to be made, I hereby bind myself, my heirs, executors, and administrators, firmly by these presents.

Sealed with my seal and signed at——, Ohio, this —— day of ——, A. D. eighteen hundred and ——.

The condition of the above obligation is such, that whereas the above bound A. B. has this day been appointed by the probate court of —— county, Ohio, guardian of the person and estate [*or*, estate only, *if so*] of

     C. D., aged —— years, [*and if the bond is for more than one, add* G. H., aged —— years,

     J. K., aged —— years, etc.]

the child, [*or*, children) of E. F., deceased, late of —— [*or*, now living, *if so*,] and which appointment the said A. B. has accepted, and has also given mortgage security for the faithful discharge of the duties of the same.

Now, if the said A. B. shall faithfully discharge all of his [*or, her*] duties, as such guardian, then the above obligation shall be void, otherwise it shall be and remain in full force.

Signed, sealed and delivered
    in presence of   A. B.   [SEAL.]

This bond approved in open court, this —— day of ——, A. D. 18—.   A. C., Probate Judge.

68. *No bond invalid for informality.*—The law provides that no bond executed by a guardian shall be void, or held invalid on account of any informality in the same, nor on account of any informality or illegality in the appointment of such guardian; and that such bond shall have the same force and effect as if such appointment had been legally made and such bond executed in proper form.[1]

69. *Guardian's bond good when signed in blank.*—All guardian's bonds will be binding on all who sign them either as principals or sureties, whether at the time of signing and sealing such bond by them, or any of them, the amounts of such bonds be filled in or left in blank, if such amounts be filled in before, or at the time of the approval or acceptance of such bonds; and such filling in may be done in the absence of any or all of the said signers, and without any express authority for that purpose from them or any of them.[2]

70. *Carelessness not justified. Difference between form and substance of bond.*—These provisions of the law, however, will not justify carelessness in drawing up the bond; for while a carelessly drawn bond may be deficient in form, and yet be valid, it is quite as likely to be deficient in substance, too, and thereby to be void.

71. There is a marked difference between the *form* of a bond and its *substance*; and while these informalities will not affect its validity, the want of the substance required will render it inoperative. Therefore, it is better to follow a fixed form, and not to undertake to frame a bond without due care, and without distinguishing between what is substance and what is mere form.

---

[1] § 6262.   [2] § 6.

72. *The bond should be signed in court.*—To guard effectually against mistakes, frauds, forgeries, and misapprehensions, the bond should be always signed at the office of the probate judge, and in his presence, or that of his clerk. The practice of permitting the bond to be carried out and signed by the parties to it, and then returned, is very improper, and fraught with many dangers.

73. A moment's reflection will convince any one of this. The infant has no part in this matter, and can give no attention to it, nor has he any control over it. It is the peculiar province of the court to give the infant the most ample protection, and narrowly watch his every interest. These bonds may often run for a great number of years, before there is any occasion to look into them, or before any inquiry is made concerning them; then some of the actors may be dead, and some dishonest, and if the surety answer to the bond that his name is a forgery, the ward may be defrauded of his whole estate. The safest guard against the possibility of this answer is to have the bond signed and attested in court, before the judge or his clerk, and witnesses.

74–9. *Form of mortgage.* If, instead of freehold securities, a mortgage is given, as specified in paragraph 40, such mortgage may be in form as follows:

Know all men by these presents: That whereas A. B., of —— county, Ohio, having applied for appointment as guardian of the person and estate [*or*, estate only, *if so*] of C. D. [*and if more than one minor is named in the bond, here name them all*], child [*or*, children] of E. F., deceased; Now therefore the said A. B., in lieu of freehold surety and in pursuance of the statute in such case made and provided, and in consideration of the trust to be imposed upon said A. B., by reason of said appointment, does hereby grant, bargain, sell and convey to the said [*here name the said minor or minors*] his [*or*, her, *or*, their] heirs and assigns forever, the following-described real estate, situate in the [city, *or*, village, *or*, township, *as may be*] of ——, in the county of ——, and State of Ohio, to-wit [*here describe the property by metes and bounds, or in other suitable way*]: and all the estate, title and interest of the said A. B., either in law or in equity, of, in and to the said premises; together with all the privileges and appurtenances to the same belonging, and all the rents, issues and profits thereof; to have and to hold the same to the only proper use of the said [*here name the said minor or minors*] his [*or*, her, *or*, their] heirs and assigns forever. And the said A. B., for himself and for his heirs, executors and administrators, does hereby covenant with the said [*here again name said minor or minors*] his [*or*, her, *or*, their] heirs and assigns, that he is the true and lawful owner of the said premises, and has full power to convey the same; and that the title, so conveyed, is clear, free, and unincumbered; and further, that he will warrant and defend the same against all claim or claims of all persons whomsoever. Provided, nevertheless, that if the said A. B. shall faithfully discharge all of his [*or*, her] duties as said guardian, then these presents shall be void.

In witness whereof, the said A. B. [*and, if he has a wife, here add*, and W. B., his wife, the latter of whom hereby releases her right and expectancy of dower in the said premises] has hereunto set his hand and seal [*or*, have hereunto set their hands and seals], this —— day of ——, in the year of our Lord one thousand eight hundred and ——.

Signed, sealed and acknowledged in the presence of us [*there must be two witnesses to each signature; but the same two can witness any number of signatures*] :

A. B.,   [SEAL.]
[W. B. *if so*]   [SEAL.]

The State of Ohio, county of ——, ss.

Be it remembered, that on the —— day of ——, in the year of our Lord one thousand eight hundred and ——, before me, the subscriber, a notary public [*or other officer authorized to take acknowledgment of deeds*] in and for said county, personally came A. B. [and W. B., *if so*], the grantor [*or*, the grantors] in the foregoing mortgage deed, and acknowledged the signing and sealing thereof to be his [*or*, their] voluntary act and deed, for the uses and purposes therein mentioned. [*And if W. B. signed, here add*] and the said W. B., wife of the said A. B., being examined by me separate and apart from her said husband, and the contents of said mortgage being by me made known, and explained to her, as the statute directs, declared that she did voluntarily sign, seal and acknowledge the same, and that she is still satisfied therewith, as her act and deed, for the uses and purposes therein mentioned.

In testimony whereof, I have hereunto subscribed my name [*if the officer have an official seal, say* and affixed my official, *or* notarial, seal]. on the day and year aforesaid.

[SEAL.]   RICHARD ROE, Notary Public,
                                    [*or. J. P. etc.*], as aforesaid.

80. *Where mortgage to be filed.* The law does not provide where in the court such mortgage must be filed; but as it is in lieu of security that would otherwise be in the bond itself, it should no doubt be filed with the bond, and not with the general papers in the case.

81. *The requisites of affidavit as to the value of land security.* The law does not prescribe the number nor character of the affidavits mentioned in paragraph 40, and in these respects they are entirely within the discretion and control of the probate judge; but by analogy to statutory provisions in other and somewhat similar circumstances,[1] we may infer that the judge should require the affidavits of at least three judicious, disinterested persons, whose opinion, from the fact of their being property owners n the vicinity of the mortgaged premises, or dealers in real estate in that vicinity, or for other good reasons, may fairly be presumed to be entitled to credit in this matter.

82. *How to proceed when mortgage security is given.* If the applicant proposes to give mortgage security, he will observe[2] that he must *first* furnish the court with an abstract of title to the property offered as security; and as this and the execution of the mortgage necessitate the expenditure of money, time and trouble which no one interested desires to have thrown away, probably the best course for the applicant to pursue would be to obtain say three such affidavits as are described in the preceding paragraph, and submit them to the probate judge, along with the statement described in paragraphs 91–99, below; and the judge can then inform him whether these affidavits are sufficient, or whether additional ones will be required, and also whether a mortgage on the property described in them would

---

[1] See ? 6076; Raff's Guide, p. 83.

[2] See par. 40, this chapter.

be satisfactory security, in case the abstract shall show it to be free and unincumbered, for the amount of the bond he must give.

83–6. *The form of the affidavits* may be, for instance, as follows; and they may be taken before the probate judge, or notary public, a justice of the peace, or other officer authorized to administer oaths:

The State of Ohio, —— county, *ss.*

Before me, Richard Roe, a notary public [*or, justice of the peace, etc.*] in and for said county, personally appeared L. O., who, being duly sworn, says that for fifteen years last past he has been a resident of and owner of a farm of one hundred and sixty acres in the immediate vicinity of the real estate owned by A. B., and described as follows [*here give a description of the real estate similar to that which must be given in the mortgage, which see; change the foregoing, as the facts require.*]

Affiant further says that said real estate of A. B. is worth, exclusive of all improvements thereon, the sum of —— dollars, to the best of his knowledge and belief.

 (*Signed*)   L. O.

Sworn to and subscribed before me, this —— day of ——, A. D. 18—.

 [SEAL.]   RICHARD ROE, Notary Public
                 [*or, J. P., etc.*] as aforesaid.

87–8. *Another form.*

The State of Ohio, —— county, *ss.*

N. S., being duly sworn, says that he, as sheriff of said county, has, during his present term of office, sold two tracts of land in the vicinity of the land of A. B. [*if one affidavit has already been taken, the sheet on which this one is written may be attached to that affidavit, if desired*], described in the annexed affidavit of L. O., and that by reason of his former residence in that vicinity, and other reasons, he is well acquainted with the value of real estate in that locality; and he verily believes that said land of A. B. is fully worth —— dollars, exclusive of all improvements thereon.

 (*Signed*)   N. S.

Sworn to and subscribed before me, this —— day of ——,
A. D. 18—.

[SEAL]   RICHARD ROE, Notary Public,
                                  —— county, Ohio.

89. *Further consideration of bonds, found where.* The steps so
far directed with regard to the bond are those which are preliminary to the appointment, and which had to be treated as a part
of that subject. The further consideration of bonds, exceptions
thereto, suits upon, sureties, rights and liabilities under, etc.,
will be found in chapter 10.

PROCEEDINGS TO APPOINT A GUARDIAN.

90. *Statement of ward's estate must be filed.* Before any
person can be appointed guardian of the person and estate, or
of the estate only, of any minor, he must file in the office of the
court having such appointment to make, a statement of the
whole estate of such minor, and the probable value thereof, and
also the probable annual rents of such minor's real estate, and
must verify the same by affidavit.[1]

91–99. *Form of.* This statement may be in the following form :

To the Honorable, the Judge of the Probate Court,
          of —— County, Ohio :

Your petitioner represents it to be necessary that the court appoint a guardian for the following named minor [*or* minors, *if
more than one*], residing in said county, to-wit:

C. D., aged —— years; [*and if more than one. add,* G. H.,
aged —— years, J. H., *aged* —— years. *etc.*], child of E. D., deceased [*or,* now living, *if so: and use the plural number of the words
minor, child, person, estate, etc., when necessary*].

Your petitioner makes this his application to be appointed
guardian for the person and estate [*or,* estate only, *if so*] of said minor ; and he represents that said minor has an estate consisting
of [*here give a not too minutely itemized, yet full statement ; as*]

1. One house and lot in Glendale, probable value......... $12,500
2. Farm, 160 acres, in Green tp., this county, probable
          value...... 5,200

---

[1] § 6259.

3. 200 acres wild land, in Louisiana, probable value......   400
4. 14 shares Little Miami R. R. stock,   "   "   1,436
5. Cash on deposit at H. W. Hughes & Co's bank.........   1,080
6. U. S. bonds, from the estate of E. F., after settlement.   1,000
7. Promissory note of H. S., from same estate..............   1,160
                                                        ————
                                                        $22,776

The probable annual rent of Glendale house and lot is.. $900
Of the 160-acre farm, (90 acres cleared)......   300
                                                        ————
                                                        $1,200

RECAPITULATION.

Probable value of real estate............................. .... $18,100
   "   "   " personal property..........................   4,676
   "   annual rents of real estate...........................   1,200

The following freeholders are offered as sureties: P. Q. and R. S.

Petitioner's post-office, ——; his residence, ——; his place of business, ——; his attorneys, ——; their office, ——.

The State of Ohio, —— county, ss.

A. B., being duly sworn, says that the foregoing statements are in all respects true and correct, to the best of his knowledge and belief.

(*Signed*)   A. B.

Sworn to and subscribed before me, this —— day of ——, A. D. ——.   A. C., Probate Judge, etc.

100. *What officer may take affidavit.*   This affidavit may be made before the probate judge, a notary public, or any officer authorized to administer oaths generally; but it would be well to make all affidavits before the judge, at least when convenient.

101. *Judge should appoint applicant, if.*—If the probate judge is satisfied that the person proposed as guardian is a proper and suitable person, and that the statement as to the estate of the minor is correctly and honestly made, he should then appoint such person, and make a minute thereof upon the journal of the court.

102-5. *Form of journal entry[1] of appointment of a guardian.*

In the matter of the guardianship of C. D.

This day came A. B., and made application to be appointed guardian of C. D., and the court being satisfied that said C. D. is a minor, of the age of —— years [*any age less than fourteen, if a male; or twelve, if a female*].* on the —— day of ——, A. D. ——, and child of E. F., deceased, late of ——, [*or, say, now living*], and that said minor is a resident of this county; and the said A. B., having filed in this office a statement, duly verified by his affidavit, of the whole estate of said minor, and the probable value thereof [*and if there be real estate, add:* and also the probable annual rents of said minor's real estate], it is, therefore, by the court ordered, that said A. B. be, and he is hereby appointed guardian of the person and estate [*or, if not of the person, say:* of the estate only] of the said C. D.

And thereupon came the said A. B., in open court, and accepted said appointment, and took an oath that he would faithfully and honestly discharge the duties devolving upon him as such guardian, and also gave and filed herein his bond in the sum of —— dollars, conditioned according to law, with —— and ——, residents of —— county, O., freeholders, as sureties [*or,* mortgage security on 160 acres of land (*or otherwise briefly describe the real estate*) situated in —— township of said county of ——.], which bond was approved of by the court.

[*If all these events did not occur on the same day, enter them as of the day on which they occurred.*]

106-7. *Form of journal entry, where the minor selects a guardian.*

If the guardian appointed is one selected by the minor of the proper age, the form of the entry should vary from the above in this: proceed to the * as in the following:

In the matter of the guardianship of C. D.

This day came the said C. D., and made choice of A. B. as his guardian, which choice is approved by the court, and the court being satisfied that said C. D. is a minor of the age of —— years [*fourteen or more if a male, and twelve if a female,—and from the * proceed as in the above form.*]

---

[1] See direction about plural number on page 41.

108–110. *Form of entry when minor notified and fails to appoint.*

If the minor has been notified to make his selection, and has failed to do so, the above form may be modified, thus:

In the matter of the guardianship of C. D.

It appearing to the court that said C. D. has been duly notified to come into this court and select a guardian for himself, upon the —— day of ——, A. D. —— [*some day prior to the day of this entry*], which he has failed to do [*or say, if the case be so*: and having selected L. P. as his guardian, who was not approved of by the court], and the court being satisfied that said C. D. is a minor child of E. F., deceased, of the age of —— years, on the —— day of ——, A. D. ——, and is a resident of this county, and the court having thereupon selected A. B. as a suitable person to act as such guardian. the said A. B. this day came and filed in this office a statement. duly verified by his affidavit, etc. [*proceed from here as in the first form of a journal entry.*]

111–113. *Form of journal entry of appointment of guardian of the person only.*

In the matter of the guardianship of C. D.

This day came A. B., and made application to be appointed guardian of the person only of C. D. And the court being satisfied that said C. D. is a minor, of the age of —— years [*any age less than fourteen for males, and twelve for females*], on the —— day of ——, A. D.——, and child of E. F., deceased, late of —— [*or, if the father or mother be living, but are unsuitable persons, say,* and child of E. F., now living, and the court being further satisfied that said parent (*or,* parents) is an unsuitable person (*or,* are unsuitable persons) to have the custody and tuition of said minor], and being further satisfied that said minor is a resident of this county, and that it is for the interest of said minor to have a guardian appointed for his person only.

It is therefore by the court ordered, that said A. B. be, and he is hereby appointed guardian of the person only of said C. D. And thereupon came the said A. B., in open court, and accepted said appointment, and took an oath that he would faithfully and honestly discharge the duties devolving upon him as such guardian, and also gave and filed herein his bond in the sum of —— dollars, conditioned according to law, with —— and ——, free-holders, as sureties [*or with mortgage security, as in preceding entry*], which bond was approved of by the court.

114–115. *Form of guardian's oath at appointment.* (See par. 39.)

A. B., guardian of C. D., a minor, being duly sworn [*or affirmed*], says that he will faithfully and honestly discharge the duties devolving upon him as such guardian, as he will answer to God [*or, as he will answer under the pains and penalties of perjury, if the guardian affirms*].

(*Signed*)   A. B.

Sworn to [*or affirmed*] and subscribed before me, this —— day of ——, A. D. 18—.   A. C., Probate Judge, etc.

116. *Oath may be indorsed on bond, or filed with it.*—This oath may very properly be indorsed upon the back of the bond, as a safe and convenient place for keeping it; or it may be on a separate paper, annexed to and filed with the bond, although this is not expressly required.

117. *What the journal entry should show, and why*—It should be remembered that these appointments may come under the review of other courts than the one where the appointment of a guardian is made, both in this state and in other states and countries; it is therefore important that the journal entry of the order, making the appointment, should in itself show all the matters requisite to give the court jurisdiction, and also those things done on the part of the guardian, which authorize him to act under the appointment.

118. *What is effective part of the appointment.*—The actual taking out letters of guardianship is nothing of itself: the entry on the court journal is the effective part of the appointment, and the letters usually issued are only a certificate of the fact.[1]

-----

[1] A guardian for a minor, appointed by the court   *   *   , has no power to act or control the property of his ward, until he has given bond, with surety approved by the court. Letters of guardianship, issued to him by the clerk, before such bond is given, confer no such power, and have no legal effect whatever. 1851. State *v.* Sloane, 20 O. 327.

A guardian derives his power to act from the appointment and giving

119. *Another form of oath—How filed in some counties.—*
In some counties it is the practice to combine the oaths as to
the amount of estate and the one just given into one form, letting it follow the statement given in paragraph —; and blanks
for these statements and oath are bound into a volume for convenience of filing and reference.   The form is substantially as
follows :

120–3. The State of Ohio, Hamilton county, *ss.*

Before me, the undersigned, judge of the probate court, in
and for said county, personally appeared A. B., who upon oath
[*or affirmation*] deposes and says that the foregoing statement is
true according to the best of his knowledge; and that he will
faithfully and honestly discharge the duties devolving upon him
as guardian for the person and estate of C. D., a minor of said
county, as required by law.

 (*Signed*)   A. B.
 Sworn to [*or affirmed*] and subscribed before me this —— day
of —— 18—.   A. C., Probate Judge.
              By A. G., Deputy Clerk.

124. *When appointment is complete.—*When the appointment
of a guardian has been made, the bond given and approved by
the court, and oath taken as already stated, then the guardian is
clothed with full powers to act in that capacity to the extent for
which he has been appointed.[1]

---

bond. Letters of guardianship need not in fact issue. Maxsom *v.* Sawyer,
12 O. 195.

A letter of guardianship is in the nature of a certificate or commission;
and, in the absence of any statutory provision requiring it, it is not essential to its validity as evidence of the appointment that it should recite the
mode and particulars of the nomination, and all reasonable presumption
must be indulged in favor of its having emanated regularly and after lawful
proceedings. Burrows *v.* Bailey, 34 Mich. 64.

The fact that the letter of guardianship, though the minors were shown to
be over 14 years of age, does not show in terms that the guardian was nominated by them, or that they were asked to nominate or to appear for that
purpose, will not justify its exclusion as evidence. *Ib.*

[1] See note 1, preceding page.

125. *What to do first after appointment.*—Immediately after his appointment, the guardian should get a suitable book for properly keeping the accounts required of him by law, as more fully set forth in chapter 9, especially paragraphs 4 and 5.

CHAPTER 4.

RESIGNATION, REMOVAL, RELEASE, ETC., OF GUARDIAN.

1. *Continuance of guardianship.*—A guardian once appointed and qualified to act, will continue in that capacity[1] until the

---

[1] "As two persons, or sets of persons, can not at the same time hold the same trust, it follows that one guardian must be removed, or a vacancy otherwise created, before the court can make a new appointment. This principle, apparently simple, has sometimes been overlooked; when, for

ward arrives at the age of majority,[1] unless such guardian sooner dies,[2] resigns,[3] is removed for cause,[4] the ward selects another suitable guardian at the proper age,[5] become legally disqualified to act, as in the case of a female guardian who marries,[6] or in case of the marriage of the ward,[7] etc.

2. *Resignation.*—The court by whom any guardian has been or may be appointed, may, for reasons satisfactory to such court, accept the resignation of any such guardian, and appoint another in his stead.[8] But the court should, in no case, accept the resignation of any guardian, until he has filed a full and true account of his guardianship, for final settlement, up to the time he tenders his resignation.

3. *Form of resignation of guardian.*

The undersigned, heretofore appointed by this court guardian of C. D., says, that he has this day filed a full, true, and just account of his guardianship up to this time, and now tenders his resignation of such guardianship, for reasons which he will show to the court, as the court may direct.

(*Signed*),   A. B.

Dated the —— day of ——, A. D. ——.

4. *Form of journal entry, in case of resignation.*

In the matter of the guardianship of C. D.

This day came the said A. B., guardian of C. D., and filed his accounts for settlement up to this time, and thereupon

---

instance, a court has issued new letters without revoking the old. . . . The appointment of a new guardian does not of itself terminate the authority of one, previously chosen. It is an act without jurisdiction, and void." Schouler's Dom. Rel. 429.

[1] See par. 22, chap. 3.

[2] See par. 11, below; also 3 Redf. on Wills, 457.

[3] See next par.

[4] See par. 17, below.

[5] See par. 23, chap. 3.

[6] See par. 35–36, chap. 3, and par. 7, below.

[7] See par. 8, below.

[8] § 6274.

thereupon tendered his resignation as such guardian, which, for reasons satisfactory to the court, is hereby accepted.

5. *Another guardian should be appointed.*—In such case, another guardian should be at once appointed, in the manner already laid down for an original appointment.[1]

6. *When ward selects another guardian.*—When the male ward arrives at the age of fourteen years, or a female at the age of twelve years, and selects a guardian, and such new guardian is appointed and qualified, the powers of the guardian previously appointed cease, without further action by the court.

7. *When unmarried female guardian marries.*—When any unmarried woman, who has been or may be appointed guardian of any minor, shall marry, such marriage of itself determines the guardianship of such woman ; and the probate court of the proper county must appoint another guardian for such minor, to which last named guardian all the estate of such minor must, on demand, be delivered up by such former guardian ; and she must forthwith render her guardianship account to the court from which she received her appointment, for final settlement.[2]

8. *When female ward marries.*—The marriage of a ward, if a female, ends the guardianship as to the person, but not as to the estate, of such ward.[3]

9. *Does marriage of male ward end guardianship?*—The authorities seem uncertain as to the effect of a male ward's marriage[4]

---

[1] See chap. 3.

[2] § 6292. See Appendix, par. 66.

[3] § 6265.

[4] "Upon the marriage of a male ward, the guardianship continues as to his estate, though it has been thought otherwise as to his person." 2 Kent. 226. (Citing a note as follows: " Reeve's Domestic Relations, 328. By the civil law, marriage did not confer on a minor the privileges of majority. Dig. 4, 4, 2; Code, 5, 37, 12. But the laws of modern nations are very diverse on the effect of marriage upon minors. Marriage is an emancipation of the minor to full rights by the French and Dutch laws. Code Civil Art. 476; Voet. ad Pand. 4, 4, 6; Vanderlinden's Inst. b. 1, c. 5, sec. 7.)

"If a male ward marry, I apprehend he has contracted a relation, and one that he had a right to contract, wholly inconsistent with a guardianship

on his wardship; but our statutes declare that the guardianship of an infant ward continues till the age of majority, and, as to males, make no exceptions. The marriage of a male ward would therefore appear to have no effect on his relations with his guardian. Of course statutory provisions override the decisions of the courts of other states and countries, and the opinions of the ablest writers.

10. *Death of ward.*—If the ward dies, the guardianship over the estate ceases, as a matter of course, and the guardian has no further power over the property. He should then settle his accounts finally, and if any thing further is to be done with the property of the ward, an administrator should be appointed.

11. *Death of guardian.*—If the guardian dies, the power he had as guardian, ceases, and his executor or administrator has no power to act in that capacity;[1] but it is the duty of such executor or administrator to render an account of his decedent's guardianship, as directed in chapter 9.

12. *Removal of guardian from the state.*—The removal from

---

of his person. As to his estate, marriage does not vary his situation. Reeve's Dom. Rel. 328. (No citations.)

"Though the court of chancery can not appoint a guardian after marriage, yet it will not determine a guardianship, or discharge an order made for a guardian because of marriage." Bacon's Abr., Guardian (E.) Citing Roach v. Garvin, 1 Ves. 159; Matter of Whittaker, 4 Johns. 378.)

"The lawful marriage of any ward, whether male or female, must necessarily effect the rights of the guardian. So far as the ward's person is concerned, there can be no question that the guardianship ends. Marriage is paramount to all other relations, and its proper continuance being inconsistent with guardianship of the person, the latter yields to it, whatever may be the sex of the ward. But as to the estate, the rule, in view of the late married women's statutes, is not so clear. If, however, a male ward marries a female, whether she be minor or adult, his guardian retains power over his estate, as before, until he becomes of age. Schouler's Dom. Rel. 425. (Citing Reeve's Dom. Rel. 328; 2 Kent's Com. 226; Bacon's Abr., Guardian, (E); Eyre v. Countess of Shaftsbury, 2 P. Wms. 103; Mendes r. Mendes, 3 Atk. 619; Ib. 1 Ves. 89; Jones r. Ward, 10 Yerg. 160.)

The marriage of a female ward terminates the guardianship; it is otherwise of the marriage of a male ward. Brick's estate, 15 Abb. (N. Y.) Pr. 12; Holmes v. Field, 12 Ill. 424; Shutt v. Carloss, 1 Ired. (N. C.) Eq. 232; Burr v. Wilson, 18 Tex. 367; Ware v. Ware, 28 Gratt. (Va. 1877) 670.

[1] Schouler's Dom. Rel. 426.

this state of any person who has been heretofore or may be hereafter appointed guardian, will, of itself, determine the guardianship of such person.[1]

13. *When ward removes from the state, what?*—When a minor, for whom a guardian has been appointed in this state, removes to another state or territory, and a guardian of such infant is there appointed, the guardian appointed in this state may be removed, and required to settle his account as hereinafter provided.[2]

14. *When and under what circumstances the guardian here may be removed.*—Such removal must not be made unless the guardian appointed in another state or territory shall apply to the probate court in this state which made the former appointment, and file therein an exemplification from the record of the court making the foreign appointment, containing all the entries and proceedings in relation to his appointment, and his giving bond, with a copy thereof and of the letters of guardianship, all authenticated as required by the act of congress in that behalf; and before such application can be heard, or any action taken therein by the court, at least thirty days' written notice must be served on the guardian appointed in this state, specifying the object of the application and the time when the same will be heard.[3]

15. *No such removal made, unless.*—No such removal can be made in favor of any foreign guardian, unless at the time of the hearing the state or territory in which he was appointed has made a similar provision as to wards removing from such state or territory; and the court may, in any case, deny the application unless satisfied that the removal of the guardian appointed in this state would be to the interest of the ward.[3]

16. *What to be done if guardian here removed.*—If the court, on such hearing, remove the guardian, the court may cause all suitable orders to be made discharging the resident guardian, and authorizing the paying over and delivery to the foreign guardian all moneys and other property in the hands of the resident guardian after his settlement.[4]

17. *May be removed for drunkenness, etc.*—The probate court

---

[1] § 6272. See note 3, p. 28; par. 71, p. 312. [2] § 6276. [3] § 6277. [4] § 6278.

may at any time remove a guardian appointed by such court, he having thirty days notice thereof, for habitual drunkenness, neglect of his duties, incompetency, fraudulent conduct, removal from the county, or any other cause which, in the opinion of such court, renders it for the interest of the ward that such guardian be removed.[1]

18. *For not filing inventory, etc.*—If the guardian fails to file an inventory, as required by law, for thirty days after having been notified so to do by the probate judge, such judge must remove him. See paragraph 5, chapter 5.

19. *Court must enforce guardian's duties.*—It is made the duty of the court by which any guardian has been or may be appointed, to enforce the return, at the prescribed times, of all inventories and accounts required to be filed in such court by such guardian, and also to enforce the performance of all other duties devolving upon guardians appointed by such court, either *with* or *without* complaint being first made, and thereupon to make and enter such judgments and orders as may be requisite in any case to promote the faithful and correct discharge of the duties

---

[1] § 6272. See also 2 Story Equity Jur. § 1289; Perry on Trusts, §§ 276 817; 3 Redf. on Wills, 458.

A guardian and his sureties are liable for any money collected by the guardian after removal, if the person paying the money does so in good faith. Sage *v.* Hammonds, 27 Gratt. (Va.) 651.

A father, who, as guardian of his minor children, received an annual income of $2,000 from their property, but refused for a period of several years to provide for their support and education, was not a suitable person to manage their estate, and was properly removed from their guardianship. *In re* Swifts, 47 Cal. 629.

Where it appeared that a guardian failed to return his account, employed the slaves of his ward in his own service, kept his own stock on his ward's land, and fed them on the corn of his ward. *Held*, this was a sufficient cause of removal. Ripitoe *v.* Hale, 1 Stew. (Ala.) 166.

The insolvency of the guardian and of one of his sureties is good cause for removal. *Re* Cooper, 2 Paige (N. Y.) 34.

Conduct of a guardian tending to alienate the ward's affections from its mother, a person of good character, is sufficient ground for removal. Perkins *v.* Finnegan, 105 Mass. 501.

Mere whim, or caprice, or choice, either in the ward or the friends, will not be a sufficient ground of removal. The objection must rest on substantial grounds of unfitness in the guardian. 3 Redf. on Wills, 458.

of such guardians, or to preserve the estate of minors for whom such guardians may have been or shall be appointed.[1]

20. *How to enforce such duties.*—It is perfectly clear from the three preceding paragraphs that the probate judge may enforce such duties by removal, if necessary, and that, in certain cases, such removal is imperatively required.

21. *Complaint, who to make; hearing of.*—Any person may complain to the probate court of the dereliction of duty in any guardian; and whenever such a complaint is made, or whenever the probate judge himself knows, or has good cause to believe, that there is ground for such a complaint, his duty is to act at once, and institute proceedings to inquire into the matter, of course giving the required notice of thirty days.

22-25. *Form of complaint.* No special form of complaint is prescribed in the cases mentioned in paragraph 19 above, but the following form may be used, and adapted also to other cases where application is made to the court to do certain things:

To the Honorable, the Judge of the Probate Court
        of —— county, Ohio;

Your petitioner represents that E. F., late of said county, died on or about the —— day of —— 18—, leaving C. D. [*and* G. H., etc., *if so; making the proper changes below, if more than one child*], his minor child, and an estate to be administered, worth about $——; that on or about the —— day of ——, 18—, A. B. was appointed guardian of said C. D.; and that said guardian has neglected and failed to file an inventory, as required by law [*or*, has removed from the state; *or*, has become a habitual drunkard; *or*, has become a lunatic; *or*, is incompetent to manage so important a trust; *or*, that said guardian's bondsman, P. Q., has died; *or mention any other cause or failure of duty*].

Your petitioner further represents that he is interested in said minor, as adult brother [*or*, as a friend; *or mention any other ground of interest in ward or estate*], and prays that citation may issue, requiring said A. B. to appear before said court, on the —— day of ——, 18—, at —— o'clock, — M., then and there to show cause, if any he may have, why he should not be re-

---

[1] § 6275.

moved [*or, give additional security; or do any other proper thing required by law for the good of said minor*].

(Signed)   N. F.

26. *Why such complaints sometimes necessary.* It may be further said of such complaints, that in many counties, especially our most populous ones, the probate judge can not know, from personal knowledge, the condition of every ward's affairs, especially of such matters as the record does not yet disclose: for instance, the removal from the state, or death, of the guardian or his sureties. It is true that such information could be conveyed orally or by letter to the judge, and that it might then be his duty to act upon such light as this would give him; but it is best to give such information in a more formal way, and to have it filed among the papers in the case.

27. *Affidavit to such complaint.* Upon the strength of such a complaint, the judge would, under most circumstances, issue a citation against the person complained of, even though the law, in some cases, authorized him to require an affidavit. As the welfare of the ward, and especially the protection and preservation of the ward's property, are so completely intrusted to his watchfulness and care, he should generally assume that even seemingly well grounded suspicion must be examined into, and the matters they relate to righted, if need be. But should he require an affidavit, it can be added or annexed to the foregoing complaint, as follows:

28–29. Form of affidavit to complaint.

State of Ohio, —— county, ss.

N. F., being duly sworn, says that the various matters and things set forth in the foregoing [*or, annexed*] complaint are true, to the best of his knowledge and belief.

(Signed)   N. F.

Sworn to and subscribed before me, this —— day of ——, A. D. 18—.   A. C., Probate Judge, etc.

30–31. Form of a citation.

The State of Ohio, —— county, ss.: Probate Court.

To A. B., guardian of C. D.:

You are hereby notified to appear *forthwith* [*or*, on the ——

day of ——, A. D. 18—, at — o'clock A. M.) at the office of the probate court of said county, to answer why you have not filed your accounts as guardian as aforesaid, according to law [*or, according to the order of said court heretofore made, if such order has been made and not complied with,* or, why you have not loaned the money of your said ward, according to law, *or state any other failure of duty or ground of complaint, as in paragraph* 23; *and also add, if desired*], and to show cause why you should not be removed from such guardianship.

Witness my hand and the seal of said court, this —— day of ——A. D, 18—.

[L. S.]   A. C., Probate Judge of said Court.

32. *How served.* This citation may be served by the sheriff, or by any disinterested person, in like manner as the notice is served when exceptions are filed to the bond.[1]

33–36. *Another form, more commonly used when served by sheriff.*

The State of Ohio, —— count,y ss.
To the sheriff of our said county, greeting:

We command you that you cite and give notice to A. B., guardian of C. D., to be and appear before A. C., judge of the probate court within and for the county aforesaid, at ——, on the —— day of ——, A. D. 18—, at — o'clock, — M., then and there to show cause, if any he may have, why he has not filed his accounts as guardian aforesaid [*or state any other failure of duty, etc., as in preceding form; and also, if desired,* and to show cause why he should not be removed from such guardianship]. And of this writ make due service and return to our said court, at the time and place aforesaid.

In testimony whereof, I have hereunto set my hand and affixed the seal of the probate court, at ——, this —— day of ——, A. D. 18—.

[SEAL.]   A. C., Probate Judge.
         By ——, Deputy Clerk.

37. *The hearing.*—Upon the appearance of the guardian, the court should inquire into the charges against him, and if the

---

[1] See pages 170, 171.

court is of the opinion, after such examination, that such person is not a proper or not a competent person to act as such guardian, he should be removed, and a new guardian should be appointed; but if, upon the hearing, the court finds that the complaint is not sustained, the motion should be dismissed, and the guardian should not be removed.

38. *The discretion of the judge* ought, no doubt, to be reasonably exercised, and with due caution, for the guardian is not without some rights, as well as the ward, and he ought not to be removed for a mere frivolous cause; but there should be some substantial reason, materially affecting the interests of the ward, either in his person or property, as the case may be.[1]

39. *What justifies removal.*—It is not every failure to perform the full and exact duties of guardian that will justify a removal: as, for instance, if a guardian should not promptly, on the very day his two years expire for rendering his account, so render it, and when cited to answer for the delinquency, should give a reasonable excuse therefor, and should then render a fair and just account, it would not be proper in such case to remove him; whereas, a guardian who habitually neglected his duties, in whole or in part, ought promptly to be removed.[1]

40. The good sense and sound discretion of the court will be brought into action in these cases to the fullest extent; for no rule that will be applicable to all cases, or even to the majority of cases, can be laid down.

41. *Proceedings when bond excepted to—notice.*—The proceedings in case of exceptions being filed against the guardian's bond, in which only ten days' notice is required, and in which a guardian may no doubt be removed, are considered in chapter 10.

42–5. *Form of journal entry upon citation to remove a guardian.*

In the matter of the guardianship of C. D.

On the motion of M. N. [*or, of the court, if it be so, without the movement of any one else*] to remove A. B. from such guardianship, on the ground that [*here state the charge as in the notice*].

This day, this motion came on to be heard, and testimony being produced, and the court being fully advised in the premises, do find that the charge made against said A. B., as guardian of

---

[1] See note 1, page 53.

C. D., is true, and that said A. B. ought to be removed from said guardianship; therefore, it is ordered by the court, that said A. B. be, and he is hereby removed from said guardianship, and his powers and authority therein revoked; and it is further ordered, that said A. B. shall file in this court a full and just account of his guardianship, within —— days, and that he also pay the costs herein taxed, at —— dollars, and in default thereof, that an execution issue therefor, against his individual property, as upon judgments at law.

46–7. *Form of entry, if charge not sustained.*

If the court, however, find that the charge is not sustained, the journal entry should be accordingly. In such case, the form of the journal entry, after stating the caption as in the last form, may be as follows :

This day this motion came on to be heard, and the court being fully advised in the premises, do find that said charge against said A. B. is not sustained, and the said motion is therefore dismissed. And it is ordered, that M. N. pay the costs herein taxed at —— dollars, within —— days, and in default thereof, that execution issue therefor, as upon judgments at law.

48. *Notice to guardian of ward's intended selection.*—As the right of the guardian, who is selected by a minor of the proper age for selecting his own guardian, to supersede the former guardian, depends upon the fact that the ward has attained that age, as such fact is not necessarily determinable by inspection in court, but may be proved or controverted by other evidence, it seems that such former guardian is entitled to notice of the intended application to the court to appoint a new guardian, of the ward's election, so as to give him an opportunity of proving the ward not to be of that age, if the fact be so.[1]

---

[1] 3 Dana, 599.

CHAPTER 5.

GENERAL POWERS AND DUTIES, ETC., OF GUARDIANS.

1. *Powers of guardian of person and estate*—Every person appointed guardian both of the person and estate of a minor, shall have the custody and tuition of his ward, and the management[1]

---

[1] The office of trustee is one of personal confidence, and can not be delegated. If a person takes upon himself the management of property for the benefit of another, he has no right to impose that duty on others, and if he does, he will be responsible. Therefore, if a trustee confides his duties or the trust fund to the care of a stranger, or to his attorney, he will be personally responsible. Perry on Trusts, § 402. See also 2 Kent's Com. 223, Schouler's Dom. Rel. 471; 3 Redf. on Wills, 527; and cases cited by these writers; also, Eichelberger's Appeal, 4 Watts, (Pa.) 84.

But under some circumstances, a trustee may deposit money in bank. See paragraph 39.

And there are circumstances where trustees must employ agents. If he acts in accordance with the usages of mankind, and prudently for the trust, as he would have done for himself, and according to the usage of business, as if a trustee appoints rents to be paid to a banker, at that time in credit, but who afterward breaks, the trustee is not answerable. So in the employment of stewards and agents, if he acts in the usual method of business. Perry on Trusts, § 401; 3 Redf. on Wills, 528–9.

It is the duty of the trustee to proceed at once, after his appointment and qualification, to receive the possession of the trust property and to protect it from loss and injury; and if there are debts or securities due and payable to the trust estate, he must proceed to collect them. If loss or damage to

of such ward's estate during minority, unless sooner removed or discharged from such trust, or the guardianship shall sooner determine from any of the causes specified in chapter 4.[1]

2. *Rights of parents.*—But the statute expressly provides that the father of such minor, or if there be no father, the mother, if a suitable person, respectively, shall have the custody of the person and the control of the education of such minor.[1]

3. *Statutory duties of guardians of person and estate.*—The following are declared by the statutes[2] to be the duties of every guardian of any minor, who may be appointed to have the cus-

---

the trust estate occurs from his negligence in these respects, he would probably be personally liable. Perry on Trusts, § 438; Schouler's Dom. Rel. 473; 3 Redf. on Wills, 540; but see last part of par. 12, below.

Unless authorized to do so by will, a trustee will become liable if he allows money to remain out and uncollected on personal security, even if it was so loaned or invested by the testator himself. It is not enough for an *executor* to apply for the payment through an attorney; he must follow the collection actively by legal proceedings, unless he can show that such proceedings would have been futile and vain. Perry on Trusts, § 440. No doubt this rule would also apply to a guardian. See Lane v. Mickle, 46 Ala. 600; Walker v. Walker, 42 Ga. 135; 3 Redf. on Wills, 540.

An infant's guardian has power to accept delivery of deed of conveyance to his ward. Barney v. Seeley, 38 Wis. 381. A guardian's responsibility for the property of his ward extends only to such as is accessible to him. Bethune v. Green, 27 Ga. 56.

Guardians can not release a debt due their wards. Horine v. Horine, 11 Mo. 649.

Guardian is ward's mere agent, having an authority not coupled with an interest. Manson v. Felton, 13 Pick. (Mass.) 206.

If a person has once accepted the guardianship, either expressly or by implication, he can not afterwards avoid its duties and responsibilities; he can only be discharged by a decree of a court having jurisdiction, and upon proper proceedings had. Perry on Trusts, §§ 268, 401. See 3 Redf. on Wills, 526.

One who, in 1854, became guardian under circumstances sufficient to put him upon inquiry as to the rights of his ward to a pension as heir of a soldier of the Mexican war, *Held* to be responsible for the amount of such pension from 1854 till his ward became of age. Clodfelter v. Bost, 70 N. C. 733.

See note 1, Page 94.

[1] § 6264.

[2] § 6269, as amended, vol. 77 O. L. p. 77.

tody of such minor and take charge of the estate of such minor, to-wit:

4. *First. Must file inventory.* — To make out and file, within three months after his appointment, a full inventory, verified by oath, of the real and personal estate of his ward, with the value of the same, and the value of the yearly rent of the real estate.

5. *Penalty.* If the guardian fails to file such inventory for thirty days after he shall have been notified of the expiration of the time by the probate judge, said probate judge must remove him and appoint a successor.

6. *Second.   Must manage estate.*—To manage the estate for the best interest of his ward.[1]

---

[1] Where a guardian, for the purpose of paying for improvements to land in the possession of or claimed by his ward, gave a lien on the accruing rents, it was held that, if the guardian had the power to incumber the land, the ward could not overreach the lien by purchasing a paramount and better title than he had when the lien was created; for the contract of the guardian, made within the extent of his power, binds the ward the same as if it were his own.   Este *v.* Strong, 2 O. 401.

If a guardian convert land scrip, receivable at the land office in the purchase of public lands, into money, by investing it in land for himself and others, and accounting with his wards for the scrip, with interest from the time of its investment, he can not, if he acted in good faith in the transaction, be charged as a trustee of the land purchased, or compelled to account for the profits growing out of the purchase.   Davies *v.* Lowrey, 15 O. 655.

Land scrip, or certificates for money paid by S., were issued under the act of Congress of May 23, 1828 (4 U. S. Stat. 286), to A., B. and C., minors, and in trust for the other heirs of S.; the certificates were not assignable on their face, and were payable in lands.   The following note was appended to the certificates: "The indorsement to be executed by (L.) guardian of said heirs."   The certificates indorsed by A. B. C., and L., guardian of said heirs, were used by L. and his partners in the purchase of lands, and the title taken by H., one of the partners, for their common benefit, the partners agreeing, respectively, to pay L. their portions of the amount of the certificates in money.   In a proceeding by the unnamed heirs of S. against H. and others in interest, charging said lands: *Held,* that L. had no authority as guardian of A., B. and C., to dispose of or transfer the interest of the other heirs in the certificates.   1860.   Stoddard *v.* Smith, 11 O. S. 581.

A party creating a lien on an estate can not be permitted to defeat that lien by any act of his own.   On this principle, where a guardian having authority for the purpose, improved the property of his ward, and gave a

7. *Third.   Must render accounts*—To render, on oath, to the proper court, an account[1] of the receipts and expenditures of such guardian, verified by vouchers or proof, once in every two years, or oftener, upon the order of the court, made upon motion of any person interested in said ward, or the property of such ward, for good cause shown by affidavit.[2]   But in all cases where the whole estate of said ward, or of several wards jointly, under the same appointment of guardianship, does not exceed two hundred dollars in value, said guardian can only be required to render such account upon the termination of said guardianship, or upon the order of said court, made upon its own motion, or the motion of some person interested in said ward or wards, or in his, her, or their property, for good cause shown, and set forth upon the journal of said court.

8. *Penalty.* Should the guardian fail to render[3] any account required in the preceding paragraph, for thirty days after he shall have been notified of the expiration of the time by the

---

lien on the accruing rents for the payment of the costs of the improvements, it is not competent for the ward, by the purchase of a paramount title, to defeat that lien.   The act of the guardian must be regarded as equally binding on the ward, as if his own, when of full age.   1826.   Este *v.* Strong, 2 O. 401.

See note 1, page 94.

" It may be remarked, in general, that, if any one of the acts which infants are disabled from doing of themselves, is requisite to be done to protect their interests, they are to be done by their guardians."   Walker's Am. Law, 257.

[1] See notes, pages 150–152, 164–166.

[2] It is believed that the meaning of this, expressed a little differently, is as follows: That the guardian must render, on oath, as often at least as once in two years, an account of his receipts and expenditures as such guardian, verified by vouchers or proof; but that any person interested in the ward, or in the ward's property may, for any cause shown by affidavit to be good, ask the court, by motion, to require such an account oftener than once in two years, and that, if the court considers the reason given to be a good one, it will grant the request.—, Ed.]

A trustee is bound to keep clear, distinct, and accurate accounts.   If he does not, all presumptions are against him, and all doubts and obscurities are to be taken adversely to him.   See Perry on Trusts, §§ 821, 911.

[3] For directions as to preparing such accounts, etc., see chapter 9.

probate judge, he will receive no allowance for services, unless the court enters upon its journal that such delay was necessary and reasonable.

9. *Fourth. Must settle fully*—At the expiration of his trust fully to account for and pay over to the proper person, all of the estate of his ward remaining in his hands.[1]

10. *Fifth. Must pay, compound, etc., debts, defend suits, etc*—To pay all just debts due from such ward, out of the estate in his hands, and collect all debts due such ward, and, in case of doubtful debts, to compound the same, and to appear for and defend, or cause to be defended,[2] all suits against such ward.

11. *Sixth. Must educate wards, when.* — When any ward has no father, or having a father who is unable or fails to educate such ward, it shall be the duty of his guardian to provide for him such education[3] as the amount of his estate may justify.

12. *Seventh. Must lend money, on what security; change of investment; penalty*—To loan or invest the money of his ward

---

[1] See note 1, page 60.

[2] Under the act of July 1, 1858 (S. & C. 673, §§ 14, 15), which require guardians of infants to "appear for and defend, or cause to be defended, all suits" against the infant, a guardian is authorized to appear for an infant to a petition for dower, and where he appears and answers as guardian, and his answer is received and acted on by the court, the effect is the same as though he had been expressly appointed guardian *ad litem*, and had appeared and answered as such. 1871. Rankin *v.* Kemp, 21 O. S. 651.

The act of 1824 (2 Chase, 1308), regulating the sales of land by executors and administrators, did not direct the mode in which the heirs should be made parties, and the courts adopted such practice as they deemed expedient. Where minor children who were not named in the petition had an appearance entered for them in court by their guardian, while the petition was pending, they were bound by the order of sale. Whatever irregularity there was in such practice, it did not affect the purchaser, who held his title as securely as a purchaser at sheriff's sale, under a judgment at law, or a decree in chancery. 1835. Ewing's Lessee *v.* Higby, 7 O. 1 pt. 198.

And see Ewing *v.* Hollister, 7 O. 2 pt. 138, where the legality of the same sale was sustained.

[3] The following extract, full of accepted law, excellent judgment, and sound, practical common sense, is commended to the careful consideration of every guardian. "The general rules of law governing all cases are that:

within a reasonable time[1] after he receives it, in notes or bonds secured by first mortgage[2] on real estate of at least double the

the guardian shall procure proper food, and clothing, for his ward, and the opportunity to acquire the elements of practical education, both secular and religious, so long as his estate, or the earnings of the ward will warrant it. Beyond this must depend upon the extent of his property and his reasonable expectations in life, with reference to which the ward may expect his guardian will afford him the opportunities of education and instruction. Every ward who has the means of subsistence without manual labor, has the right to have that means applied, to a reasonable extent, in procuring him indispensable support and education. Beyond this the guardian would not be expected, ordinarily, perhaps, to expend more than the income of the estate in procuring that extent of instruction which is merely ornamental, and which comes more especially within the range of the elegant arts, or the higher studies connected with education, which may tend to gratify the taste, or the laudable ambition of the ward, but which do not, in any sensible degree, qualify him for the essential duties of life. And if the estate of the ward is very large, the guardian would not be expected to expend all the income, probably, for the mere purpose of the indulgence of the ward, or in vain attempts to accomplish such attainments as were not within the compass of his capacity. The guardian is to exercise a reasonable discretion in this as in all other respects; and while he denies his ward no reasonble indulgence, which is consistent with the extent of his fortune and fairly within the range of reasonable support and education, according to his just expectations in life, he is at the same time to hold such a firm and steady hand over all the expenditures, for the benefit of his ward, as will commend itself to the approbation of a prudent and just judge, who may be called to examine and adjust his accounts; and will not leave the ward, when he comes to control his own affairs, to entertain sorrow or regret that he had not fallen under a more discreet and prudent guardianship." 3 Redfield on Wills, 456–7. See note 2, page 90.

The guardian is the proper judge as to the school or university at which his ward shall be educated; and the court will compel the obedience of the ward to the selection, unless some reasonable objection is shown. But if there are two or more guardians appointed for the ward, and they disagree as to the mode of education, the court will exercise its own discretion on the subject, and will not regard itself bound by the wishes of the majority upon the subject. Tyler on Inf. & Cov. § 174. (Citing Tremain's case, Strange, 168, and Hall v. Hall, 3 Atk. 721.

A guardian will not be permitted to do any thing prejudicial to his ward, and courts will not construe any of his acts so as to prejudice them. Torrey v. Black, 65 Barb. (N. Y.) 417.

[1] See note 1, page 67.

[2] Mortgages on real estate are considered proper investments in all of the

value of the money loaned or invested, exclusive of improvements, timber, or minerals, subject to destruction or exhaustion, in bonds of the United States, or of any state on which default has never been made in the payment of interest, or bonds of any county or city in this state, issued in conformity to law; or, with the consent and approbation of the probate court, in productive real estate within this state, the title to which must be taken in the name of the guardian as such; and to manage such investments, and when deemed proper, change the same into any other investment of the above classes; but no real estate so purchased can be sold by the guardian, except with the consent and approbation of the probate court; and if said guardian fail

---

United States; and mortgages upon real estate, of which the borrower is the absolute owner in fee simple, taken with proper caution as to the amount and title, are considered safe and proper investments. In all cases the trustee must use great care and diligence in ascertaining the valuation, situation, condition, and productiveness of the real estate or other property upon which it is proposed to make a loan of the trust money; for he will be liable for the loss if he is guilty of any negligence in this respect. Perry on Trusts, § 458.

But trustees can not lend money on mortgage to one of themselves. Ib. § 461.

It is a universal rule that trustees can not invest money in personal securities; and even if they have a discretion as to the kind of investments they may make, it is not sound discretion to invest in personal securities. In the words of an eminent authority [Lord Kenyon]. "No rule is better established than that a trustee can not lend on a mere personal security, and it *ought to be rung in the ears* of every one who acts in the character of trustee." Ib. § 453.

A guardian lending trust funds to a man in active business, without security, will be held responsible for its loss. Clark *v.* Garfield, 8 Allen (Mass.) 427; of similar tenor, Lee *v.* Lee, 55 Ala. 590.

A guardian or trustee, in the absence of specific directions, may, by the common law of England, loan on mortgage of real estate or invest in government stocks only, unless otherwise directed by order of court. A trustee investing in the ordinary mode is not responsible for loss if he act honestly and with the common prudence and skill of competent men. The law does not require of him the care and skill of the most cautious or shrewdest money-makers. Miller *v.* Proctor, 20 O. S. 442.

If a guardian, instead of loaning his ward's money, use it himself, though his liability is greater thereby, it is not a breach of the bond, so long as he has the money ready to pay over on legal demand. Case *v.* State (Hocking Dist. Ct. 1852), 10 W. L. J. 163.

to loan or invest the money of his ward within such reasonable time, he must account on settlement for such money and interest thereon, calculated with annual rests;[1] and also to settle and adjust, when necessary or desirable, the assets which he may receive, in kind, from an executor or administrator, as may be most advantageous to his wards; but before such settlement and adjustment will be valid and binding, it must be approved by the probate court, and such approval entered on its journal; and with the like approval, to hold the assets as received from the executor or administrator, or what may be received in the settlement and adjustment of said assets.   (See also par. 14, below.)

13. *Eighth.—Must obey court.*   To obey and perform all orders and judgments of the proper courts touching the guardianship.

---

[1] Where a guardian had an opportunity to show any excuse for failure to invest the money of his ward, but introduces no evidence, the court will not presume inability to invest to excuse him from interest.   Nor will it excuse him that if the money had been invested in certain stocks, then deemed the best in the city, it might have been wholly lost.   1834.   Armstrong *v.* Miller, W. 562.

The object for which a guardian is appointed is to keep his ward's funds safely and to render them productive.   If he fails to invest them productively, when he could do so, he is chargeable with interest.   Armstrong *v.* Miller, 6 O. 118, 124.

It is a general rule that trustees should loan more on real estate of a fixed and permanent value, and not so much on property with houses of a perishable nature, or upon property of a fluctuating or contingent value. But a gurdian or trustee who, in good faith and with ordinary prudence, invests in a mortgage security to two-thirds the market price of unimproved lands adjacent to a growing city, or in a new state, the value of which land is generally estimated on fair anticipations of an influx of population, and contingent thereon, is not liable for depreciation in value, caused by financial derangement or diminished immigration, which could not have been reasonably foreseen.   In re Spencer's appeal.   1861.   (Logan Co. Common Pleas.)   3 W. L. M. 408.

Trustees must invest trust funds in their hands in the manner directed, within a reasonable time, though they are subject to no specific directions as to the time and manner of investment,'or they will be charged interest on the fund, and will be required to make good any loss or damage suffered on account of such delay.   What is reasonable time depends on circumstances. One year has been so held in several cases, more especially relating to administration.   The U. S. Supreme Court, in Barney *v.* Saunders, 16 How 543, held three months to be reasonable time within which to invest trust

14. *How guardians. etc., may invest funds.* Guardians, trustees, executors, and administrators may, when they have funds belonging to the trust which are to be invested, invest the same in the certificates of the indebtedness of this state or of the United States, or in such other securities as may be approved by the court having control of the administration of the trust.[1]

15. *Duties of guardian of the estate only.* When the guardian

---

funds paid to a banker, and charged the trustee for the sum lost by failure of the banker after that time, *except* small amounts paid in from time to time, derived from rents, interest and dividends. Guardians and trustees are held to a stricter rule in relation to investments than executors acting as trustees, as guardians generally take an estate ready to be invested. See Perry on Trusts, § 462; 2 Kent's Com. 230–1; Tyler on Inf. and Cov., §175; Schouler's Dom. Rel. 475; Barney *v.* Saunders, 16 How. 543; Ashley *v.* Martin, 50 Ala. 537; *Re* Mott, 26 N. J. Eq. 509; Bradford *v.* Bodfish, 39 Ia. 681; Colburn *v.* State, 47 Ind. 310.

In the absence of statutory provisions similar to the foregoing, the *general* rule established by the courts is that guardians must be charged with uncompounded interest, at the legal rate, from the time beyond which it was unreasonable for him to retain it unproductive to the ward, subject to the qualification that if the guardian has made more from the money in any way than such interest, he must account for all he has made; and also, that if he was bound to have made any specific designated investment, he should account for all the income that would have resulted therefrom, or to such interest, at the option of the ward; and the court might, in its discretion, subject the guardian to the payment of compound interest. Perry on Trusts, § 468–472; Tyler on Inf. and Cov. § 175.

[1] § 6413. This section further provides that "Whenever money coming into the hands of an executor, administrator, trustee, agent, assignee, attorney, or officer, shall be stopped therein by reason of litigation or other lawful cause, and the same will probably be so detained for more than six months, such executor, administrator, trustee, agent, assignee, attorney, or officer, may invest the same during such detention in the same manner that trust funds are now authorized by law to be invested, or in such other manner as the probate court or other court having jurisdiction of the pending litigation, or person aforesaid, may direct."

By mentioning who *may* invest money so stopped, and omitting guardians from this list, the law seems to prohibit them from investing money temporarily stopped in their hands. In such case, especially if the sum were considerable, it would be judicious to apply for an order of court, directing in what manner such funds should be cared for during such detention.

See paragraph 12, above, and notes thereto.

is appointed to take charge only of the estate of the minor, his duties are the same as those above specified in paragraphs 3–13, except that he will not be required to perform the *sixth* duty there mentioned, if a guardian of the person of such minor has been appointed.[4]

16. *Duties of guardian of person only; must protect, control, maintain, and educate his ward, etc.*—When a guardian is appointed to have the custody, maintenance, and education of a minor, his duties are as follows:[2]

17. *First.* To protect and control the person of the ward.

18. *Second.* To provide a suitable maintenance[3] for his ward, when necessary, which must be paid out of the estate of such ward in the hands of the guardian of such estate, upon the order of the guardian of the person of such ward.

19. *Third.* When such ward has no father or mother, or having a father or mother, and such parent is unable or fails to maintain or educate such ward, it is the duty of the guardian so appointed, to provide for him such maintenance and education as the amount of his estate may justify, which must be paid out of the estate of such ward in the hands of the guardian of such estate, upon the order of the guardian of the person of such ward.

20. *Fourth.* To obey and perform all the orders and judgments of the proper court, touching the guardianship.

21. *How enforced.* How these duties are to be enforced is specified in chapter 4.

22. *Stock in building associations held by trustees, etc.* All shares of stock held in such associations by or in the name of a minor, or by or in the name of a guardian or trustee of a minor, may, at the discretion of the board of directors, and with the consent of such trustee or guardian, be paid to such trustee or guardian, and it will be a valid payment.[4]

---

[1] § 6270.

[2] The guardian is the judge in the first instance, of what are necessaries for the infant, his ward. If he, acting in good faith, refuses his consent to the ward's taking a journey, undertaken only for the purposes of pleasure and companionship with her friends, another person who advances money for the expenses of the journey, can not recover it from the ward, after majority, as "necessaries." McKanna *v.* Merry, 61 Ill. 177.

[3] § 6271.   [4] § 3836.

23. *Guardians' and parents' powers as to custody and education of minor.* For the sake of avoiding confusion, it may be well to summarize the various provisions of the law relating to the respective right of the parents and guardians in this matter, which provisions might seem, at a hasty glance, to be in conflict in some respects: *First.* The guardian of the *person only* of a minor has the custody and must provide for the education of such ward, as the parents of such ward must be either dead, or are unsuitable persons to be intrusted with these duties.[1] *Second.* The guardian of the *person and estate* of a minor does not have the custody of the person, nor the control of the education of such ward, unless the ward has neither father nor mother, or unless such parents are respectively unsuitable persons to be intrusted therewith.[2] *Third.* The guardian of the *estate only* has nothing to do with the custody of the person, nor with the education of his ward, except to pay the proper bills therefor out of the ward's estate.[3]

24. *Certain minors may not marry, unless guardian, etc., consent.* Male persons under the age of twenty-one years, and female persons under the age of eighteen years, must first obtain the consent of their fathers, respectively, or in case of the death or incapacity of their fathers, then of their mothers or guardians, before they can be joined in marriage.

25. *Others may.* Male persons of the age of eighteen years, and female persons of the age of sixteen years, not nearer of kin than second cousins, and not having a husband or wife living, may be joined in marriage, if consent as above directed be first obtained.[4]

---

[1] § 6255; § 6260; *Third* of § 6271.　See par. 18, chap. 3; pars. 16–19, chap. 5.

[2] § 6255; § 6264; *Sixth* of § 6269.　See pars. 19, 33, chap. 3; pars. 1, 2, 11, chap. 5.

[3] §§ 6270, 6269.　See paragraphs 15, 18, 19, this chapter.

[4] § 6384.

The marriage contract of one affected with congenital imbecility of mind, to a degree rendering him incapable of consent, is void *ad initio.* A court of chancery, in the exercise of its ordinary powers, will entertain jurisdiction, at the suit of the imbecile's guardian, to declare such marriage a nullity. Waymire *v.* Jetmore, 22 O. S. 271.

Mutual promises to marry in the future, though made by parties competent to contract, and followed by cohabitation as husband and wife, do not

26. *Such consent must be witnessed and certified.* If any of the persons intending to marry are under age, and have not had a former wife or husband, the consent of the parents or guardians must be personally given before the probate judge, or certified under the hand of such parent or guardian, attested by two witnesses, one of whom must appear before said judge, and make oath that he saw the parent or guardian, whose name is annexed to such certificate, subscribe, or heard him or her acknowledge the same; and the probate judge is authorized to administer such oath, and thereupon issue and sign a proper license,[1] and affix thereto the seal of the court.[2]

27. *What the minister or justice must know before performing the marriage ceremony.* Every minister, or justice of the peace, must, before he solemnizes any marriage between parties, either of whom is required by the provisions of paragraph 24 above, to obtain the consent of his or her parent or guardian (except in cases where license has been obtained from the judge of the probate court), be satisfied that the marriage bans have been duly published, and also that the consent of such parent or guardian has been obtained, either by acknowledgment in presence of such minister or justice of the peace, or by a certificate under the signature of such parent or guardian, and attested by one or more credible

---

constitute a valid marriage. Duncan *v.* Duncan, 10 O. S. 181; but where the person who solemnized the marriage had no license, it was held that it was to be inferred that the parties openly and mutually consented to a contract of present marriage—then to become husband and wife—and when they thereafter cohabited as such, that this constituted a legal marriage, and the man having then a wife living, might properly be convicted of bigamy, on proof of such second marriage. Carmichael *v.* State, 12 O. S. 553.

Marriages contracted in this state by male persons under the age of eighteen, and females under the age of fourteen, are invalid, unless confirmed by cohabitation after arriving at those ages respectively; and such marriage, not so confirmed, does not subject a party to punishment for bigamy for contracting a subsequent marriage while the first husband or wife is living. Shafher *v.* State, 20 O. 1.

[1] In an action for damages by a father, for the wrongful issuing of license for the marriage of his daughter, evidence of the bad character of the husband may be received and considered by the jury in aggravation of damages. Larwill *v.* Kirby, 14 O. 1.

[2] § 6390.

witnesses, who must be present for the purpose of satisfying such minister or justice of the peace, that such certificate was actually signed by the parent or guardian, for the purpose aforesaid.

28–31. *The form of certificate* required in the two preceding paragraphs may be as follows :

I hereby certify, that I give my consent, as guardian of C. D., that he [*or,* she, *as the case may be*] may marry O. P.

Witness my hand, this —— day of ——, A. D. ——.

A. B.,
Guardian of C. D.

Attest :
 V. W.,
 X. Y.

32. *Effect of marriage on the guardianship.* The effect of the ward's marriage on his or her guardianship has been stated on page 50.

33. *When foreign guardian of foreign ward may demand or receive property of his ward in this state.*—In any case in which a guardian not appointed in this state and his ward are both non-residents of this state, and the ward is entitled to money or other property in the lawful custody of any executor, administrator, or other person in this state, such guardian may, by the order of the probate court of the proper county, upon filing therein the proofs named in paragraph 14, of chapter 4, and giving notice to such custodian as therein prescribed, be permitted to demand, receive, or recover, by suit, such money or other property, and remove the same, unless the terms of limitation attending the right by which the ward owns the same, conflict with such removal.[1]

34. *Guardian and others interested may get direction of court.*—Any executor, administrator, guardian, or other trustee, may maintain a civil action in the court of common pleas against the creditors, legatees, distributees, or other parties, asking the direction or judgment of the court in any matter respecting the trust, estate, or property to be administered, and the rights of the parties in interest, in the same manner, and as fully as was for-

---

[1] § 6279.

merly entertained in courts of chancery; and in case any executor, administrator, guardian, or other trustee, after being requested in writing by any creditor, legatee, distributee, or other party in interest to bring such action, fail for thirty days so to do, the creditor, legatee, distributee, or other party making such request, may himself institute such action.[1]

35. *General principles and observations.*—The statutes by no means point out the entire duties of trustees,[2] especially of those treated of in chapters 21 and 22 of this book, nor the manner in which these duties must be performed. Numerous, extensive, and learned treatises have been written upon these subjects, taking for the basis of their contents the immense mass of decisions of the courts of the various states of the United States and of England, as well as the common law, most of which are accepted as

---

[1] § 6202.

An action by executors against devisees, distributees, and heirs, asking the direction and judgment of the court touching the construction of the testator's will, and the duties of the executors thereunder, and although praying, among other things, for an order to sell lands, in pursuance of the supposed intention of the testator, for the payment of legacies, is appealable from the common pleas to the district court. Townsend *v.* Townsend, 24 Ohio St. 1. See also Steinberger *v.* Steinberger, 19 Ohio, 106.

An action brought for the mere purpose of obtaining the opinion of the court upon the construction of the will, can not be maintained in cases where no trust is involved. Collins *v.* Collins, 19 Ohio St. 468.

When no trust is involved, and no advice or guidance to an executor or other trustee is required, parties claiming under or against a will can not maintain an action for the mere purpose of obtaining the court's opinion as to its meaning or legal effect. Corry *v.* Fleming, 29 Ohio St. 147.

A trustee who is also executor, there being two claimants to a fund, may ask the direction of the court. First Presbyterian Society *v.* Same, 25 Ohio St. 128, 133.

A trustee in doubt as to his powers, has a right to apply to a court of equity to define them, and give judicial sanction to his acts. Wiswell *v.* First Congregational Church, 14 Ohio St. 31.

[2] Guardians are trustees. Schouler's Dom. Rel. 437–9; Redf. on Wills, 440, n. 15; Bouv. Law Dic. 616; Hill on Trusts, 49. Other writers on trusts show that they consider them such, as a matter of course, without expressly saying so, by treating of their duties, etc., in their works on trusts and trustees. It also follows that they are from the fundamental principles of trusteeship as prescribed by all authorities and as defined in law and other dictionaries, which see.

binding in this state, or at least as worthy of being followed by our courts having special jurisdiction in such matters, where the statutes make no special provisions.

36. Though not infrequent references are made throughout this volume to many of these treatises and decisions, it may be well here to attempt a summary of some other well-defined and generally accepted principles governing guardians and trustees.

37. The reader should also bear in mind that in relation to *some* trustees, and especially executors and administrators, the statutory provisions are quite minute in many particulars. Though these provisions do not apply in express terms to guardians and trustees, yet if the statutes are silent on any given point of practice as to guardians or other trustees, they would most probably be looked to, whenever, in the nature of things, they would be as fitting in the one case as the other. The court, being without guide in the one case and being compelled to adopt *some* course or plan, would most likely, and very properly, adopt the plan pointed out in the other case, so far as applicable.

38. *Guardian subject to these principles.*—In the management of his ward's estate, a guardian is bound by the principles which regulate the general conduct of all trustees.[1]

39. *As to deposits of money in bank.* If a guardian deposits money *in his own name* in a bank, and the money is lost by the bank's failure, or otherwise, he will be personally responsible for such money. But if he, *as guardian*, deposits it in a bank in good credit and repute, till the proper time for paying it to creditors, for use in paying the current expenses of supporting and educating the ward, or till it can be judiciously invested, etc., and the bank fails, he will not be responsible. He must act in regard to this as a prudent man would in his own affairs, and must keep the account of such funds separate from the account of his own.[2] His bank book and bank account for such

---

[1] Schouler's Dom. Rel. 461.

[2] Although the following authorities do not all *mention* guardians, the general principles are those which govern them in such circumstances, as well as executors and other trustees.

In Shaw *v.* Bauman, 34 O. S. 25 (in which a justice of the peace was held

funds should show that the account is with "A. B., as guardian of C. D."

40. *Rule as to proper care and diligence.* No doubt the rule is that where trustees, including guardians, act within the scope of their authority, in good faith and according to the best of their judgment, and exercise such prudence, care and diligence as men of ordinary prudence, care and diligence manifest in like matters of their own, they will not be held accountable for

——

liable for money officially collected by him, and deposited *in his own name* in a bank which failed), the court used this language (p. 32   "The rule in equity is well settled, . . . that if a trustee deposits the funds of a trust estate in bank, in his own name, individually, with his own private funds, he thereby becomes debtor to the trust estate, and a creditor of the bank; and in case the trust funds are lost through the insolvency of the bank, the trustee becomes individually liable for the loss.   (Citing Wren *v.* Kirton, 11 Ves. 377; Macdonnell *v.* Harding, 8 Eng. Ch. 177; *Re* Stafford, 11 Barbour, 353; Brown *v.* Recketts, 1 John. Ch. 303; Ins. Co. *v.* Lynch, 11 Paige, 520; Phillips *v.* Lamar, 27 Geo. 227.)   See also McLain *v.* McGregor, 1 C. S. C. R. 327 ; (*or,* W. & B. Digest, "Trusts," 55.)

·   A trustee may deposit money temporarily in some responsible banking-house ; but he will be liable for the money in case of a failure of the bank, or for its depreciation, if he deposits it to his *own credit,* and not to the separate account of the trust estate. . . . It is the duty of the trustee to withdraw the money from the bank upon the slightest indication of danger or loss. . . . He will be liable if he keeps money in bank an unreasonable length of time. . . . 1 Perry on Trusts, §§ 443–7, 914; (citing numerous English and American authorities, especially to the first sentence of this paragraph.)   See also Schouler's Dom. Rel. 474.

In all cases, however, in which a trustee places money in the hands of a banker, he should take care to keep it separate, and not mix it with his own in a common account; for, if he should so mix it, he would be deemed to have treated the whole as his own, and he would be held liable to the *cestui que trust* for any loss sustained by the banker's insolvency. 2 Story on Equity Jurisprudence, § 1270.   Also, Hill on Trustees, 375, 376; Perry on Trusts, §§ 444, 463; Schouler's Dom. Rel. 474; 3 Redf. on Wills, 539.

But, with respect to losses sustained by the failure of bankers, or other persons into whose hands the money of the testator has been deposited by the executor, the rule, at least in equity, seems to be that where the deposit was made from necessity, or conformably to the common usage of mankind, the executor will not be responsible for the loss. 2 Williams on Executors 1545, 1546; 3 Redf. on Wills, 529.

An executor will not be liable for money allowed to remain with bankers who fail, where it is not an unreasonable sum for the executor to keep in

losses happening from their management of the trust funds.[1] But this rule will only protect the guardian as long as he manages the trust fund strictly as the law requires him to do.[2]

41. It has also been held that the maxim that every person is presumed to know the law, is not always applicable to trustees; on the contrary, they may be exonerated from losses resulting from their ignorance of the law, in cases where they exercise proper diligence and precaution, and act upon the advice of counsel.[3]

42. *Guardian responsible for criminal acts of his agents.* Though a trustee is not responsible for the crimes of strangers, he is responsible for the criminal acts of agents employed by himself about the trust funds.[4]

43. *Must pay right person.* Guardians, and others having trust money to distribute, must see that it reaches the person

---

bank, or where it was only reasonable for the money to be deposited there under the circumstances. Smith on Equity, paragraph 355.

" . . If a guardian deposits his ward's money in his own name, and it is lost, he is accountable for it. Tyler on Inf. and Cov., §175.

[1] Miller *v.* Proctor, 20 O. S. 442; State *v.* Guilford, 18 O. 500; Perry on Trusts, §§441, 914; Tyler on Inf. and Cov., §175; Schouler's Dom. Rel. 468, 469, 479; 3 Redf. on Wills, 535, 563, 453, n. 6; Morley *v.* Morley, 2 Ch. Ca. 2; Jones *v.* Lewis, 2 Ves. 241; Massey *v.* Banner, 1 J. & W., 247; Att'y. Gen. *v.* Dixon, 13 Ves. 534; *Ex p.* Belchier, Amb. 220; *Ex p.* Griffin, 2 Gi. & J. 114; Taylor *v.* Benham, 5 How. 233; King *v.* Talbot, 50 Barb. 453; 40 N. Y. 86; Neff's App., 57 Penn. St. 91; King *v.* King, 37 Ga. 205; Campbell *v.* Campbell, 38 Ga. 301; White *v.* Parker, 8 Barb. 48, 53; Glover *v.* Glover, 1 McMullin (S. C.), 153; De Peyster *v.* Clarkson, 2 Wend. 77, 106; Smith v. Smith, Marsh. (Ky.) 238; Lovell *v.* Minot, 20 Pick. 116; Ashley *v.* Martin, 50 Ala. 537; Longmire *v.* Herndon, 72 N. C. 629; State *v.* Morrison, 68 N. C. 162; Love *v.* Logan, 69 N. C. 70; Atkinson *v.* Whitehead, 66 N. C. 296; Genet *v.* Tallmadge, 1 Johns. Ch. (N. Y.) 3; *In re* Spencer's Appeal (Logan Co. O., C. P.) 3 W. L. M. 408; Lay *v.* O'Neil, 29 La. Ann. 722. See also last three pars. of note 1, p. 67.

In 3 Redf. on Wills, 541, it is stated that trust funds must be kept and invested not only with that care, skill and watchfulness which the trustee would exercise in regard to his own funds of like character and amount, but with that which the most vigilant exercise about such matters (citing, at end of a long paragraph, 1 Lewin, 211 *et seq.*, and cases there cited). But the rule in Ohio is as stated above. See Ohio cases referred to in this note.

[2] See paragraphs 12, 37.

[3] Miller *v.* Proctor, 20 O. S., 442; see also 3 Redf. on Wills, 565.

[4] Perry on Trusts, §441; Schouler's Dom. Rel. 471; 3 Redf. on Wills, 542.

entitled to receive it, for if paid to the wrong person, by mistake or otherwise, they are still liable to pay it to the rightful claimant.[1]

44. *Guardian can in no way derive profit from ward's property.* —It is a well settled rule in equity, that a trustee is not permitted to so manage the subject of his trust as to make profits or gain therefrom, either directly or indirectly, for himself. The beneficiaries in the trust have a right to expect and require the exercise of his best judgment, care and diligence on their behalf, and the gains resulting therefrom inure to their sole benefit. Among other things, this would effectually prevent a trustee from buying up a debt or incumbrance to which the trust estate is liable for less than the amount due thereon, and appropriate the difference as a profit to himself.[2]

---

[1] Perry on Trusts, §926; 3 Redf. on Wills, 538. But not for interest thereon, *Ib.* 445-6.

[2] Cox *v.* John, 32 O. S. 532; Perry on Trusts, §§ 427-432, 464, 621; Schouler's Dom. Rel. 468-9, 478, 510, 511; 3 Redf. on Wills, 533-5; 2 Kent's Com. 229; 4 do. 371, note c; Tyler on Inf. and Cov., § 175.

Among recent cases outside of Ohio, not cited in above works, see Berkmeyer *v.* Kellerman (Conn.), 3 Cin. Law Bulletin, 19; Lowry *v.* State, 64 Ind. 421; Chanslor *v.* Chanslor, 11 Bush (Ky.), 663; Wood *v.* Safford, 50 Miss. 370; State *v.* Peebles, 70 N. C. 10.

What such trustee may not do directly, he is not permitted to do through the intervention of an agent or attorney. Cox *v.* John, 32 O. S. 532.

An administrator [and this applies with equal force to guardians.—*Ed.*] can not, therefore, be allowed, directly, or through his attorney, to compromise, adjust, and settle claims against the estate for which he is acting, for less than their face, and to put the difference in his own pocket. *Ib.*

And the rule is the same, whether the attorney, through whom such compromise and settlement is effected, acts for the administrator officially or personally; and whether he acts, in making such settlement, as the attorney of the administrator, solely, or for him and others, with a view to their joint profit. What the administrator may not do singly, the policy of the law will not permit him to participate in doing. In either case the discounts obtained from creditors must inure to the benefit of the estate. *Ib.*

It is the peculiar province of equity to take cognizance of transactions growing out of relations of trust, and to prevent those holding such positions from using them and their influence for their own aggrandizement. Berkmeyer *v.* Kellerman.

All the power, influence and skill of one occupying such a relation is to be used for the advantage of the beneficial owner and not for personal gain;

45. *Guardians can not speculate with, nor use ward's money in business.*—Trustees can not use any part of the trust fund in their own speculations or business. Should they nevertheless do so, all profits whatsoever derived from such use must be accounted for as the property of the beneficiaries; and should any loss result from such use of the funds, it must be borne entirely by the trustee.[1]

46. In case of such use by a guardian, the wards may, on arriving of age, elect to take either (1), all the profits made in such

and all increase, gains or profits, whether arising from the natural increase in value of the property or from the management of the trustee, are the absolute property of the beneficiary. *Ib.*

One standing in the relation of a parent and guardian, in fact, of a minor, having the custody and control of such minor and of his property during his minority, is bound to the most scrupulous good faith in the management of the estate. *Ib.*

If a guardian convert land-scrip, receivable at the land-office in the purchase of public lands, into money, by investing it in land for himself and others, and accounting with his wards for the scrip, with interest from the time of its investment, he can not, if he acted in good faith in the transaction, be charged as a trustee of the land purchased, or compelled to account for the profits growing out of the investment. 1846. Davies *v.* Lowrey, 15 O. 655.

[1] See Schouler's Dom. Rel., § 427–432.

Trustees can not make a profit from trust funds by using them in any kind of trade or speculation, nor in their own business; nor can they put the funds into the trade or business of another, and receive a *bonus* or other profit or advantage. In all such cases, the trustees must account for every dollar received from the use of the trust money, and they will be absolutely responsible for it if it is lost in any such transactions. By this rule, trustees may be liable to very great losses, while they can receive no profit; and the rule is made thus stringent, that trustees may not be tempted from selfish motives to embark the trust fund upon the chances of trade and speculation. Perry on Trusts, § 429.

If a trustee stands by and sees his co-trustee employ funds in that manner, he will be equally liable; and the same rule applies if the trustees simply continue the trade or business of the testator. It is their duty to close up the trade, withdraw the fund, and invest it in proper securities at the earliest convenient moment; and this is so, although the trustees may have been the business agents or partners of the testators. If the person from whom the trust fund comes authorize his trustees to continue the fund in a trading firm, it will be a breach of trust to allow the fund to remain after a change in the firm, as by the death or withdrawal of one of the part-

way; or (2) interest compounded annually on all funds so employed during the time of such wrongful use; and of course, in case of loss, could recover the funds so lost, with interest, by suit if necessary, on the guardian's bond.[1]

47. *Guardian should generally use only the income.*—No part of the capital of the infant should ever be used for its maintenance without first obtaining an order of court permitting this to be done.   It is probable that in case the capital is small and the ward can not be maintained on the income, and the guardian so uses a part or all of the capital, the court would, upon satisfactory proof that it was necessary to do so, ratify such action. But there are cases where it has refused, and the burden would always be on the guardian to show this necessity.   The proper and safe plan would be to get an order of the court in every such case, before infringing on the capital at all.[2]

48. *Capital used for education.*—Courts are much more willing

------

ners. If the trustees are directed to continue the testator's trade, they can invest none of his general assets in the business. They are confined to the fund already embarked in the trade. *Ib.*, ¾ 151, 156, 459; 2 Kent's Com. 230; Corcoran *v.* Allen (1877), 11 R. I. 567.

See also references in note 2, page 77.

[1] See par. 12, this chapter. Perry on Trusts, ¾¾ 462, 464, 621; Schouler's Dom. Rel. 170, 478, 510–511; 3 Redf. on Wills, 535.

See also note 2, page 77; as to suit on bond, see chap. 10.

[2] Cohen *v.* Shyer, 1 Tenn. Ch. 192; Johnston *v.* Haines, 68 N. C. 511. See U. S. Dig. G. 262, 275.)

If a guardian has not infringed upon the capital, he can not be held responsible for the profits nor interest of the estate, though he may have spent for his ward more than the interest of a given year that year, or less another year, if, during the entire guardianship, he has not expended more than the entire interest, and has disbursed it reasonably and suitably to the circumstances of his wards, and legally in other respects. Speer *v.* Tinsley, 55 Ga. 89.

[3] Perry on Trusts, ¾ 618–19; Tyler on Inf. and Cov., ¾ 176; Schouler's Dom. Rel. 457; Story's Eq., ¾ 1355.

"The order in which the ward's property should be expended for his support and education is as follows: First, the income of the property; next, if that proves insufficient, the principal of personal property; lastly, if both are inadequate, the ward's real estate, or so much of it as may be necessary." Schouler's Dom. Rel. 457–8.

It is competent for the probate court to fix the amount to be expended in

to permit the use of ward's capital to properly educate him for business or life than for mere maintenance, as it is then considered to be not expended so much as converted into a different and useful form.[1]

49. *Purchase of ward's property by guardian, at his sale.*—It is a well settled principle, applied with great strictness in this state,[2] that a trustee can not, either directly or indirectly, purchase the property he holds in trust.[3] Of course, this would prevent a guardian from purchasing land of his ward at sales

the maintenance and education of the ward, and to say how far the principal of the funds belonging to the ward shall be encroached upon. Wiggle *v.* Owen, 45 Miss. 691.

The pension of wards from the U. S. on account of their dead father's military services may be used for their support, but to justify an allowance therefrom to their surviving mother for their past support would require a stronger showing than for a future allowance, and should only be made under special circumstances. Welch *v.* Burris, 29 Iowa, 186.

[1] Perry on Trusts, § 518.
See "*sixth*," page 64.

[2] "This principle . . . has been pushed to a vigorous extent in our own courts."—Chief Justice Lane, in Dunlap *v.* Mitchell, 10 O. 117, 120.

[3] Welsh *v.* Perkins, 8 O. 52, 55; —— *v.* ——, 6 Dana, 171; Armstrong *v.* Huston, 8 O. 552, 554; Dunlap *v.* Mitchell, 10 O. 117, 120; Glass *v.* Greathouse, 20 O. 503; Sheldon *v.* Newton, 3 O. S. 494; Barrington *v.* Alexander, 6 O. S. 189; Riddle *v.* Roll, 24 O. S. 572; Piatt *v.* Longworth, 27 O. S. 159; Rammelsberg *v.* Mitchell, 29 O. S. 22; Beard *v.* Westerman, 32 O. S. 29. See also Perry on Trusts, §§ 602 v, 602 w, 194-210, 787; 3 Redf. on Wills, 531; 537, 551; 2 Kent's Com. 229; 4 Kent's Com. 433, n. (e); Tyler on Inf. and Cov., § 175.

Courts of equity will presume without proof that such contracts are fraudulent, and declare them void, or at least will throw upon the purchaser in such cases the entire burden of proving the entire fairness of the transaction, and that it was advantageous to the ward. Perry on Trusts, §§ 194, 195, and the many cases there cited. See also Jacox v. Jacox, 40 Mich. 473; Morrison v. Kinstra, 55 Miss. 71.

Such a sale, having proven very advantageous to the ward and injurious to the guardian, was sustained. Redd *v.* Jones, 30 Gratt. (Va.) 123.

A guardian having bought his ward's land and paid for it, restitution will not be required when the infant, having come of age, seeks a disaffirmance of the contract. Green v. Jones, 14 N. Y. S. C. 492; (1876.)

Such purchase held good, on full payment of purchase money, the sale being fair and price good. Small v. Small, 74 N. C. 16; Blackmore v. Shelly, 8 Humph. (Tenn.) 439; Elrod v. Lancaster, 2 Head, (Tenn.) 571.

treated of in chapter 6; and should he, nevertheless, attempt so to buy, the beneficiary can have the sale set aside [1]

50. Such sale would be good, if ratified by the wards after they became of age.[2]

51. *Guardian's purchase with ward's money.*—If a guardian of a minor purchases property with the ward's funds and takes the title in himself, a trust will result to the ward,[3] who may take the land at what it cost, or the money, with interest, when he becomes of age.[4]

Also when bought to save property from sacrifice, at auction. But trustee held to account for profits made in reselling. 3 Redf. on Wills, 555–6.

"Where a gurdian purchases for himself at sales of his ward's property, his conduct will be closely scrutinized. But where no fraud appears, and the sale appears beneficial to the ward, the more reasonable doctrine is that the transaction is sustainable in equity, subject to the ward's subsequent election, on reaching majority, to disaffirm the sale. The guardian meanwhile takes the legal title; more especially if the sale was conducted through a third party, who afterward conveyed to him." Schouler's Dom. Rel. 469; also 511.

To similar effect, 3 Redf. on Wills, 537, n. 21, 555; Doe r. Hassell, 68 N. C. 213; Lee r. Howell, 69 N. C. 200.

It is believed that the only way such sales could be rendered safe for the purchaser at all in Ohio, would be by their ratification by the ward some time after his becoming of age.—*Ed.*

[1] Perry on Trusts, ? 602 w; Schouler's Dom. Rel. 469; Beam r. Froneberger, 75 N. C. 540. See also par. 180, chap. 6; notes on pp. 126, 163–5.

For general principles concerning this point, see Ohio case cited in note 3, p. 80.

[2] Dunlap r. Mitchell, 10 O. 117.

[3] Perry on Trusts, ? 127; Tyler on Inf. and Cov., ? 175; 3 Redf. on Wills, 557; 4 Kent's Com. 371, n. (c); Freeman r. Kelly, 1 Hoff. 90; Harrisburg Bank r. Tyler, 3 Watts & S. 373; Martin v. Greer, 1 Geo. Dec. 109; Moffit r. McDonald, 11 Humph. 457; Kirkpatrick v. McDonald, 11 Penn. St. 387; Wilhelm r. Folmer, 6 Penn. St. 296; Day v. Roth, 18 N. Y. 488; Lathrop v. Gilbert, 2 Stoct. 344; McLarren r. Brewer, 51 Me. 402; Thompson's App. 22 Penn. St. 16; Pugh v. Pugh, 9 Ind. 132; Valle r. Bryan, 19 Mo. 423; Neil r. Keese, 13 Tex. 187; Hancock r. Titus, 33 Miss. 224; White v. Parker, 8 Barb. 48; Vason v. Bell, 53 Ga. 416; Chanslor v. Chanslor, 11 Bush, 663; Sterling v. Arnold, 54 Ga. 690; Kepler r. Davis, 80 Penn. St. 153 . . (applying rule); Armitage v. Snowden, 41 Md. 119; Morgan v. Johnson, 68 Ill. 190.

[4] —— v. ——, 5 Dana. 224; Alexander v. do., 46 Ga. 283.

6

52. There can be no doubt but that the guardian could also be sued on his bond for the amount so appropriated to his own use.[1]

53. *Contracts between guardian and ward.*—The relation between guardian and ward is one of great influence over the ward, and while it exists, no contracts between them can be made.[2] But if a contract or conveyance is made by the ward to the guardian just after attaining his property, and before a full settlement is made, and while the influence of the guardian is still in full force, courts will examine it in all its aspects; and the guardian claiming under such a conveyance must satisfy the court that the transaction was fair and proper, and that it did not proceed from undue influence, or from fear, hope, or other unworthy motive induced in the mind of the ward by the conduct of the guardian.[3]

54. *Gift from ward to guardian.*—Much the same principles apply to gifts from wards to their late guardians. It has been said that, although a gift from a ward may be a highly moral act, and alike creditable and honorable to him, yet, if the court

---

[1] Armitage v. Snowden, 41 Md. 119.

[2] Perry on Trusts, § 200; Schouler's Dom. Rel. 512; Dawson v. Massey, 1 B. & B. 226; Blackmore v. Shelly, 8 Humph. 439; Bostwick v. Atkins, 3 Comst. 53; Gallatian v. Cunningham, 8 Cow. 361; Clarke v. Devereaux, 1 S. C. 172.

If a party having an infant under his influence and control, against whom he is prosecuting a suit in which no defense is made for the infant, intends to insist on the rights of an ordinary adversary, he ought first to surrender the advantages arising from his fiduciary or quasi-fiduciary character. 1867. Long v. Mulford, 17 O. S. 484.

The jurisdiction which courts of equity employ to protect infants is not confined to cases of a strictly fiduciary character. The principle on which relief is given applies to all cases where influence is acquired and abused, and confidence reposed and betrayed. In cases of a fiduciary character, influence is presumed; in others, its existence must be proved. *Ib.*

[3] Perry on Trusts, § 200; 3 Redf. on Wills, 443; Tyler on Inf. and Cov. § 178; Schouler's Dom. Rel. 512–14. See note 1 on page 163. Richardson v. Linney, 7 B. Mon. (Ky.) 571; Andrews v. Jones, 10 Ala. 400; Eberts v. Eberts, 54 Penn. St. 110; Dawson v. Massey, 1 B. & B. 229; Wright v. Proud, 13 Ves. 136; Wedderburn v. Wedderburn, 4 M. & C. 41; Aylward v. Kearney, 2 B. & B. 463; Mulhallen v. Marum, 3 Dr. & W. 317; Cary v. Mansfield, 1 Ves. 379; Garvin v. Williams, 44 Mo. 465; 11 Am. Law Reg. (N. S.) 656.

is not entirely satisfied by clear demonstration that the gift was properly made, it will be set aside. Nothing can be allowed to stand that proceeds from the pressure of the relation of guardian and ward fresh upon the mind of the ward.[1]

55. The statement that a gift from a ward to his late guardian is creditable and honorable, etc., is much more applicable to England, where the law does not provide for any compensation to the guardian, than it is to this state and to the United States generally, where the guardian is allowed reasonable pay for his time, trouble, and services. But this is an additional reason why such gifts here should be closely scrutinized by our courts.

56. *The ward may recover property wrongfully conveyed by guardian.*—If a trustee wrongfully conveys any of the trust property, real or personal, to a purchaser with notice[2] of the trust character of such property, the beneficiary may pursue and recover

---

[1] Perry on Trusts, § 200; Tyler on Inf. and Cov., § 178; Schouler's Dom. Rel. 513–15; Hatch *v.* do., 9 Ves. 297; Hylton *v.* do., 2 Ves. 518; Pierce *v.* Waring, same, and 1 Ves. 380, and 1 P. Wms. 120 n.; 1 Cox, 125; Wood *v.* Downes, 18 Ves. 126; Johnson *v.* Johnson, 5 Ala. 90; Williams *v.* Powell, 1 Ired. (N. C.) 460; Caplinger *v.* Stokes, Meigs, 175; Somes *v.* Skinner, 16 Mass. 348; Whitman's App., 28 Penn. St. 348; Hawkins App., 32 Penn. St. 263; Scott *v.* Freeland, 7 Sm. & M. 420; Garvin *v.* Williams, 44 Mo. 465.

[2] Where a guardian has the legal power to sell or dispose of the personal estate of his ward in any manner he may think most conducive to the purposes of his trust, a purchaser who deals fairly has a right to presume that he acts for the benefit of his ward. He is not bound to inquire into the state of the trust, nor is he responsible for the faithful application of the money, unless he knew or had sufficient information at the time that the guardian contemplated a breach of trust, and intended to apply the money, or was, in fact, by the very transaction applying it to his own private purposes. Field *v.* Schieffelin, 7 Johns. Ch. 150; Conrad *v.* Griffey, 16 How. 37, 38; Elliott *v.* Merryman & Notes, 1 Lead. Cas. Eq. 74, 110.

Among the duties of a guardian prescribed by statute are the education of the ward in such amount as the estate may justify, the investment of the money of the ward, and generally the management of the estate for the best interest of the ward. These duties involve discretion. While it may be a general principle, although not indeed universally true, that a purchaser having notice of a trust is bound to see to the proper execution of the trust, the principle does not prevail where the purchase money is to be applied by the trustee himself to purposes requiring time, deliberation, or discretion on his part. Clyde *v.* Simpson, 4 O. S. 445, 464; Coonrod *v.* Coonrod, 6 O. 115, 116; Story's Eq. § 1134 (Redfield's Ed. § 977a.)

the property, or he may hold the trustee responsible personally; and if the trustee purchases land in his own name with the trust funds, the beneficiary may have the land, or hold the trustee responsible for the trust fund so expended, with interest.[1]

57. *Ward's labor and services.*—The guardian, occupying, as he does, to a considerable extent, the place of a parent, may, when circumstances render it expedient, compel the ward to contribute to his own maintenance by such labor and services as he is capable of rendering without detriment to his health, character, and reasonable education; and this would be especially true of a ward whose income is insufficient for his support. But the guardian can not receive such services rendered to himself, nor their proceeds when rendered to others, without being responsible and liable to account for the same, just as he must for other property or thing of value belonging to his ward, and he can set off against any claims for board, etc., of the ward, the real value of the services rendered by the ward to the person furnishing such board, care,[2] etc.

58. *Where ward resides with guardian.*—But when the ward resides with his guardian as a member of his family, the courts

---

[1] Perry on Trusts, §§ 828-844; Schouler's Dom. Rel. 470. See also Branch v. Du Bose, 55 Ga. 514; Shelton v. Lewis, 27 Ark. 190; Younce v. McBride, 68 N. C. 532; Lemley v. Atwood, 65 N. C. 46.

[2] See Schouler's Dom. Rel. 499; Tyler on Inf. and Cov. 265; Starling v. Balkum, 47 Ala. 314; Lewis v. Edwards, 44 Ind. 333; also, note 2, p. 64.

If a guardian of a minor knows that the minor and her mother have agreed with a third person as to the services of the minor, the compensation therefor, and the payment therefor to the minor, and permit the agreement to be executed, and the amount to be paid to the minor, without objection, he is estopped from collecting the amount as guardian. (27 Ind. 534; 31 Ind. 76; 32 Ind. 309.) Boulton v. Black, Sup. Ct. Ind. 1880; 5 Cin'ti Law Bul. 129.

A minor had a guardian other than his father, and such guardian contracted with the minor's father for the sale of the minor's time during the remainder of his minority, and paid the father for the time according to the contract. *Held*, that the amount could not be allowed to the guardian on the settlement of his account with the probate court, without his showing affirmatively that his ward was at least no worse off than if he had his money, with interest, on arriving at his majority. Bannister v. do., 44 Vt. 624.

Guardians should keep their wards employed when able to earn their own support, rather than permit them to consume in idleness the principal of

generally consider that such services as children render are a fair equivalent for their board, and are not disposed to allow the guardian any compensation for the ward's mere maintenance, nor the ward for his services.[1]   However, the court should consider the circumstances of each particular case, taking into account the age, sex, strength, and other elements affecting the usefulness of the services of the ward, the amount of time he may have been compelled to work when he ought to have been at school, etc., and do substantial justice accordingly.   It can readily be seen a strong boy, kept at work on a farm most of the time between the years of, say twelve and twenty, is not on an equal footing with a sickly child between the years of four and eight, capable of and doing little or no work.   And a guardian who would permit his ward to be improperly deprived of suitable means of education, taking into account the amount of his ward's estate and other circumstances, is not fit for his trust, and ought to be promptly removed.[2]

59. *Allowance of fixed sum for ward's maintenance.*—In English chancery practice it is the general rule that when the appointment of a guardian is sought, a fixed sum for the support of the ward is asked for at the same time.   Though this rule is not general in the United States,[3] yet it is not uncommon, especially when the minors are living with their mother and have property of their own, for the care of which a guardian of

their patrimony.   State. *v.* Clark, 16 Ind. 97; Clark *v.* Clark, 8 Paige (N. Y.) 152.

Where a minor is living with A., under his control, and B. hires his services from A.; in an action by A. to recover for such services, B. is estopped by his contract from denying A.'s right to control his services.   1833.   Lowry *v.* Button, W., 330.

[1] Schouler's Dom Rel. 449, 500.

When a guardian takes his ward into his own family, an intention to maintain such ward gratuitously may be inferred from circumstances.   Proof of an express promise is not necessary.   1869.   Crosby *v.* Crosby, 1 S. C. 337.

[2] Where a ward has been properly maintained and educated, it is no ground for removal of the guardian that he has merely given his notes for the expenses, there being no complaint by the creditor.   Sweet *v.* Sweet, Spears (S. C.) Ch. 309.   See note 3, p. 64; also, note 1, p. 53; last part of note 2, p. 90.   ("Removal of G.")

[3] Schouler's Dom. Rel. 459, 461.

the estate has been appointed, to represent to the court the amount of income or property the wards each have, and to ask the court to fix an amount per annum which the mother may be allowed for the maintenance and education of each ward. This sum may be changed in amount from time to time, as the needs of the ward or the change in value of the ward's property may require. This is the most convenient and desirable, and a safe way of proceeding, when the circumstances are such as to justify its adoption.

60. *Costs of litigation, etc.; who must pay.*—It may be stated as a general rule that all costs and expenses, including reasonable attorney fees, fairly incurred by the guardian in suits for receiving, properly administering, and protecting the trust fund, must be allowed to him by the court; and he should also be allowed those of suits decided against him, if he was honest and acting in good faith in such suits, and they were such as a reasonable and prudent man might reasonably have undertaken or resisted in the management of his own affairs.[1]

61. *Suit on uncertain claims.*—It should be borne in mind that there may be claims of such uncertain validity, both in favor of the trust estate and against it, that it might amount to a breach of trust to abandon them in the one case or to pay them in the other, without a decree of court to direct the guardian what he should do in relation to them. In such cases he should get the sanction of the court, and his costs and proper expenses will be allowed.

62. *Obligations of parents and guardians as to support of minor*

---

[1] Perry on Trusts, §§ 891–903, 910; Schouler's Dom. Rel. 462; Moore *v.* Shields, 69 N. C. 50; McNickle *v.* Henry, 4 Brews. (Pa.) 150.

A guardian will not be allowed to charge the estate of his ward with any part of the expenses of a controversy on the settlement of his accounts, when the controversy was occasioned by his own fault. Blake *v.* Pegram, 109 Mass. 541; see also Moore *v.* Shields, 69 N. C. 50.

The court has, however, full power to assess the costs, in such cases, against the guardian, the trust fund, or otherwise, as in its discretion shall seem just and right. § 6288. Perry on Trusts, §§ 892, 910.

But if a suit is made necessary by the misconduct or failure of the guardian to do his duty, or by his mere caprice or obstinacy, or by his refusal to account, or by his careless manner of keeping correct accounts, etc., he must pay the costs. Ib. §§ 900–903, 910.

children considered. The general rule is that a father must support his minor children, if he is able to do so, and in such case the guardian can not apply any part of the income of the infant's estate to its support, or at least not without an order of the court. But the courts now look with more liberality than formerly to the circumstances of each case, and take into consideration the respective estates; and if that of the infant is much larger than that of the father, or when, though able to support such children, he is yet not able to support them in such a manner as their future prospects, fortune, and expectations justify or require, the court may order their maintenance out of their separate estate.[1]

63. The application for the maintenance of the minor out of his own income may be made by the father, or by the guardian.

64. *How order for maintenance granted.* If the estate belongs absolutely to the minor, and no conflicting interests can arise, the order for maintenance may be made on an application and without suit; but if there are opposing and complicated interests, the court will not act without a regular suit and notice to all parties.[2]

65. *A mother not compelled to maintain her children.* A mother is entitled to maintenance of her children out of their funds, whether she is living with the husband by whom she had the children, or is living with a second husband, or is a widow.[3]

---

[1] See 2 Kent's Com, pp. 191–192, text and notes; Perry on Trusts, §§ 612–615; Schouler's Dom. Rel. 322, 326, 459; Story's Eq. §§ 1316, 1347 f; 1354 a. See also notes on page 79.

G. was guardian of his children as to property bequeathed to them. G. was wealthy, and maintained and educated his children without charge against them. When he died, his estate was ample to pay all his debts and leave a large surplus to his heirs, but his estate became insolvent by losses incurred after his death. On suit by his creditors against his administrators, *held,* that the guardianship account was not chargeable for the benefit of these creditors, with the cost of educating and maintaining the children. Griffith *v.* Bird, 22 Gratt. (Va.) 73.

[2] Perry on Trusts, § 617.

[3] Perry on Trusts, § 613; Schouler's Dom. Rel. 326; 2 Kent's Com. 191; Haley *v.* Bannister, 4 Mod. 275; Hodgson *v.* do., 4 Cl. & Fin. 323; 11 Bligh (N. S.) 62; Ll. & Goo. Sugd. 259; Ll. & Goo. Plunk. 137; Lanoy *v.* Athol, 2 Atk. 417; *Exp.* Petre, 7 Ves. 403; Beasley *v.* McGrath, 2 Sch. & L. 35; Greenwell *v.* do., 5 Ves. 194; Douglas *v.* Andrews, 12 Beav. 310;

66. *Stepfather need not maintain stepchildren, unless.* A stepfather need not support his wife's children, and is entitled to maintenance out of their income, unless their maintenance costs him nothing.[1] But if they are taken into his house as a part of his family, he is bound to maintain and educate them as if they were his own children.[2]

67. *Effect of ward's death.* If the ward dies, all of his property, both real and personal, at once vests, subject to the payment of debts and legal charges, in the heirs of such ward, and the guardian must at once render his account.[3] The guardian can not proceed to settle such decedent's estate, but an administrator must be appointed for that purpose,[4] and to him the guardian must turn over all of such ward's personal property. The ward's heirs of course become the joint owners of his real es-

---

Heyward *v.* Cuthbert, 4 Des. 445; *Re* Bostwick, 4 John. Ch. 100; Whipple *v.* Dow, 2 Mass. 445; Dawes *v.* Howard, 4 Mass. 97; Bruin *v.* Knott, 1 Phil. 573; Anderton *v.* Yates, 5 De G. & Sm. 202; Smee *v.* Martin, 1 Bunb. 131; Hughes *v.* Hughes, 1 Bro. C. C. 387.

But it is also held that the mother, after the death of the father, being then the head of the family, and having control of the minor children, is bound to support them, if she is of sufficient ability. Schouler's Dom. Rel. 325; Dedham *v.* Natick, 16 Mass. 140. See page 69, *ante.*

[1] 2 Kent's Com. 192; Perry on Trusts, § 613. Also, Appendix, par. 12.

[2] 2 Kent's Com. 192; Schouler's Dom. Rel. 378, 499; Mulhern *v.* McDavitt, 82 Mass. 401. See also Douglas' Appeal, 82 Pa. St. 169; Bradford *v.* Bodfish, 39 Iowa, 681.

[3] Schouler's Dom. Rel. 424–5; Tyler on Inf. & Cov. § 177; 1 Bouvier's Institute, 147.

[4] Raff's Guide to Executors and Administrators, 50; Schouler's Dom. Rel. 425.

Where a judgment was recovered against H. by the guardian of a minor, and the minor dying, the judgment was paid to her administrator, the debtor may have an injunction against the collection of the judgment by the guardian. But he must make the administrator a party, that he may contest the payment if he desires. 1833. Harper *v.* Seely, W. 390.

F. inherited land from his father. A guardian was appointed for him, who, under an order of the court, sold a portion of the land for the support and education of his ward. F. died before coming of age. The guardian had money in his hands arising from the sale of the land. *Held,* that the money was to be regarded as personal property acquired by the intestate ward, and passed as such to his half brothers and sisters, children of his mother by a second marriage. Armstrong *v.* Miller, 6 O. 118.

tate, and with its partition among them or otherwise, the guardian has nothing whatever to do.[1]

68. *When one of two or more guardians ceases to act.*　When there are two or more guardians appointed for the same minor, and one dies, removes from the state, is removed, resigns, or, being an unmarried female, marries, or otherwise ceases to be a guardian, this does not affect the powers or duties of the remaining guardian or guardians, but he or they will continue as if such former one had never been appointed.[2]

69. In such a case, however, the situation of those left to act, might be so changed as to require a settlement of their accounts, and a new bond might be demanded. Of all this, the probate judge is the sole judge, and must act as circumstances seem to require, in each particular case.

70. *Ward can not manage nor dispose of his estate.*—It is the guardian's duty not to permit the ward to sell, or otherwise dispose of his estate, real or personal; but on the contrary, to control the same himself, keep it and make it as productive as possible, unless the real estate be ordered to be sold by the proper court. And if the ward persist in selling or attempting to sell his estate, the guardian should not give up the possession thereof to the purchaser; and if he does sanction such sale, and surrender possession under it, he is guilty of a breach of his fiducial duties.[3]

71. *Guardian's duty as to ward's character, etc.*—A guardian should fill the place of a good parent. He should maintain the ward in a manner suitable to his condition in life; should provide him the opportunities of education, and use his authority to compel the ward to embrace the opportunities offered. The education should not consist of schooling merely, but the morals of the ward should be carefully attended to, and the authority of

---

[1] Where a guardian, under an order of court, had sold the land of his infant ward, who died before coming of age, a bill by parties claiming to be next of kin to recover the proceeds remaining in his hands, was sustained, though the demand was for money only. Armstrong *r.* Miller, 6 O. 118. See par. 2, chapter 11.

[2] 3 Redfield on Wills, 532; Schouler's Dom. Rel. 438; *Re* Reynolds, 18 N. Y. Supreme Ct. 41; Pepper *v.* Stone, 10 Vt. 427.

[3] 4 Dana, 631.

the guardian should be judiciously used and kindly advice and warning given, to the end that the associations of his ward be proper ones, and his moral deportment, so far as possible, unexceptionable.[1] Education includes also the proper training of the ward, so as to fit him for some of the useful pursuits of life, such as a trade, profession, or business. The guardian assumes fidelity to these things and the like when he accepts the appointment, gives the bond, and solemnly takes the oath required.[2]

72. *Repairs.*—It is the guardian's duty to make the proper repairs on ward's real estate, and pay for them out of the income.

---

[1] As the guardian is bound to promote the moral welfare of the person intrusted to his care, he may warn off from the ward's premises any persons improper for him to associate with, and, if necessary, expel them forcibly. This right is to be reasonably construed ; and in the use of means and the amount of force necessary to effect this object, he is allowed a liberal discretion, such as a parent might exercise under like circumstances. And in many other respects the rights of a guardian resemble closely those of a parent. Schouler's Dom. Rel. 455 (citing Wood e. Gale, 10 N. H. 247).

[2] "The guardian's duties as to the ward's person are those of protection, education and maintenance. In exercising them, he is bound to regard the ward's best interests. Guardians, as we have seen, are seldom appointed where there is not some property. But even though the ward is penniless, we are not to suppose that one vested with the full right of custody can neglect with impunity those offices of tenderness which common charity as well as parental affection suggest. For to the orphan he stands in the place of a parent, and supplies that watchfulness, care, and discipline which are essential to the young in the formation of their habits, and of which, being deprived altogether, they would better die than live.

"It is, however, to be always borne in mind that while the father is bound to educate and maintain his children absolutely and from his own means, no such pecuniary responsibility is imposed upon the guardian. The latter need only use for that purpose the ward's fortunes. Hence, in supplying the wants of his ward, he is to consider, not the style of life to which they have been accustomed, so much as the income of their estate at his disposal. Whatever their social rank may have been, he may, provided they are left destitute, place them to work, or if they are too young and feeble, surrender them to some charitable institution. He should, however, act with delicacy and prudence; he may properly consider in this connection the habits and tastes of the children and the wishes of their relatives; and he can relieve himself of responsibility by asking judicial guidance." Schouler's Dom. Rel. 455.

73. *How guardian may collect interest due ward on registered government bonds.*—See chapter 25, paragraphs 21-37.

74. *Other duties, etc.*—As to the guardian's duties relating to the lease of land, sale of real and personal estate, bonds, etc., see the chapters respectively devoted to those subjects.

CHAPTER 6.

SALE OF WARD'S PROPERTY.

1. *When ward's personal property may be sold.* The guardian of the person or estate, and of the estate only, can, when for the interest of the ward, sell all or any part of the personal estate of the ward.[1]

---

[1] § 6280.

It would not be prudent for the guardian to make any important change in the character of any considerable part of the ward's estate, such as selling the personal property and investing the property in real estate, without first obtaining, for his protection, an order of court permitting or directing him to do so. See Story's Eq., § 1357; Perry on Trusts, §§ 606, 607; Schouler's Dom. Rel. 466, 480; paragraph 12, chap. 4. Of course, he must even then act in good faith for the best interests of his ward. See par. 40, chap. 5.

The guardian may dispose of the personal estate of his ward as he may think most beneficial for the ward, and a person who purchases, in good faith and for value, such property, with no knowledge of fraudulent intent on the part of the guardian, is not responsible for a misapplication of the proceeds. Strong v. Hope (Ham. Co. Dist. Ct. 1879); 4 Cinti. Law Bul. 1034; Field v. Schieffelin, 7 Johns. (N. Y.) Ch. 150; Woodward v. Donnally, 27 Ala. 198.

This applies to every species of personal property, though it is not usual to sell family pictures, plate, watches and personal ornaments, but to keep them, by which to remember their former owners. And in other peculiar cases, as where the ward is nearly of age, and is soon to enter upon a well-stocked farm, which is his own property, the guardian will be justified in not selling off the stock. (Reeve's Dom. Rel. 326; Tyler on Inf. and Cov. 262; Schouler's Dom. Rel. 475.)

But see paragraphs 44–46, and notes thereto, of chapter 5, as to conducting any business for ward's benefit.

2. *Who may sell ward's real estate, and why.* Whenever necessary for the education, support, or payment of just debts of any minor, or for the discharge of any liens on the real estate of such minor, or whenever the real estate of such minor is suffering unavoidable waste, or a better investment of the value thereof can be made, and the court shall be satisfied that a sale thereof will be for the benefit of any minor, the probate court by which a guardian of the person and estate, or of the estate only, has been appointed, may, on the application of such guardian, order the real estate of such minor, or a part thereof, situate in this state, to be sold.[1]

----

[1] § 6280.

The court of common pleas that appointed a guardian may empower him to sell the land of a minor situate in another county. Where a guardian's sale has been examined and confirmed by the court, and the journal entry shows that a bond has been directed and sureties approved, it will be presumed that the bond was executed. The law does not require the bond to be carried into the record. Maxsom *v.* Sawyer, 12 O. 195.

A military land-warrant was issued to the widow and minor child of a deceased soldier of the Mexican war, under the act of Congress of February 11, 1847, which provided that the guardian of such minor may, " upon being duly authorized by the orphans' or other court having probate jurisdiction, have power to sell " the warrant; and the guardian of the minor, with the widow, assigned the warrant without being authorized to do so by the probate court, to a person who knew all the facts of the case, but supposed the assignment gave him a clear title to the warrant : *Held*—The assignment of the guardian, without the authority of the proper court, did not transfer the right of the minor in the warrant to the purchaser. Mack *v.* Brammer. 28 O. S. 508.

A sale made by an administrator, on the joint application of himself and the guardian of the minor heirs, for the support of such heirs and the widow, is void. The application may not have been fatally defective—too many may not vitiate; but the guardian alone could make application for this purpose, and the administrator had no power to apply for or execute the sale for this purpose. Newcomb's Lessee *v.* Smith, 5 O. 117.

Formerly, the guardianship of a minor female expired, by operation of law, when the ward arrived at the age of twelve years. A guardian appointed for such ward, when under the age of twelve years, could not, as such guardian, by petition filed after the ward arrives at the age of twelve years, sell the ward's land. A sale, under an order of court, upon such petition, was void. Perry *v.* Brainard, 11 O. 442. See note 4, page 25.

Under the act relating to guardians, passed February 9, 1824 (2 Chase

3. *Guardian may ask for sale of real estate of two or more wards; guardians may join.* Where any person is such guardian for two or more minors whose real estate is owned by them,

1317, Swan's Rev. Stat. 441), the only power to authorize a guardian to sell the real estate of his ward, prior to the creation of the probate court, was vested in the court of common pleas of the county in which the guardian was appointed. Foresman *r.* Haug, 36 O. S. —.

The provision in section 3 of the amendatory act of February 23, 1846 (2 Curwen, 1237, Swan's Rev. Stat. 417), requiring guardians to be governed, "in the execution of any order of sale" of the real estate of their wards "by the same regulations that may be prescribed, and in force when such order is made, for the sale" of lands by administrators, does not prescribe the court to which application may be made by the guardian to obtain such order of sale, but relates to the manner in which the order is to be *executed* after it has been granted by the proper court. *Ib.*

As to compelling guardian to pay over to administrator, for the payment of debts in pursuance of an agreement to that effect, the proceeds of a sale made by the guardian, see Bradstreet *r.* Shank, (Hamilton District Court) 5 Cinti. Law B .l. 362.

A guardian can receive nothing but money in payment for a sale of his ward's property. He can not receive his own note in payment, and if he does so, and afterwards fails to account for and pay over in money the proceeds of the sale, his ward may maintain an action against the purchaser for the purchase-money, or set aside the sale. 17 Barb. 15; 51 Ind. 148; 14 Ind. 324; 43 Ind. 203.

The appellee herein who purchased the property of the guardian, insists that he had a right to expect he would apply his individual note on the purchase-money due Esther Bevis, who was a married woman, and that Stover was acting as her agent, as the law did not permit him to apply it on the amount due his ward, upon the principle that it will be presumed, in the absence of notice to the contrary, that the trustee will do his duty in the management of the business of his trust. But Stover, being only the agent of Esther, had no right to accept any thing for his principals. Bevis *r.* Heflin (Sup. Ct. Ind. '79), 3 Cin. Law Bul. 1132. See also Story on Agency, § 98, and note 2, next page.

The estate of a ward in remainder in land, depending on the life of his father, may be sold in the manner prescribed by law for guardian's sale of ward's land, during the life of the father. Garland *v.* Loring, 1 Rand (Va.) 396.

The provisions of the statute relating to guardian's sales must be complied with, or the sale will be void. Cooper *v.* Sunderland, 3 Iowa, 114; Frazier *v.* Steenrod, 7 Iowa, 339; Shanks *v.* Seamonds, 24 Iowa, 131; Wells *v.* Cowherd, 2 Metc. (Ky.) 514; Bell *v.* Clark, same, 573; Mattingly *v.* Read, 3 same, 524. Watts *v.* Pond, 4 same, 61; Carpenter *v.* Strothers, 16 B. Mon.

jointly, or in common, the guardian may in one application ask for the sale of the interest of all, or any number of his wards, in such real estate; and where different persons are guardians of minors so interested jointly, or in common, in the same real estate, such guardians may join in one application; and on the hearing, in either case, the court may authorize the sale of the interest of one or more, or of all such wards, as, in its discretion, it may deem right and proper.[1]

4. *Jurisdiction of courts in such sale.* The probate court has concurrent jurisdiction in the sale of lands on petition by executors, administrators and guardians, and the assignment of dower in such cases of sale;[2] and such jurisdiction, once acquired, is exclusive of that of every other probate court.[3]

5. *The petition for sale of real estate; must contain what; town lots.* The application for the sale of real estate must be by petition, which must set forth specifically: *First*—The value and

---

(Ky.) 289; Burnett *v.* Churchill, 18 same, 387; Wyatt *v.* Mansfield, same, 779; Banker *v.* Hopewell, Metc. (Ky.), 260; Megowan *v.* Way, same, 418; Leary *v.* Fletcher, 1 Ired. (N. C.) L. 259; Ducket *v.* Skinner, 11 same, 431; Sprnil *v.* Davenport, 3 Jones (N. C.), L. 42; Pendleton *v.* Trueblood, same, 96.

[1] § 6280.

[2] § 625.

Concurrent jurisdiction conferred upon probate courts, in the sale of land on petition of executors, administrators and guardians, by section 3 of the act of March 11, 1853 (3 Curwen, 2041, S. & C. 1213), vests in the probate court of the several counties only such jurisdiction in regard to ordering such sales as was possessed by the courts of common pleas in such counties respectively. Foresman *v.* Haag, 36 O. S. —.

Hence, where, at the time of the passage of said act, the court of common pleas in a particular county was authorized to order the sale of the lands of a ward, on the application of his guardian, the probate court of such county could not order such sale. *Ib.*

The probate court of Pickaway county duly appointed, in 1853, guardians for certain minors residing in Scioto county, and on proceedings instituted by the guardians in the probate court of Cuyahoga county, certain real estate of the wards, situate in the county last named, was, in 1854, sold by order of that court, the sales confirmed, and the deeds executed accordingly. *Held,* that the proceedings in the probate court of Cuyahoga county were void for want of jurisdiction. *Ib.*

See also 4th, 5th and 6th paragraphs of note 1, page 95.

[3] § 627.

character of all personal estate belonging to such ward that has come to the knowledge or possession of such guardian. *Second*—The disposition made of such personal estate. *Third*—The amount and condition of such ward's personal estate, if any, dependent upon the settlement of any decedent's estate, or the execution of any trust. *Fourth*—The annual value of the real estate of the ward, with a pertinent description of such real estate. *Fifth*—The amount of rent received, and the application thereof. *Sixth*—The proposed manner of re-investing the proceeds of the sale, if asked for that purpose. *Seventh*—Each item of indebtedness, or the amount and character of the lien, if the sale is prayed for the discharge thereof. *Eighth*—The age of the ward, where and with whom residing. *Ninth*—If there be no personal estate belonging to such ward in possession or expectancy, and none has come into the hands of such guardian, and no rents have been received, the fact must be stated in the petition : If it is desired that the land sought to be sold, or any part thereof, shall be laid out in town-lots, that fact must be stated, and the reasons therefor, and the manner in which the same is to be laid out.[1]

---

[1] The statute for the sale of infants' estates by guardians requires that the petition of the guardian shall contain a description of all the real estate of the ward, and, when the contrary does not appear, it will be presumed that the real estate described in the petition includes all that the ward owns. Mauarr *e.* Parrish, 26 O. S. 636.

In a proceeding under the statute for the sale of lands of a minor by a guardian, the petition described the lots as Nos. 73, 74 and 75, in East Ironton, and as having come to the ward by descent. The appraisement and order of sale described them as Nos. 173, 174 and 175, the latter being the true description of the lots actually owned by the ward, and which came to her by descent. In an action by the ward against the purchaser of one of the lots, at a sale by the guardian in pursuance of said order of the probate court, it was held, that it is to be presumed that the ward owned only the three lots sold, and that there was a mere mistake in numbering them in the petition, and that the petition was sufficient to give the court jurisdiction. *Ibid.*

The failure of the court to require an additional bond of the guardian, before allowing the order of sale, or to appoint appraisers who have the proper qualifications, in this case residence in the county, although it may be ground for error, does not render the proceedings void, or the sale invalid. *Ibid.*

For construction of former law, see Armstrong *v.* Miller, 6 O. 118; Stall

6. *Dower of widow.* If there is a claim of a widow for dower, that should also be set out in the petition,[1] and in case dower should already have been assigned to the widow in the premises described in the petition, under proceedings previously instituted by her, a description of that portion of the premises covered by the dower should be given in the petition.

7. *Liens, leases, partitions, etc.* The petition should contain a statement of the mortgages,[2] judgments, vendor's liens, or other liens existing against such real estate, known to the petitioner; and if there be any questions relating to the title of the ward, whether growing out of trusts, equities, or any other matter, they should be specifically stated; as well as any leases of any portions of such real estate, with the terms of the same. If the ward holds the real estate in common with others, that fact should be set forth in the petition; in which case the petition should ask for a sale of the ward's undivided interest— leaving a division of the premises for the joint action of the purchaser at the sale, and those holding in common with the ward— fact should be set forth in the petition; and in all cases the nature and extent of his interest, or the title in and to the real estate prescribed in the petition should be clearly and fully mentioned.

8. *Who are defendants.*—The ward (or wards) is the defendant to the petition,[3] together with the other parties in interest designated above.

9–23. *Form of petition.*—The form of petition, journal entries, etc., will be given as if there were but one ward. Should there be more, the necessary changes are easily made:

---

v. Macalester, 9 O. 19; Este *v.* Strong, 2 O. 401; and Maxsom *v.* Sawyer, 12 O. 195.

[1] See paragraph 4, this chapter.

[2] The mortgage lien remains in full force, if the mortgagee is not made a party to the suit. Holloway *v.* Stuart's admr, 19 O. St. 472.

See also note 1, above.

[3] § 6282.

A ward will not be bound by a decree affecting his property, where the guardian was a party to the suit, but not the ward; nor will a court of equity entertain a bill to enforce such decree against the ward, it being, as to him a nullity. Este *v.* Strong, 2 O. 401.

—— county, Ohio, *ss.*, Probate Court [*or*, Court of Common Pleas].

A. B., guardian of C. D., a minor, plaintiff,

vs.

Said C. D., a minor, aged —— years, X. Y., L. D., T. U., G. H., trustee [*and name all other persons whose rights this suit affects, and give age of each minor defendant*].

Petition to sell real estate.

The plaintiff represents that he is the duly appointed and qualified guardian of C. D., now of the age of —— years, and residing with ——, at ——.

[*If there was never any personal property, say :*] That no personal estate of any kind, belonging to said ward, ever came to the possession or knowledge of the plaintiff. [*But if there ever was any personal estate, then say, instead of the above :*] That all of the personal estate belonging to said ward, that ever came to the possession or knowledge of the plaintiff, consisted of [*Here describe it generally ; as, farming implements, horses, cattle, notes, moneys, bonds and mortgages, state stocks, bank stock, etc., etc.,*] and was of the value of —— dollars. That the plaintiff has disposed of said estate in full [*or if in part only, say, to the amount of —— dollars*] as follows, to-wit : Expended for said ward in clothing, —— dollars ; boarding, —— dollars ; tuition, books, etc., —— dollars ; in payment of a certain mortgage held by X. Y. upon lot No. —, in Glendale, —— dollars ; for taxes on same lot, —— dollars ; paying mechanics' lien thereon, —— dollars [*And so of any other general expenditure ; and if any such liens as mentioned above are in force and unpaid, state the facts accordingly*].

That there is no personal estate of said ward dependent upon the settlement of any decedent's estate or the execution of any trust, nor in expectancy ; [*or if the fact be otherwise, instead of the above, say,* That there will be the amount of —— dollars, *or*, an amount not yet ascertained, supposed to be about —— dollars, coming to said ward from the estate of E. D., not yet finally settled ; *or such an amount* will be due to said ward from the

trust estate in the hands of ·G. H., who was made trustee by E.
D., and which will probably be paid, *state when*].

That said ward is the owner of the fee simple [*or, life estate or
leasehold, as the case may be*] of the following described real estate, situate in —— county, Ohio, and described as follows, to-
wit: [*Here describe it by metes and bounds,* or in other proper
way, as carefully as should be done in a deed*], which real estate is
worth annually —— dollars; [*or if wild land, say, which is wild
land, and yields no income.*]

That the plaintiff has received —— dollars, in rents, from all
the real estate of his ward, and has expended the same as follows:
In repairs, —— dollars; taxes on real estate, —— dollars [*etc.,
etc., as the facts are, and if any money is remaining on hand, so
state, and the amount; or if all the lands yield no income at all, say,
instead of the above,* That the plaintiff has received no rents
whatever from any of said ward's real estate.]

That the sale of said real estate is necessary for the maintenance and education of said ward [*or if it is proposed to reinvest
the money arising from the sale, say or add,* That the plaintiff believes it will be for the interest of said ward to sell said real estate and reinvest the money arising therefrom in (*state stocks,
loans upon mortgage or otherwise*).]

That said ward is indebted to J. K. for necessaries in clothing,
in the sum of —— dollars; to L. M. for boarding, —— dollars; to
O. P. for tuition, —— dollars, etc.; [*or if the fact be so, say,*
There is no indebtedness of the said ward.]

That X. Y. has a lien on said real estate, by way of mortgage,
to secure the sum of —— dollars now due [*or not yet due, as the
case may be*], and T. U. has a mechanics' lien for —— dollars,
which accrued in the lifetime of E. D., father of said ward [*or
if no liens exist, say,* There are no liens upon said real estate to
the knowledge of the plaintiff.]

[*If there be a widow's dower on the land, say:*] That L. D.,
widow of E. D., has a dower estate in said lands.

[*If it is desired to lay out the land, or part of it, in town lots,
say:*] That it is desired to lay out said land [*or if a part only of
it, say,* That part of said land described as follows: *and here
describe or otherwise clearly designate the part to be so divided*] into
town lots, for the reason that said land [*or, tract last designated*]

is situate within the corporate limits of the village. of —— [*or
otherwise give the reasons according to the facts*], for which reason
said land would sell for more money than if not so divided.

[*And also state clearly any other facts directed by law or required
by the circumstances of the case to be stated.*

The plaintiff therefore prays that said C. D. [*and if there be a
widow, or persons holding liens, add their names*] may be made defendant [*or defendants, as the case may be*] to this petition. [*If
there be a widow and lienholders, add,* 'That dower may be set off
to said widow and the rights and liens of said lienholders may
be adjusted], and that plaintiff may be ordered to sell said real
estate [*and if it is proposed to reinvest the money, add,* and to reinvest the money arising therefrom as is hereinbefore proposed],
and for other proper relief, etc.   A. B., Guardian of C. D.

24. *Verification and form of.*—The petition must be verified by
the oath of the guardian,[1] which may be in form as follows : [2]

25-26. The State of Ohio, —— county, *ss.* :

A. B., being duly sworn, says that he is the plaintiff mentioned in the foregoing petition, and that the facts therein stated
are true, as he verily believes.   A. B.

Sworn to before me, and signed in my presence, this —— day
of ——, A. D. ——.   A. C., Probate Judge, etc.

27. *Who administers oath.*—This oath may be administered by
any officer authorized to administer oaths generally.[3]

28. *Notice of filing petition, how served, etc.*—"Upon such petition being filed, verified by the oath of the guardian, the court
shall order the petitioner to give notice to his ward, who shall be
defendant to the petition, of the filing and demand thereof, and
the time when the same will be heard, in such manner as to the
court shall seem reasonable and proper."[4] This is the language
of the former as well as the present law.   It was never construed

---

[1] § 6282.   [2] §§ 5105, 5107.   [3] § 5107.

[4] § 6282.   See also section 6406, found in paragraph 37, this chapter.

The act of 1824 (2 Chase, 1308), regulating the sales of land by executors
and administrators, did not direct the mode in which the heirs should be
made parties, and the courts adopted such practice as they deemed expedient.
Where minor children who were not named in the petition, had an ap-

so as to require the petitioner *in person* to give the notice; ho
may do so by some third person, or by the sheriff or other officer, as the court may direct or permit.

29. *Journal entry, ordering notice of sale, and time of hearing.*

Said A. B., as guardian of B. C., plaintiff, having filed his petition for the sale of real estate of said B. C., it is now ordered
that said A. B. give notice in writing to his said ward, defendant
herein, of the pendency and prayer of said petition: and the
hearing of this cause is set for ——, the —— day of ——, A. D.
18—, at —— o'clock — M.

30. *Code of common pleas to govern in probate court, so far as
applicable.*—"The provisions of law governing civil proceedings
in the court of common pleas shall, so far as applicable, govern
like proceedings in the probate court, when there is no provision on the subject in this title."[2]

31. *Since when.*—Previous to the adoption of the codified law[3]

pearance entered for them in court by the guardian, while the petition was
pending, they were bound by the order of sale. Whatever irregularity there
was in such practice, it did not affect the purchaser, who held his title as securely as a purchaser at sheriff's sale, under a judgment at law or a decree in
chancery. 1835. Ewing's Lessee *v.* Higby. 7 O. 1 pt. 198.

And see Ewing *v.* Hollister, 7 O. 2 pt. 138, where the legality of the same
sale was sustained.

Where a record of a proceeding in the court of common pleas sets out
that it was "shown to the court that *due notice* had been given to the defendants: *Held*, that this language imports a finding by the court that the
notice which the law required under the circumstances had been regularly
given. Evidence will not be received to contradict this finding of the
court. Where jurisdiction is shown, or must be presumed, the judgment or
order of the court can not be collaterally impeached." Richards *v.* Skiff et
al., 8 Ohio St. 586.

A sale of the ward's land, by his guardian, without the notice required by
law, is void for want of jurisdiction of the court ordering such sale. Lyon
v. Vanatta, 35 Iowa, 521 ; Musgrave *v.* Conover, 85 Ill. 374.

If, however, the notice is defective merely, the jurisdiction is saved, and
the proceeding can not be attacked collaterally. Lyon *v.* Vanatta, 35
Iowa, 521.

[1] See Swan & Critchfield's Statutes, p. 675, § 24.

[2] § 6411.

[3] See 75 O. L. pp, 836–970.

governing procedure in probate courts, and now being Title II of Part Third of the Revised Statutes, the foregoing provision was not in force.[1]

32. *Infants; how served; law found where.*—Title I of Part Third of these statutes contains the law governing "Procedure in the courts of common pleas and superior courts, and district courts on appeal" referred to in paragraph 30, above; and this Title I contains the following provision, which is no doubt applicable to the service of notice in probate courts.

33. "When the defendant is under the age of fourteen years, the service [of summons] must be upon him, and also upon his guardian, or his father; or, if neither his guardian nor his father can be found, then upon his mother, or the person having the care of such infant, or with whom he lives; if neither of these can be found, or if the defendant is a minor over fourteen years of age, service upon the defendant alone shall be sufficient; and the manner of service may be the same as in the case of adults."[2]

34. *Infant's age; why stated.*—So that service may be properly made on the minor defendants, their ages should be stated in the petition, as already shown.[3]

35. *Should the notice be served by the guardian?*—The law as found in the chapter last mentioned does not seem to forbid the guardian's making the service; yet it seems better that it should be made, if not by the sheriff or other officer, at least by a disinterested party, rather than by the guardian, who, as plaintiff, stands in the relation of antagonist to all the defendants, and consequently, in theory at least, if not in fact, may be interested

---

[1] The nearest approximate provision in the old law was as follows: "In the exercise of the jurisdiction conferred by this act, the probate judge shall have the same powers, perform the same duties, and be governed by the same rules and regulations as are provided by law for the courts of common pleas, and the judges thereof, in vacation, so far as the same may be consistent with this and other acts now in force." Swan & Critchfield, p. 1217, § LVIII. It seems to have been the belief of the codifying commission and of the legislature that this differed in meaning from section 6111, as no reference whatever is made to it at the end of the section. See close of section 6412, also new.

[2] § 5047.   [3] See par 9, above.

in their not being served at all, and in having it appear of record that they have been duly notified.

36. It may well happen that one of the defendant wards, or possibly the only defendant, may be a child less than, say, two years old. To serve a written notice on such a defendant, except as directed in paragraph 33, would be a most useless absurdity; and it would be an absurdity almost equally great, should the parents of the ward be dead, and the plaintiff be compelled to serve the notice on such infant, and upon himself as its guardian.

37. *How other defendants to be notified.*—The law contained in the chapter mentioned is entirely silent as to how the defendants, not the wards of the petitioner, are to be notified. But it is provided in another place that when notice of any proceedings in a probate court are required by law, or deemed necessary by the probate judge, and the manner of giving the same is not directed by statute, the probate judge must order notice of such proceedings to be given to all persons interested therein, in such manner and for such length of time as he may deem reasonable.[1]

38–9. *Form of Journal entry of Order of the Court as to Notice to Defendants.*

A. B., Guardian of C. D.,
    vs.   } *Petition to sell land.*
Said C. D., his Ward.   }

This day came the said A. B., as guardian of C. D., and filed his petition, duly verified, asking for the sale of the real estate of his ward, for the allotment of dower and the adjustment of liens upon said land, and for its division into town lots; whereupon it is by the court ordered, that said A. B., by the sheriff, [*if so*] shall cause notice thereof to be given to said C. D., and to L. D., *his* mother or father, *etc.*; and also to L. D., *if there be a widow,* and to X. Y. and T. X., *if there be lienholders*], in writing, personally, and by leaving copies thereof at the usual place of residence of each of those who can not be served personally, —— weeks [*or,* days] before the day of the hearing of said application to sell] said real estate; which time of hearing is hereby

---

[1] § 6406.

fixed by the court, for the —— day of ——, A. D. ——, at — o'clock. — M.

40. *Service of summons or notice.*—If the court directs that service of notice be made by the sheriff, the service will probably be in the form of a summons, as in civil actions, in which case no form or instructions are considered necessary except as given in par. 16; but the following would be a sufficient form of notice, even if served by the sheriff or other officer.

41. *Form of Notice to Defendants.*

To C. D., L. D., X. Y., and T. U.:

You are hereby notified that on the —— day of ——, A. D. 18—, A. B., as guardian of C. D., a minor child of E. B., deceased, late of —— county, Ohio, filed in the probate court of —— county, Ohio, a petition, the object and prayer of which is, to procure said court to order the sale of the real estate of the said C. D., situate in the county of ——, Ohio, and described as follows, to-wit: [*Here describe it as in the petition; and if the prayer is, to reinvest the money, add,* and to authorize the said guardian to reinvest the funds in *here state the manner, as in the petition: and if dower is to be assigned, add,* and that dower may be assigned to said L. D., in the premises; *and if liens are set out in the petition, add,* and that the liens of the other defendants may be adjusted; and, *if so,* for the division of said land into town lots.]

The application therefor will be for a hearing by said court, on the —— day of ——, A. D ——, at — o'clock, — M., at which time an order will be asked as prayed for in said petition.

(*Signed*)   A. B., Guardian of C. D.

Dated this —— day of ——, A. D. 18—.

42. *When and how to be served.*—A true copy of this notice should be given personally to each of the defendants, as long, at least, before the day set for the hearing, as is directed in the order of court, or left at their usual place of residence with some one there found, or if no one is there found, then left in some place at the residence where it will most probably be discovered upon the return of the family; but service on minors must be as stated in paragraphs 32–36 above.

43. *Return of.*—The notice should then be returned to the court,

with an affidavit by the person serving it on the back thereof, of the service, and its manner of service.

44–45. *Form of such Affidavit.*

The State of Ohio, —— county, *ss.*

A. B., being duly sworn, says that on the —— day of ——, A. D. 18—, he served the within notice on the within named C. D., L. D., X. Y. and T. U., by leaving with each of them personally a certified copy thereof (*or if not personally, as to any of them, then say, as to those not served personally, by copy left at the usual place of residence of* [*here naming them*] *who could not be seen personally*).

    (*Signed*)   A. B.

Sworn to and subscribed before me, this —— day of ——, A. D. 18—.   A. C., Probate Judge, etc.

46. *Directions to sheriff, etc.*—If the notice or summons is to be served by the sheriff, directions to that officer as to where the persons to be served reside or may be found should be left for or given to that officer, in such way as may be customary in the county where the proceedings are pending.

47. *Service by publication; affidavit required, etc.*—The law provides that service by publication may be made on any defendant who resides out of the state; or whose residence is unknown; or who, though a resident, has departed from the county for the purpose of avoiding service; or who keeps himself concealed for the same purpose; or which is a foreign corporation, having no agent in this state on whom service can be made. In any such case, when the residence of a defendant is known, it must be stated in the publication; and, immediately after the first publication, the party making the service must deliver to the clerk copies of the publication, with the proper postage, and the clerk must mail a copy to each defendant, directed to his residence named therein, and make an entry thereof on the appearance docket. In all other cases, the party making the service, his agent or attorney, must, before the hearing, make and file an affidavit that the residence of the defendant is unknown, and can not, with reasonable diligence, be ascertained.[1]

-----

[1] § 5048.

48. Before such service can be made, an affidavit must be filed that service of a summons can not be made in this state, on the defendant to be served by publication, and that the case is one of those mentioned in the preceding paragraph. After filing such affidavit, service by publication may be made.[1]

49. When an heir or a devisee of a deceased person is a necessary party, and it appears by affidavit that his name and residence are unknown to the plaintiff, proceedings against him may be had without naming him; and the court must make an order respecting the publication of notice, but the order must require no less than six weeks' publication.[2]

50–56. *Form of Affidavit for Service by Publication.*

—— county, Ohio, *ss.*, Probate Court.

A. B., guardian of C. D., plaintiff,   } *Affidavit to obtain publication,*
                vs.   } *etc.*
    Said C. D. *et al.*, defendants.)

State of Ohio, —— county, *ss.*

A. B. being sworn, says that he is the said plaintiff [*or*, the attorney of the said plaintiff]. * that the said defendant, A. V., is a resident of Fairfield, in the State of Iowa, † that service of summons on him can not be made in this state, and that the case is one of those mentioned in § 5048 of the Revised Statutes of Ohio.

[*If the defendant's residence be unknown, omit the matter between the * and †, and insert instead*]. that the residence of said B. V. is unknown to affiant, and can not with reasonable diligence be ascertained.

[*If there be a non-resident defendant, A. V., whose residence is known, and another defendant whose residence is not known, and can not be ascertained, omit nothing above, and insert, at the †, the matter concerning B. V. as given.*]

[*If there be an heir or devisee, as mentioned in paragraph* 49, *insert also.*] that the residence [and name, *if so*] of the said defendant. heir of ——, mentioned in the petition in said cause, is [*or*, are] unknown to said plaintiff; *and omit or retain*

---

[1] § 5049.   [2] § 5053.

*the matter concerning A. V. and B. V., as the circumstances
require.*]

Sworn [*or,* affirmed] to and subscribed before me this —— day
of ——, 18—.   II. M., Notary Public, —— county, Ohio.

57. *Form of Notice by Publication.*

LEGAL NOTICE.

A. V., who resides at Fairfield, in the State of Iowa [*add, if so,*
B. V., whose residence is unknown, and the unknown heirs of
L. V.] will take notice that A. B., guardian of C. D., a minor
child of E. B., deceased, late of —— county, Ohio, (*and proceed
substantially the same as in form of notice in paragraph* 41 *above.*]

58. *Publication made where, and how long.*—The publication
must be made six consecutive weeks, in a newspaper printed in
the county where the petition is filed; or, if there be no newspaper printed in the county, then in a newspaper printed in this
state, and of general circulation in such county; and if it is
made in a daily newspaper, one insertion a week will be sufficient. It must contain a summary statement of the object and
prayer of the petition, mention the court wherein it is filed, and
notify the person or persons thus to be served when they are
required to answer.[1]

59. Service by publication is deemed complete at the date of
the last publication, when made in the manner and for the time
prescribed in the preceding paragraphs; and such service must
be proved by affidavit.[2]

60–62. *Form of Proof of Publication.*

The State of Ohio, —— county, ss.

P. F. being sworn, says that he is the publisher [*or,* bookkeeper
or otherwise, as the fact may be], of the ——, a newspaper printed
and of general circulation in said county, and that a notice, of
which the annexed is a true copy, was published in said paper
on —— of each week for six consecutive weeks, beginning on
the —— day of ——, 18—.

[*The following may be added, if so*]:   Affiant further says that
a daily and weekly edition of said newspaper is published; that

---

[1] § 5050.   [2] § 5051.

said notice appeared in the daily edition, the circulation of which in said county exceeds that of the weekly edition. and that the cost of publication in the daily does not exceed that in the weekly edition.

Sworn to and subscribed before me, this —— day of ——, 18—.

RICHARD ROE, Notary Public. —— county, Ohio.

63. This affidavit might be made by the guardian or other person connected with the case, but it is customary and best to have it made by some one connected with the paper printing it.

64. *Is a guardian ad litem necessary in such sales?* There is no provision made in the chapter mentioned in paragraph 29, for a guardian *ad litem* in suits for such sales, nor is there any allusion to such guardian. But section 5003 is a part of Title I., mentioned above, and is as follows: "The defense of an infant must be by a guardian for the suit, who may be appointed by the court in which the action is prosecuted, or by a judge thereof, or by a probate judge."

65. It may be stated as a general principle of law, so well established as to need no citations of authorities to sustain it, that every defendant is entitled to a hearing in court, and that he is not bound by the action of the court unless this is granted him. Can a minor, as the law now is, be said to have such a hearing in such matters as are now under consideration, unless he appears by a guardian *ad litem*, or by some person acting substantially in that capacity?[1]

---

[1] Section 6144, relating to sale of lands by executors or administrators to pay debts of decedents, expressly provides that "It shall not be necessary, unless the prayer of the petition for a sale is contested, to appoint guardians *ad litem* for infant heirs or devisees or other persons having the next estate of inheritance from the deceased who are defendants; and no such guardian shall have authority to waive notice or service of summons." See also, in such case, Ewing *v.* Hollister, 7 O. 2d pt. 138.

But the law relating to sales by guardians contains no such provision. In the case of only one child-defendant, supposed in paragraph 36, and similar cases, who would there be to make a contest, if no guardian *ad litem* is appointed, no matter how great the need of a contest might be?

Under the chancery act of 1810, and the supplementary act of 1812, proceedings in a court of common pleas were held binding against minors

66. It may be safely said that it is good practice, and the only safe and prudent course to pursue, to appoint a guardian for the suit in *all* cases where a guardian sells real estate of his ward. There is no good reason to be urged against it, except the attendant expense; and if it be granted, for argument's sake, that the law does not require it, would not cautious persons be deterred from bidding on lands to which the ward, or some one under him, might set up a claim long afterwards, and thus more loss result than could occur by a compliance with the probable, if not the certain, meaning of the law?

67. *As to duties, appointment, etc., of guardians ad litem*, see chapter 23.

68. *How widow may elect to be endowed out of proceeds of sale—effect of such election.* In actions for the sale of real estate by guardians, the widow of any decedent who has a dower interest therein, being a party, may file her answer, and waive the assignment of dower by metes and bounds, and ask the court to have the estate sold free of dower, and to allow her in lieu thereof such sum of money, out of the proceeds of the sale, as the court deems the just and reasonable value of her dower interest therein; and the answer of the widow will have the same force and effect, in all respects, as the deed of release to the purchaser of such estate of the dower interest therein of such widow.[1]

69. *Guardian of insane widow may act for her.* If the widow shall have been adjudged insane or imbecile, her guardian may, with the consent and approval of the judge of the court in which the action is pending, file such answer in her behalf, and

---

who were made defendants and served by publication, though no guardians had been appointed. Morgan *v.* Burnett, 18 O. 535.

Is was held to be error, on a bill of revivor, to decide against infant defendants, until a guardian *ad litem* had been appointed. St. Clair *v.* Smith, 3 O. 355.

It is not mere irregularity, but is error in fact, to take judgment against infant defendants without the appointment of a guardian *ad litem*. The remedy, under New York Code of Procedure, is by motion to set aside the proceedings. McMurray *v.* same, 9 Abb. (N. Y.) Pr. N. S. 315; 41 How. Pr. 41.

[1] § 5719, 5720.

it will have the same force and effect as if she were not under
disability, and filed the same personally.[1]

70-73. *Answer of decedent's widow, waiving dower in land,
and asking for its value in money.*

A. B., guardian of C. D.,   —— county, ss..
        v.   Probate Court.
Said C. D. and others, defendants.   Answer of widow.

The said L. D., widow, [by A. D., her guardian. *if so*]. hereby
consents to the sale of said premises prayed for in plaintiff's petition in this cause, and waives the assignment of dower in said
premises to her by metes and bounds, or in rents and profits,
and asks the court to allow her, in lieu of said dower, such sum
of money, out of the proceeds of such sale, as the court may
deem to be the reasonable value of her dower interest in said
premises.

      L. D., (widow's own signature.)
      [*or*, L. D.,
           By A. G., her attorney].
      [*or*, L. D.,
           By A. D., her guardian.]

State of Ohio, —— county, *ss.*

L. D., being duly sworn, says that she is the widow mentioned in the foregoing answer, and that the several matters
and things set forth in said answer are true.

                     L. D.

Sworn (*or*, affirmed) to and subscribed before me, this ——
day of —— A. D. 18—.

      A. C., Probate Judge,
      [*or, other competent officer.*]

74. *Verification not required.* The foregoing answer, when
made by the guardian, need not be verified on oath.[2]

75. *Minor heir not to be prejudiced by collusive assignment of
dower.* If, during the minority of an heir, dower be assigned to
a widow not entitled thereto, or if she recover the same by de-

---

        [1] § 5721.   [2] § 5103.

fault, fraud, or collusion of the guardian, such heir may, on coming of age, have an action against such widow to recover the lands wrongfully awarded.[1]

76. *Hearing of petition—appraisers appointed—town lots laid off.* At the time appointed for the hearing of said petition, and upon being satisfied that the notice named in the order (and re-required in par. 28) has been given, and that such real estate ought to be sold, the court must appoint three freeholders of the county where the real estate proposed to be sold is situated, who are not of kin to the petitioner, to appraise such real estate; and if the petition seeks to have the land, or any part of it, laid out into town lots, and the court finds that it will be to the advantage of the ward to have the same done, the court must also authorize the survey and platting of the land for that purpose.[2]

77–88. *Form of Order of Appraisement, and Findings of Court.*

[*Omit parts not applicable to case in hand, and change singular to plural number when necessary.*]

A. B., guardian of C. D.,   —— county, ss. Probate Court.
v.   Decree for appraisement, etc., in pro-
Said C. D. and others.   ceedings to sell ward's land.

This cause coming on this day to be heard, upon the petition of plaintiff, exhibits and testimony, and upon the return of the notice heretofore ordered, and the answers of G. L., the guardian *ad litem*, of L. D., the widow, and of [*name them*] the other defendants; and the court being fully advised in the premises finds:

That all the defendants herein have been duly and legally served with process, and have been duly notified of the pendency and prayer of the petition, as prescribed by law.

That the statements of said petition are true, and that the real estate described therein ought to be sold, as prayed for in said petition.

That it would be for the advantage of said ward to have said land [*or, a part of said land*] laid out into town lots, as prayed for in said petition [*or otherwise, as the court may deem best.*]

---

[1] § 5717.

[2] § 6283.

S

That said L. D., widow of said E. D., is entitled to dower in said real estate.

That said L. D., widow, waives, as in her answer herein set forth, assignment of her dower in said premises, and desires that the same may be sold free and clear of her said dower, and that the court set off to her, out of the proceeds of the sale of said premises, such a sum of money as may be just and reasonable, in lieu of her said dower interest. [*Of course, omit this when not so, and find such other things as each case may require.*]

Therefore it is ordered:

That G. H., I. J., and K. L., judicious freeholders of this county, [*or, if the lands are in another county, say of* —— *county*], and not of kin to the petitioner, be and are hereby appointed appraisers in said cause, and that they be sworn as required by law, before entering upon the discharge of their duties as said appraisers.

That said appraisers, upon actual view of the premises, described in said petition, appraise the same at its fair cash value, free from [*or, subject to, as may be*] the dower of said L. D., widow of E. D., deceased.

That said appraisers assign and set off to said L. D., widow, as her dower therein, the one equal third part in value of said real estate described in said petition.

That said appraisers divide said real estate [*or, a part of said real estate, and designate what part*] into town lots, and make a correct survey and plat of said land so divided, first calling to their assistance, if they deem it necessary, a competent engineer or surveyor.

[*And make such further orders as the case may require.*]

And that said appraisers make return of their appraisement and other doings hereunder to this court, on or before the —— day of ——, A. D. 18—.

89. *Guardian usually suggests appraisers.* It is customary for the guardian to suggest the names of the appraisers, he being presumably better acquainted with suitable persons therefor in the vicinity of the land than the court, and if no objection is known or made to them, the court usually appoints those so suggested.

90. *When appraiser fails to act.* In the sales of lands by executors, etc., it is provided that when any person appointed by the court as an appraiser fails to discharge his duties, . . . the executor or administrator may apply to the court making the order of appraisement and have another appraiser appointed thereby;[1] though, in such cases, in sales by guardians, the law is silent, the same course as indicated in this paragraph should be pursued. But to avoid all doubts, as well as delays, such persons should be selected as will attend to the matter, first consulting each one as to whether he can and will do so, if appointed, and see that he appears at the proper time and place.

91–97. *Certificate to the appraisers, and form of.* The court should then issue a certificate to the appraisers, of their appointment,[2] which may be as follows:

—— county, Ohio, ss.   Probate Court.

A. B., guardian of C. D.,
      vs. } *Appraisers certificate of appointment.*
Said C. D. and others.

To G. H., I. J., K. L.:

You are hereby notified that you have been appointed by said probate court of —— county, Ohio, as appraisers in said case; and you are hereby ordered, upon your oaths, and upon actual view of the premises described below—

To truly and impartially appraise. at its fair cash value, free from [*or, subject to, as may be*] the dower of L. D., widow of E. D., deceased, the following described real estate. to-wit [*here clearly describe the property*]:

You are further ordered to assign and set off to said L. D., widow, as her dower therein, the one equal third part of said real estate.

[*And give such further orders as are found in the preceding decree for appraisement, and no others.*]

You will make return of your appraisement by the —— day of ——, A. D. 18—.

Witness my hand and the seal of said court, this —— day of ——, A. D. 18—.

                                    A. C.,

    [L. S.]   Probate Judge.

---

[1] See paragraph 37, chapter 5.   [2] § 6284.

98. *If no dower to assign, what to omit.* If there be no dower to be assigned, all the above relating thereto must be omitted; and should no assignment of dower be required, an order of appraisement and sale may be made at the same time by the court; and in that case the report of the appraisers need not be presented for confirmation until after the sale, and until the report of sale is also ready to be submitted.

99. *Oath of appraisers.* The appraisers must take an oath to truly and impartially appraise said real estate at the fair cash value; and this oath must be indorsed on the certificate of their appointment, or order of sale issued by the court.[1]

100–103. *Form of appraisers' oath* may be as follows:

The State of Ohio, —— county, ss.

G. H., I. J., and K. L., being duly sworn, say that they will truly and impartially appraise the below [*or,* within] described real estate, and will faithfully and impartially discharge all the duties enjoined upon them by law, as appraisers of the real estate of C. D., a minor ward, under an order of the probate court of said county, in the case of A. B., guardian of said C. D., against said C. D. and others, according to the best of their understanding and ability.
G. H.,
I. J.,
K. L.

Sworn to and subscribed before me, this —— day of ——, A. D. 18—.
L. L.,
Justice of the Peace [*or other proper officer*].

104. *How appraisers to proceed.* The appraisers must actually go upon the premises, when about to perform their duty, being *first* sworn as above; and if dower is to be assigned in several tracts, it may be set off all in one tract, or in the several tracts, as the appraisers shall think proper. When assigned, the dower should be clearly described in their return, so that any one with the description, can go upon the land and find the boundaries of the dower, or be able distinctly to separate it from the remainder of the estate.

105. *Dower assigned in rents, etc.* Where no division can be

---

[1] § 6284.

made by metes and bounds, dower must be assigned in a special manner, as of the third part of the rents, issues and profits.[1]

106. *Appraisers duty in such cases.*   In such cases, the appraisers should ascertain and report to court, what are the rents, issues, and profits of the land, clear of taxes, reasonable repairs, and such like expenses.[2]   And in that case, too, the property should then be appraised subject to such dower incumbrance.

107. *How returned to court.*—The assignment of dower and appraisement should be attached to the certificate of the appointment and returned to the court, within the time named in such certificate, and be signed by the appraisers.

108–109. *Form of Appraisement and Assignment of Dower.*

(*Here is the most appropriate place for the oath of appraisers, given in pars. 100–103; then add:*)

In obedience to the order of the court hereto attached, we, the undersigned appraisers, being first duly sworn, and upon actual view of the premises described in said order, do set off and assign to L. D., widow, etc., for her dower estate * in said real estate, so much thereof as is contained within the following bounds, to-wit : [*Here give the particular description. by metes and bounds ; or say, if the case be so*], we do find that a division thereof can not be made by metes and bounds, and do therefore set off and assign to said L. D., as and for her dower therein. the sum of —— dollars yearly, during her life, that being one-third of the estimated net annual rents, issues, and profits of said real estate.   And we do) estimate the real cash value of said real estate (incumbered by said dower, so assigned) at —— dollars.

Signed by the Appraisers.

---

[1] § 5714.

[2] In Hillgartner *v.* Gebhart, 25 O. S. 557, the court held that "one-third of the net rents, issues, and profits, is the measure of the dower interest in such cases.   By this measure the doweress is compensated for 'one full and equal third part of all the lands, tenements, and real estate' which is her primary right.   The net rents, issues, and profits, are equivalent to the use of the estate.   In ascertaining the net rents, the expenses of reasonable repairs and taxes should be deducted from the gross rents ; but no deduction shoul l be made for expenses of water rent or insurance."

See also Dunseth *v.* Bank, 6 O. 77, 79 ; 2 Scribner on Dower, 661, 662 ; Hale *v.* Jones, 6 Johns (N. Y.), 258 ; Riley *v.* Clamorgan, 15 Mo. 331 ; Beavis *v.* Smith, 11 Ala. 32.

110. If there be no dower to be assigned, the above form can be used, leaving out all the matter, as to dower, within the parentheses.

111. When several tracts are described in the petition, and dower is assigned in one tract for all, the preceding form may be used to the *, and then continue as follows: "in all the real estate mentioned in said petition, the following described tract (or tracts) to-wit: [*Here describe the dower.*] And we do appraise the value of said several tracts as follows: The one containing —— acres, in which dower has been assigned, and subject to and incumbered by said dower, at —— dollars; the one containing —— acres, which is not incumbered by dower, at —— dollars," etc.

112. *Guardian to execute additional bond before sale.*—Upon the appraisement of said real estate being filed, signed by the appraisers, the court must require the guardian to execute a bond, with sufficient freehold sureties, payable to the state in double the appraised value of such real estate, with condition for the faithful discharge of his duties, and the faithful payment and accounting for of all moneys arising from such sale according to law.[1]

113–118. *Form of Journal Entry approving Appraisement, Plat, and Survey, Widow's Dower, ordering Guardian's Bond, etc.*

A. B., guardian of C. D. } *Decree approving appraisers' report in*
vs.
Said C. D. and others. } *proceedings to sell ward's lands.*

This day came the appraisers heretofore appointed in this case, and filed their report herein [*say, if so,* including the survey and plat, heretofore ordered by the court, of the lands to be divided into town lots, as prayed for in said petition, and the assignment of dower to L. D., widow of E. D.,] all of which, being examined, the court finds has been duly made.

It is thereupon ordered by the court that said report [including said plat and survey], be approved and confirmed.

---

[1] § 6285.

A sale made without giving such bond, held to be void. Ryder *v.* Flanders, 30 Mich. 336; Stewart *v.* Bailey, 28 Mich. 251.

[That said L. D., widow, hold in severalty the lands so assigned and set off to her, as her dower estate in said real estate; [*or if an amount of money is assigned to her, say*], and that said L. D., widow, shall receive the sum of —— dollars annually, during life, as and for her dower estate in the lands in the petition described, and that the same be and is hereby made a lien and charge upon said lands, and that the same shall be payable annually, [*or, quantity, etc., as the case may be*], on the —— day of ——, of each year during her life, and in default of payment thereof, an execution shall issue therefor against said lands, as upon judgments at law.]*

That said A. B. execute, within —— days, to the State of Ohio, a bond with sufficient freehold sureties, to the acceptance of the court, in the sum of —— dollars [*double the amount of the appraised value of the real estate*], conditioned according to law.

119. *If no dower, what to do.*—If no dower is assigned, or no plat and survey made, then leave out of the above form all matter relating to the dower, or plat and survey, or both, as the facts may require.

120-126. *Form of Guardian's Bond where Real Estate is to be Sold.*

Know all men by these presents, that we, A. B., of —— county, Ohio, P. Q., of —— county, Ohio, and R. S., of —— county, Ohio [*or if all of same county, say here, all of —— county, Ohio, and omit accordingly*], are held and firmly bound unto the State of Ohio, in the sum of —— dollars [*double the amount of the appraised value of the real estate*], for the payment of which we hereby jointly and severally bind ourselves, our heirs, administrators, and assigns firmly by these presents.

Sealed with our seals, and signed at ——, this —— day of ——, A. D. ——.

The condition of the above obligation is such, that whereas the above bound A. B. was, heretofore, appointed guardian of the person and estate [*or of the estate only, if such be the case*] of C. D., minor child of E. D., deceased, late of —— [*or, then living, if such was the case*], and which appointment the said A. B. accepted, and gave bond and made the oath required by law. And whereas the said A. B., as such guardian, has made application to the probate court of —— county, Ohio, for an order to sell certain real estate of his said ward, which, under proceedings there duly had, has been appraised at the sum of —— dollars; and whereas said court has ordered said A. B., as guardian as aforesaid, to execute a bond as such guardian, according to the statute in such case made and provided:

Now, therefore, if the said A. B. shall faithfully discharge his duties as guardian of said C. D., and shall faithfully make payment and account for all moneys arising from such sale, according to law, then the above obligation will be void; otherwise it will be and remain in full force.

Signed, sealed, and delivered in   A. B., [SEAL.]
our presence: P. Q., [SEAL.]
    J. N.   R. S., [SEAL.]
    V. W.

This bond approved by me, this —— day of ——, A. D. ——.
                              A. C., Probate Judge.

127. *Order of sale; how made.*—Upon such bond being filed and approved by the court, it must order the sale of such real estate,[1] at auction, for not less than two-thirds of the appraised value thereof, providing in the order for reasonable notice and the place of such sale in the county in which such real estate is situate, and what credit to be given for the payment of the purchase-money.[2]

128. *Deferred payments secured by mortgage.*—The deferred payments of the purchase-money must be secured by a mortgage executed by the purchaser on the real estate sold, and they

---

[1] Where, by virtue of proceedings and an order of sale in the probate court, a guardian sells, at public sale, and conveys the land of his ward, but by mistake, such proceedings, order of sale, and conveyance do not embrace all the land that was intended by the guardian to be sold, and was supposed to be bought by the purchaser, a court of equity will not interfere, as against the minors, to correct such mistake, and to give to the purchaser the additional land intended to be sold, and supposed to be purchased, but which was not in fact sold or conveyed. Dickey *v.* Beatty, 14 O. S. 389.

The guardian's deed made under such orders of the court has usually only the effect of a quitclaim, except so far as he may have covenanted on his part that he has complied with the statute requisites, and that he is the guardian duly authorized; and, in general, he can not bind his ward by any covenants of warranty in the deed. Schouler's Dom. Rel. 483.

[2] § 6286.

[2] § 5404. See par. 30, this chapter.

must bear interest at the legal rate per annum from the day of sale, payable annually.[1]

129. *May be sold at private sale, when.*—If it is made to appear to such probate court that it will be more for the interest of the ward to sell such real estate at private sale, it may authorize the guardian to sell the same at private sale, either in whole or in parcels,[2] and upon such terms of payment as may be prescribed by the court; but in no case can such real estate be sold at private sale for less than the appraised value thereof.[1]

130. *Decree, etc., when town lots are laid out.*—If the petition includes an application for the laying out into town lots of the land to be sold, or any part thereof, and the court approve the survey and plat made for that purpose, the court must also authorize the guardian, on behalf of his ward, to sign, seal, and acknowledge the plat in that behalf for record according to law.[1]

131–146. *Form of Decree for Sale.*

—— county, Ohio, *ss.,* Probate Court.

A. B., guardian of C. D.,
    vs.   } *Decree for sale in proceedings to sell land.*
Said C. D., and others.

This cause coming on this day further to be heard, and it appearing to the court,

That the appraisement hereto ordered has been made and confirmed by the court;

That said A. B., guardian, the plaintiff above named, has given bond in double the amount of said appraisement, with P. Q. and R. S. as sureties, conditioned as provided by law, and which bond is approved by court.

[*Here, say, if so*] That it has been made to appear upon satisfactory evidence to the court, that it would be more for the interest of said ward to sell the lands described in the petition in this cause, in parcels [*or,* in whole.]

---

[1] § 6286. See paragraphs 177, 178, this chapter.

[2] Sheriffs, administrators, and guardians making public sale of lands, may, in their discretion, divide a tract levied upon and appraised entire, and sell in parcels, being responsible for the abuses of that discretion. Stall v. Macalester, 9 O. 19.

It is therefore ordered by the court:

That the petitioner proceed to sell the lands in the petition described.

[*If private sale is ordered, here order.*]

That the petitioner may sell lands at private sale, at not less than the appraised value thereof, in parcels. [*If so, and, in such case, omit the two next succeeding paragraphs, unless advertisement of notice is nevertheless desired.*]

That the petitioner shall give notice —— weeks [*or, days*] consecutively, of the terms and time and place of sale, prior thereto, in some newspaper printed and of general circulation in —— county, Ohio [*the county where the lands lie; or the court may name the newspaper, and if none be printed in that county, then the court may order the notice to be given in some paper of general circulation in that county, or by hand-bills, or both, or in any other way the court may think proper.*][1]

That said sale shall be at public auction, at the door of the court-house of —— county [*the county where the lands lie, or, on the premises*].

That said sale shall be for one-third cash in hand on the day of sale, one-third in one, and one-third in two years from the day of sale [*or such other terms as the court think proper*]; the deferred payments to be secured by a mortgage, executed by the purchaser to the said C. D., on the premises sold, and to bear interest at the rate of —— per centum per annum, from the day of sale, payable annually.

That said A. B., guardian, is hereby authorized, on behalf of said C. D., his ward, to sign, seal, and to acknowledge the plat of the sub-division of lands into town lots, heretofore approved by court, for record according to law.

That the petitioner make return of his proceedings herein immediately after such sale is made [*or the court may fix a day for the return to be made*].

147. *When decree for private sale may be made.*—Should the foregoing decree for sale be made without any reference to a private sale, and it should at any time afterward be made to ap-

---

[1] As to manner of notice, when not provided by statute, see par 37, this chapter.

pear that such private sale ought to be had, the findings and order of the court, relating to private sale, in the preceding decree, may be made as a separate decree.

148. *How decree for private sale obtained.*—The method usually adopted for satisfying the court that a private sale would best subserve the interests of the ward, is to procure the affidavits of at least three men of good character and recognized good judgment, living in the vicinity of the land, or for other reasons presumed to know the facts and needs of the case, though the judge exercises his discretion about this, and *may* act on the application of the guardian alone. Such application may be as follows :

149–152. *Form of Application to Sell Real Estate at Private Sale.*

——, county, Ohio, *ss.*, Probate Court.

<table>
<tr><td>A. B., guardian of C. D.,
      vs.
Said C. D. and others.</td><td>}</td><td>*Application to sell land at private sale.*</td></tr>
</table>

The undersigned applicant represents that it would be best for the interest of the said A. B., to sell the real estate described in the petition in this cause, at private sale, for the following reasons. [*Here give the reasons.*]

The applicant therefore asks for an order authorizing him to sell said real estate at private sale.

A. B.. Guardian as aforesaid.

153–157. *May be sworn to—Form of oath.*—The facts in the foregoing application may be sworn to, if desired, as follows, and such application would then have the force of an affidavit :

The State of Ohio, —— county, *ss.*

A. B., being duly sworn, says that the various matters set forth in the foregoing application are true, as he verily believes.

A. B.

Sworn to and subscribed before me, this —— day of ——, A. D. 18—.   A. C., Probate Judge,

    [SEAL.]   [*or other proper officer.*]

158–160. *The form of affidavit for private sale,* mentioned in paragraph 148, may be as follows:

The State of Ohio, —— county, ss.

D. E., being duly sworn, says that * he has read [*or,* has heard read; *or,* that he knows the facts set forth in] the application to which this affidavit is annexed; that he has no interest whatever in the matters therein referred to, and that it will be more for the interest of the said C. D. to sell said land at private sale, as he verily believes. C. D.

Sworn [*or,* affirmed] to and subscribed before me, this —— day of ——, A. D. 18—.

N. E., Notary Public, —— county, Ohio.

161–165. *Another form.*—Three or more affidavits similar to the above, may be combined into one, in form, as follows:

State of Ohio, —— county. ss.

D. E., G. H., I. K., and L. M., being duly sworn, each for himself says that [*and continue from the * exactly as above to the signatures. Each affiant must then sign his name, as follows:*]

D. E.,
G. H.,
I. K.,
L. M.

Sworn [*or,* affirmed] to and subscribed before me, this —— day of ——. A. D. 18—.

N. E., Notary, Public, —— county, Ohio.

166. *Precipe for order of sale.*—Upon request, in writing, of the guardian, the probate judge, or clerk of the court of common pleas, will issue the order of sale, which will be simply by giving the guardian a copy of the order, duly certified to as being a correct copy of the journal entry.

167–170. *Form of Precipe for Order of Sale.*

—— county, Ohio, *ss.*, —— court.

A. B., Guardian of C. D., } *Precipe for order of sale in proceedings*
vs. } *to sell land.*
C. D., and others. }

Issue the order of sale in this case.

A. B., Guardian of C. D.

171. *Notice of sale.*—When the guardian has fixed upon a time when he will offer the property for sale, he should advertise the time, place, and terms of sale, in accordance with the order of court.

172–175. *Form of Notice of Sale.*

GUARDIAN'S SALE.

In pursuance of an order of the probate court of —— county, Ohio, made on the —— day of ——, A. D. ——, in the case of A. B., guardian of C. D., *against* his ward, the undersigned will, on the —— day of ——, A. D. ——, at 12 o'clock [*or any other hour named*], at the door of the court house, in —— county [*or, on the premises, as the court may order*], offer at public sale, the following described real estate, situate in —— county, Ohio, to-wit [*Here describe it.*]

Terms of sale, one-third cash on the day of sale, one-third in one and one-third in two years from the day of sale, to be secured by mortgage on the premises sold, and the deferred payments to bear interest at the rate of 6 per centum per annum, payable annually [*or otherwise, as the court may have directed*].

Appraised at $——.

A. B., Guardian of C. D.

176. *Where sale must be made.*—All sales of lands under order of sale must be made at the court house of the county in which the land is situate, unless otherwise ordered by the court;[1] but, as a general rule, it will be for the interest of the ward to sell the land on the premises.

177. *Guardian may subdivide and sell—his risk in so doing.*— If the lands are in one entire tract, and appraised as such, the guardian may, in his discretion, subdivide the tract, and sell such subdivisions separately; but in that case, the whole together must sell for two-thirds of the appraised value of the entire tract,[2] else the sales will be all set aside; and the court may set them aside, at the costs of the guardian himself. Or, if any of such sales were confirmed, and the result of all the sales together should prove to be less than two-thirds the appraised vale of the

---

[1] § 5404.

[2] Stall *v.* Macalister, 9 O. 19; see same, p. 24.

entire tract, the guardian would probably be held bound for any loss occasioned to his ward thereby.

178. *Best to get order of court.*—If it is deemed advisable to subdivide the entire tract, it is far better to have an order of court specially authorizing it, when the appraisement is ordered, and then let the subdivisions be appraised separately.

179. *How sale conducted.*—The sale should be made by the guardian, by a professional auctioneer, or other person as may seem best for the interests of the ward ; and after having dwelt a sufficient length of time to be assured that no more bids can be had, it should be struck off to the highest bidder, if he offers two-thirds or over of the appraised value.

180. *Appraisers, etc., can not buy.*—Purchases of real or personal property, by the officer making sale thereof, or by an appraiser of such property, will be considered fraudulent and void; but this section does not affect, unless for fraud, sales by executors, administrators, or guardians, prior to March 29, 1841.[1]

---

[1] § 5404. See also paragraphs 49, 50, chap. 5.

An appraiser of land at an administrator's sale, stands in such a relation, that his purchase, although without actual fraud, will be set aside, in equity, at the instance of the heirs. 1838. Armstrong v. Huston's Heirs, 8 O. 551.

The principle of equity which prevents those from acquiring a title, to whose discretion or agency the management of a sale is confided, applies not only to trustees, executors, attorneys, and agents, but to every person to whose integrity or judgment is committed the execution of any step needful in making the sale. Ib. 554.

Fullness of price, absence of fraud, and fairness of purchase are not sufficient to countervail this rule of policy. To give it effect, it is necessary to recognize a right in the former owner, to set aside the sale in all cases, on repayment of the money advanced. Ib.

In proceedings in partition, an appraiser, in the absence of fraud, prior to the act of March 29, 1841 (1 Curwen, 793), might become a purchaser at the sheriff's sale. The rule of policy applied in the case of Armstrong v. Huston, 8 O. 552, is a rigorous one, and will not be extended to a case not strictly in point.

Applies also to attorneys in a case (see second paragraph of this note, also, Wade v. Pettibone, 11 O. 57).

In such proceedings, the acts of the guardian of a minor, done in good faith, are binding upon his ward.

Where a minor, in such case, on arriving at full age, ratifies the acts of

181. *Report of sale—confirmation and deed.*—Upon the return day of the order of sale issued by the court, such guardian must make a report of the sale by him made; whereupon, the court, on being satisfied that such sale was fairly and legally made, must confirm the same, and order the petitioner to execute a deed of conveyance for the real estate so sold, upon the purchaser securing the deferred payments of the purchase money in the manner prescribed in paragraph 128.[1]

182. *If no sale made, what to do.*—And if no sale is made, for want of bidders, or other cause, a return of that fact should be made on the order of sale issued; for every order of sale issued,

---

his guardian, by receiving and appropriating the proceeds of the sale, with full knowledge of the facts, he is estopped in equity from taking advantage of a mere irregularity in the proceedings. 1846.   Bohart *v.* Atkinson, 14 O. 228.

A purchase of real estate at a judicial sale, by one who, at the appraisement under which such sale was made, served as an appraiser, is not, under the provisions of section 441 of the code [now ? 5404], strictly void, but is voidable only; and will "be considered fraudulent and void" only on an interposition or proceeding by a party in interest directly for the purpose of avoiding such sale.   1862.   Terrill *v.* Auchauer, 14 O. S. 80.

Section 441 of the code, provides that "no sheriff or other officer making the sale of property, either personal or real, nor any appraiser of such property, shall, either directly or indirectly, purchase the same; and every purchase so made shall be considered fraudulent and void."   *Held*, that a purchase by an appraiser was not strictly void, but voidable only, and will be "considered fraudulent and void" only on an interposition or proceeding by a party in interest directly for the purpose of avoiding the sale.   Ib.

[1] ? 6287.

The report should show that he in all respects complied with the requirements of the law and the order of the court, in giving notice, in offering the premises at the time and place mentioned in the notice, and in the time allowed for the payment of the purchase money.   It is not sufficient that the report state generally that notice was given and the sale made according to law; but must set forth particularly *how*, and *for what length of time* the notice was given; and *when* and *where* the property was offered; together with the terms of sale, and whether the same were complied with by the purchaser.   It is the province of the court, and not of the executor or administrator, to say whether his proceedings were according to law. Raff's Guide, pp. 150–1.

The foregoing extract relates to the report of sale by executors and administrators, but it is equally applicable to reports of guardian's sales.

is noted on the execution docket, and it is important, in order to make a clear record, that every order of sale should be returned to the court whence issued, whether it has been acted upon or not, and with the action, if any was had, and why not, if none was had.

183–185. *Form of return to an Order of Sale, when a Sale has been made.*

In obedience to the within [*or*, attached] order, I duly advertised the real estate therein described for sale, for —— consecutive weeks [*or*, days] before the day of sale, in ——, a newspaper published and of general circulation in said county, stating in in said notice the time, place, and terms of said sale; and on the —— day of ——, A. D. ——, I attended, at the door of the court house, of said county [*or*, on the premises, *as the order directs*], at the hour of — o'clock, that being the time and place specified in said notice for said sale, and then and there, at public auction, offered said real estate [subject to the dower estate of L. D., therein, *if so*], when H. S. offered for the same the sum of —— dollars, which, being the highest and best bid that was offered, and more than [*or*, equal to] two-thirds of the appraised value of said premises, I then and there sold the same to him [subject to said dower estate, *if so*], for that sum.

Terms of Sale—One-third of the purchase money to be paid in hand, one-third in one year, and one-third in two years from day of sale, with interest on the two deferred payments, said deferred payments to be secured by mortgage on the premises sold.

A copy of said notice, with proof of publication, is hereto attached and filed. Dated this —— day of ——, A. D. 18—.

A. B., Guardian of C. D.

186. *Attached copy of notice, etc.*—A copy of the notice should be attached to the order issued, and returned with it, with an affidavit of its due publication.

187–8. *Forms of the Affidavit proving the Publication of the Notice of sale*

State of Ohio, —— county, ss.:

X. Y., being duly sworn, says that he is the publisher [*or*, foreman, *or otherwise, as may be*] of the ——, a newspaper printed* and in general circulation in said county, and that a notice, of which the annexed is a true copy, was published in said paper on —— day of each week for —— consecutive weeks, beginning on the —— day of ——, 18—.

189–192. If said paper be a daily, the following may be added :

Affiant further says that a daily and weekly edition of said newspaper is published ; that said notice appeared in the *daily* edition ; that the circulation of the *daily* in said county exceeds that of the *weekly*, and that the cost of publication in the *daily* does not exceed that in the *weekly*.

Sworn [*or*, affirmed] to and subscribed before me, this —— day of ——, 18—.   S. C., Notary Public —— county, Ohio.

193–4. When the affidavit is made by the guardian, the foregoing may be altered as follows. A copy of the notice must be attached to the affidavit in either case :

A. B., being duly sworn, says that the —— is a newspaper printed [*and conclude as above after the*].

195. *If no newspaper in the county.*—If no newspaper is published in the county where the petition is filed, the court should point out the mode of advertising the sale in the order of sale, in which case all the foregoing must be modified accordingly.

196. *When not sold for want of bidders.*—The law in the chapter on guardians does not direct what course to pursue when the land can not be sold for want of bidders ; but in such case, no doubt, the law stated in paragraph 30 would govern, and this would necessitate action under section 5416, which is as follows :

197. " When real estate, taken on execution and appraised, and twice advertised and offered for sale, remains unsold for want of bidders, the court from which the execution issued shall, on motion of the plaintiff, set aside such appraisement, and order a new appraisement to be made, or set aside such levy and appraisement, and award a new execution to issue, as the case may require ; and when such real estate, or any part thereof, has been three times appraised as aforesaid, and thereafter twice advertised and offered for sale, and then remains unsold for want of

bidders, the court may direct the amount for which the same shall be sold."

198. *Report when no sale is affected.*—After having twice advertised and offered the land for sale, as directed in the preceding paragraph, the guardian should make the following report:

199–203. *Form of Report, Sale not made.*

—— County, Ohio, ss., —— court.

<table>
<tr><td>A. B., guardian of C. D.,
vs.
Said C. D. et al.</td><td>}</td><td>Report of no sale in proceedings for sale of land.</td></tr>
</table>

In pursuance of the order of court in this case, I gave notice of sale by publication in the ——, a weekly newspaper of general circulation in said county of ——, for at least four successive weeks prior to the —— day of ——, 18—; and on that day, at — o'clock. forenoon, upon the premises, in accordance with said notice of sale. I offered the real estate in the petition described for sale. subject to the dower estate of Y. B. therein; and no bids being offered, said premises were not sold.

I thereupon gave notice of sale by publication [*and continue as already stated in this form*].

—— ——, 18—.   A. B., Guardian.

204. *Form of order of reappraisement.*—The order of reappraisement may be as follows:

<table>
<tr><td>205–6. A. B., guardian of C. D.,
vs.
Said C. D. et al.</td><td>}</td><td>Order of reappraisement in proceedings to sell land.</td></tr>
</table>

On motion to the court by ——, counsel for the plaintiff, and it appearing that the real estate described in the petition has been twice offered for sale and not sold for want of bidders*, it is ordered that the appraisement heretofore made may be set aside, and that said premises be reappraised by the oaths of D. H., O. B., and F. S.; and that said plaintiff thereupon proceed to sell said premises subject to such reappraisement, in accordance with the former order of this court.

207. *Order to sell at a fixed price.*—Follow the preceding form to the*, then proceed as follows :

208. It is ordered that said plaintiff proceed to sell said premises according to law, and the previous order of this court, at a sum not less than —— dollars.

209. *Report of private sale.*—The circumstances being so various under which private sale might be ordered, no general form can well be given ; but the instructions for forms of report of sale, found on preceding pages, should be followed. so far as applicable.

210. *Affidavit required in case of private sale.*—Before the court can confirm a sale by a guardian, made under an order allowing such officer to make private sale, the court must require such officer to make and file an affidavit that such private sale has been made after diligent endeavor to obtain the best price for the property, and that the sale reported is for the highest price he could get for the property.[1]

211. *Form of affidavit, etc.*—The affidavit should be attached to the report of sale, and may be in form as follows :

212–215. The State of Ohio, —— county, *ss. :*

A. B., being duly sworn, says that the private sale of property, made by order of court, as represented in the report to which this is attached, was made after diligent endeavor to obtain the best price possible for said property. and that the sale reported is for the highest price that he could get for said property.

A. B.

Sworn to and subscribed before me, this —— day of ——, A. D. 18—.   A. C., Probate Judge [*or other officer*].

216. *Confirmation of sale.*   When any return is duly made to the court, the proceedings should be examined carefully by the court, and if found fair, legal, and correct, the sale must be confirmed,[2] and a deed, and mortgage, if required, will be ordered.

---

[1] § 6412.

[2] 6287.

If the court had no jurisdiction to make such sale, it will be void. Perry *v.* Brainard, 11 O. 442.

If guardian dies before giving deed, his successor should complete the sale, giving deed. Lynch *v.* Kirby, 36 Mich. 238.

217–19. *Form of Order of Confirmation.*

A. B., guardian of C. D., } Order of confirmation in proceedings to
vs.
Said C. D. and others. } *sell land.*

This day this cause came on to be heard, upon the motion of the petitioner to confirm the sale made in obedience to the order heretofore made in this case; and the court having carefully examined the proceedings of petitioner upon said order of sale, and finding them in all matters correct, and being satisfied that said sale was fairly and legally made, it is ordered that the same be, and it is hereby approved and confirmed, and it is further ordered that the petitioner make a deed of all the right, title and interest of the said C. D. in and to said lands to the purchaser named in the petitioner's report of sale herein, upon the said purchaser's executing to said guardian a mortgage upon the premises, to secure the deferred payments of the purchase money, with interest at the rate of six per centum per annum, payable annually.

And it is further ordered that the petitioner pay the costs of these proceedings, taxed at —— dollars, out of said money for which said land was sold, within —— days, and in default thereof, that execution issue therefor against the property of said C. D., as upon judgments at law.

220. *Entry, if liens adjusted.*—If there are any mortgages or other liens to be adjusted, the journal entry must of course be modified, so as to conform to the findings of the court as to them, and to any order the court may make as to their payment out of the money for which the real estate was sold.

221. *Taxes, etc., must be paid out of proceeds.*—Among the liens which must be ordered paid out of the proceeds of such sale, are taxes and penalties that may be due against the land sold.[1]

222–228. *Guardian's Deed.*[2]

Know all men by these presents, that, by virtue of the law in such case made and provided, and of an order and decree of the

---

[1] § 2854.

[2] Guardian's deeds often contain recitals of facts which may be convenient or desirable as a history of the proceedings, but which are not necessary to the validity of the deed. The following form may be used, if preferred:
Whereas, heretofore, to-wit, on the —— day of ——, A. D. 18—, A. B., the

probate court within and for the county of ——, and state of Ohio, made on the ——— day of ——, A. D. 18—, in case No. ——, in said court, and of other proceedings had by and in said court in said case, all of which will more fully appear by the records of said court, to which reference is hereby made, authorizing A. B., as guardian of C. D., minor child of E. F., deceased, to sell the hereinafter described real estate of said C. D., and in pursuance of a sale duly made and reported to said court, and by it confirmed on the —— day of ——, A. D. 18—, and in consideration of the sum of —— dollars paid [or, secured to be paid, *as may be*] to said guardian by D. M., the purchaser at said sale, the said A. B., as guardian as aforesaid, does hereby grant, bargain, sell and convey to the said D. M., his heirs and assigns forever, all the right, title and in-

---

duly appointed and qualified guardian of C. D., a minor, filed, as such guardian, in the probate court of —— county, Ohio, being the court by which he was so appointed, a petition against his said ward, asking, upon legal cause therein set forth, for an order to sell the following described real estate, belonging to said ward in fee simple [or, for life, *or otherwise, as the case may be*], situate in the county of ——, Ohio, that is to say [*here describe the real estate, by metes and bounds, etc.*]; and whereas, the said C. D. was duly notified of the pendency of said petition, and the objects and prayer therein; and whereas, upon proceedings duly had thereon in said court, it was, on the —— day of ——, A. D. 18—, by said court ordered, that the said A. B. should proceed to sell said real estate according to law, at public vendue, upon giving —— days' notice of the time and place of such sale; and whereas, the said A. B., in accordance with said order, made such sale at the door of the court house [*or, on the premises, if it be so*], on the —— of ——, day of ——, A. D. 18—, to H. S., for the sum of —— dollars, he being the highest and best bidder therefor, and that being more than two-thirds the appraised value thereof; and whereas, the said A. B. made return of his said proceedings and sale to said court, and the said court having carefully examined the same, on the —— day of ——, A. D. 18—, finding the same correct, did approve and confirm the same, and ordered the said A. B. to make a deed of said real estate to the purchaser thereof.

Now, therefore, be it known, that by virtue of the powers conferred by law on the said A. B., as guardian as aforesaid of the said C. D., and by virtue of the powers and authority given said A. B., in the proceedings and orders aforesaid, and in consideration of the said sum of —— dollars, by the said H. S. paid, and secured, according to law, to be paid to the said A. B., as guardian as aforesaid, the said A. B., as guardian as aforesaid, does hereby grant, bargain, sell and convey unto the said H. S., his heirs and assigns forever, all the right, title, interest, claim, and demand of the said C. D., in law and equity, in and to the said premises.

To have and to hold the same to the said H. S., his heirs and assigns forever, in as full and ample a manner as the said C. D., or the said A. B., as guardian as aforesaid, might, could, or ought to convey the same.

In witness whereof, the said A. B., as guardian as aforesaid, has hereto set his hand and seal, this —— day of ——, in the year of our Lord one thousand eight hundred and ——.　　　　　　　A. B., [SEAL.]
Guardian of C. D.

terest of the said C. D. in and to the following described real estate, situate in [*fully describe the property, stating, in proper cases, whether sold free from, or subject to dower; and if subject to dower, describe it*]. To have and to hold the same, with the appurtenances, to the said D. M., his heirs and assigns forever. In testimony whereof the said A. B., as guardian as aforesaid, has hereunto set his hand and seal, this —— day of ——, in the year A. D. eighteen hundred and ——.   A. B.,   [SEAL.]

As Guardian of C. D.

The State of Ohio, —— county, ss.

Be it remembered, that on the —— day of ——, A. D. 18—, before me, the undersigned, a notary public [*or*, mayor, *etc.*] within and for said county, personally came A. B., as guardian of C. D., the grantor in the foregoing deed, and as such acknowledged the signing and sealing thereof to be his voluntary act and deed for the uses and purposes therein specified.

RICHARD ROE, Notary Public as aforesaid.

230. *To whom note and mortgage given.*—The notes and mortgage for deferred payments may be given either to the ward, or to the guardian as such; but the latter is the better practice.

231–8. *Form of Mortgage.*

KNOW ALL MEN BY THESE PRESENTS:

That H. S., of —— county, Ohio, in consideration of —— dollars [*naming here the entire unpaid part of the purchase price*], to him paid by A. B., as guardian of C. D., a minor, the receipt whereof is hereby acknowledged, does hereby grant, bargain, sell, and convey to the said A. B., guardian as aforesaid, his heirs[2] and assigns forever, the following described real estate, situate in [*here fully describe the real estate conveyed*]; and all the estate, title, and interest of the said H. S., either in law or in equity, of, in, and to the said premises; together with all the privileges and appurtenances to the same belonging, and all the rents, issues, and profits thereof; to have and to hold the same to the only proper use of the said A. B., as guardian as aforesaid, his heirs and assigns forever.

And the said H. S., for himself, and for his heirs, executors,

---

[1] If acknowledged before a J. P., omit the words "*and official seal.*"

[2] The word "heirs," not "successors," must be used. 10 O. 1; W. 144.

and administrators, does hereby covenant with the said A. B., guardian as aforesaid, his heirs and assigns, that he is the true and lawful owner of the said premises, and has full power to convey the same; that the title, so conveyed, is clear, free, and unincumbered; and further, that he will warrant and defend the same against all claim, or claims, of all persons whomsoever.

Provided, nevertheless, that if the said H. S. shall pay or cause to be paid his two certain promissory notes of even date herewith for —— dollars each, with interest thereon from date till paid at six per cent. per annum, payable annually; one of said notes being due and payable one year after date, and the other two years after date, each to the order of A. B., as guardian of C. D., and being given to secure the unpaid balance of the purchase money of said premises, then these presents shall be void.

In witness whereof, the said H. S. has hereunto set his hand and seal, this —— day of ——, in the year of our Lord one thousand eight hundred and ——.

H. S. [SEAL.]

Signed, sealed, and acknowledged in }
presence of us :   T. M., }
                                R. C.   }

The State of Ohio, county of ——, ss.

Be it remembered, that on the —— day of ——, in the year of our Lord one thousand eight hundred and ——, before me, the subscriber, a notary public [*or other officer, as may be*] in and for said county, personally came H. S., the grantor in the foregoing mortgage deed, and acknowledged the signing and sealing thereof to be his voluntary act and deed, for the uses and purposes therein mentioned.

In testimony whereof, I have hereunto subscribed my name, *and affixed my notarial seal*, on the day and year aforesaid.

[SEAL.]   N. E.,
Notary Public as aforesaid.

Sale of Lands in this State by Foreign Guardians.

239. *Application for sale—security.*—All applications for sale of real estate by guardians to minors, who live out of this state, must be made in the probate court of the county where the lands

are situate; and if situate in more counties than one, then in one of the counties in which a part of such real estate is situate; and additional security will be required of such guardian, when deemed necessary, and such as may be approved by the probate court of the county in which such application is made.[1]

240. *The proceedings*, in case of a foreign guardian making application to sell real estate of his ward lying in this state, will be the same precisely as that in the case of a guardian appointed here; the necessary variations in the forms already given, to adapt them to such a case, can be readily made.

241. *Order of court for security—form of.*—If the probate court, in which such application of a foreign guardian is made, deems it necessary to require additional security to that already given by the guardian, in the state or county where he was appointed, an order of court should be made so requiring it after the appraisement is made; and in so doing, the usual order made after the appraisement, the form of which has heretofore been given in paragraphs 113–118, may be used to the *, and then proceed as follows:

242. And the court deeming it necessary that an additional security should be given by said guardian, it is therefore further ordered, that the said A. B., within —— days, execute to the State of Ohio, a bond with sufficient freehold sureties, to the acceptance of this court, in the sum of —— dollars [*double the amount of the appraised value of the real estate*], conditioned according to law.

243–46. *The form of bond* will be like that already given in paragraphs 120-126, but the condition will be modified thus:

The condition of the above obligation is such, that whereas the above bound A. B., has heretofore been, by the ——- court of —— county, State of —— [*or*, Dominion of Canada, *etc., as the case may be*], duly appointed and qualified as guardian of C. D., a minor child of E. F., deceased, late of —— [*or*, then and now living, *if such is the case*], and which appointment the said A. B. accepted, and is still authorized to act under; and whereas the said A. B., as such guardian, has made application to the probate court of —— county, Ohio, for an order to sell certain real estate of his said ward, situate in the county of ——, Ohio, and which

---

[1] § 6290. See par. 1, chap. 25.

is particularly described in the petition of said application, which real estate, under proceedings there duly had, has been appraised at —— dollars; and whereas said court has ordered said A. B., as guardian as aforesaid, to execute a bond as such guardian, according to the statute in such case made and provided.

Now, therefore, if the said A. B. shall faithfully discharge his duties, as guardian of said C. D., and shall faithfully make payment and account for all moneys arising from such sale, according to law, then the above obligation will be void, otherwise to be and remain in full force.

A. B., [SEAL.]
C. D., [SEAL.]
E. F., [SEAL.]

This bond approved by me, this —— day of ——, A. D. ——.

A. C., Probate Judge of said —— county.

247. *If no bond be given, what to do.*—In case the foreign guardian can not or does not give the bond required, no further proceedings can be had, and no order of sale can be made; and in such case, the court should simply dismiss the proceedings at the costs of the guardian.

248. In such case, if it be necessary still to sell the lands of a foreign minor, a guardian must be appointed in this state, as directed in chapter 3.

249. *If given, what.*—If, however, the bond be given by the foreign guardian, and approved by the court, then the matter will proceed as heretofore directed in other cases.

250. *If bond not required.*—If no bond is required by the court, then so much of the order confirming the appraisement, and assignment of dower, if dower there be, as relates to giving a bond will be omitted; and in that case, the fact that no further bond is deemed necessary by the court, should be stated; and the order of sale may then be included in, and follow the order confirming the appraisement and assignment of dower.

251. *Remedy of purchaser, if guardian's sale invalid.*—The statute provides that if, upon the sale of property on execution, the title of the purchaser is invalid by reason of a defect in the proceedings, the purchaser may be subrogated to the right of the

creditor against the debtor, to the extent of the money paid and applied to the debtor's benefit, and, to the same extent, will have a lien on the property sold, as against all persons, except bona fide purchasers without notice; but this will not be construed to require the creditor to refund the purchase money, by reason of the invalidity of any such sales; and that this shall apply, also, to all sales by guardians.[1]

252. *How possession gained of lands sold at guardian's sale.*— Persons occupying lands sold at guardian's sale may be evicted by proceedings before a magistrate, in the manner provided in the chapter relating to Forcible Entry and Detainer, sections 6599–6612.[2]

253. *Kind of title guardian's sale conveys.*—As in other judicial sales, the general rule is that the guardian sells only such title to the land as the ward has, and the purchaser must make inquiry as to the title, and the authority of the guardian to sell. The guardian makes no warranty, and if he does, he only binds himself personally.[3]

------

[1] §§ 5410, 5411.   [2] § 6600.

[3] Black v. Walton (1877), 32 Ark. 321.   See note 1, p. 120.

CHAPTER 7.

LEASE OF WARD'S REAL ESTATE.

1. *Power of guardian to lease for three years.*—A guardian of the person and estate, or of the estate only, of any minor may lease the real estate of his ward for any term not exceeding three years and not extending beyond the minority.[1]

2. *Power to lease for fifteen years to save property from sale.*—Such guardian may also lease the real estate of his ward for any term not exceeding fifteen years, although such term extend beyond

---

[1] § 6295.

The guardian should, of course, rent his lands to the best possible advantage, and see that the rent money is well secured; he should see that the tenant uses the lands, houses, etc., as not abusing them; that the premises are kept in reasonably good repair, without extraordinary expense. See par. 72, chapter 5, as to repairs.

A guardian leased his ward's land in January, several years, where it was customary to lease lands in the spring. In an action against the guardian it was shown that the land would have rented for more money in the spring than in January, and the guardian was made to pay the difference to the ward. Knothe v. Kalser, 5 T. & C. (N. Y.), 4.

A guardian is not liable for an error of judgment in having leased the lands of his wards for a less rent than could have been obtained, where he acts in manifest good faith, having first secured the approval of the probate court. McElheny v. Musick, 63 Ill. 329.

the minority, whenever the court appointing him finds, on his application, that such lease will be to the advantage of the ward, and is necessary to secure the improvement of the real estate and to increase its rents, and that such increase is needed for the support and education of his ward or to pay his liabilities or any liens on, or claims against his estate, and that by such lease a sale of real estate for these purposes may be prevented.[1]

3. *Application for power to make such lease.*—Such application must be by petition, which must contain a description of the real estate and a particular statement of its value and the value of all other property or effects of the ward, and his income and expenses. a detailed statement of the improvements proposed and the liabilities or expense of support and education to be provided for, the rent of the real estate as it is, and the probable increase of rent if the improvements are made, the means intended to be used in making the improvements and the proposed terms and time of the lease; and such other facts as shall be pertinent to the question whether the authority for making the lease should be granted.[2]

4. *Who may unite in application.*—In such application the guardian may act on behalf of two or more wards, and two or more guardians of different wards may unite, when all the wards are jointly or in common interested in the real estate.[3]

5. *Rules as to parties and notice.*—The same rules apply in such matters as to parties and notice as in application for sale of real estate. (See chapter 6.)

6. *Dower.*—The widow's dower may be one of the liens on the real estate of a minor, but as probate courts have jurisdiction, in the assignment of dower, only in cases of *sales* of real estate to pay debts.[4] the court could not, in a proceeding to *lease* the real estate, assign such dower, and it seems that no conflicting liens could be adjusted in such proceeding.

7–12. *Form of application.*—The petition may be substantially as follows, varying it to suit the number of guardians or wards, and in other respects as the facts of each case may require:

---

[1] § 6296.   [2] § 6297.   [3] § 6298.   [4] See par. 4, chap. 6.

—— county, Ohio, *ss.* Probate Court.

<table>
<tr><td>A. B., as guardian of C. D., plaintiff.
vs.
Said C. D., a minor, aged 10 years,
L. D., X. Y. [*etc., naming all persons whose rights this application affects*], defendants.</td><td>*Petition to Lease Ward's Land.*</td></tr>
</table>

Said plaintiff says that he is the duly appointed guardian of said C. D., minor; that said minor is the owner in fee simple of the following described real estate, situate in the city of Cincinnati, county of Hamilton, and State of Ohio, to-wit: Lot No. [*describe it, as in a deed*]; that said lot is probably worth —— dollars. is totally unimproved, and produces no income whatever [*or, if improved and rented, say,* that the gross receipts derived therefrom for the past —— years have been —— dollars per year; *or, state the income for each year*], that there has been expended on said lot, during that time, amounts as follows: for taxes, —— dollars; for street improvement, —— dollars; [*if improved, for repairs,* —— dollars; *etc., as may be*]; that there is a mortgage on said property to secure a note of —— dollars, given by E. D., the father of said C. D., during his life, to said X. Y., and due in three months from this time; that said L. D., widow of said E. D., has a dower interest in said lot, for which she has agreed in writing to accept —— dollars, if paid within three years; that there are no other liens upon said lot.

Plaintiff further says that said C. D. has other property, as follows: [*here describe his property as directed above, each piece separately, if necessary; or, if so,* says that said C. D. has no other property]; that the gross annual income of said C. D. is —— dollars [*or, for the past* —— years has averaged —— dollars per year]; that his expenses, in addition to the taxes [*etc.*] above mentioned, during the past —— years, have been, for clothing, —— dollars; for tuition and other educational expenses, —— dollars, [*etc.*]; being an average of —— dollars per year; that the amount of said expenses per year will increase in the future by reason of [*state why, if so.*]

Plaintiff further says that said lot, by reason of its location, is valuable for business purposes, and will probably become more so year by year; and that its sale, either to satisfy said mort-

gage or for the assignment of said dower, will be extremely dis-
advantageous to said C. D.; that said lot can be leased for a
period of twelve years to G. T., a responsible person, upon the
following terms.   Said G. T. will erect thereon a [*describe the
structure*], which would be a permanent improvement, for the
purpose of carrying on therein the business of [*state what—or,
here state such facts as are pertinent, and tend to show that the
lease should be made*], and will pay, during said twelve years, an
annual ground rent of —— dollars, payable semi-annually.

Plaintiff further says that said ground rent, together with the
personal property above mentioned, would be sufficient to pay
off said liens and to support and educate said C. D.; but that if
said lot is not leased, it must be sold to satisfy said liens.

Wherefore plaintiff prays that he may be ordered by the court
to lease said lot upon the terms and conditions above specified,
or upon such other terms and conditions as the court may direct.   A. B., Guardian as aforesaid.

13. *Verification.*—This petition must be verified in the same
way as petition on page 102.

14. *Proceedings on preliminary hearing.*—On the hearing, the
court must appoint three disinterested freeholders of the county
in which the real estate is situate, who are not of kin to the petitioner, to view the premises and report under oath their opinion of the probable cost of the improvements proposed, whether
the same and the proposed lease would be for the best interest
of the ward or wards, and if so, upon what terms the lease should
be made; and the report must be returned on or before a day
named in the order for the final hearing of the case.[1]

15. *Forms of appointment.*—The forms for the appointment of
the freeholders alluded to in the preceding paragraph, as well as
of their oath, report, etc., can readily be adapted from the similar forms in chapter 6.

16. *Hearing and orders thereon.*—On the final hearing, if the
report of the freeholders be in favor of the lease, and the court
be of opinion that it will be to the advantage of the ward or wards
to improve and lease the real estate, and that such lease is necessary to secure the improvements and increase the rents, and that

---

[1] § 6298.

such increase is needed for the support and education of the ward or wards, or to pay his or their liabilities or liens or other claims against his or their estate, and that by such lease a sale of real estate for any of these purposes may be prevented, the court must make an order authorizing the lease to be made on such terms and in such manner as the court shall think proper.[1]

17. *How the improvements may be made.*—In the lease made in pursuance of such order, it may be provided that the improvements must be made by the tenant as part of the rent, or by the guardian, either out of the rent or other means of the ward or wards, as the court may have directed.[2]

18. *When such lease extending beyond minority shall determine.*—Any lease made by a guardian to extend beyond the minority must, nevertheless, determine when the ward, if there be but one, arrives at full age, or if more than one, when all of them arrive at full age, unless such ward or wards then confirm the same; and in case of the death of the ward, if there be but one, or of all of them, if more than one, the lease must also determine, unless the legal representatives of such ward or wards confirm the same; if there be more than one ward, and some, but not all, die, the lease will continue till the survivor or survivors reach full age.[3]

19. *Lien of tenant for improvements.*—When such lease is determined by reason of the death or majority of the ward or wards, the tenant will have a lien on the premises for any sum or sums expended by him in pursuance of the lease in making improvements, and for which compensation shall not have been made, either by the rent or otherwise.[3]

---

[1] § 6299.   [2] § 6300.   [3] § 6301

CHAPTER 8.

TAXATION AND TAX TITLES, AS AFFECTING GUARDIAN AND WARD.

1. *Guardians must pay ward's land tax.*—Every person must pay tax each year for the lands or town lots of which he or she may have the care as guardian.[1]

2. *And list same for taxation.*—It is the duty of every person

---

[1] §§ 2845, 2847. Under the statute relating to taxation, the guardian of minors is charged with the duty of representing the real estate of their wards in listing it for taxation and payment of taxes as well as in the general management of such estate, and as such guardian he may represent his ward's estate under the statute above cited [2 S. & C., p. 509, petitioning for road improvements], either to ask for or oppose such improvement.

Where minor children, who are tenants in common of the lot of land, reside on the same, they are resident owners, but whether each is to be counted, or all counted as one. *Quære.*

If the names of such minors, and of the guardian individually, are signed to a petition by direction of the guardian, and in his presence, it is equivalent to his signing as guardian. Campbell *v.* Park, 32 O. S. 544.

seized of or holding real estate (as guardian or otherwise) to list the same for taxation with the county auditor, on or before the third Monday of May next, after the same shall be subject to taxation; and in case of neglecting to list the same as aforesaid, the county auditor must, when the same shall be thereafter listed, charge upon each tract so neglected to be listed, the taxes for each year they shall have been omitted, after becoming liable for taxation, together with twenty-five per centum penalty and six per centum interest thereon, in addition to the taxes of the current year.[1]

3. *Penalty for neglect.*—If any guardian neglect or refuse to list[2] or pay the taxes on the same, in the manner above indicated, such guardian is made liable, in an action, to his ward, for any damage sustained by such neglect or refusal.[3]

4. Therefore, if by reason of the guardian's neglect to list the lands, there be a penalty suffered to be charged against the lands, he will be liable to pay the ward that penalty.

5. So if, by failure to pay the taxes, the lands be subjected to the payment of a penalty, or be sold for the taxes at delinquent or forfeited sale, the guardian will be liable to the ward for any such penalty, or for the penalty and interest required to be·paid to redeem them; or, in case the lands are thereby lost, then for the value of the lands.

6. *Must pay out of his own funds, if necessary.*—It seems that the guardian must in all cases list and pay the taxes upon the lands of his ward, whether he has money of the ward's in his hands or not, because it is expressly made the duty of guardians and executors having lands in charge to pay the taxes. The statute makes a difference between them and agents and attor-

---

[1] § 2846.

[2] Where three executors of an estate reside in the same township—two of them within the corporate limits of a village, the others without such limits, and the three have possession, in law, of the taxable moneys, credits, bonds, and stocks of the estate, the same must, in view of the equities and analogies of the statute (which does not expressly provide for such case) be entered for taxation—one-third as of the place of residence of each executor. Harkness *v.* Mathews, 10 Ohio St. 431.

This would very probably apply to guardians, also.

[3] § 2848.

10

neys, as these latter are only required to pay the taxes, and made liable for the consequences of not paying them, when they have funds of the principal in their hands.[1]

7. So that, if the guardian have no personal estate in his hands, and the ward has no means but the land itself, the guardian may make application to court for an order to sell the lands;[2] or, if he does not think it best to pursue this course, or does not do so in time to pay the taxes, he must then pay them from his own funds.

8. *Compensation and lien for such advances.*—Every guardian, having the care of lands as aforesaid, who is put to any trouble or expense in listing or paying the taxes on such lands, or who has to advance his own money for listing or paying the taxes on such lands, will be allowed a reasonable compensation for the time spent, the expenses incurred, and money advanced, which must de deemed in all courts a just charge against the ward.[3]

9. *When guardian or trustee sells land, tax paid out of proceeds.*—Whenever any land is sold by guardians or trustees, the court must order the taxes and penalties, and the interest thereon against such lands, to be paid out of the proceeds of such sale.[4]

10. *Guardian must list the personal property of ward for taxation.* The personal property of every ward must be listed by his guardian, of every minor child, idiot, or lunatic having no guardian, by his father, if living; if not, by his mother, if living; and if neither father nor mother be living, by the person having such property in charge; of every wife by her husband, if of sound mind; if not, by herself; of every person for whose benefit property is held in trust by the trustees, etc.[5]

---

[1] § 2850.

[2] In such case the tax is a debt of the estate, and if the administrator have not personal assets to pay for the same, he may apply for an order to sell lands for that purpose. Welsh v. Perkins, 8 Ohio, 52

[3] § 2851.

[4] § 2851.

[5] § 2734. This same section of the law provides that "every person of full age and sound mind must list the personal property of which he is the owner, and all moneys in his possession, all moneys invested, loaned, or otherwise controlled by him, as agent or attorney, or on account of any

11. *Where personal property must be listed.* Every person required to list property on behalf of others, must list the same in the same township, city, or village, in which he would be required to list it if such property were his own; but he must list it *separately* from his own, specifying, in each case, the name of the person, estate, company, or corporation, to whom it belongs.[1]

12. *When property to be listed, and as of what day.* Each person required to list property must, annually, upon receiving a blank for that purpose from the assessor, or, within ten days thereafter, make out and deliver to the assessor a statement, verified by his oath, of all the personal property, moneys, credits, investments in bonds, stocks, joint-stock companies, annuities, or otherwise, in his possession, or under his control, on the day preceding the second Monday of April of that year, which he is required to list for taxation, either as owner or holder thereof, or as parent, guardian, trustee, or otherwise.[2]

13. *How ward's property should be listed.* The guardian should get two such blanks from the assessor, and list the personal property of his ward on a different blank from that on which he lists his own. This latter he should list as the property of C. D.; the former he should list as the property of C. D., as guardian of A. B.

14. *How county treasurer may collect from guardian.* The law provides that, among other means, the county treasurer may adopt to compel the payment of taxes, he may distrain (seize) goods and chattels of the delinquent,[3] and also provides that if he is unable to collect, by distress (seizure), the taxes assessed upon any guardian (among others), then such treasurer must apply to the clerk of the court of common pleas in his county, at any time after his semi-annual settlement with the county

---

other person or persons, company or corporation whatsoever, and all moneys deposited subject to his order, check, or draft; and all credits due or owing from any person or persons, body corporate or politic, whether in or out of such county; all money loaned on pledge or mortgage of real estate, although a deed or other instrument may have been given for the same, if between the parties the same is considered as security merely."

The guardian must list all such **property of his ward.**

[1] § 2735. See note 2, page 145.   [2] § 2736.

[3] §§ 1094, 1095, 1104.

auditor, and said clerk must cause a notice to be served upon such guardian, requiring him forthwith to show cause why he should not pay such taxes; and if he fails to show a sufficient cause, the court, at the term to which said notice is returnable, must enter a rule against him for the payment of such taxes and the cost of such proceeding, which rule will have the same force and effect as a judgment at law; and be enforced by attachment or execution, or such process as the court directs.[1]

15. *Release of ward's tax title by guardian.*   When any minor has title to any real estate by tax title only, the guardian of such minor may, if he deem it advisable, by deed of release and quitclaim, convey such minor's interest or title to the person entitled to redeem such real estate, upon receiving from such person the full amount paid for such tax title with the penalty and interest allowed by law in that behalf.[2]   As to what this penalty and interest are, see paragraph 19, below.

16. *Effect of tender to release.*   If any such guardian tenders such deed to the person so entitled to redeem such real estate, and such person refuses to accept the same, and pay as aforesaid, such person, in any proceeding thereafter instituted to redeem or recover such real estate can not recover costs.[2]

17. *Lands sold for taxes may be redeemed within two years.*   All lands and town lots which have been, or may hereafter be sold for taxes at delinquent sale, under the laws of this state, may be redeemed at any time within two years from and after the sale thereof; and all lands belonging to minors, insane persons, and others,[3] which have been or may hereafter be sold for taxes, may be redeemed at any time within two years from and after the expiration of such disability.[4]

18. *As to general validity of tax title.*   Although the statutes indicate that a tax title is good after two years, it is in effect not much, if any thing, more than a lien on the land for the taxes paid, and the penalties and interest prescribed by law, as the courts almost universally find some way of restoring the lands

---

[1] § 1097.   [2] § 6194.

[3] The others are married women, persons in captivity, and persons serving in the army or navy of the United States during actual war.

[4] § 2890.

to their rightful owner, if these items are paid ; and this is quite just and right. Twenty-one years' possession under a tax title would generally not be disturbed; but then it would be the lapse of time, rather than the tax deed, that would make the title good.

19. *How lands may be redeemed.* Any person desiring to redeem any land or town lot sold at delinquent tax sale, under or by virtue of any law of this state, within one year after the sale thereof, or within one year after the expiration of any of the disabilities named in paragraph 17, above, may deposit with the county treasurer, upon the certificate of the county auditor, particularly describing such land or town lot, and specifying the same, an amount of money equal to that for which such land or town lot was sold, and the taxes subsequently paid thereon by such purchaser, or those claiming under him, together with interest, and fifteen per centum penalty on the whole amount paid, including costs, and one dollar to pay the expenses of advertising, as provided by law; and any.person desiring to redeem any land or town lot so sold for taxes, after the expiration of one year from the sale thereof, and within the time limited by law for such redemption, may deposit with the county treasurer, upon the certificate of the county auditor, particularly describing such land or town lot, and specifying the same, an amount of money equal to that for which such land or town lot was sold, and the taxes subsequently paid thereon by such purchaser, or those claiming under him, together with interest and five per centum penalty on the whole amount paid, including costs, and one dollar to pay the expense of said advertising.[1]

---

[1] §2891. The proceeding to redeem is essentially *in rem;* and it is not necessary that any person be named as party defendant. Plumb *v.* Robinson, 13 O. S. 298. Parol evidence admissible to show trust estate. *Ib.*

Validity of title can not be drawn in question in a proceeding to redeem. Masterson *v.* Beasley, 3 O. 301; nor authority of agent questioned. *Ib.*

Right of appeal under former laws. Street *v.* Francis, 3 O. 277; Rawson *v.* Boughton, 5 O. 328. Married women can redeem. Plumb *v.* Robinson, 13 O. S. 298.

CHAPTER 9.

ACCOUNT AND SETTLEMENT, AND COMPENSATION OF GUARDIAN.

1. *When settlements must be made.*—As already stated in chapter 6, the guardian must make a settlement of his account with the court, under oath, at least once in every two years, and at such other times as the court may, either upon its own motion or upon the motion of any interested person, require;[1] and he

---

[1] § 6269.

The account required by section 14 of the guardian act of April 12, 1858

must make a final settlement in the same manner, at the expiration of his trust,[1] whether by resignation, removal, marriage of a female guardian,[2] removal from the state, choice of another guardian by the ward at a proper age,[3] the arrival of the ward at full age, death of the ward,[4] or from other cause.[5]

2. In either of the above cases, the court should at once require the guardian to make a full and final settlement[6] of his account, and a failure to comply would be a breach of his bond.[7]

3. *Object of account, and how made.*—The language of the statute requiring the guardian to render, on oath, to the proper court, an account of *the receipts and expenditures*, means, of course, *all* the receipts and expenditures, and the account should be a full statement of all the transactions of the guardian and condition of the ward's estate. The object of the account is to

---

(S. & C. 670; ? 6269 Rev. Stat.), to be rendered by a guardian to a probate court at least once in every two years, when rendered and judicially passed upon by the court, is a settlement within the meaning of section 31 of the act. (? 6289; see pars. 50, 51.)

Under the provisions of said section 31, every settlement so made by a guardian is final between the guardian and the ward, unless an appeal is taken therefrom, or the settlement is opened in accordance with the provisions of the section. Woodmansee *v.* Woodmansee, 32 O. S. 18.

A failure by a guardian to settle his accounts within the time prescribed by law is clearly a breach of his bond. Hocking District Court, 1852. Case *v.* State, 10 W. L. J. 163.

A guardian, appointed in Pennsylvania, received the assets of his ward, and removed, with the assets of his ward, to Ohio, and died, without settlement of his accounts as guardian: *Held*, that the ward could sustain a bill in equity, in the courts of Ohio, for an account against the personal representative of the guardian. Pedan *v.* Robb, 8 O. 227.

[1] ? 6269. A probate court, in settling an account, would act upon equitable principles. Perry on Trusts, ? 407.

[2] ? 6292.   [3] ?? 6258, 6272.   [4] See par. 67, chap. 5.   [5] ?? 6269, 6272.

[6] Upon closing his final account in the probate court, an amount being due his ward, the guardian induces her to sign a receipt for the money as though paid, agreeing to be responsible to her for said amount with interest: *Held*, an action may be maintained upon such agreement by the ward, and the sum actually due from the guardian recovered, without in any way opening and reviewing the accounts which had been settled in the probate court. Lindsay *v.* Lindsay, 28 O. S. 157.

[7] 10 W. L. Journal, 167. See notes above.

show the court and the parties in interest what these transactions have been and what this condition is, and to perpetuate this of record. For these and other reasons, the account should be so clear and definite that it may be understood both by the court and all parties in interest without the presence of the guardian, and without making it necessary to call him into court for the purpose of explaining any of its items.

4. *Should get blank book for accounts.*—As soon as the guardian is ready to enter upon the discharge of his duties, he ought to procure a convenient sized blank account book, sufficiently large to last him during his appointment. And if he be guardian of several wards, he should procure as many such books as he has wards, or one sufficiently large to open in it a separate account with each of them.

5. *Account of each ward separate.*—It does not matter whether they be all the children of the same parents, and derive their property from the same source or not, since, as each ward has a separate and exclusive share of such property, to which his co-wards have no claims whatever, the accounts of each must be kept separate and distinct.

6. *Should charge himself with what.*—The guardian should charge himself with all moneys, goods and chattels, notes,[1] bonds, mortgages, or other evidences of debts due to the ward from any source, which come to the guardian's knowledge; also all rents received by the guardian, as well as those which may be lost, all

---

[1] A guardian is liable to his ward for accepting from an administrator or other party a note or other obligation in lieu of money coming to the ward's estate, when the same proves uncollectible. Bescher v. State, 63 Ind. 302. But see page 67, as to assets from estate.

Where a person occupies the double relation of administrator of a decedent's estate, and guardian of his minor heirs of such estate, and it becomes his duty as such administrator to pay over a fund in his hands for distribution to himself as guardian for the minor heirs, the law will, in general, presume such payment to have been made. Wilson v. Wilson, 17 O. S. 150.

Where a party acting in a double capacity is possessed of a fund in one capacity, which it is his duty (so to speak) to tranfer to himself in another, such transfer will in law be presumed. *Ib.* 156.

But this legal presumption may be rebutted; and where he charges himself with the fund in his account as administrator, but fails to credit himself in that account, with its payment to himself as guardian, and in an attempted settlement of his account as guardian, refrains from charging him-

earnings of the ward, and all interests upon money due the ward, and if lands be sold, with the proceeds thereof, giving the dates when the amounts were received, and entering the principal and interest separately.

7. *As to interest on funds in his hands.*—He is not chargeable with interest[1] upon money in his hands, unless he apply the same to his own use, or derive some benefit from the loan of it, or unless he unreasonably and unnecessarily delayed investing it or paying it over to the proper person, especially if the claim of such person was drawing interest.[2]

8. *Should credit himself with what.*—He should credit himself with all payments he actually makes for the ward, whether for board, clothing, tuition, just and proper debts due from the ward, incumbrances on the estate, taxes upon personal and real property, repairs upon real property, insurance in proper cases, expenses of the guardianship, as probate fees, reasonable attorney's fees in proper cases,[3] etc., etc.

If the guardian has advanced money for his ward, when no funds of the ward were in his hands, to pay taxes, or to redeem land of the ward from a mortgage that was about to be fore-

---

self therein with such fund, the legal presumption of a transfer of the fund is rebutted; and in an action by his former wards on his bond as administrator, for the recovery of the fund, he will be estopped to deny that he still holds the same as administrator. *Ib.*

[1] See page 67, as to when the statutes makes him liable for interest. Also, pages 79, 81, 84, and notes thereto.

[2] "The proper mode of taking the account of trustees is to treat all the income of the trust received during the current year as unproductive, and to charge against the income of the current year all the disbursements, including the compensation or commissions of the trustees for the same year, and to strike a balance, upon which, as a general rule, interest is to be allowed, but in such a way as not to compound it. If, however, these balances are too small to invest, or for any reason the trustees might equitably keep them on hand, interest upon them will not be allowed upon them until the balances so accumulate as to be properly invested, or until the trustees ought to invest them." Perry on Trusts, § 468.

[3] It is stated in Perry on Trusts (§ 432), Redfield on Wills (vol. 3, pp. 537, 557), and by other writers, as a strict rule, that an attorney, being a trustee, can make no charge against the trust estate for services rendered by him in his professional capacity to the estate of which he is trustee; the learned author first named above citing thirteen English, three New York, and one

closed, the land being of more value than the amount of the mortgage, he will be allowed interest on the money so advanced, and may credit himself, in his account, with the same.

9. *Bad debts, what to do about.*—If there are any bad debts due the ward, rents not collectible, etc., they should be entered in the form of a note or otherwise in the account, with an explanation as to why they were not collected. If this is not done, interested parties may, in after years, learn of them for the first time, and charge the guardian with negligence in not collecting them, by which time he might have forgotten, or be unable then to show why they were not collected. For this reason it is sometimes well, especially if a debt be large, to reduce it to judgment, and get the sheriff's or other officer's return of "no goods" as evidence of the impossibility of collecting. Still, expenses should not be

---

North Carolina cases to sustain this rule; the others, so far as observed, citing *some* of the same cases.

That this rule is not of universal application is shown by the following extract from a note in Schouler's Domestic Relations (page 500): "Where commissions at the court's discretion are allowed, special services performed by the guardian may be considered in fixing the rate of commission, but not as an additional charge. . . . McElhenny's Appeal, 46 Penn. St. 347. Even in New York the unfairness of an inflexible rule, applicable to all who hold trust moneys, has led to the assertion of a doctrine in a recent case, which threatens to disturb the chancery rule, formerly considered as well settled, namely, that services of a professional or personal character, rendered the ward, may be allowed to the guardian, besides the usual commission, on the ground that they were rendered not as guardian but as an individual. Morgan *v.* Morgan, 39 Barb. 20. In Maine, Massachusetts and other states where the court allows what is reasonable, the guardian may charge specific sums for special services, instead of or in addition to a commission; *provided* the whole does not exceed a fair rate of compensation. Longley *v.* Hall, 11 Pick. 120; Rathbun *v.* Colton, 15 Pick. 471; Emerson, appellant, 32 Me. 159; Dixon *v.* Homer, 2 Met. 420; Roach *v.* Jelks, 40 Miss. 754; Evarts *v.* Mason, 11 Vt. 122."

In view of the authorities given in the two preceding paragraphs, and of the fact that the English rule forbids trustees receiving any pecuniary compensation whatever, the first paragraph of this note may be said to state the English, rather than the American rule; and in view of the further fact that Ohio is one of the states where the court is to allow reasonable compensation, the concluding part of the second paragraph of this note may be considered as the rule in this state; and as far as known to the writer, it is in accordance with the practice of our probate courts.

needlessly incurred in this way.[1] But the guardian must make every reasonable effort to collect such debts, and if he does not succeed, he should note the result as directed in paragraphs 18–22, below.

10. *Guardian must take receipts.*—For every payment the guardian makes, he should take a receipt. It is required by statute, that his accounts be verified by vouchers or proof; and unless he makes it an invariable rule to pay out *no* money without getting a proper receipt for it, he will be unable to prove to the court, as he must do on settling, that the payments were made.

11. *As to form of account.*—The form of the account may be such as will be most readily prepared and understood by persons having a limited knowledge of accounts. The plainest form of "single entry" will be found to meet the necessities of nearly all the transactions of guardians; the most complicated statements perhaps will be where loans and investments have been made; but whatever the transactions may have been, they should be definitely stated.

12. The account should clearly show the debits and credits of the guardian, and refer by number or otherwise, to the vouchers produced; the footings should be made and the balance struck; and the whole statement should be so complete that any person, including the ward after he shall have arrived at full age, can tell, from the account, without explanation, exactly how the guardian stands with the trust.

13–15. *Form of account.*—The following form and statement of an account is given as an example, showing the transactions of a guardian, and of the manner of striking the balance, and showing the condition of the estate of the ward at the time of filing the account. Another form substantially the same is given on pages 254-6.

---

[1] "Ordinary prudence and diligence is the rule; and for culpable negligence subjecting the estate of his ward to loss he may make himself personally liable, even though the demand be against a person residing in another state. He is not to sue in all cases where ordinary modes of collection fail; for the expenses of litigation are to be weighed against the chances of realizing a benefit." Schouler's Dom. Rel. 474. See page 86, above.

[2] § 6269, as amended, Vol. 77, O. L., p. 77. See par. 7, chapter 5.

Current account of A. B., Guardian of the person and estate

RECEIPTS.	$	cts.
STATEMENT OF ASSETS RECEIVED, OTHER THAN MONEY AND LANDS.		
1878.		
Sept. 10.. From J. L., administrator of said decedent, the following property on distribution in kind, to-wit:		
2 U. S. $500.00 4 per cent. bonds..................$1,000 00		
14 shares L. M. R. R. stock........................ 1,400 00		
1 note on H. S 1,160 00		
$3,560 00		
CASH RECEIPTS.		
Sept. 10.. From J. L., administrator, on distribution of the estate of said E. D., dec'd...................................	1,080	00
Oct. 1.... interest on U. S. bonds...............................	10	00
" 1.... 1 mo's rent of house in Glendale.......................	75	00
" 15.... quarterly dividend L. M. R. R. bonds..................	28	00
1879.		
Jan. 2... 3 mo's rent house in Glendale........................	225	00
" 2... interest on U. S. bonds...........................	10	00
" 15... quarterly dividend L. M. R. R bonds.................	28	00
March 1. 1 year's rent of farm in Green township, Hamilton County, Ohio...................................	350	00
April 1.. 3 mo's rent of house in Glendale	225	00
" 1.. amount of note of H. S	1,160	00
interest at 6 per cent., 1 year.......................	69	60
" 1.. quarterly dividend L. M. R. R. bonds................	28	00
July 1.. 3 mo's rent of house in Glendale....................	225	00
" 1.. interest on U. S. bonds...........................	10	00
" 10.. quarterly dividends L. M. R. R. bonds..............	28	00
Oct. 1... interest on U. S. bonds...........................	10	00
" 1... 8 mo's rent of house in Glendale....................	225	00
" 15... quarterly dividend L. M. R. R. bonds...............	28	00
1880.		
Jan. 2... 3 mo's rent of house in Glendale....................	225	00
" 2... interest on U. S. bonds...........................	10	00
" 12... quarterly dividend in L. M. R. R. bonds............	28	00
March 1. 1 year's rent of farm in Green township............	350	00
" 1. for fallen timber, Green township.................	32	00
April 1.. 3 mo's rent of house in Glendale....................	225	00
" 1.. interest on U. S. bonds...........................	10	00
" 16.. quarterly dividend L. M. R. R. bonds..............	28	00
July 1.. interest on U. S. bonds...........................	10	00
" 1.. 3 mo's rent of house in Glendale....................	225	00
" 16.. quarterly dividend. L. M. R. R. bonds..............	28	00
Total Cash Receipts	4,985	60
Total expended and invested (see next page)	4,755	25
Balance of cash on hand, Sept. 10, 1880.....................	230	35

of C. D., minor child of E. D., dec'd., with estate of said minor :

	EXPENDITURES.	Voucher.	$	cts
1878.				
Sept. 1..	Paid, probate court, letters of guardianship..........	1	4	60
" 20..	" probate court, filing inventory...................	2	1	25
Dec. 10..	" taxes on farm in Greene towns'p..........	3	31	60
" 10..	" taxes on house in Glendale....................	4	242	15
" 10...	" on personal property...................	5	49	15
" 19..	" repairing house in Glendale....................	6	66	25
March 1.	" back taxes, Louisiana land.....................	7	25	50
1879.				
Feb. 16.	" repairing fences on farm....................	8	28	40
" 16.	" repairing barn on farm...................	9	32	50
" 16.	" suit of clothing for ward	10	51	00
" 27.	" under clothing " "	11	8	50
" 27.	" repairing shoes " "	12	1	50
Sept. 1...	" tuition and room rent at college.................	13	120	00
" 1...	" car fare: furnishing ward's room at college...	14-16	105	10
" 1...	" cash to ward for incidentals..................	17	10	00
" 1...	" boarding for ward.................	18	215	00
" 1...	" suits of clothing, underwear, etc., for ward ...	19	42	00
" 1....	" boots and shoes for ward	20	19	00
" 1....	" books and stationery for ward..................	21	20	00
Dec. 15..	" taxes on Louisiana land......................	22	1	50
" 15..	" taxes on farm in Greene township	23	31	60
" 15..	" taxes on house in Glendale.....................	24	250	00
" 15..	" taxes on personal property...................	25	52	10
1880.				
Jan. 10...	" bills for clothing for ward.........................	26	45	00
" 10....	" cash to ward for incidentals..................	27	5	00
" 10...	" boarding for ward..................................	28	60	00
May 1..	" boarding " "	29	60	00
June 25..	" cash to ward for traveling expenses home, and incidentals...............................	30	15	00
" 25..	" clothing for ward	31	30	00
Sept. 1..	" ward's tuition and room rent at college.........	32	120	00
" 1...	" books and sundries for ward.....................	33	40	00
" 1...	" boarding and sundries for ward.................	34	215	00
" 1...	" cash to ward for incidentals.....................	35	15	00
" 1...	" ward's car fare, etc., to college.....................	36	20	00
" 1...	" guardian's compensation for all services to date.......................................	37	160	00
" 1...	" tax on Louisiana land.................	38	1	25
1879.	Total expenditures................		2,255	25
Dec. 10...	Loaned cash to M. D., on mortgage note, at 7 per cent., payable annually..		1,500	00
1880.				
Aug. 1....	Purchased, as investment, U. S. Government bond..		1,000	00
	Total expended and invested............................		4,755	25

	STATEMENT OF ASSETS OTHER THAN REAL ESTATE, NOW ON HAND.		$	cts
1880.				
Sept. 18..	Cash.................................		$230	35
	U. S Government bonds..........................		2,000	00
	L. M. R. R. bonds...................................		1,400	00
	Mortgage note of M. D..............................		1,500	00
	Total.................................		5,130	35

16. The entries showing the balance of cash, bonds, stocks and other property in the hands of the guardian, should be carried to the next account, and should be the first entries therein.

17. *The final account* must show that the guardian has settled with and paid to the ward all the remaining and unexpended money and property which came to the possession of the guardian.

18–21. *Bad debts, how noted.* Should there be uncollectible debts, they may be noted as follows in the final account:

"The following debts were uncollectible, and are still due, though every proper and reasonable effort has been made to collect them:

> From B. C., rent of Avondale house for January and February of 18—, at $25.00 per month $50.00
>
> From J. L., admr. as aforesaid, said ward's share of the estate of said E. D., not paid over to said guardian 870.00

(Etc., etc.)

"Said B. C., though previously a good tenant, failed in business in December, 18—, with no assets whatever which his creditors could obtain, as proceedings against him by other creditors demonstrated; and therefore, though said guardian often asked for the payment of said $50, no legal proceedings were ever had to recover it.

"Said administrator failed to pay over a large amount of money belonging to said estate, for which said guardian, with others, brought suit on his bond, which proved to be of no use, as will be seen by reference to records and papers in case No. ——, of the court of common pleas of this county.

"(Etc., etc.)"

22. Or, the guardian can charge himself with these items on the debtor side of the account, and credit himself with them on the other side, and explain them in a foot-note, or in any other clear and satisfactory way.[1]

---

[1] A guardian is presumably liable to his ward for the nominal amount of debts due his ward's estate, which he has failed to collect; if they were not

23. *Guardian must make affidavit to the account—its form.*
The guardian must make oath to the account, which oath may
be in form as follows:

24–5. The State of Ohio, ——county, *ss:*

A. B., guardian of C. D., a minor, being duly sworn, says that
the foregoing account is in all respects true, just and correct, to
the best of his knowledge and belief. [*If any property sold at
private sale by order of court is therein accounted for, here add*]
and that the private sale of the property therein mentioned as
made by order of court, was made after diligent endeavor to
obtain the best price for the same, and that the sale reported
is for the highest price that could be obtained for said property.

A. B.

Sworn to and subscribed before me, this —— day of ——,
18—.   A. C., Probate Judge.

26. *Form of Journal Entry when the Accounts are Filed.*

In the matter of the guardianship of C. D.

This day came A. B., guardian of said C. D., and filed his accounts, as such guardian, for partial [*or,* final] settlement.

COMPENSATION OF GUARDIAN.

27. *The amount of guardian's compensation.* The statute fixes
no definite amount or mode of ascertaining what compensation
shall be allowed to the guardian for his services, but this is left
wholly to the judgment and discretion of the court. It is simply provided that every guardian shall be allowed by the court
settling his accounts, the amount of all his reasonable expenses
incurred in the execution of his trust; and also such compensation for his services as the court shall deem reasonable.[1]

28. Ordinarily, perhaps, as good a rule as can be adopted, at
least where the guardianship is of short continuance, is to allow
the same fees as are allowed to executors and administrators,
which is six per centum on the first thousand dollars, four per

---

collectible for their face, that is for him to show in defense.   Scigler *a.*
same, 7 S. C. (1876) 317.

[1] §6268. See note 3, p. 153.

centum on all over that and not exceeding five thousand dollars, and two percentum on all over that amount.

29. These percentages are what would properly be allowed *once only* on the principal of the ward's estate, after which the percentage should be on the income only;[1] otherwise, by making short investments, and re-collecting frequently, the estate would soon all be the guardian's, and not the ward's. For extraordinary services or trouble, such additional sum as under all the circumstances is thought by the court reasonable and proper.[2]

30. But no absolute rule can be given, either for ordinary or extraordinary services. The court must estimate these services from all the circumstances of the particular case, taking into consideration the trouble incident to the guardianship, whether of the person or estate, or both, the responsibility of the guardian in handling the moneys; of training, educating, and caring for the person of the ward; and the fact whether these things have been faithfully done, etc., etc.

31. *For care of real estate.* The trouble incident to the care of real estate is also a proper subject to be considered in fixing the compensation.

32. *For taxes paid, etc.* The guardian is entitled to his expenses, and a reasonable compensation for his time and

---

[1] Where more than one account is filed by an executor or administrator, the rule for the allowance of commissions remains unchanged. Upon the filing of the second, or any subsequent account, the computation is taken up where left by the preceding account, and the money contained in the preceding account, or accounts, is added to what is subsequently accounted for, and the computation of the commissions is made as though the moneys were all comprehended in one account. For example: If an estate amount to six thousand dollars; and in the first account nine hundred dollars be accounted for; in the second, four thousand dollars, and in the third and final one, eleven hundred dollars; on the settlement of the first account, the commissions would be six per cent.; of the second, six per cent. on one hundred dollars, and four per cent. on three thousand nine hundred dollars; and of the third, four per cent. upon one hundred dollars, and two per cent. on the residue. But an executor or administrator may claim compensation for extra services upon the filing of every account. Raff's Guide, page 160.

[2] See note 3, page 153, as to compensation for special services as attorney.

trouble in listing lands for taxation, and paying the taxes thereon.[1]

33. *When no compensation allowed.*—But if the guardian fails to render, upon oath, to the proper court, an account of his receipts and expenditures as such guardian, verified by vouchers or proof, at least once in every two years, he will, unless excused by court, receive no allowance for his services. This is the peremptory command of the law.[2]

34. *Compensation of guardian's executor, etc.*—As already stated, if the guardian dies before settlement of his accounts, and his executor or administrator settles them, such executor or administrator making such settlement must be allowed such compensation for the same as the court with which the settlement is made shall deem reasonable.[3] In such case there should undoubtedly be an apportionment of the compensation, and the deceased guardian's actual necessary expenses incurred as guardian, and a reasonable compensation for his services to the time of his death, should be allowed to his estate.

35. *Notice of filing accounts to be published.*—It is the duty of the probate judge to cause notice to be published in some newspaper of the county, of the filing of any accounts by guardians and trustees, specifying the time when such accounts will be heard, which must not be less than three weeks after the publication of such notice. The probate judge may then, for cause, allow further time to file exceptions to said accounts; and the costs of such notice must be paid, if more than one account be specified in the same notice, in equal proportions by the guardians or trustees, respectively.[4]

36. *Who may file exceptions to account.*—Any person interested in such account may file exceptions to it at any time before the day set for the hearing, pointing out the particular items excepted to.

37. *The hearing.*—When the day of hearing arrives, the judge should examine closely the account, and compare the same with

---

[1] See par. 8, chap. 8.

[2] See par. 8, chap. 5.

[3] See par. 11, chap. 4.

[4] § 6402.

11

the vouchers, and see that the footing of figures are all correct; and this the judge should do whether exceptions are filed or not.

38. *Examination of accountants under oath.*—The probate judge has full power and authority to examine guardians and trustees under oath touching their accounts; and if he thinks proper to do so, he may reduce such examination to writing, and require such guardian or trustee to sign the same; and such examination must be filed with the papers in the case.[1]

39. *Guardian and ward can not sue each other, until.*—It may be remarked here that a guardian is not liable in an action by his ward, until he has been called on by the judge of probate to settle his account, and has refused; or has settled, and a balance has been found due to the ward.[2]

40. And on the other hand, if the guardian has advanced money for his ward, he can not sue his ward therefor, when he arrives at full age, but must have it adjusted by a settlement of his accounts with the probate court.[3]

---

[1] § 6403.

[2] Schouler's Dom. Rel. 502, 506; also Gibbs *v.* Lum, 29 La. Ann. (1877), 526.

[3] Davis *r.* Ford, 7 O. 2d pt., 104, 109. See more fully note 1, page 165, 166; also Schouler's Dom. Rel. 502.

A guardian may, in his account, filed for settlement in the probate court, charge all proper debts due him from his ward, although accruing prior to the guardianship. Such accounts will be scrutinized with great jealousy, but they must be settled in that way, since the guardian can not sue his ward or himself. Such accounts may be filed for settlement at any time when the probate judge will receive them. When so filed, the probate judge has no discretion to refuse to settle them, though he disallowed items not proper charges, and he must receive such account once in every two years at least, and whenever guardianship is terminated. If the probate judge refuse to settle such account, and dismiss it for want of jurisdiction, there is no remedy by appeal to the common pleas. The remedy is by mandamus to require the judge to proceed and settle the account. A resignation of the guardian does not abate the proceeding on the account, but the court should proceed to settle it. The probate court exercises but a limited jurisdiction, but having power to settle guardian's accounts, would generally follow the analogies of the chancery jurisdiction over the same subject. And in chancery, allowances for maintenance and repairs will be limited to the income of an estate, unless made on order of the chancellor, or unless very pecu-

41. *When to settle with ward, and take his receipt.*—Some probate judges direct the guardian to settle in full with his ward after he arrives of age, file his receipt as a voucher, and to present the final account closed up, the judge of course reserving the right to review and change the account. Other judges require the guardian to come to court with his vouchers and his account completed, *except* as to his compensation and the amount due the ward, the respective amounts of which the court decides. In such case, the guardian must afterward pay the ward the amount so found due, and take his receipt therefor.[1]

42. The latter practice is more in accordance with the spirit of the law than the former, and, if the views of the judge and guardian as to proper compensation, etc., disagree, it is more convenient.

---

liar circumstances exist, when claims incurred by a guardian without authority, beyond the income, may be allowed as a charge on the principal. Walker & Bates Digest, art. Guardian.

[1] One standing in the relation of a parent and guardian in fact, of a minor, having the custody and control of such minor, and of his property during such minority, is bound to the most scrupulous good faith in the management of the estate, and where, on such minor's coming of age, he attempts to make a settlement of his trust with him, a court of equity will examine the transaction with extreme jealousy, to see that no undue influence has been exercised, that the parties have been put on an equal footing, by full disclosures, and that no advantage has been taken. Berkmyer *v.* Kellerman, 32 O. S. 239.

Where a party occupying such a relation, claims any benefit or advantage from a settlement with his ward on his coming of age, of his trust transactions, the burden of proof is on him to show that he has made full disclosures, that he has exercised no undue influence, and that such settlement is fair and equitable. *Ib.*

A conveyance by such minor on the day he comes of age, of all of his real estate to the persons occupying such relations, in execution of such a settlement made for such minor by others not authorized to bind it, and while he is still under their influence and control, and not advised of his rights, is not binding, and can only be upheld in a court of equity by clear proof, that under all the circumstances it is just and equitable. *Ib.*

If the settlement relied on to uphold such conveyance embraces distinct and several claims of two or more, who hold such relations to the child, such conveyance may be sustained as to one, and set aside as to the others, ac-

43–46. *Form of Journal Entry of Confirmation of Accounts*

In the matter of the guardianship of C. D.

Notice of the filing of the account of A. B., as guardian of C. D., heretofore filed for partial [*or, final*] settlement, having been duly given by publication in —— ——, a newspaper of this county, and this day being the day named therein for a hearing of said account, the same came on this day to be heard;* and no exceptions thereto being filed, the court carefully examined the same, and finding it in all things true and correct, it is ordered that the same be and it is hereby confirmed and settled.

And the court does further find that there is in said guardian's hands none of said ward's money [*or, a balance of* —— *dollars of said ward's money*; *and if on final settlement, add, which he is hereby ordered to pay to said C. D., or whomsoever is entitled thereto*].

47. [*Or, if there be exceptions filed and overruled, begin at the* *, *and say:*] Upon the account and the exceptions thereto filed by —— ——, and having heard the testimony, and the court being fully advised in the premises,* finds that the said exceptions are not well taken, but that said account is true and correct; where-

---

cording as the equity of the case will warrant. *Ib.* See also notes on pp. 82, 165.

Suit on a guardian's bond, *Held:* 1. A receipt signed by a ward after he became of legal age, acknowledging that he had received from his guardian a certain sum "in full of all demands," etc., was not conclusive evidence of a settlement between the guardian and ward, and could be explained or contradicted by parol evidence. 2. The final report of the guardian, which had not been allowed and approved by the court, was not competent evidence to show a settlement. If the facts in the case were true, the guardian was a competent witness to prove them; but his simple *ex parte* statement, though verified by oath, was not competent evidence to prove such facts. The unapproved and allowed report was nothing but an *ex parte* sworn statement. Beedle *v.* State, ex rel. (Sup. Ct. Ind., Nov. '78.) 3 Cin. Law Bul. 902.

Where a ward, on coming of age, joined with her brothers, sisters, mother, and step-father in executing a release of a farm, etc., to her guardian, who was her eldest brother, in order to carry out a family arrangement of what had before been done, *Held:* that the ordinary presumption as to a release "from a ward just out of the leading strings" did not apply. Cowan's Appeal, 74 Pa. St., 329.

upon it is ordered, that the said account ought to be, and it is hereby confirmed and settled. And the court further finds, that there is remaining in the hands of said guardian, a balance of —— dollars of his ward's moneys [*and if on final settlement, add,* which he is hereby ordered to pay to *whomsoever is entitled thereto*].

48. [*Or, if the exceptions are allowed, proceed as in the last form to the *, and then say:*] do find that the exceptions are well taken, and they are therefore allowed; and the court further finds that in all else, the said account is true and correct; whereupon it is ordered that the items objected to in said exceptions be not allowed in said account, and that in all things else the same be and it is hereby confirmed and settled. And the court further finds that there is remaining in the said guardian's hands a balance of —— dollars of his said ward's moneys; [*if on final settlement, conclude as before.*]

49. *To whom guardian must pay balance in hand at settlement.*— When a final settlement is made and an amount found in the hands of the guardian, he must pay that balance over to the ward, if of full age, or to the succeeding guardian, if one be appointed, the ward not being of age, or to the administrator of the ward, if dead. whether of age or not, or into court, if the court so order it to be done, and in either case the guardian should take a receipt therefor.

50. *Effect of settlement with court.*—The settlement made in the probate court of the accounts of a guardian will be final between him and his ward, unless an appeal be taken therefrom to the court of common pleas in the manner provided by law.[1]

51. *When and how ward may review the settlement.*—But any such ward has the right of opening and reviewing such settle-

---

[1] § 6289; as to appeals, see chap. 24.

The account required of the guardian, to be rendered at least every two years to the probate court, when rendered and judicially passed on by the court, is a settlement within the meaning of section 31 (6289): and under the provisions of that section, every settlement is final between the guardian and ward, unless an appeal is taken therefrom, or it is opened under the provisions of that section. Woodmansie *v.* Woodmansie, 32 O. S. 18.

When a guardian closes his account with his ward, by filing a final settlement in the probate court, an amount being due his ward, for which he in-

ment, for fraud or manifest mistake, by civil action in the court of common pleas of the county in which such settlement was made, or the county where such guardian may reside when the petition is filed, at the option of the plaintiff in such action, at any time within two years after the said ward shall arrive at full age.[1]

duces her to sign a receipt as for money paid, he agreeing to be responsible to her for the amount, with interest, an action may be maintained upon such agreement by the ward, and the sum actually due recovered from the guardian, without in any way opening or reviewing the accounts which had been settled in the probate court. Lindsay *v*. Lindsay, 28 O. S. 157.

A guardian can not sustain an action against his ward while the relation of guardian and ward subsists, for advances made to his ward, as evidenced by a balance due to him on settlement with the court. Davis *v*. Ford, 7 O. 2 pt. 104. The action to recover any balance that may be due him from his late ward must be brought in the proper court, after such balance is declared in the probate court, and after the relation between them ceases to subsist. *Ib.*

But a guardian may, in his account filed for settlement in the probate court, charge all proper debts due from his ward, although accruing prior to the guardianship; for he can not bring an action against himself or his ward while the relation continues. When so filed, the probate judge has no discretion to refuse to settle them, though he should scrutinize them with great jealousy, and disallow items which are not proper charges. *Ib.*

After a ward becomes of age, he stands in the relation of creditor to his guardian. His cause of action is then complete; and if he fails to bring suit within the time limited by statute thereafter, the claim is barred. Coleman *v*. Willis, 46 M. 236.

The accounts rendered from time to time by a guardian during ward's minority, and approved by the probate court, are only *prima facie* correct, and do not bind the ward when he is able to show that they are erroneous. Willis *v*. Fox, 25 Wis. 646.

[1] In the absence of fraud, account can not be attacked by ward after two years. High *v*. Snedicor, 57 Ala. 403.

Only upon clear and satisfactory proof will a final settlement, made by a guardian with his ward after she has arrived at majority, be impeached after a lapse of a long interval of time—as here, nearly a quarter of a century. Railsback *v*. Williamson, 88 Ill. 494.

The final settlement of a guardian made in the probate court, unless revoked, reopened or appealed from, is conclusive upon the parties; it can not be attacked collaterally, in a suit by the ward on the guardian's bond, for the allowance to a third person of an unjust and fraudulent claim in such settlement. Holland *v* State, 48 Ind. 391.

52. *Guardian should get final release from ward.* After the guardian has fully settled his accounts and paid over any balance due to the ward, and taken a receipt therefor, it would be good and prudent practice to ask the late ward, some time after the settlement, to examine, in person, or with an accountant or attorney, the accounts to his own satisfaction, and if explanations are then wanted, to ask for them; and if all matters are found to be satisfactory. then to give to the guardian a full release[1] and discharge from all obligations arising from the guardianship.

53. *Form of.* Such release might be in form as follows, or be varied to suit the facts:

54. I have examined, in person (*or*, by attorney; *or*, in person and with the assistance of H. M.. my attorney) the accounts and final settlement of A. B., my late guardian, and find said accounts and settlement to be in full, just. fair, and satisfactory; and for a valuable consideration to me paid. I hereby release him from any further obligations on account of or arising from his relations to me as said guardian.

(Date)   C. D.

55. *Such release no defense, when.* Such a release would not protect the guardian from any fraud, deception. or manifest mistake.[2]

---

[1] A valid release from the ward, absolving the guardian from all liability to account, and her acceptance of the consideration of the release, in satisfaction of her demands. bars her of all right to call him to account for the profits derived from the unauthorized use of her estate. Satterfield *v.* John, 53 Ala. 127; Cheever *v.* Congdon, 34 Mich. 296.

[2] Lindsay *v.* Lindsay, 28 O. S. 157; Beedle *v.* State, 62 Ind. 26; Bruce *v.* Doolittle, 81 Ill. 103; Monnin *v.* Beroujon, 51 Ala. 196; Trader *v.* Lowe, 45 Md. 1; Womack *v.* Austin, 1 S. C. 421.

"As before stated, a release executed upon proper advice. with ample time for mature deliberation, and upon full information, is *prima facie* valid; and the burden is upon the party disputing it to impeach it." Perry on Trusts, § 923.

CHAPTER 10.

BOND.

EXCEPTIONS TO—RELEASE FROM—SUITS ON.

1. *Already treated in part.* It having been deemed necessary to specify in chapter 3, paragraphs 37–89, who must give bond and who need not, its form, requisites, and certain journal entries concerning it, these matters need not be again mentioned here.

EXCEPTIONS TO THE BOND.

2. *Who may file exceptions, and when.* At any time after the bond has been given, any person, whether of kin to the ward or not, who may judge the bond to be insufficient, may appear on behalf of the minor, in the court where the appointment of the guardian was made, and there file exceptions to the bond of such guardian, as to the sufficiency of the amount of the penalty thereof, or the sureties therein.[1]

3–6. *Form of exceptions.* These may be in the following form:

Exceptions taken by M. N., in behalf of C. D., a minor, to the bond of A. B., as his guardian.

And now comes M. N., on behalf of said minor, and excepts to the bond of said guardian, because, (1.) The amount of the penalty thereof is not sufficient. (2.) The sureties are not sufficient.

M. N.,
For C. D.

7. *Notice of, must be given to guardian.* When the exceptions are so filed, notice thereof must be given to the guardian whose bond is excepted to, requiring him to appear before the court

---

[1] § 6261.

within a reasonable time, not exceeding ten days, and show cause against the allowance of the exception.[1]

8. *How served.* The law provides that when notice of any proceeding in a probate court is required by law, or deemed necessary by the probate judge, and the manner of giving the same is not directed by statute, the probate judge must order notice of such proceedings to be given to all persons interested therein, in such manner and for such length of time as he shall deem reasonable.[2]

9. In this case the statute fixes the time within the limit of ten days, but not the form of the notice, nor the manner of serving. The following

10–14. *Form of notice*—would meet all the requirements of the case, the court therein fixing the day and hour of hearing the exceptions.

To A. B., guardian of C. D. :

You are hereby notified, that on the —— day of ——, A. D. 18 —, M. N., on behalf of the said C. D., filed in the probate court of —— county, Ohio, exceptions to your bond as guardian of C. D. You are therefore required to appear before said court on the —— day of ——, A. D. 18 —, at — o'clock, —. M. [*not exceeding ten days from the date of the notice*], and show cause, if any you have, why said exceptions should not be allowed by the court, and you be required to give further security.

Witness my hand and the seal of said court, this —— day of ——, A. D. 18 —.

[L. S.]   A. C.,
                                      Probate Judge, etc.

15. *When served.* The notice should be served upon the guardian without delay, as he will otherwise be adjudged not to have had sufficient time to prepare himself to meet the exceptions, and the court will therefore not act upon them on the day fixed upon in the notice.

16. *By whom served, and how service proved.* The notice may be served and returned by the sheriff of the proper county, as

---

[1] ? 6261.

[2] ? 6406

other process is served and returned by him, or it may be served by the person taking the exceptions, or by any one else. If served by any one other than the sheriff, an affidavit of service should be made on the back of the notice by the person making the service, and returned to the court on or before the day set for the hearing.

17–20. *Form of affidavit in proof of service.* Such affidavit may be in the following form :

The State of Ohio, —— county, *ss.*

M. N., being duly sworn, says, that on the —— day of ——,
A. D., 18— he served the within notice upon the said A. B., by giving him personally a true copy thereof.

    (*Signed*)   M. N.

Sworn to and subscribed before me, this —— day of ——,
A. D. 18—.   A. C.,
   [SEAL.]   Probate Judge, etc.

21. *Adjournments.* Upon the day set for the hearing, the court may, undoubtedly, upon good cause shown, adjourn the hearing, at the instance of either party, to any other day ; but no adjournment should be had without good cause, nor should it then be so long as to occasion unreasonable delay upon either side. But the whole matter of adjournments is within the sound discretion of the court.

22. If an adjournment is at any time had, the same ought to be noted on the the journal of the court, and may thus :

23. *Form of Journal Entry of Adjournment.*

In the matter of the exceptions of M. N. to the bond of A. B., as guardian of C. D. This matter is continued until the —— day of ——, A. D. ——, at —— o'clock — M.

24. *Final hearing.* Upon the final hearing of the exceptions to the bond, the court will hear the parties testify, and such other witnesses, including the sureties, if they are offered, as either party may produce; and arguments of counsel may also be heard.

25. *Court may require additional sureties, etc.* Upon such hearing, the court may either dismiss the exceptions, or require the

guardian to find additional sureties, or security in a larger amount, or make such other order as the case may require.[1]

26–28. *Form of journal entry.* If the exceptions are dismissed, the following entry should be made:

In the matter of the exception of M. N. to the bond of A. B., as guardian of C. D.

This day this matter came on to be heard, upon the allegations of the parties and the testimony offered, and the court, being fully advised in the premises, find the exceptions are not well taken ; and it is therefore ordered by the court that the same be dismissed, and that the said M. N. pay the costs herein, taxed at —— dollars, within —— days, and in default thereof that an execution issue therefor, as upon judgments at law.

29. *If exceptions sustained, what?* If the court, however, sustain the exceptions, in any or all particulars, then an order must

---

[1] § 6162. The proper court has the power to require the guardian to give an additional bond for the discharge of the general duties of the office. Suit may be brought upon the additional bond before the original bond given by the guardian is exhausted, or the sureties thereon shown to be worthless. Where it does not clearly appear to have been the intention that such additional bond was to be subsidiary to, and security for, the original bond, the obligors in the additional bond are liable for breaches of it, either in a separate suit against them and the obligors in the original bond upon both bonds. In such case the additional bond is a primary concurrent security. Allen v. State, 61 Ind. 261; same, 3 Cin. Law Bul. 747.

The late court of common pleas, acting as a probate court, had authority to require a guardian to give a second bond, in case the first had become insufficient. (Hocking District Court, 1852.) Case v. State, 10 W. L. J. 163.

The sureties on a second bond required a guardian, on the first having become insufficient, providing for a faithful discharge of his duties, are liable for failure to pay over all money of his ward, whether received prior or subsequent to the bond. *Ib.*

In a suit by a guardian against the sureties of a former guardian, under section 7 of the act of April 17, 1857 (S. & C. 621), the defendants are not precluded by the proviso contained in said section from denying the fact of the plaintiff's guardianship, though after judgment against their principal. 1866. Shroyer v. Richmond, 16 O. S. 455.

The liability of a surety on a new bond is prospective only. Lowry v. State, 64 Ind, 421.

be made accordingly; and, in such case, the entry may be in the following form:

30–32. *Form of Journal Entry, sustaining Exceptions, Revoking Letters, and Assessing Costs.*

In the matter of the exceptions of M. N. to the bond of A. B., as guardian of C. D.

This day, this matter came on to be heard, upon the allegations of the parties, and the testimony offered; and the court, being fully advised in the premises, find that the sureties upon said bond are insufficient [*or, if the case be so, say,* the amount of said bond is insufficient by the sum of —— dollars]—[*or, if both of these facts are found by the court, then state them both as found*]; it is therefore ordered by the court that the said A. B., within —— days [*a reasonable time to be fixed by the court*], give bond as guardian, as aforesaid, in the same amount as the former bond, with additional sureties, to the satisfaction of the court [*or, if the finding require it, say,* give an additional bond, as guardian, as aforesaid, in the sum of —— dollars]; and it is further ordered by the court, that in case the said A. B. shall fail to comply with the foregoing order within the time limited in that behalf, then he shall be removed from his office as guardian of the said C. D., and his powers and authority as such guardian shall thenceforward cease and determine.

And, it is further ordered, that the said A. B., out of his own private estate [*or, in a proper case, say,* out of the estate of said C. D.], pay the costs herein within —— days, and in default thereof, that execution issue therefor, as upon judgments at law.

33. *Costs, who to pay; court decides.* If the sureties have become insufficient by insolvency or removal, or the like, subsequent to the giving of the bond, without fault on the part of the guardian, there does not seem to be good reason why he should pay the costs, unless, indeed, he has wilfully or unnecessarily caused costs to be made by resisting the matter, when he knew, or had good reason to suppose, that the sureties had become insufficient; in which case he ought, of course, to be adjudged to

pay the costs himself, as he should do, also, in case the sureties were originally insufficient.

34. The question of who shall pay costs, is one for the court to determine, upon the whole circumstances of the case, exercising a sound discretion therein.

35. *Court must act of its own motion.*—But even if no exceptions are filed by any one, the statute nevertheless makes it the duty of the court, by whom any guardian is appointed, to require, of its own motion, such guardian to give an additional bond, whenever, in the opinion of the court, the interests of the ward of such guardian demand the same.[1]

36. It is the peculiar province of the probate court, as has been said before, to watch, with an unsleeping eye, the interests of the minors who, in law, can not help themselves; therefore, whenever the judge, from any source, becomes aware that the bond of a guardian was originally, or has become, of less security, in any respect, than it ought to be, his duty is to inquire promptly into the matter, without waiting for any one to file exceptions, and require an additional bond to be given, if, in his opinion, the interest of the ward require it.

37. *Guardian's right to notice, etc., in such case also.*—The guardian, however, has rights in this matter, too, and ordinarily, where the court is about to act on its own motion, the guardian should have a day in court; and a notification similar to that given where exceptions are filed, so modified as to show that it is a movement of the court itself, should be served upon the guardian; and proceedings and orders similar to those made where exceptions are filed, should be had when the court acts upon its own motion.

THE RELEASE OF SURETIES.

38. *How surety of guardian released.*—Any surety of a guardian may, at any time, apply to the proper probate court to be released from his bond of such guardian, by filing his request therefor with the judge of such court, and giving ten day's no-

---

[1] § 6261.

tice to such guardian when application will be made to such court to release such surety.[1]

39–40. *Form of the Request to be Released by Surety.*

To the Probate Court, —— county, Ohio:

The undersigned, a surety on the bond of A. B., as guardian of C. D., requests to be released from said bond.

P. Q.

41–45. *Form of Notice to the Guardian.*

To A. B., guardian of C. D.:

Sir: On the ——day of ——, A. D. 18—, I filed with the probate judge of —— county, Ohio, a request to be released from the bond on which I am surety for you, as guardian of C. D.——.

The matter will be heard, by said probate judge, on the —— day of ——, A. D. 18—, at —— o'clock, — M. [*this day must be ten days from the day the notice is served*], at which time you must give a new bond, with sureties to be approved by the court, otherwise you will be removed from such guardianship.

Dated —— day of —— A. D. 18—.

[Signed]

P. Q.

46. *The service of such notice* may be by leaving a copy thereof with the guardian at the time above directed.   Such service may be made, unless otherwise ordered by the judge, by some disinterested person, who should afterwards appear before the probate judge, or some other officer authorized to administer oaths, and make affidavit on the back of the notice as to its service. The notice itself should then be filed in the probate court as evidence of service.

47–49.—*The form of the affidavit of service* may be as follows:

State of Ohio, —— county, *ss.*

M. N., being duly sworn, says, that on the ——s day of ——, A. D. 18—, he served the within notice upon A. B. personally, by leaving with him a true copy thereof.

[Signed],

M. N.

---

[1] 6273.

If proper notice is not served as required by law, a surety's discharge would be void.   Dupont *v.* Mayo, 56 Ga. 304.

Sworn to and subscribed before me, this —— day of —— A. D·
18—.   A. C., Probate Judge, etc.

50. *Journal entries.*—There should be an entry of these proceedings upon the journal of the court. as each step is taken.

51-52. *Form of Entry Noting the Filing of the Request.*

In the matter of the guardianship of C. D.

This day came P. Q., a surety on the bond of A. B., as guardian of C. D., and filed his written request to be released as
such surety.

53-54. *Form of Entry Requiring New Bond.*

In the matter of the guardianship of C. D.

This day came P. Q., a surety on the bond of A. B., as guardian of C. D., and produced here to the court the notice to A. B.,
of his application to be released as such surety, and it being
proved to the satisfaction of the court. that said notice was duly
given to said A. B., by copy served upon him personally by M.
N., on the —— day of ——, A. D. ——. [*a day ten or more days before the day of hearing.*] it is therefore ordered that said A. B.
shall give a new bond in the sum of —— dollars, as guardian as
aforesaid, conditioned according to law, with surety to the acceptance of the court, within —— days.

55. *Entries when new bond given.*—If the new bond be given
within the time limited therefor in the last order, then an entry
should be made of its approval or rejection, as the case may be.

56-57. *Form of Entry where the Bond is Approved.*

In the matter of the guardianship of C. D.

This day came A. B., guardian of C. D., and gave a new bond
as such guardian, in the sum of —— dollars, conditioned according to law, with —— —— and —— ——, as his sureties thereto,
in accordance with the former order of this court, which last
named bond and sureties are approved by the court.   And it is
thereupon ordered that said P. Q., a surety upon the former bond
of said A. B., as such guardian, be and he is henceforth released
upon said former bond, for and on account of the acts of said A.
B., as guardian as aforesaid, from this time forth.

58. *Guardian removed if bond not given.*—If the guardian fails to give bond when directed by the court to do so, he must be removed and his letters must be superceded.[1]

59-60. *Form of journal entry where Bond is not approved or not given.*

In the matter of the guardianship of C. D.

This day being the day fixed by the court, by the former order herein, when the said A. B. should give a new bond as guardian of C. D., in the sum of —— dollars, conditioned according to law, and with sureties to the acceptance of the court, the said A. B. failed to give such bond : it is therefore ordered by the court, that the said A. B. be, and he is hereby removed from the said guardianship of the said C. D., and that his letter of guardianship be, and is hereby superseded, and his powers as such guardian henceforward revoked.

61. *As to release of sureties, if guardian removed.*—In case the guardian is removed from the trust, there is no necessity of releasing the sureties on the bond, by an order to that effect, because the removal of itself releases the sureties, and makes the bond of no force as to the guardian's future acts.

62. *New guardian should be at once appointed.*—In case of removal of the guardian, a new guardian ought to be immediately appointed, so that the estate, as well as the person of the ward, may be properly taken care of.

63. *Extent of old surety's liability.*   The original surety will not be released until such guardian so gives bond; but such original surety will be liable only for the acts of such guardian from the time of the execution of the original bond to the filing and approval by the court of such new bond.[2]

----

[1] § 6273.

[2] § 6273.   State v. Page, 63 Ind. 209.

The estate of a deceased surety on a guardian's bond is liable for a default which occurs after the surety's death.   Cotton v. State, 64 Ind. 573; 47 Ind. 316; 59 Ind. 485.

A guardian giving another bond upon order of court for other and better security, does not release the sureties upon the original bond, nor render those upon the new bond primarily liable.   McGlothlin v. Wyatt, 1 Lea (Tenn.) 717.

12

64. *As to joint bonds.* If two or more trustees or guardians have given a joint bond, it is in the nature of an agreement to be answerable for each other's acts and defaults. The remedy for a breach of trust in such cases is a suit upon the bond, in the name of the proper person, for the benefit of those interested, against all the joint makers and sureties of the bond; and any breaches of trust, committed by either or all the guardians, may be given in evidence, and a judgment against all will be rendered, although the breach of trust was committed by one alone. But the estate of a guardian who had died before the wrongful act of a co-guardian, would not be liable for such act.[1]

SUITS ON THE BOND.

65. *How suit on bond brought, and by whom.* When a guardian, by any misconduct, neglect of duty, etc., forfeits his bond, or renders his sureties liable, any person injured thereby, or who is by law entitled to the benefit of the security, may bring an action thereon, in his own name, against the person and his sureties, to recover the amount to which he is entitled by reason of the delinquency. Such action may be prosecuted on a certified copy of the bond, and the custodian of the bond must deliver such copy to any person claiming to be so injured, on tender of the proper fee.[2]

---

[1] Perry on Trusts, § 126.

[2] § 4991. See note 1, page 172; note 2, page 177.

Abandoning the custody of estate into others' hands, under mistaken impression of what the law is, does not release sureties. Cotton *v.* Wolf, 14 Bush. (Ky.) 238.

The bond of a guardian whose appointment is void, is good as a common law obligation, and the sureties are liable for all property coming into such guardian's hands, by reason of such appointment. *Ib.* See also Corbitt *v.* Carroll, 50 Ala. 315.

A guardian is liable in his bond for using his ward's money in his own business, as well as for disposing of any of ward's propery for his own use. Lowry *v.* State, 64 Ind. 421.

An action of assumpsit will not lie at the suit of an administrator, appointed under the laws of this state, to recover moneys, the proceeds of the lands of the plaintiff's intestate lying in Pennsylvania, which descended to the wards of the defendant, and were sold by him, as guardian, under authority of the orphan's court of that state. To that court, and within the

66. *Effect of judgment.* A judgment for one delinquency does not preclude the same or another party from an action on the same instrument for another delinquency.[1]

67. *Extent of remedy by suit on bond.* The remedy provided in the two preceding paragraphs is not confined in its application to the specific duties laid down in the statutes, and set forth in the different chapters of this book, and especially in the 5th, but extends to all duties of the guardian as such, and applies to negative as well as positive acts, in this respect; as, if an injury occurs to the estate of the ward, by the fraud or neglect of the guardian, he will be liable, as much as if an injury was occasioned by his direct act.[2]

68. If an unjust judgment be rendered against his ward, by reason of the guardian failing to defend the action, knowing of its pendency, he would no doubt be liable to the ward in damages therefor.

69. So, too, if waste is permitted on the real estate of the ward, by the negligence of the guardian, he will undoubtedly be liable therefor.

70. *Separate liability of guardian.* It should be remembered, that as to the guardian himself, it is not the bond he gives that raises any liability upon his part, but that, while he is liable for any breach of the condition of the bond, he is, nevertheless, per-

---

jurisdiction of that state, the defendant and his sureties are responsible for the faithful administration of his trust. 1846. Donley *v.* Shields, 14 O. 359.

Where a guardian's bond recites the appointment of a guardian by the proper authority, the obligors are estopped to deny the fact thus recited, or to question the validity of the appointment. 1866. Shroyer *v.* Richmond, 16 O. S. 455.

A suit against the sureties in a guardian's bond may be sustained without a previous adjustment of the amount due from the principal. 1835. State *v.* Humphreys, 7 O. 1 pt. 223.

[1] § 4994.

[2] Litt. 123. If a loss occurs from any want of care, attention, or diligence on the part of the trustee, he may be held responsible for not taking such action as was called for. Perry on Trusts, § 256; Cotton *v.* State, 64 Ind. 573.

England *v.* Downes, 6 Beav. 269, 279; Townley *v.* Bond, 2 Conn. & Laws, 405; James *v.* Frearson, 1 Y. & C. Ch. Ca. 270; Taylor *v.* Millington, 4 Jur. (N. S.) 204; Exp. Greaves, 25 L. J. 53; 2 Jur. N. S. 253; Malzy *v.* Edge, 2 Jur. (N. S.) 8.

sonally liable for the same matters, acts, or omissions of duty, if no bond be given, or if the bond, being given, should prove defective or inefficient.

71. *Liability of the sureties on the bond.* On the other hand, the sureties of a guardian have no liabilities except those raised by the giving of the bond. It is the bond, as to them, that creates the liability, and the acts or omissions of duty on the part of the guardian, simply fix that liability. Therefore, if the bond should be utterly void, there would be no liability on the part of the sureties at all.

72. But if the bond be sufficient to commence a liability on the part of the sureties, then any failure to perform any of the duties of the guardian, will be a breach of the condition of the bond, and the sureties will be liable accordingly. In other words, if, in such case, the guardian be liable to respond in damages, then the sureties are also liable.[1]

73. *When suit on guardian's bond must be brought.* Generally, an action on a guardian's bond must be brought within ten years after the cause of action accrues.[2]

74. If a person entitled to bring such action is, at the time the cause of action accrues, within the age of twenty-one years, a married woman, insane, or imprisoned, such person may bring such action within ten years after such disability is removed.[3]

---

[1] A ward whose guardian was indebted on final settlement may, after return of "no property," as to him, maintain a bill against the administrator and distributees of a deceased surety of the guardian, to subject to the satisfaction of the decree, money remaining in the hands of the administrator, derived from a sale of the surety's property, for which judgments had been rendered against him on final settlement in favor of the distributees. Anderson v. Thomas, 54 Ala. 104.

[2] § 4984. Under the act of 1831 (3 Chase, 1768), suit on bond limited, as in an action against principal alone. State v. Conway, 18 O. 234; State v. Blake, 2 O. S. 147; State v. Newman, 2 O. S. 567. But under this section the limitation was held to be ten years, even where the bond was given before the adoption of the code. King v. Nichols, 16 O. S. 80; State v. Orr, 16 O. S. 522.

But where the action is not on the official bond, but against the officer alone, it is barred in six years. Mount v. Lakeman, 21 O. S. 643.

Action against officer does not accrue until demand is made. Keithler v. Foster, 22 O. S. 27.

[3] § 4986. Party relying on the statute can not avail himself of successive

75. For other modifications of paragraph 73 above, see the chapter of Revised Statutes, including sections 4974–4992.[1]

76. *Sureties may be made parties to judgment.* Sureties to the bond of a guardian or trustee, may be made parties to a judgment thereon against the principal, by action.[2]

77. *Where guardian may be sued.* Generally speaking, actions must be brought where the subject of the action is situated; or in the county where the cause of action, or some part of it, arose; or in the county where the defendant resides, or may be summoned;[3] but actions against a guardian may be brought in the county wherein he was appointed or resides, and summons may issue to any county, in such cases.[4]

78. *When non-resident guardian may be served by publication.* In actions against guardians, when the defendant has given bond as such in this State, but at the time of the commencement of the action is a non-resident of the State, or his place of residence can not be ascertained, service may be had by publication.[5]

---

disabilities. Whitney *v.* Webb, 10 O. 513; Carey *v.* Robinson, 13 O. 181; Cozzens *v.* Farnan, 30 O. S. 491.

The statute is personal and can not be extended to a party not within its saving. Bronson *v.* Adams, 10 O. 135.

Where the interests of two defendants are joint and inseparable, and the rights of one are saved, it inures to the benefit of the other. Sturges *v.* Longworth, 1 O. S. 544; Bradford *v.* Andrews, 20 O. S. 208; Meese *v.* Keefe, 10 O. 362; Riddle *v.* Roll, 24 O. S. 572; Trimble *v.* Longworth, 13 O. S. 431.

The grantee or heir of one protected from the operation of the statutory bar is entitled to the benefit of that protection. Ford *v.* Langel, 4 O. S. 464; Carey *v.* Robinson, 13 O. 181.

Under the act of 1831 (3 Chase, 1768), in connection with the act of 1834 (32 v. 10), it was held that the disability of infancy in a female was removed at the age of eighteen years. Slater *v.* Cave, 3 O. S. 80.

The four years limitation prescribed in the act for the settlement of estates, within which suits are to be commenced against executors and administrators, applies to an action instituted on a guardian's bond, and the disability of infancy will not save the plaintiff from the operation of the statute. 1867. Favorite *v.* Booher's Adm'r. 17 O. S. 548.

[1] § 4984.

[2] § 5371.

[3] §§ 5022–5032.

[4] § 5031.

[5] § 5048.

79. *Guardian may sue in his own name.* The general rule of our law is, that all suits must be brought in the name of the real party in interest; but a guardian may bring an action without joining with him the person for whose benefit it is prosecuted.[1] All pleadings in such cases must clearly show that he is acting as such guardian, and not for himself individually.

80. *How guardian's bankruptcy affects his liability.* The guardian's liability to his wards is not affected by such guardian's discharge in bankruptcy.[2]

81. *Special proceedings to compel guardian to pay money found due on settlement.* If, after thirty days from the time the guardian's accounts are settled, and an amount is found to be due to any person, or a balance in his hands, which the court orders him to pay over to any person, he neglects or refuses so to pay, the person so interested may file, in the probate court of the county where such settlement or order was made, a petition, briefly setting forth the amount and nature of the claim; whereupon a citation must issue from said court, against such guardian, setting forth the filing of the petition, and the amount claimed by the petitioner, and commanding the guardian to appear before said court on the return day thereof, to answer said petition and show cause, if any there be, why judgment should not be rendered and execution awarded against such guardian, for the amount claimed by such petitioner, and found to be due upon such settlement or order. This citation must be made returnable not less than twenty, nor more than forty days from its date, and must be served and returned by the sheriff or other proper officer, as in the case of a summons, and may be issued to any county in the state.[3]

82–88. *Form of Petition by Ward in Such Case.*

State of Ohio, ——— county, ss.

Probate Court.   } Petition to compel Guardian to pay money
  C. D. *v.* A. B.   }   in his hands.

The petitioner, C. D., says the defendant, A. B., was the duly

---

[1] §§ 4993–4995.   [2] *Re* Maybin, 15 Bank. Reg. 468.

[3] § 6195, as amended, 78 O. L. p. 76.

appointed and qualified guardian of petitioner, and as such, on the —— day of ——, A. D. 18—, upon his final settlement with the probate court of this county, there was, by said court, found in his hands the sum of —— dollars, balance of his accounts, belonging to the petitioner, and ordered to be paid over accordingly, by said court, and which amount it was the defendant's duty to have paid to the petitioner within thirty days after the day of the settlement aforesaid, which time has elapsed, but which he has refused and neglected to do, and still so neglects and refuses, although the same has been repeatedly demanded of him.

The petitioner therefore asks judgment and execution against said defendant for said sum of money, with interest thereon from the —— day of ——, A. D. 18—, and his costs.

(*Signed*)   C. D.

The State of Ohio, —— county, *ss.*

C. D., being sworn, says that he is the plaintiff above mentioned, and that the allegations contained in the foregoing petition are true, as he verily believes.

                                                       C. D.

Sworn to and subscribed before me, this —— day of ——, A. D. 18—.

                              RICHARD ROE.
                    Notary Public, —— county, O.

89–93. *Form of Petition by a Creditor of the Ward.*

State of Ohio, —— county, *ss.*

Probate Court.   } Petition to compel Guardian to pay money
    M. N. *v.* A. B. }   in his hands.

The petitioner, M. N., says that the defendant, A. B., is the guardian of C. D., a minor, and as such, on the —— day of ——, A. D. 18—, in a settlement of his accounts then had, in the Probate Court of this county, the said court found that the said ward was indebted to the petitioner in the sum of —— dollars, and that said A. B. had money in his hands of said ward sufficient to pay the same, and thereupon ordered the defendant to pay the same; and which amount it was the duty of the defendant to have paid within thirty days after the day of the settlement aforesaid, which period has elapsed, but which he has refused and neglected to do, and still so neglects and refuses, although the same has been repeatedly demanded of him.

The petitioner therefore asks judgment and execution against said defendant for said sum of money, with interest thereon from the —— day of ——, A. D. 18—, and his costs.

   (*Signed*)   M. N.

The State of Ohio, —— county, *ss.*

M. N., being duly sworn [*and conclude as in the preceding form*].

94. *Form of petition in other cases.*—The preceding forms can readily be adapted to meet the case of a succeeding guardian claiming the balance in the former guardian's hands, and other cases that may arise.

95–99. *Form of the Citation upon Petition being Filed.*

The State of Ohio, —— county, ss.   Probate court.

   To the sheriff of said county, *greeting:*

C. D. }
  v. } *Citation.*
A. B. }

You are hereby commanded to make known to said A. B. that said C. D. has this day filed in said court a petition claiming the sum of —— dollars, as due to him upon defendant's settlement with the probate court of this county, as guardian of C. D., and command him to appear on the —— day of ——, A. D. 18—, and answer said petition, and show cause, if any he has, why judgment should not be rendered and execution awarded against him for the amount claimed, and interest.   You will make due service of this citation, and return the same upon the day last above mentioned.

Witness my hand and the seal of said court, this —— day of ——, A. D. 18—.

   (*Signed*)   A. G., Probate Judge.

100. *How to proceed, if guardian has become a non-resident.*—No

doubt that, under the provisions of law given in paragraph 30, or in paragraph 37, of chapter 6, a guardian who had become a non-resident, or whose residence had become unknown, could be notified by publication, as directed in paragraphs 47–63 of the same chapter, making, of course, such changes in the forms there given as the facts might require.

101–103. *Form of notice by publication, in suit to compel distribution,* may be as follows; or varied to suit the circumstances and facts:

LEGAL NOTICE (OR, NOTICE).

A. B., a resident of Cameron, in the county of Clinton, in the state of Missouri [*or,* whose residence is unknown], will take notice that C. D., his late ward, filed in the probate court of Wayne county, in the State of Ohio, a petition claiming the sum of —— dollars, and interest, as due to him upon the defendant's settlement with the probate court of said county, made on the —— day of ——, A. D. 18—, as guardian of said C. D., and also for costs, and praying for a judgment and execution therefor against the defendant.

The day fixed for the hearing thereof is on the —— day of ——, A. D. 18—, at which time, unless you answer and show cause to the contrary, a judgment and order will be asked, as prayed for.

(*Signed*)   C. D.

CHAPTER 11.

PARTITION.

1. *Law governing partition; why given here.*—As very many ward's estates, and, consequently, the the duties of their guardians, are affected by the provisions of law governing partition, it is deemed best, for the convenience of these persons, to give here fully the substance of these provisions, except so far as they relate to the partition of property belonging to religious societies. But as the guardian, in such matters, would probably always employ an attorney conversant with the practice of courts of com-

mon pleas, in which court proceedings for partition are had,[1] it is not deemed necessary to encumber this chapter with the forms with which such attorneys are familiar in the standard books of pleadings.

2. *Power of guardian to act for ward in partition.*—The guardian of a minor, idiot, or insane person, may, on behalf of his ward, do and perform any act, matter, or thing respecting the partition of an estate which such minor, idiot, or insane person could do under this chapter if he were of age and of sound mind; and he may elect, on behalf of such ward, to take the estate, when the same can not be divided without injury, and make payments therefor on behalf of such ward.[2]

3. *Powers of foreign guardian.*—A person appointed according to the laws of any other state or country, to take charge of the estate of an idiot or insane person not a resident of this state,

---

[1] See paragraph 6, below.

[2] § 5772.

The finding of the court, that the person assuming to act as guardian in partition proceedings under the act of 1820 is such guardian, imports absolute verity, and is sufficient, *prima facie*, to show that the court had obtained jurisdiction over the ward, Merritt *v.* Horne, 5 O. S. 307; and under that act, where all the persons interested in the land had the same guardian, he might appear *ex parte*, and process was unnecessary to give the court jurisdiction. Goudy *v.* Shanks, 8 O. 415.

In proceedings in partition, the acts of a guardian of a minor, done in good faith, are binding upon his ward. Bohart *v.* Atkinson, 14 O. 228.

Where a minor, in such case, on arriving at full age, ratifies the acts of his guardian, by receiving and appropriating the proceeds of the sale in partition with full knowledge of the facts, he is estopped in equity from taking advantage of a mere irregularity in the proceedings. 1846. *Ib.*

If, upon sale of the land under such a proceeding, the husband of the infant, acting as her guardian, with a full knowledge of the facts, acknowledges such person to have been guardian, and receives from him as such the consideration money for the property, he will be estopped to prove that such person was not duly appointed, and can not, after the death of the wife, controvert the jurisdiction of the court over the infant. The estoppel is equally effectual at law and in chancery. One who has induced another to part with his money or property, and has taken the fruits of a judicial proceeding, is precluded from afterward questioning its regularity, or, by evidence aliunde, impairing its effect. 1855. Merritt *v.* Horne, 5 O. S. 307.

Sections 2 and 9 of the statute of 1820 (2 Chase, 1162) authorized guard-

may, upon being duly authorized in this state to take charge of such estate situated in this state, act in the partition of such estate to the same extent that the guardian of an idiot or insane person is authorized to do by the last preceding paragraph.[1]

4. *Who may be compelled to partition.*—Tenants in common, and coparceners, of any estate in lands, tenements, or hereditaments within the state, may be compelled to make or suffer partition thereof in manner prescribed below.[2]

5. *Where proceedings for partition may be had.*—When the

---

ians of minors to bring petition and do any act necessary to make partition of the land of their wards. Where one was a guardian of all interested in the land, having the right both to institute and defend, or consent to proceedings, no process of an adversary nature was necessary to confer jurisdiction upon the court. 1838. Goudy's Lessee *v.* Shank, 8 O. 415.

[1] § 5773.

[2] § 5754.

Neither reversioners nor remaindermen can have partition, the right only extending to those who have the possession, or an immediate right to the possession of the lands sought to be aparted, Tabler *v.* Wiseman, 2 O. S. 207; Davison *v.* Wolf, 9 O. 73; but the owner of a life estate in the whole, or a part of the tract, who also owns an interest in the remainder, may have partition. Morgan *v.* Staley, 11 O. 389; Tabler *v.* Wiseman, above.

A right of entry, without actual seizin, there being no intervening estate, will entitle a party to partition. Tabler *v.* Wiseman, above.

A partition operates only upon the possession, and does not create any new title, Tabler *v.* Wiseman, 2 O. S. 207; McBain *v.* McBain, 15 O. S. 337; and when parties to a proceeding for partition are made such by publication and without actual notice, they are not estopped thereby from setting up their legal title. McBain *v.* McBain, *supra.*

An answer to a petition for partition, denying that the plaintiffs have any title to or interest in the premises, does not oust the court of jurisdiction. Perry *v.* Richardson, 27 O. S. 110.

The fact that two actions for partition were prosecuted at the same time does not vitiate the regular proceedings in the one upon which partition is made. Smith *v.* Barber, 7 O. 2 pt. 118.

The regularity of proceedings in partition can not be inquired into in a collateral proceeding. Wilson *v.* Bull, 10 O. 250; Bohart *v.* Atkinson, 14 O. 228.

A purchaser from one tenant in common can not drive the owner of a paramount title, upon later purchasers of an interest in the land from other tenants in common. Dennison *v.* Foster, 9 O. 126.

When separate interests have been acquired under an erroneous partition chancery will exercise jurisdiction to bring all parties before the court, and

estate is situate in one county, the proceedings must be had in that county; and when situated in two or more counties, the proceedings may be had in any county wherein a part of such estate is situate.[1]

6. *Who may file petition, and what to set forth.*—A person entitled to partition of an estate may file his petition therefor in the court of common pleas, setting forth the nature of his title, and a pertinent description of the lands, tenements, or hereditaments of which partition is demanded, and naming each tenant in common, coparcener, or other interested person, as defendants therein.[2]

7. *The order of partition.*—If the court find that the plaintiff has a legal right to any part of such estate, it must order partition thereof in favor of the plaintiff, or all parties in interest, appoint three disinterested and judicious freeholders of the vicinity to be commissioners to make the partition, and order a writ of partition to issue.[3]

8. *The writ of partition.*—The writ of partition may be directed to the sheriff of either of the counties in which any part of the

---

while it preserves all substantial rights, will so mould them, in making a new division of the land, as to impose burdens where, in equity, they ought to fall, and thus diminish, as far as practicable, the evils of previous errors. Dawson v. Lawrence, 13 O. 544.

[1] § 5755.

[2] § 5756.

Where judicial proceedings are offered in evidence, a party to them can not avoid their effect on the ground of a slight mistake in his name; the mistake must be such as that the person can not be identified, or as to describe another, and therefore the record is good if it contain the name *Pillsby* for *Pillsbury.* Pillsbury v. Dugan, 9 O. 117.

The plaintiff is bound to set forth in his petition the title and interests of the several tenants, and to sustain the same by proof, Harman v. Kelly, 14 O. 502; the owner of the premises, although they are misdescribed in the petition, may come in and defend, and when it appears that a part of the persons claimed to be tenants in common have no interest in the land, the petition can not be maintained, *Ib.*; and a title in fee, acquired by possession, may be shown to defeat the partition. *Ib.*

A plaintiff who has the like interest in several tracts, can not join as defendant in a single action for partition the different persons who each own an interest in only one of the tracts. Prentiss' case, 7 O. 2 pt 129.

[3] § 5757.

estate lies, and must command him that, by the oaths of the commissioners, which oath may be administered by him, he cause to be set off and divided to the plaintiff, or each party in interest, such part and proportion of the estate as the court shall order.[1]

9. *Duty of commissioners in making partition.*—In making such partition, the commissioners must view and examine the estate, and, on their oaths, set apart the same in such lots as will be most advantageous and equitable, having due regard to the improvements, situation, and quality of the different parts thereof.[2]

10. *Their duty when partition of more than one tract demanded.* When partition of more than one tract is demanded, the commissioners must set off to each plaintiff or party in interest, his proper proportion in each of the several tracts, unless the several tracts are owned by the same proprietors in the same proportion in each tract, in which case the whole share of any proprietor, in all the several tracts, may be set off to such proprietor according to the best discretion of the commissioners.[3]

11. *Amicable partition.*—Before a writ of partition is issued, the person of whom partition is demanded may appear in court, in person or by attorney, and consent to a partition of the estate, agreeably to the prayer and facts set forth in the petition. Such amicable partition, when made and recorded, will be valid and binding between the parties thereto.[4]

12. *Commissioners to appraise land when they can not divide it ; election of party to take at appraisement.*—When the commissioners are of opinion that the estate can not be divided according to the demand of the writ without manifest injury to the value thereof, they must return that fact to the court, with a just valuation of the estate; whereupon, if the court approve of the return, and one or more of the parties elect to take the estate at such appraised value, the same must be adjudged to him or them, upon his or their paying to the other parties their proportion of

---

[1] § 5758.

[2] § 5759. In making partition among several tenants in common of several tracts of land, owning in the same proportion, it is regular to assign to any one, or to each one, an entire tract. 7 O. 2 pt. 118.

[3] § 5760.

[4] § 5761.

the appraised value thereof, according to their respective rights, or securing the same as provided below.[1]

13. *Terms of payment when estate taken by party; execution of conveyances.*—If one or more of the parties elect to take the estate at the appraised value, the terms of payment, unless the court, on good cause shown, by special order, direct and require the entire payment to be made in cash, or unless all the parties in interest agree thereon, must be one-third cash, one-third in one year, and one-third in two years, with interest, the deferred payments to be secured to the satisfaction of the court; and on payment being made in full, or in part, with sufficient security for the remainder, as above provided, the sheriff must, according to the order of the court, make and execute a conveyance to the party electing to take the same.[2]

---

[1] § 5762.　A person residing thereon, but having no interest therein, was made a party to a proceeding to partition the land among the tenants in common, and a valuation being returned, he elected to take the same thereat, and the election being confirmed and deed made: Held, that he took a good title to the land.　Rogers *v.* Tucker, 7 O. S. 417.

A husband and wife united in a proceeding for partition, pending which the wife died, and a valuation being returned, the husband elected to take the land and received a deed: Held—

1. That he took the estate of the other coparceners, and the heirs of the wife could not claim that his election inured to their benefit.

2. That as to the interest which had been his wife's and in which he had curtesy, it was not affected by the election and deed, and the husband having died, the heirs were entitled to recover the land, Foster *v.* Dugan, 8 O. 87; and a husband, who is also a tenant in common, is competent to make partition of the wife's real estate, but the right he or his grantee acquires by the proceeding in partition does not extinguish her right, which survives to her or her heirs.　Foster *v.* Dennison, 9 O. 121.

When a division of the land has been reported by the commissioners, and possession was taken in severalty under it, and improvements made, it will not, after the lapse of several years, be disturbed, although no entry of confirmation of the report was made by the court.　Piatt *v.* Hubbell, 5 O. 243.

[2] § 5763.　A sale in partition of real estate held in common divests the wife of a co-tenant of her inchoate right of dower therein, and passes the entire estate to the purchaser.　Weaver *v.* Gregg, 6 O. S. 547.

Where there is no statutory requirement in cases of partition, requiring a mortgage on the premises to be given to secure the price, a guardian may, in order to affect the partition, allow his ward's money to be secured on other real estate; and if a loss accrue, the guardian will not be liable if he acted

14. *Sale of the estate when the parties do not elect to take the same.* If no such election to take the estate be made, the court may, at the instance of a party, make an order for the sale thereof at public auction, by the sheriff who executed the writ of partition, or his successor in office.[1]

15. *How such sale conducted, and terms thereof.*—All such sales must be made at the door of the court-house, unless the court, for good cause, direct the same to be made on the premises, and must be conducted in all other respects as a sale upon execution, except that it will not be necessary to appraise the estate; but the estate can not be sold for less than two-thirds of the appraised value thereof, as returned by the commissioners; and unless the court, by special order, direct and require, on good cause shown, the entire payment to be made in cash, the purchase money will be payable one-third on the day of sale, one-third in one year, and one-third in two years thereafter, with interest.[2]

16. *Confirmation of sale, and execution of conveyances.*—On the return by the sheriff of his proceedings, the court must examine the same; if sale has been made, and the court approve such sale, the sheriff, on receiving payment of the consideration money, or taking sufficient security therefor, to the satisfaction of the court, must execute and deliver a deed to the purchaser.[3]

---

in good faith and with ordinary prudence. *In re* Spencer's Appeal, 3 W. L. M. 408.

When at a partition among devisees, one of them had an inchoate right of dower in premises set off to another, which subsequently ripened into a perfect estate, she will not be estopped to claim her dower against her co-partitioners, but the court will enforce contribution from all the parties to the partition, to make good to the person in whose share the dower is assigned his equal share in the estate remaining after the assignment of dower. Walker *v.* Hall, 15 O. S. 355.

[1] § 5764.

[2] § 5765. One of the terms of a sale on partition being that possession of the premises was reserved to the tenants till the expiration of a current lease, and the deed to the purchaser not having been delivered till after the expiration of the lease, it was held that the tenants, and not the purchaser, were entitled to the rents reserved in the lease. Black *v.* George, 26 O. S. 629.

[3] § 5766. A misrecital in a sheriff's deeds does not estop the purchaser from showing what the fact was, and may be corrected. Glover *v.* Ruffin, 6 O. 355.

17. *Distribution of proceeds ; sheriff's liability.* The money or securities arising from a sale of, or an election to take, the estate, must be distributed and paid, by order of the court, to the parties entitled thereto, in lieu of their respective parts and proportions of the estate, according to their just rights therein ; and all receipts of such money or securities by the sheriff will be in his official capacity, and his sureties on his official bond will be liable for any misapplication thereof.[1]

18. *Proceedings when estate has been once offered and not sold.*— When the estate has been once offered and not sold, an alias writ for the sale thereof may issue as often as need be ; and the court may order a revaluation, by three judicious and disinterested freeholders of the vicinity, to be appointed by the court, and direct a sale of the estate at not less than two-thirds of such revaluation, or, if the court deem it for the interest of the parties, it may order a sale without such revaluation, at not less than such sum as it may fix.[2]

19. *When successor of sheriff who made sale to execute conveyance.*—When a conveyance of land sold, or elected to be taken, is not made by the officer who made the sale, the court, being first satisfied that such sale or election was regularly made, and

---

A deed executed by the sheriff during his term of office, but acknowledged after his term had expired, is good, Foster *v.* Dugan, 8 O. 87 ; but a sheriff's deed without a seal is insufficient to pass the title. Merritt *v.* Horne, 5 O. S. 307.

The purchaser of land at a sale on partition, takes the same discharged of the lien of a judgment against a tenant in common therein, rendered after the order of sale was made, and the remedy of the judgment creditor is against the co-tenant's interest in the proceeds of sale. Cradelbaugh *v.* Pritchett, 8 O. S. 646.

[1] § 5767. A failure of the sheriff to return or pay over the purchase money or securities by him received, does not affect the title of the purchaser. Goudy *v.* Shank, 8 O. 415 ; see also Collins *v.* Skillen, 15 O. S. 382 ; and Griffin *v.* Underwood, Ib. 389.

The sheriff can not release a mortgage given for the deferred payments, although it was given to the sheriff himself for the use of specified parties entitled to the payments, and the purchaser, and those claiming under him, are affected with constructive notice of the lien of the parties for whose use the mortgage was made. Welsh *v.* Freeman, 21 O. S. 402 ; Preston *v.* Compton, 30 O. S. 299.

[2] § 5768.　　13

that the purchase-money has been fully paid or secured, may, on motion, order the sheriff of the county, or officer performing the duties of sheriff, to execute and deliver to the purchaser, or person electing to take the property, a deed for the lands so sold or elected to be taken.[1]

20. *When widow is entitled to dower, or an interest is subject to a life estate.*—When a widow is entitled to dower in an estate of which partition is sought, dower must be assigned her therein, except in the following cases: 1st. When an assignment thereof has already been made. 2nd. When she has, by answer, elected to be endowed out of the proceeds of a sale of the estate,[2] and the commissioners do not make partition, but return a valuation of the estate. 3d. When the right of dower extends only to an undivided interest in the estate. In the latter case, and in cases where an undivided interest is subject to a life estate, and the tenant for life has not, by answer, elected to receive the value of his estate out of the proceeds of a sale of the interest, the commissioners may, if an appraisement of the estate is to be returned, assign the dower, or set off the life estate, or, if they find it for the interest of the parties so to do, they may appraise the whole interest, and the widow and the tenant for life will receive the value of their interests out of the proceeds of a sale thereof.[3]

21. *Commissioners appointed to partition estate to assign dower.*—The commissioners appointed by the court to make partition must set off to such widow her dower in the estate; and in the performance of such duty they must be governed in all respects by, and the proceedings must conform to, the provisions prescribing the duties of commissioners in assigning dower, in section 5707 to 5725, inclusive, of the Revised Statutes.[4]

---

[1] § 5769.

[2] See paragraphs 68–73, chapter 6.

[3] § 5770. Dower being assigned in a partition action by an annuity charged on the lands, and the court having ordered that the parties, or their representatives or assigns, should pay the installments as they became due, and, in default of payment, that execution should issue therefor, it was held that the order was void for uncertainty, and that the remedy of the doweress was by action to enforce the lien on the land. Miller *v.* Peters, 25 O. S. 270.

[4] § 5771.

22. *Actions by one parcener against another, etc.*—Ono tenant in common, or coparcener, may recover from another his share of rents and profits received by such tenant in common or coparcener from the estate, according to the justice and equity of the case; and ono parcener may maintain an action of waste against another; but no parcener will have or possess any privileges over another, in any election, division, partition, or matter, to be made or done, concerning lands which have descended.'

---

¹§5774.

CHAPTER 12.

OCCUPYING CLAIMANTS TO REAL ESTATE.

RIGHTS AND OBLIGATIONS OF GUARDIANS AND WARDS WHO ARE, OR HAVE CLAIMS ADVERSE TO, SUCH CLAIMANTS.

1. *What position ward may occupy.*—The ward may be either the occupying claimant, or the adverse claimant not in possession referred to in the succeeding paragraphs.

2. *In what cases such claimant to be paid for improvements.*—A person in the quiet possession of lands or tenements, and claiming to own the same, who has obtained the title to and is in possession of the same without fraud or collusion on his part, can not be evicted or turned out of possession by any person who sets up and proves an adverse and better title, until the occupying claimant, or his heirs, are fully paid the value of all lasting and valuable improvements made on the land by him or by the person under whom he holds, before receiving actual notice by the commencement of suit on such adverse claim to turn him out of possession, unless such occupying claimant refuse to pay to the person so setting up and proving an adverse and better title the value of the land, without improvements made thereon as aforesaid, upon demand of the successful claimant, or his heirs, as provided below, when, 1st. Such occupying claimant holds a plain and connected title, in law or equity, derived from the records of a public office; or, 2d. Holds the same

by deed, devise, descent, contract, bond, or agreement, from and under a person claiming title as aforesaid, derived from the records of a public office, or by deed duly authenticated and recorded; or, 3d. Under sale on execution, against the person claiming title as aforesaid, derived from the records of a public office, or by deed duly authenticated and recorded; or, 4th. Under a sale for taxes authorized by the laws of this state, or the laws of the territory north-west of the river Ohio; or, 5th. Under a sale and conveyance made by executors, administrators, or guardians, or by any other person or persons, in pursuance of an order of court, or decree in chancery, where lands are or have been directed to be sold;[1] or, has possession under tax title.[2]

---

[1] § 5786. The office of township trustee, in which the leases of school lands made by them are recorded, is, as to such leases, a public office within the meaning of this section.   Hart *v.* Johnson, 6 O. 538.

The words "by deed duly authenticated and recorded" mean a deed to a person under whom the occupant claims, and not a deed to the occupant himself, overruling Glick *v.* Gregg, 19 O. 57; but it must be a deed apparently conveying an estate which will justify him in making improvements; therefore, a tenant for life obtaining his title and possession with knowledge of the quantity of his estate, is not entitled to the benefit of the statute.   Beardsley *v.* Chapman, 1 O. S. 118.

A purchaser of real estate at an administrator's sale, if evicted by the heir, is entitled to the benefit of this statute, Longworth *v.* Wolfington, 6 O. 9; and so is a purchaser upon a sale under execution, Seller's *v.* Corwin, 5 O. 398; but a purchaser from a judgment debtor of land actually levied upon by execution is not so entitled.   Vincent *v.* Goddard, 7 O. 2 pt. 188.

A person entering upon land, under color of title, paying taxes and making improvements as owner, being ejected at law, can not sustain a bill in equity for compensation and reimbursement against the rightful owner, Winthrop *v.* Huntington, 3 O. 327; but where the rightful owner asked to have his title quieted against claimants under a sale similar to that in Winthrop *v.* Huntington, the court required him to reimburse the defendant for taxes paid on the land.   Nowler *v.* Coit, 1 O. 519.

The provisions of this statute do not extend to the case of valuable improvements made by a tenant in common under a will by which, in the contingency of his dying without issue, the survivor took the estate.   Taylor *v.* Foster, 22 O. S. 255.

A partition which was made regardless of a claim for improvements, valid under this statute, will not be enjoined when the occupying claimant is in adverse possession, and the claimant in partition will have to prosecute ejectment.   Penrod *v.* Danner, 19 O. 218.

An occupying claimant will not be presumed to know any defects or re-

[2] § 5787.

3. *Damages, value of improvements, etc., determined by jury.*—If the court renders judgment against the occupying claimant,[1] a jury must be impaneled as the law provides, which must immediately view the premises, and, on oath, assess the value of all lasting and valuable improvements made on such land by the occupying claimant before he received notice of the adverse claim as above mentioned. The jury must also assess the damages, if any, sustained by waste, and the net annual value of the rents and profits of the land which the occupying claimant has received since the receipt of said notice by service of said summons; and must deduct the amount thereof from the estimated value of such improvements; and the jury must also assess the value of the land at the time judgment was rendered, without these improvements or damages sustained by waste.[2]

4. *Judgment and execution on verdict for plaintiff.*—If the jury report a sum in favor of the claimant not in possession, on the assessment and valuation of the valuable and lasting improvements, the assessment of damages for waste, and the net annual value of the rents and profits, the court must render a judgment therefor, without pleadings, and issue execution thereon, as in other cases; or, if no such excess be reported, then, and in

---

citals that appear in deeds prior to the deed of his grantor; and if a recital in that or in his own deed shows that the premises once belonged to a third person, it will not defeat the occupant's claim to the benefit of this statute. Beardsley *v.* Chapman, 1 O. S. 118

The mere fact that the occupant had notice of the claim which is successfully asserted is not conclusive evidence of fraud and collusion on part of the purchaser, but he may show, notwithstanding such notice, that he purchased in actual good faith, and made his improvements in the honest belief that the land was his own. Harrison *v.* Castner, 11 O. S. 339.

[1] This is a separate proceeding, in which the party prevailing is entitled to costs, though he be the party ejected. Martin's case, 1 O. 156.

[2] §§ 5788, 5789.

An occupying claimant is entitled to recover, as well for improvements made by himself, or the person under whom he claims, before his title commenced, as for those made afterward. Shaler *v.* Magin, 2 O. 235; Davis *v.* Powell, 13 O. 308. But he can not recover for improvements made outside of the land described in his title-deeds. Waldron *v.* Woodcock, 15 O. 13.

either case, the claimant not in possession can not maintain a suit for mesne profits.[1]

5. *Proceedings if verdict is for occupying claimant.*—If the jury report a sum in favor of the occupying claimant, on the assessment and valuation of the valuable and lasting improvements, deducting therefrom the damages, if any, sustained by waste, together with the net annual value of the rents and profits which the defendant has received after commencement of the action, the successful claimant, or his heirs, or, if they are minors, their guardians, may either demand of the occupying claimant the value of the land without the improvements so assessed, and tender a deed of the land to the occupying claimant, or may pay the occupying claimant the sum so allowed by the jury in his favor, within such reasonable time as the court shall allow.[2]

6. *When a writ of possession will issue.*—If the successful claimant, his heirs, or their guardians, elect to pay, and do pay, to the occupying claimant, the sum reported in his favor by the jury, within the time allowed by the court, then a writ of possession must issue in favor of the successful claimant, his heirs, or their guardians.[3]

7. *When claimant elects to receive value of land.*—If the successful claimant, his heirs, or their guardians, elect to receive the value of the land without improvements, so assessed to be paid by the occupying claimant, and tender a general warranty deed of the land conveying such adverse or better title, within the time allowed by the court for the payment of the money, and the occupying claimant refuse or neglect to pay the same to the successful claimant, his heirs, or their guardians, within the time limited, a writ of possession must be issued in favor of the successful claimant, his heirs, or their guardians.[4]

8. *When occupant may have action for title.*—The occupying claimant, or his heirs, can not be evicted from the possession of

---

[1] § 5792.   [2] § 5793.   [3] § 5794.

[4] § 5795.

It is necessary that the successful claimant who elects to convey his land tender a deed with covenants of warranty; but it is not necessary that the deed be made by himself, provided it conveys the title; and the occupying claimant is not entitled to interest upon the valuation until the election is made. Wilkins *v.* Huse, 15 O. 285.

such land, except as is provided in the two preceding paragraphs, where an application is made for the value of improvements; and in all cases where the occupying claimant, or his heirs, pay into court the value of the land, without improvements, within the time allowed by the court, when an election has been made by the successful claimant, his heirs, or their guardians, to surrender land under the provisions of this and the preceding paragraphs of this chapter, such occupant, or his heirs, may, at any time after such payment is made, bring an action in the court where judgment of eviction was obtained, and obtain judgment for the title of the land, if the same had not been previously conveyed to such occupant as aforesaid.[1]

---

[1] § 5796.

CHAPTER 13.

ROAD LAWS, ETC., AS DIRECTLY AFFECTING GUARDIANS AND WARDS.

1. *As to new roads and changes in old ones; notice to guardian.* When application is made for laying out, altering, changing the width of, or vacating any county road, the principal petitioner must give at least six days' notice, in writing, to the owner or his agent, if residing within the county; or, if such owner be a minor, idiot, or insane person, to the guardian of such person, if a resident of the county, through whose land the road is proposed to be laid out and established, or through whose land the road which it is proposed to alter or vacate may have been previously established, and also six days' notice to the viewers and surveyor named in the order of the commissioners, of the time and place of meeting, as specified in the order of the county commissioners concerning the road, and of the day by which claims for compensation must be filed; and the principal petitioner, if the road is proposed to be laid out, altered, or vacated, on any lands owned by a non-resident of the county, must cause a notice to such non-resident to be published for four consecutive weeks in some newspaper published in such county; but if there be no newspaper published therein, then in some newspaper in an adjoining county to that in which the lands sought to be affected by the road are situate, which notice shall state the time and place of the meeting of the viewers and surveyor, as specified in the order of the commissioners, and also the substance of the petition.[1]

---

[1] §§ 4638, 4645, 4642.

2. *Guardians and others may appeal in such matters.*—An appeal from the final order of the county commissioners establishing a county road, or altering or vacating, in whole or in part, a state or county road, or changing the width of a county road, may be taken to the probate court of the same county by any person having an estate in fee, for life, or years, in any lands or tenements, situate in any township in the county, in or through which township such new, altered, changed, or vacated road passes, or by the husband of any married woman, or guardian of any ward, having such an estate.[1]

3. *Guardians need give no appeal bond.*—Appellants must, to perfect such appeal, give such appeal bond as the law prescribes, on or before the twentieth day after the entry of the order appealed from; but minors, idiots or lunatics, or their guardians, respectively, may appeal without giving bond, by causing an entry to that effect to be made within the period aforesaid, by the county auditor, in the record of the commissioners.[2]

4. *Appeals by claimant of damages; notice to guardian.*— The law also provides that every claimant of compensation and damages, on account of the establishment or alteration of a county or township road, or alteration of a state road, or change in width of a county road, may appeal to the probate court from the final decision of the county commissioners or township trustees, confirming the assessment of compensation and damages made by the viewers in his behalf, or the refusal of the viewers to award damages to him, and also provides how such appeal shall be perfected and docketed, and how notice must be served on all interested parties; and that service of notice upon a guardian will be sufficient service upon his ward.[3]

5. *Powers of guardians as to two-mile assessment pikes.*—Certain improved free roads, designated as two-mile assessment pikes, from the fact that they are constructed at the expense of property situate within two miles of them, may be built by the county commissioners, if a majority of the resident landholders, most to be benefited, subscribe a petition asking for such road. To get such a road constructed, proceedings must be had in the probate court, viewers and a surveyor must be appointed, surveys, re-

---

[1] §4688.   [2] §4689.   [3] §§4699–4701.

ports, and assessments must be made, damages may be claimed and recovered, and other things done which do not come within the scope of this volume to describe in detail.[1]

6. In all these matters, the guardian of any minor, idiot, or insane person may act for his ward, and all his acts will be binding upon the ward;[2] and in determining the majority above mentioned, minor heirs must not be counted for or against the road, unless represented by legal guardian; and the action of such guardian will be binding upon such minor heirs; and all heirs or owners, either adults or minors, to any undivided estate, will be entitled to only one vote.[3]

7. *Assessments for streets, etc.; duties of guardians as to, etc.*—The law also provides[4] how assessments upon property may be made for various public improvements, including the laying out, improving, etc., of streets, alleys, and other public highways[5] in municipal corporations; and among other things it is provided that, in cities of the first class, or in corporations in counties containing a city of the first grade of the first class, when a petition, subscribed by three-fourths in interest of the owners of property abutting upon any street or highway of any description, is regularly presented to the council for the purpose, the cost of any improvement of such street or highway may be assessed and collected in equal annual installments, proportioned to the whole assessment, in a manner to be indicated in the petition, or if not so indicated, then in the manner which may be fixed by council; and the interest on any bonds issued for the improvement, by the corporation, must be assessed, together with the annual installments provided for upon the property so improved; but where the lot or land of one who did not subscribe the petition is assessed, such assessment must not exceed twenty-five per cent. of the value of his lot or land after the improvement is made; provided, that whenever in the title of the Revised Statutes which relates to municipal corporations, the petition of the owners of

---

[1] §§ 4829–4864.

[2] § 4834. See, also, 4859.

[3] § 4836.

[4] §§ 2262 and following.

[5] § 2263.

property is required, a married woman shall have the same authority to sign that she would have if unmarried; and the guardians of infants or insane persons may sign such petition on behalf of their wards, only when expressly authorized by the probate court, on good cause shown.[1]

---

[1] § 2272. For numerous notes of decisions as to such assessments, see notes to §§ 2263 and 2264, Rev. Stat. of Ohio.

CHAPTER 14.

SCHOOL LAWS, AS AFFECTING GUARDIAN AND WARD.

1. *Suspension and expulsion of pupils from school; rights of guardians.*—No pupil can be suspended from school by a superintendent or teacher except for such time as may be necessary to convene the board of education of the district or the directors of the sub-district, and no pupil can be expelled except by a vote of two-thirds of such board or directors, and not until the parent or guardian of the offending pupil has been notified of the proposed expulsion, and permitted to be heard against the same; and no scholar can be suspended or expelled from any school beyond the current term thereof.[1]

2. *Children must attend school, unless.*—Every parent, guardian, or other person having charge or control of any child between the ages of eight and fourteen years, must send such child to a common school for at least twelve weeks in each school year, at least six weeks of which shall be consecutive, unless the board of education, or the board of directors, as the case may be, having control of the school district or sub-district in which such parent or guardian resides, excuse such child from attendance, when it appears to the satisfaction of such board that the child's bodily or mental condition is such as to prevent its attendance at school, or application to study, for the time required, or that its time and labor are essentially necessary for the support of an indigent parent, brother, or sister, or that it is being otherwise

---

[1] § 4014.

furnished with the means of education for a like period of time, or has already acquired branches of learning ordinarily taught in common schools; but if the common school of the district or sub-district in which such parent or guardian resides is distant two miles from his residence by the nearest traveled road, he will not be liable to the provisions of this paragraph, nor to the subsequent paragraphs of this chapter.[1]

3. *Unlawful to employ children who have not attended school.*— No manufacturer, owner of mills or mines, agent, overseer, contractor, landlord, or other person, is permitted to employ any child under fourteen years of age during the established school hours of the locality, who has resided in this state during the school year next preceding the commencement of such employment, and is under the control of a parent or guardian, and is not dependent upon its own resources for support, unless such child has attended some common or private school for the term of at least twelve weeks during the school year next preceding the commencement of such employment, and delivers to its employer a certificate of that fact from the clerk of a board of education, or the clerk of a board of directors, or the teacher of the school which it attended; nor can such employment continue for a longer period than forty weeks during any school year, unless such child deliver to such employer a certificate of excuse from the proper authority, for any of the reasons mentioned in the preceding paragraph.[2]

4. *How books supplied, if guardian can not purchase.*—If it be shown to the satisfaction of the board of education that the parent or guardian has not the means wherewith to purchase for his child or children the necessary school books to enable him to comply with the requirements of this chapter, the board may furnish the same, free of charge, to be paid for out of the contingent fund at the disposal of the board.[3]

5. *Penalties against violation of preceding provisions.*—A parent, guardian, or other person who fails to comply with the provisions of this chapter, will be liable to a fine of not less than two nor more than five dollars for the first offense, nor less than five nor more than ten dollars for each subsequent

---

[1] § 4023.   [2] § 4024; see par. 5, chap. 15.   [3] § 4026.

offense; such fine must be collected by the clerk of the board of education, in the name of the state, in an action before any court having competent jurisdiction; and the money so collected by each clerk must be paid to the county treasurer, and be applied to the use of the common schools of his district.[1]

---

[1] § 4027.

CHAPTER 15.

APPRENTICESHIP OF WARD.

1. *Wards may be bound out upon approval by the probate court.*
The guardian of a female under twelve years of age, or a male
under fourteen years of age, may, if it be necessary, bind such
minor to any suitable person, until such minor shall arrive at
the age of twenty-one if a male, or eighteen if a female, or for
a shorter period; but no such indenture can be executed unless
the probate court appointing such guardian shall first approve
such binding, and the terms and conditions of the indentures,
and evidence such approval by a certificate under the seal of the
court, indorsed upon the indentures.[1]

2. *As to other provisions on same subject.* The preceding paragraph contains all the law as to the ward's apprenticeship found
in that chapter of the Revised Statutes which is devoted to
guardians and trustees; but the following are other provisions
relating to the duties of guardians and others as to such appren-
ticeships.

---

[1] § 6293.

3. *By whom indenture to be executed.* The indenture or covenant of service must be signed and sealed by the father; or, in case of the death or inability of the father, by the mother or guardian; or, in case of an orphan or destitute child, by the trustees of the township, of the one part, and by the master or mistress of the other part.[1]

4. *Must state minor's age.* The indenture or covenant of service must contain a statement of the age and time of service of the minor, and, if such age is unknown, then it must be inserted according to the best information; which age must, in relation to the term of service, be deemed and taken as the true age of such minor.[2]

5. *What covenant indenture must contain.* The indenture or covenant by which a minor is bound, must contain a covenant, on the part of the master or mistress, to send the minor to a common school for at least twelve weeks, in each school year during the apprenticeship, after the minor is eight years of age, and at the expiration of the term of service, to furnish the minor with a new Bible, and two good suits of clothes; and all money or property stipulated to be paid by the master or mistress, must be secured to, and for the sole use and benefit of the minor.[3]

6. *To be recorded when and by whom; effect of not recording.* The master or mistress must cause the indenture or covenant of service to be recorded within three months from the execution thereof, by the clerk of the township, or clerk of the municipal corporation where the master or mistress resides; and on failure so to do, the minor will be discharged from service, and the master or mistress remain liable for the payment of all property stipulated to be paid by the covenants.[4]

7. In such case, the minor would no doubt be again as completely subject to the control of the guardian as though the articles of apprenticeship had never been entered into.

8. *Duties of guardians, etc., as to apprentices; may complain to justice.* It is the duty of parents and guardians, and the trustees of townships, to inquire into the usage of a minor who is bound, and to defend him or her from the cruelty, neglect, or breach of covenant of the master or mistress, for which purpose

---

[1] §3120.   [2] §3121.   [3] §3122; see par. 3, p. 206.   [4] §3123.

14

such parent, guardian, or trustees, or the minor, by his or her next friend, may complain against the master or mistress, before any justice of the peace in the township where the master or mistress resides; and such justice must summon the master or mistress forthwith to appear before him, and if he can reconcile the parties to each other, he must make such order therein as the right and justice of the case requires.[1]

9. *Jury to try complaint.* If the justice be unable to settle and accommodate the difference in dispute between the parties, he must issue a venire to any constable of the township to summon five disinterested freeholders. to be therein named, to meet at a time and place certain, not exceeding three days thereafter; the jurors. or such other persons as the justice may appoint in case of their failure to attend, when met and qualified, must proceed to hear the evidence in the case; and if they find the master or mistress guilty of a breach of the indenture or covenant, or of neglect or refusal to furnish necessary food or clothing, or of cruelty toward the minor, they must render their verdict in writing accordingly, and assess such damages as the minor may have sustained.[2]

10. *Judgment thereon, and its effect.* The justice must thereupon enter the verdict in his docket, and must render judgment thereon for the damages so found, and costs. against the master or mistress. and award execution accordingly; and the indenture or covenant of service will be void from the rendition of judgment; but if the jury find the defendant not guilty, the justice must render judgment for costs against the parent, guardian, next friend, or trustees—if the complaint of the trustees was without probable cause—as the case may be, and issue execution accordingly.[3]

11. *Proceeding when apprentice becomes dissolute.* If the conduct and habits of the apprentice, clerk, or servant, become immoral and dissolute, in disregard of the commands of his or her master or mistress, and their authority be exerted for his or her reformation without effect, the master or mistress may complain to any justice of the peace of the township, who must give notice to the parent, guardian, or trustees, and such proceedings

---

[1] §3126.   [2] §3127.   [3] §3128.

must be had, as to summoning and impanneling a jury, as are provided in paragraph 8 of this chapter; and if, upon such investigation, the jurors are of opinion that the master or mistress should be discharged from his or her covenants, they must certify the same in writing to the justice, who must enter the same upon his docket; and thereupon the indenture will be void; but no judgment for costs can be entered against the parent, guardian, or trustees; but the same must be paid, except the costs of witnesses for the minor, by the master or mistress.[1]

12. *When guardian, etc., is liable.*—No parent, guardian, or trustee, will be liable upon any covenant contained in an indenture or covenant of service, unless the same contain an express covenant therein that the said parent, guardian, or trustee, is made individually liable.[2]

13–15. *Form of indenture to bind out a ward.*

Articles of agreement made this —— day of ——, A. D. 18—, by and between A. B., as guardian of C. D., a male [*or,* female] minor of the age[3] of —— years, on the —— day of ——, A. D. 18—, and G. H. witnesseth; that the said A. B., as guardian as aforesaid, hereby binds the said C. D. unto the said G. H., until the said C. D. shall arrive at the age of twenty-one years [*or, eighteen years. as the case may be; or if for any shorter period, name either the number of years that is agreed upon, or the age up to which the minor is agreed to be bound*], to learn the art of a printer [*or whatever art or business is agreed upon*]; and the said A. B., as guardian as aforesaid [*or if it be agreed that he is to be individually liable, say, instead of "as guardian as aforesaid," individually*[4]]. hereby covenants and agrees with said G. H., that the said C. D. shall faithfully serve the said G. H. and work under his direction at the employment aforesaid, during the term aforesaid, and conduct himself in a proper, becoming, and respectful manner towards the said G. H., and obey all his reasonable requests and demands.

And the said G. H. hereby covenants and agrees with the said A. B., as guardian as aforesaid, that he will this day [*or if another day be fixed, when the minor is to commence the service, say, on the*

---

[1] § 3129.   [2] § 3134.   [3] See paragraph 4.   [4] See paragraph 12.

—— day of ——, A. D. 18—] receive the said C. D. into his service for the term and for the purposes aforesaid, and that he will faithfully and in good faith teach or cause him to be taught the art and mysteries of the trade of printing [*or such other business or art as is agreed upon*]. so that said C. D. shall be as thoroughly instructed and learned therein as his capacity will permit; and will send the minor to a common school for at least twelve weeks in each school year, during his apprenticeship, after he is eight years of age; and at the expiration of said term of service, will furnish said C. D. with a new bible. and at least two good suits of clothes [*and if any money or property be agreed to be paid to the minor, say,* and will pay the said C. D. the sum of —— dollars, *or,* will give the said C. D. a good saddle-horse, saddle and bridle, *or,* a set of good tools of said trade. etc., at the expiration of the term aforesaid, *or add any other agreements between the parties*].

In witness whereof, we have hereto set our hands and seals.
   (*Signed.*)   A. B., [SEAL.]
                                      Guardian of C. D.
                                        G. H., [SEAL.]

16. *Entry of approval by court.*—As has been seen. terms and conditions of the indenture must be approved of by the court which appointed the guardian; and as every movement of the court must appear on its journal, this approval should be entered thereon.

17-18. *Form of journal entry of the approval of the court of the binding out of a minor by his guardian.*

In the matter of the guardianship of C. D., in binding his ward to G. H.

This day came the said A. B., guardian of C. D., and produced to the court articles of indenture duly made and executed on the —— day of ——, A. D. 18—, by the said A. B., as guardian as aforesaid, and the said G. H., whereby the said C. D. is bound unto the said G. H., upon the terms and covenants in said indenture named, and the court being satisfied that said G. H. is a proper person for the purposes aforesaid, and that the terms and covenants of said indenture are legal, proper, and just; the binding, terms, and conditions aforesaid are, by the court, hereby approved.

19. *Form of judge's certificate of approval of indenture.*

The State of Ohio, —— county, ss.

I, A. C., probate judge of —— county, Ohio, hereby certify, that on the —— day of ——, A. D. 18—, the probate court of said county examined the within indenture, and approve the binding and the terms and conditions therein, as will fully appear by the records of said court.

Witness my hand and the seal of said court, this —— day of ——, A. D. 18—.

[L. S.]

A. C.,
Probate Judge, etc.

20. *Character, etc., of proposed master.*—A minor may be bound to serve another person, of full age, of sound morals, and of capacity to teach what is required, and to govern the minor; for none other, it is supposed, would be approved of by a court which did its duty.

21. The person to whom the minor is bound must be capable of contracting; therefore, such minor can not be bound to a married woman, an infant, an insane or imbecile person.

CHAPTER 16.

CHARITABLE, REFORMATORY AND PUNITIVE INSTITUTIONS, AS AFFECTING GUARDIANSHIP OF MINORS, ETC.

BOYS AND REFORM SCHOOL.

1. *When guardian, etc., may send ward to.*—Male youth, not over sixteen nor under ten years of age, may be committed to the reform school by any judge of a police court, judge of the court of common pleas, or the probate court, when, on complaint and proof by the parent, guardian, or next friend. of any such youth, supported by the sworn statement of two respectable witnesses, it is shown that he, by reason of his incorrigible or criminal conduct, is beyond the control of such parent, guardian, or next friend, and that, from regard to his future welfare and the protection of society, he should be placed under restraint.[1]

GIRLS AND INDUSTRIAL HOME.

2. *Vicious or criminal girl; duty of judge and guardian.*—When a girl above the age of nine, and under the age of fifteen years, is brought by an officer, or other inhabitant, of any municipality or township, before the probate court of the proper county, upon complaint, under oath, that she has committed an offense against a law of the state, punishable by fine and imprisonment, other than by imprisonment for life, or that she is leading a vicious or criminal life, the probate judge must forthwith issue an order, in writing, addressed to the father of the girl, if living and resident of the municipality or township where she is found, and if not, then to her mother, if she is living and so resident, and if there is no father or mother resident, as aforesaid, then to her guardian, if so resident; if not, then to the person with whom the girl resides; which order must require such father, mother, guardian, or other person, to appear before the probate judge at the time and place therein named, to show cause, if there is any, why said girl should not be committed to the industrial home.[2]

3. *May be sent to industrial home.*—If the probate judge, after such time as is prescribed by law in such cases,[3] deems the accused to be a proper subject for the industrial home, he must commit her to that institution, in the manner provided by law.[4]

4. *Detention and discharge of; may be returned to guardian.*— A girl duly committed to the home must be kept there, disciplined, instructed, employed, and governed, under the direction of the trustees, until she is either reformed and discharged, or bound out by them, according to their by-laws, or has attained the age of eighteen years; but the trustees have the right to discharge and return to the parents, guardian, or protector, any girl, who, in their judgment, ought, for any cause, to be removed from the home, and in such case the trustees must enter upon their records the reasons for her discharge, a copy of which record, signed by their secretary, must be forthwith transmitted to the probate judge by whom the girl was committed.[5]

---

[1] §753.   [2] §769.   [3] §§770, 771.   [4] §770.   [5] §773.

5. *May be bound out ; who her guardian in such case.*—Any girl so committed may be bound out as apprentice or servant for a term not longer than till she arrives at the age of eighteen years, under conditions and restrictions imposed by the statutes ;[1] and the trustees of the industrial home will be her guardians while so bound out, and must take care that the terms of the contract are faithfully fulfilled, and that she is properly treated, and must cause every grievance to be redressed.[2]

WARDS IN CHILDREN'S HOMES ERECTED BY COUNTIES OR DISTRICTS.

6. *Management, etc., of such homes.*—The statutes provide for the erection and maintenance of children's homes, under the control of trustees and a superintendent.[3] Among the further provisions are the following :

7. *Who may be admitted to the home.*—The home is to be an asylum for all persons resident of the county where such home is located, under sixteen years of age (and such other persons under such age from other counties in the state, where no home is located, as the trustees of such home and the party, parties, or authorities having the custody and control of such children, by contract, agree upon), who, by reason of abandonment by parents, or orphanage, or neglect, or inability of parents to provide for them, in the opinion of the trustees, are suitable persons for such provision, and they must be admitted by the superintendent, on the order of a majority of such trustees, accompanied by a statement of facts signed by them, setting forth the name, age, birthplace, and present condition of the persons named in such order, which statement of facts contained in the order, together with any additional facts connected with the history and condition of said persons, must be, by the superintendent, recorded in a book provided him for that purpose by the commissioners of such county, which book must be at all times open for inspection.[4]

8. *Children neglected and abused by guardians, etc., may be sent to the home.*—Children who are under the custody of parent, guardian, or next friend, and who, by reason of neglect, abuse, or from the moral depravity, habitual drunkenness, incapacity

---

[1] ⸹⸹ 575-7.   [2] ⸹ 578; see chap. 15.   [3] ⸹⸹ 929-956.   [4] ⸹ 931.

or unwillingness of such legal custodian to exercise proper care or discipline over them, are being brought up to lead idle, vagrant, or criminal lives, may, if the trustees of the township in which they have a legal settlement, after a careful and impartial investigation of the condition and facts, as they exist, deem it manifestly requisite for the future welfare of such children, and for the benefit and protection of society, be committed to the guardianship of the trustees of a county or district children's home.[1]

9. *Power of trustees over children.*—All the inmates who have been neglected or abandoned, as aforesaid, or who have been by the parent or guardian voluntarily surrendered to the trustees, will be under the sole and exclusive guardianship and control of the trustees, during their stay in said home, and until they arrive at the age of sixteen years; and said trustees also have power to discharge any of the inmates of said home; and when so discharged, the parent or guardian resumes power and authority; and the trustees may return any of the inmates of said home to the parents or guardians of such inmates, when they believe them capable of caring and providing for themselves, or their parents or guardians for them.[2]

SAME, AS TO CHILDREN'S HOMES OF CITIES.

10. *Powers of trustees and managers.*—In cities of the first and second class, where children's homes or industrial schools may be established under the incorporation law of the state, the trustees and managers of such institution may take under their guardianship all children who may be placed under their care and management in either of the following modes :

11. *First*—Children under sixteen years of age, who are voluntarily surrendered by the father and mother, or in case of the death, or long continued or willful absence of the father, by the mother, or by their guardian, to the care of such trustees and managers, they being by virtue of such surrender invested with the same power over the persons of the children as the parents or guardians.

12. *Second*—Children under sixteen years of age who, upon

---

[1] § 945.
[2] § 932.

the application of the trustees and managers, may be committed to their care by any judge of probate court, or mayor of such city, on account of vagrancy or exposure to want and suffering, or neglect or abandonment by their parents or guardians, or other persons having custody of such children, or in accordance with the request of their mother or next friend in case of habitual intemperance, abuse, or neglect of their father.[1]

13. *May act as guardian of children, and procure them homes.*— The trustees and managers will have the guardianship of such children during their minority, and may, when it may seem proper, place them in suitable homes, having scrupulous regard to the religious and moral character of the persons with whom such children are placed, in order to secure to them the benefits of good example and wholesome instruction, and the opportunity of becoming intelligent and useful men and women.[2]

14. *Children may be apprenticed.*—The law then further provides that such children may be bound out, and on what conditions, etc.[3]

15. *Trustees may remove children from unsuitable homes.*—The trustees and managers may remove a child from a home when, in their judgment, the same has become an unsuitable one, and they must, in such cases, resume the same power and authority as they originally possessed; but they may return a child to parents or a surviving parent or guardian, or when they believe the child to be capable of caring and providing for himself, may discharge him to his own care.[4]

IN HOUSES OF REFUGE.

16. *When infant received into.*—The board [of directors of house of refuge of municipal corporation] may, at its discretion, receive into such institution infants under the age of sixteen years, committed to their custody in either of the following modes, to-wit:

17. *First*—Infants committed by the mayor of the corporation, or any judge or justice of the peace of the county, on complaint and due proof by the parent, guardian, or next friend of such infant, that, by reason of incorrigible or vicious conduct,

---

[1] § 2181; 78 O. L. 154.   [2] § 2182; 78 O. L. 154.
[3] §§ 2183–4; 78 O. L. 154.   [4] § 2185; 78 O. L. 154.

such infant has rendered his control beyond the power of such parent, guardian, or next friend, and made it manifestly requisite that, from regard to the future welfare of such infant, and for the protection of society, he should be placed under the guardianship of the board of directors of such house of refuge and correction.

18. *Second*—Infants committed by the authorities aforesaid, where complaint and due proof have been made that such infant is a proper subject for the guardianship of the directors of such institution, in consequence of vagrancy, or of incorrigible or vicious conduct, and that from the moral depravity of the parent, guardian, or next friend, in whose custody such infant may be, or other cause, such parent, guardian, or next friend, is incapable or unwilling to exercise the proper care and discipline over such incorrigible or vicious infant.

19. *Third*—Infants who are without a suitable home and adequate means of obtaining an honest living, or who are in danger of being brought up to lead an idle or immoral life, may be committed to the guardianship of the directors of such institution, by the trustees of any township within the county in which such institution is situated, or by the mother, when the father is dead, or has abandoned his family, or does not provide for their support, or is an habitual drunkard.[1]

20. *Infants entitled to private examination and trial, unless.*—Infants under the age of sixteen years, who are accused of an offense punishable by imprisonment in a county in which a house of refuge and correction is situated, will be entitled to a private examination and trial, to which only the parties can be admitted, unless one of the parents, the guardian, or other legal representative demands a public trial, in which case all proceedings must be in the usual form.[2]

21. *How expenses shall be paid.*—The expense of maintaining infants committed to a house of refuge and correction, by a court or magistrate of the county in which such institution is situated, or by the police or other court of the corporation, for offenses against a law of the state, or for trial, or as a witness, must be paid by the county; and the expense of infants committed by

---

[1] § 2050.   [2] § 2056.

[township trustees must be paid by the township, and of those committed by] parents and guardians must be paid by them, except in cases where the board otherwise determine; all which expense must be ascertained and fixed by the board.[1]

22. *Guardian or other party may apply to the board.*—If a parent, guardian. master to whom an infant has been apprenticed, a person occupying the position of parent, protector, or guardian, in fact, or a relative by blood or marriage, not further remote than first cousin to such infant, feels aggrieved by the commitment of an infant to the directors of a house of refuge and correction, by a person authorized to commit such infant, he may make a written application to the board, at such time as the directors, by rule or resolution, provide for hearing applications, not later than the next regular meeting of the board, to have the infant delivered to him; which application must state the ground of the applicant's claim to the custody of such infant, and the reason for claiming such custody.[2]

23. *Decision of application.*—Within ten days after hearing such application. the directors must decide; and if they be of opinion that the welfare of such infant will be promoted by granting the application, they must make an order to that effect; otherwise they must decline the application.[3]

24. *Action against directors.*—The applicant may, if the application be declined, upon first giving security for the payment of costs, commence an action against such directors in the court of common pleas or superior court of the county in which the house is situated, for the recovery of the infant, or his liberation ; which action must be conducted in all respects as actions under the code of civil procedure, except the case will have precedence of all others in the time of trial.[4]

25. *Other provisions.*—There are many other provisions as to such houses of refuge and infants who may be wards.[5] for instance, a prescribed simple form of record of proceedings for commitment, unless the minor, his guardian or parent object,[6] terms and conditions of binding out to apprenticeship, similar to those already specified,[7] etc., which it is not considered necessary to give here in full.

---

[1] § 2071. [2] § 2075. [3] § 2076. [4] § 2077.
[5] §§ 2031–2107. [6] § 2060. [7] §§ 2062–2066.

CHAPTER 17.

INTOXICATING LIQUORS.

DUTIES, RIGHTS, AND LIABILITIES OF GUARDIANS AND WARDS, WITH REFERENCE
TO THE SALE OF INTOXICATING LIQUORS, AS PROVIDED IN CHAPTER 7, TITLE
V, PART FIRST, REVISED STATUTES.

1. *The action for injury or to means of support, by causing intoxication.*—Every husband, wife, child, parent, guardian, employer, or other person injured in person or property, or means of support, by any intoxicated person; or in consequence of the intoxication, habitual or otherwise, of any person, after the giving and during the existence of the notice provided for in the next paragraph, has a right of action in his or her own name, severally or jointly, against any person or persons who, by selling or giving intoxicating liquors, have caused the intoxication, in whole or in part, of such person; and the owner of any building or premises, and the person renting or leasing the same, having knowledge that intoxicating liquors are to be sold therein, in violation of law, or, having leased the same for other purposes, knowingly permit intoxicating liquors to be sold therein, that have caused the intoxication, in whole or in part, of such person, are liable severally or jointly with the person or persons

selling or giving intoxicating liquors as aforesaid, for all damages sustained, as well as exemplary damages.[1] See par. 8.

---

[1] § 4357. Under the seventh section of the act of May 1, 1854, (52 v. 153), contractors who had in their employ hired hands with teams, wagons, and other implements, were empowered to bring suit and recover damages against any person who, unlawfully, sold intoxicating liquors to such hands, whereby they became drunk, unable themselves to work, prevented other hands and teams from working to advantage, and hindered and delayed the progress of the work, and thus injured the contractors in their property and means of support. Duroy r. Blinn, 11 O. S. 331.

Under this section as amended April 18, 1870, (67 r. 101) a justice of the peace had no jurisdiction against the owner or lessee of premises where the unlawful selling takes place, Bowers v. Pomeroy, 21 O. S. 184; injuries to the "person" of the plaintiff to support an action must be actual violence, or some physical injury to the person or health; injury to "means of support," does not imply that the plaintiff was at any time, in whole or in part, without present means of support; it is sufficient that the means of future support have been cut off or diminished; and the rule of damages is the amount of diminution; injury to "property" may be the sale of chattels, and the plaintiff need not first demand them of the vendee; and the liability of defendant is not confined to cases of injury resulting from drunkenness, immediately and during its continuance, but extends, as well, to cases where the injury results from insanity, sickness, or inability, induced by intoxication. Mulford r. Clewell, 21 O. S. 191.

Before the amendment of 1870, where the action was from injuries resulting from habitual intoxication, it was not essential to recovery that the deendant should have been the sole cause of such habitual intoxication; one who contributes to cause that condition by illegal sales, which of themselves tend, and are calculated, to produce that result, is presumed to have intended it, and is liable for the damages resulting, though others may, by their illegal acts, have contributed thereto without his knowledge, and without preconcert with him; and where the damages resulting arise from incapacity for business and loss of estate, caused by such intoxication, and it becomes impossible to separate the damages caused by others from those caused by the defendant, he is liable for all such damages, if the natural and probable consequences of his illegal acts were to cause such injury; and the statement of the vendee, a physician who was in the habit of getting intoxicated, made when purchasing, that he wanted the liquor for a patient, and for medical purposes, does not, in the absence of proof to the contrary, raise a presumption that it was a sale to the patient. Boyd v. Watt, 27 O. S. 259.

And under the amendment of 1870 separate actions might be brought against different defendants, and satisfaction and discharge of the cause of action against one afforded no defense in the other case, if in fact the intox-

2. *Notice to seller or owner of premises; its record and effect; penalty.*—Such husband, wife, child, parent, guardian, or other interested person liable to be so injured by any sale of intoxicated liquors to any person, and desiring to prevent the sale of intoxicating liquors to such person, must give notice, either verbally or in writing, before a witness, to the person or persons so selling or giving the intoxicating liquors, or to the owner or lessor of the premises wherein such intoxicating liquors are given or sold, or file with the township or corporation clerk in the township or municipal corporation wherein such intoxicating liquors may be sold, notice to all liquor dealers not to sell to such person any intoxicating liquors from and after ten days from the date of so filing such notice. Such notice so filed must be entered by the clerk in a book kept for the purpose, and opened to inspection by all interested persons. Such notice may be so erased as not to be legible, at the request of the person who filed it; but while it stands unerased, it inures to the benefit of all persons interested, as though served by each. By refusing to record such notice, the clerk would be subject to fine and forfeiture of office.[1]

3. *To whom damages to minor must be paid.*—All damages recovered by a minor, under this chapter, must be paid either to such minor or to his or her parent, guardian, or next friend, as the court may direct.[2]

4. *Sale works forfeiture of lease.*—The unlawful sale or giving

---

ications were separate and distinct, Miller *v.* Patterson, 31 O. S. 419; but the sale or giving away of liquor must, to give a right of action, be unlawful, Baker *v.* Beckwith, 29 O. S. 314; but it is not necessary that the sale should be in violation of the act of 1854; if sold in violation of any law prohibiting the sale, or if furnished in violation of the supplementary act of April 5, 1866 (63 *v.* 149), the right of action accrues under the amendment of 1870; and it is not error for the court to refuse to charge that if the jury award exemplary damages they should not consider the fact, if such they find the fact to be, that certain of the illegal sales were made on Sunday. Sibila *v.* Bahney, 34 O. S. 399.

[1] § 4358, 4359, 4360.

[2] § 4361.

A married woman has the same right to bring suits, and control them and the amount recovered, as an unmarried woman, under this chapter, § 4361.

away of intoxicating liquors works a forfeiture of all rights of the lessee or tenant under any lease or contract of rent upon premises where such unlawful sale or giving away takes place; and all suits for damages under this chapter must be by a civil action in any court having jurisdiction thereof.[1]

5. *Sellers must not give publicity to notice.*—Saloon-keepers, grocers, or others, are forbidden, under fine of ten to fifty dollars, from posting, printing in any newspaper, or in any other way giving publicity that the notice above mentioned has been given.[2]

6. *Party fined not entitled to exemptions.*—For all fines, costs, and damages assessed against any person in consequence of the sale of intoxicating liquors, as provided in the foregoing paragraphs, the real estate and personal property of such person, of every kind, without exception or exemption, except to heads of families and widows, as specified in section 5430; and such fines, costs, and damages will be a lien upon such real estate until paid.[3]

7. *Liability of owner of premises for fines, etc.*—If a person rent or lease to another, any building or premises to be used or occupied, in whole or in part, for the sale of intoxicating liquors, or permit the same to be so used or occupied, in whole or in part, such building or premises so leased, used or occupied, will be held liable for, and may be sold to pay, all fines, costs, and damages assessed against any person occupying the same; proceedings may be had to subject the same to the payment of any such fine and costs assessed or judgment recovered, or any part thereof, which remain unpaid, either before or after execution issues against the property of the person against whom such fine and costs or judgment have been adjudged or assessed; when execution issues against the property so leased or rented, the officer must proceed to satisfy the same out of the building or premises so leased or occupied.[4]

8. *Guardian's liability.*—If such building or premises belong to a minor, insane person, or idiot, his guardian having control thereof, will be liable and must account to his ward for all damages on account of such use and occupation, and the liabilities for the fines, costs, and damages aforesaid; and all contracts

---

[1] § 4361.   [2] § 4362.   [3] § 4363.   [4] § 4364.

whereby any building or premises are rented or leased, and used or occupied, in whole or in part, for the sale of intoxicating liquors, will be void, and the lessor will, on and after such selling or giving intoxicating liquors, be considered and held to be in possession of such building or premises.[1]

9. *Criminal provision as to selling such liquor to minor.*—Whoever sells intoxicating liquors to a minor, except upon the written order of his parent, guardian, or family physician, is liable to a fine of not more than fifty, nor less than five dollars.[2]

---

[1] 4364, [2] § 6941.

15

CHAPTER 18.

REAL CONTRACTS OF WARD'S ANCESTOR.

REAL CONTRACTS OF WARD'S ANCESTOR.

1. *Action to complete contract for land.*   When a person, who has entered into a written contract for the sale and conveyance of an interest in land, dies before the completion thereof, and his executor, administrator, or other legal representative, desires to complete the contract, he may file a petition therefor in the court of common pleas or probate court of the county in which the land, or any part thereof, is situate; if the petition be filed in the probate court, service may be made therein as in civil actions; and the heirs at law, devisees, or other legal representatives of the deceased vendor, when not plaintiffs, must be made defendants in the action.[1]

2. *When court may order conveyance; deed, and its effect.*   The court, after causing to be secured to and for the benefit of the estate of the deceased its just part and proportion of the consideration of the contract, may authorize the executor, administrator, or other legal representative to complete the contract, and to execute a deed for and on behalf of the heirs at law to the purchaser, which must recite the order, and will be as binding on the heirs at law, and all other persons interested, as if it had been made by the deceased in his lifetime.[2]

3. *Heirs at law or devisees may compel conveyence.*   The heirs at law or devisees of a person who purchased an interest in land

---

[1] § 5800.   [2] § 5801.

by written contract, and died before conveyance thereof to him, may compel such conveyance as the deceased might have done.[1]

4. *So may guardian of minor heirs or devisees.* The provisions of the three preceding paragraphs enable the guardian of any minor heirs of any person who had entered into such a written contract for the purchase of land or other real property, to compel the conveyance to be made, in the same manner as such person might have done if living.

5–12. *Form of petition when guardian desires to complete a purchase for minor heir.*

—— county, ss., Court of Common Pleas [*or*, Probate Court].

A. B., guardian of C. D., plaintiff,
vs.
O. P., defendant. } *Petition to complete contract for sale of land.*

Plaintiff says that he is the duly appointed guardian of said C. D., a minor child of E. D., deceased, late of —— county, Ohio; that on the —— day of ——, A. D. 18 —, the said E. D., then in full life, entered into a contract, in writing, with said O. P. for the sale of the following described real estate, situated in [*here describe the property, as should be in a deed*].

Plaintiff further says, that said sale was to be on the following terms [*state the terms*], as will appear by said contract [*or, a copy of said contract*]. hereto annexed.

[*Here state in plain language all other pertinent facts, as for instance:*] Plaintiff further says, that said E. D., during his lifetime, paid to said O. P. [*here state what he paid, and when*]. and that plaintiff, as guardian as aforesaid, is ready and willing to pay the balance due on said contract.

Plaintiff therefore prays, that said O. P. be ordered to execute and deliver to said C. D. a good and valid deed in fee simple for said land, and that plaintiff, as guardian as aforesaid. be authorized and directed to pay to said defendant the amount still due, as above stated, at the time of the delivery of said deed as aforesaid; and that in default of his making such deed, that the

---

[1] §5802. The order of the probate court in such cases may be appealed from. See paragraph 1, chapter 24.

As to the effect of the right of dower in such cases, see Raff's Guide, chapter XII.

decree of the court shall operate as such deed, and transfer and convey the title of said land to said C. D., as fully and effectually as such deed would do.   A. B., guardian.

[or, E. H., att'y. for plaintiff.]

The State of Ohio, —— county, ss.

A. B., being sworn, says that he is the plaintiff above named, and that the various matters set forth in the foregoing petition are true, as he verily believes.   A. B.

Sworn to [or, affirmed] before me, and signed in my presence, this —— day of ——, A. D. 18 —.   E. C.,

Notary Public, —— county, O.

13. *Other forms in such cases.*—For other forms easily adapted to the matter in the preceding paragraphs relating to real contracts, see paragraphs 43–59, chapter 19.

CHAPTER 19.

GUARDIANSHIP OF LUNATICS, IDIOTS AND IMBECILES.

1. *Probate court must appoint.*—The probate court, upon satisfactory proof that any person resident of the county, or having a legal settlement in any township thereof, is an idiot,[1] imbecile, or lunatic, must appoint a guardian for such person.[1]

2. *Will be guardian of ward's minor children.*—Such guardian will, by virtue of such appointment, be the guardian of the minor children of his ward, unless the court shall appoint some other person as their guardian.[2]

3. *Who is an imbecile?*—An imbecile, in this chapter, must be understood to mean a person who, not born idiotic, has become so.[2]

4. *When wife may be appointed guardian.*—When any person having a wife shall be declared to be an idiot, imbecile, or lunatic, the probate judge may appoint the wife of such person his guardian, if it be made to appear to the satisfaction of the judge that she is competent to discharge the duties of such appointment.[3]

5. *Her and her sureties' liability.*—Any married woman appointed such guardian will, in her said capacity, have power to enter into official bonds, and she and her sureties thereon will be liable in the same manner, and to the same extent, as though said bond was executed by an unmarried woman.[3]

---

[1] § 6302.

Under the act of January 29, 1824, to provide for the safe keeping of idiots, etc. (2 Chase, 1318), a county can not be charged with the maintenance of an idiot, lunatic, or insane pauper, until after the appointment of a guardian by the court. Tp. *v.* County, 10 O. 283.

[2] § 6302.   [3] § 6303.

6. *Laws applicable to such guardians; their settlement.*—All laws relating to guardians for minors and their wards, and all laws pointing out the duties, rights, and liabilities of such guardians and their sureties, in force for the time being, are applicable to guardians for idiots, imbeciles, and lunatics, and their children, except as otherwise specially provided; but in the settlement of the accounts of such guardians, no voucher can be received from or allowed as a credit to the guardian of any idiot, imbecile, or lunatic, which is signed or purports to be signed by such idiot, imbecile, or lunatic; and any settlement of the account of any such guardian heretofore made, in which any such receipt shall have been allowed as credit to such guardian, will be held and deemed absolutely null and void, and any settlement made by any such guardian must, at any time within two years after the appointment of another guardian, or after the disability of such ward may be removed, or such ward may die, be opened up and reviewed. on the motion of such newly appointed guardian, or legal representative. or of any interested person.[1]

7. *Notice of motion to reopen settlement.*—Notice of such motion must be given by publication or otherwise as the probate judge may direct.[1]

8. *Form of motion to open up settlement.*—Such motion may be in form as follows:

9. Probate Court of ——— county, Ohio.

In the matter of guardianship ⎱ *Motion to re-open settlement of*
      of C. D.   ⎰   *A. B., late guardian of C. D.*

G. H., guardian [*or, other interested person*], represents that said A. B., in his settlement of his accounts as said guardian, received credit on a certain voucher [*briefly describe it*], which voucher purports to have been signed by said C. D.

Said G. H. therefore moves the court to open up and review said settlement, and to declare the same null and void.

G. H., Guardian [or, otherwise, as may be].

10. Form of Notice of Such Motion.

To A. B., late guardian of C. D.

You are hereby notified that a motion has been filed in the

---

[1] § 6304.

probate court of —— county to open up the settlement of your accounts as said guardian, and to have the same declared null and void, because of the credit you received on a certain voucher [*briefly describe it*], purporting to have been signed by said C. D.; and that said motion will be for hearing on the —— day of ——, 18—, at — o'clock — M.   G. H., Guardian [*etc.*]

11. *How served.*—This notice may be served by G. H., by the sheriff, by publication, or otherwise, as the court may direct. If served by publication, the third person, instead of the second, may be used, but need not be, as follows: "A. B., late guardian of C. D., is hereby notified that" [*etc., giving same in substance as above*].

12. *Proof of service.*—Proof of service of notice may be required, as in paragraphs 44–45, in chapter 6.

13. *Suits by guardian of idiot, imbecile, or lunatic, and revivor of same.*—Such guardian may sue in his own name,[1] describing himself as guardian of the ward for whom he sues, and when his guardianship ceases, by his death, removal, or otherwise, or by the decease of his ward, any suit, action, or proceeding then pending will not abate, if the right survive, but his successor as guardian, or such idiot, imbecile, or lunatic, if he be restored to his reason, or the executor or administrator of such idiot, imbecile, or lunatic, as the case may require, must be made party to the suit or other proceeding, in like manner as is or may be provided by law for making an executor or administrator party to a suit or proceeding of a like kind, where the plaintiff dies during its pendency.[2]

14. *How insane person must sue.*—The action of an insane person must be brought by his guardian.[3]

---

[1] Must sue in his own name. Wageman *v.* Brown, 1 W. L. J. (Clermont co., O. S. C.) 454.

[2] § 6305.

Parties who are united in interest must be joined, as plaintiffs or defendants; but if the consent of one who should have been joined as plaintiff can not be obtained, or, if he is insane, and the consent of his guardian can not be obtained, or he has no guardian, and that fact is stated in the petition, he may be made a defendant. § 5007.

[3] § 4998.

15. *How insane person must defend.*—The defense of an insane person must be by his legally appointed guardian, or, if there is no guardian, or the guardian has an adverse interest, by a trustee for the suit, appointed by the court; and if the insanity of a party be discovered, or he become insane, after the action is brought, it must be thereafter prosecuted or defended by his guardian, or his trustee appointed, as provided in this paragraph.[1]

16. *Guardian must deny what, in answer.*—The guardian of a person of unsound mind must deny, in his answer filed in court, all allegations of the petition prejudicial to such defendant.[2]

17. *Duties and compensation of guardian ad litem and trustee.*—The court must require a guardian ad litem, or a trustee appointed under paragraph 15, above, faithfully to discharge his duty, and, upon his failure so to do, may remove him, and appoint another in his stead; and the court may fix a compensation for his services, which must be taxed in the costs against the insane person.[3]

18. *How insanity of a party determined.*—When the insanity of a party is not manifest to the court, and the fact of insanity is disputed by a party or an attorney in the action, the court may try the question, or impanel a jury to try the same.[4]

19. *Sale of real estate by guardian of idiot, imbecile, or lunatic.* Whenever the sale of the real estate of such ward is necessary for his support, or the support of his family, or the payment of his debts, or such sale will be for the interest of such ward, or his children, the guardian may sell the same under like pro-

---

[1] ₴ 5000.

Prior to the adoption of the act from which this section was taken, the court could appoint a guardian *ad litem* to defend the suit for a lunatic non-resident defendant, brought into court by publication; and no decree could be taken against him without an answer from his guardian *ad litem*. Sturges *v.* Longworth, 1 O. S. 545.   See note 1, page 272.

[2] ₴ 5078.

The probate court has no power to set a guardian over the person, property, and minor children of a man upon ex parte affidavits that he is insane, without notice to him of the proceeding while he is a resident of the county, and in no way concealed.   (Guernsey Co. O. C. P., 1858).   Cox *v.* Cox, 1 W. L. M. 96.

[3] ₴ 5001.   See par. 31, chap. 23.   [4] ₴ 5002.

ceedings[1] as are or may be required by law to authorize the sale of real estate by the guardian of a minor.[2]

20. *May be at private sale.*—If it be more for the interest of such idiot, imbecile, or lunatic, or his children, the probate court, upon the petition of the guardian, may authorize him to sell said real estate at private sale, either in whole or in parcels, and upon such terms of payment as shall be prescribed by the court.[2]

21. *Petition and hearing thereof—Order of court.*—Said petition must contain a pertinent description of the real estate proposed to be sold, a statement of its value as nearly as can be ascertained, and the facts on which the application is founded. If, upon hearing, the court shall be satisfied that it will be more for the interest of the ward that said real estate should be sold at private than at public sale, the court may make an order authorizing said sale, and prescribing the terms thereof.[2]

22. *Additional bond of guardian.*—Before making such sale, the court must take from said guardian a sufficient bond for the faithful performance of his duty in the premises, and for accounting for the proceeds of all sales made under said order; but the guardian can not be authorized to sell the real estate at private sale for less than its full appraised value.[2]

23. *When wife a party: her expectancy of dower.*—If the ward have a wife, she must be made a defendant to the petition; and if she file her answer[3] consenting to the sale free and discharged of all right and expectancy of dower therein, such answer will, on the sale being confirmed, be a full release of her expectancy of dower, and unless in such answer she waive any allowance in lieu of dower, the court must allow her, out of the proceeds of the sale, such sum in money[4] as is the just and reasonable value of her expectancy of dower.[2]

24. *Dower of insane, etc., widow: how assigned or sold by guardian.*—The guardian of an idiot, imbecile, or insane widow, who has or is supposed to have a right of dower in any lands or ten-

---

[1] See chapter 6. The forms there given can be readily adapted to the requirements of the sale of lands under this chapter.

[2] § 6306.   [3] See paragraphs 70–73, chapter 6.

[4] This sum is usually computed by means of the tables of mortality in use among life insurance companies. For one of such tables, see Raff's Guide, page 331.

ements, of which her husband was seized as an estate of inheritance, or in any land held by bond, article, or other evidence of claim, where the dower has not been assigned, has power to sell, compromise, or adjust the same upon such terms as he may deem for the interest of such widow, and as the probate court of the county in which the guardian was appointed shall approve; and after such approval, the guardian may execute and deliver all needful deeds, releases, and agreements for the sale, compromise, or assignment of such dower.[1]

25. *Guardian should make written report.*—The guardian should make a clear report in writing to the court of every act done by virtue of the power given in the preceding paragraph, and get the court's approval thereof. What these acts will be depend so much upon the circumstances of each case that no general forms can be given; but somewhat similar forms are found in chapter 6.

26. *Leasing and improving by guardian.*—Such guardian may also, in like manner as the guardian of a minor, and on like proceedings,[2] be authorized to lease and improve the real estate of his ward; and if the lease extend beyond the time of the restoration of such ward to sound mind, or his death, such lease will determine on his restoration or death, unless the same be confirmed by such ward or his legal representatives.[3]

27. *Rights of tenant.*—If such lease determine by reason of the restoration of the ward or his death, the tenant will have a lien on the premises for any sum or sums expended by him in pursuance of the lease in making improvements, and for which compensation shall not have been made either by the rent or otherwise.[3]

28. *Long lease by guardian may be authorized by court.*—Such guardian may also be authorized by the probate court to lease the real estate of his ward or any part thereof for any limited term of years or by perpetual lease, with or without the privilege of purchase, whenever the court, on his application, shall find that the same is necessary for the support of his ward, or the support of his family, or that such leasing will be for the best interests of him or them.[4]

29. *Lease for three years without order of court.*—Such guardian

---

[1] § 6307.   [2] See chapter 7.   [3] § 6308.   [4] § 6309.

may lease the real estate of his ward for any term not exceeding three years, without any application to the court.[1]

30. *Application for authority to make long lease.*—The application for authority to make such long lease or leases must be by petition, setting forth the character of the idiocy, imbecility, or lunacy of the ward; whether curable or incurable; temporary or confirmed, and its duration; the number, names, ages, and residence of the family of the ward, including the wife or husband of the ward, and of those who have the next estate of inheritance from said ward, all of whom, as well as the ward, must be made defendants; and the petition must also contain a description of the real estate; its value, and the amount for which it can probably be leased; the reasons for the proposed lease, and the terms, covenants, conditions, and stipulations on which it is proposed to lease the same.[2]

31–36. *Form of petition for long lease.*—The following form may be used, of course changing the statements to conform to the facts of the case:

State of Ohio, —— County, ss.   Probate Court.

A. B., as guardian of C. D.,
   plaintiff,
       vs.

Said C. D., H. D., wife of said C. D., and M. D., a minor, aged 15 years, L. D., a minor, aged 11 years, and J. D., a minor, aged 4 years, children of said C. D., defendants.

Petition for authority to lease land.

Petitioner represents that said C. D. is an insane person whose insanity, as plaintiff is informed by said C. D.'s physicians, and as he verily believes, is hereditary and violent, incurable and confirmed; that said C. D. has been insane since the month of ——, 18—; that he has a family consisting of his co-defendants above named, all residing on the farm of said C. D., in said county, said farm being more definitely described below; that the three defendants last above named are the only children of

---

[1] § 6309.   [2] § 6310.

said C. D., and are, therefore, together with said H. D., the persons who have the next estate of inheritance from said C. D.; that said farm contains one quarter section of land, described as follows: [*Here describe the land as it should be in a deed*]; that said farm is probably worth sixteen thousand dollars; that it can be leased for eleven hundred dollars, money rent, per year, if leased for a term of five years, with the privilege of purchase at the expiration of lease, at the price of $16,000.00; that if not so leased, plaintiff believes it can not be leased at as favorable terms, if at all; that said C. D. owns said farm in fee simple, unincumbered, and personal property amounting to about $2,000.00 in value, and nothing else; that said defendants are all dependent on the income of said property, and they can not work said farm themselves, said defendant J. D. being the only son, and too young to do any work; that it is proposed to lease said farm upon the following terms, covenants, conditions, and stipulations, to-wit: [*Here give them; or, if this can be done, say,* upon the terms, covenants, conditions, and stipulations set forth in the proposed lease to G. L., a true copy of which is hereto appended, and made a part hereof].

Plaintiff therefore prays the court that he may be authorized to lease said farm on the terms, etc., and in the manner designated above.   A. B. [*or,* H. M., attorney for plaintiff].

The State of Ohio, —— county, *ss.:*

A. B., being sworn, says that he is the plaintiff in the foregoing petition, and that the various matters therein stated are true, as he verily believes.   A. B.

Sworn to before me, and signed in my presence, this —— day of ——, 18—.   J. H., Notary public, —— county, Ohio.

37. *Proceedings on the application.*—On filing the petition, the same proceedings[1] must be had as on petition for sale of the real estate of a minor, except that the appraisers must appraise not only the value of the real estate, but also the value of its annual rent upon the terms, covenants, conditions, and stipulations of the lease as proposed in the petition; and the appraisers must also state in their report their opinion whether the proposed lease

---

[1] See chapter 6.

will be to the interest of the ward and his family; and they may also suggest any change in the terms, covenants, conditions, and stipulations proposed in the petition; on the return of the appraisement, the guardian will not be required to give an additional bond; but, in case of sale under the terms of the lease, he must be required to give such bond before the confirmation of the sale.[1]

38. *Final hearing and orders.*—Upon the final hearing, if the prayer of the petition be granted, the court may prescribe the terms, covenants, conditions, and stipulations of the lease, either in accordance with those set forth in the petition or otherwise, and authorizing the lease to be made by public or private letting, as may be deemed best; but in no case can the leasing be allowed for a less rent than that named in the report of the appraisers, and the lease can not take effect till the same, with the security therein, is approved and confirmed.[2]

39. *Completion of real estate contracts.   Additional bond.*—The guardian of an idiot, imbecile, or lunatic, whether appointed by a court in this state or elsewhere, may complete the real contracts of his ward, or any authorized contract of a guardian who has died or been removed, in like manner and by like proceedings as the real contract of a decedent may, under an order of court, be specifically performed by his executor or administrator; but in all cases when the guardian, by virtue of such contract or the completion thereof, shall receive or be entitled to receive any moneys not amply covered by his bond, the court must require of him an additional bond, with sureties, in respect of such moneys.[3]

40. *The law relating to such contracts.*—The provisions of the statutes concerning real contracts of a decedent, mentioned in the preceding paragraph, are given in the next two paragraphs.[4]

41. When a person who has entered into a written contract for the sale and conveyance of an interest in land dies before the completion thereof, and his executor, administrator, or other legal representative, desires to complete the contract, he may file

---

¹ § 6311.   ² § 6312.   ³ § 6313.

[4] As these two sections are brief, they are given here for the convenience of having all the law and the forms relating to this matter together, though the two paragraphs will also be found in chapter 18.

a petition therefor in the court of common pleas or probate court of the county in which the land, or any part thereof, is situated ; if the petition be filed in the probate court, service may be made therein as in civil actions; and the heirs at law, devisees. or other legal representatives of the deceased vendor, when not plaintiffs, must be made defendants in the action.[1]

42. The court, after causing to be secured to and for the benefit of the estate of the deceased. its just part and proportion of the consideration of the contract, may authorize the executor. administrator, or other legal representative, to complete the contract, and to execute a deed for and on behalf of the heirs at law to the purchaser, which must recite the order, and will be as binding on the heirs at law, and all other persons interested, as if it had been made by the deceased in his lifetime.[2]

43–52. *Form of petition* mentioned in paragraph 41, above.

State of Ohio, —— county, *ss.*　Probate court [*or,* court of common pleas].

<table>
<tr><td>A. B., guardian of C. D.. an insane person, plaintiff,
vs.
E. G.. II. I., K. L.. L. D., a minor over 14 years of age, defendants.</td><td>} Petition to complete contract for sale of land.</td></tr>
</table>

Plaintiff represents that on the — day of — A. D.. 18—, the said C. D., then of sound mind, and under no legal disability, entered into a contract in writing with the said E. G., for the sale of the following described real estate, situate in the county of——, and State of Ohio, to-wit : [*describe the property*] upon the following terms : [*state the terms*] as will appear by said contract [*or,* a copy of said contract] hereto attached. [*Here set forth in plain language all other pertinent facts, as for instance :*]

That said E. G. paid to said C. D., while yet of sound mind, the first, second, and third installments, and has paid to said plaintiff, since the insanity of said C. D., the fourth installment of said purchase-money.　And plaintiff says that said E. G. is ready and willing to pay the balance due upon said contract, as soon as a valid deed can be made to him for said premises.

---

[1] § 5800.　　　　　　　　　　[2] § 5801.

Plaintiff further represents that all the other defendants named are heirs at law of said C. D., now insane.

Plaintiff therefore prays that said heirs at law may be made defendants to this petition, and that said plaintiff may be authorized, upon payment of the residue of said purchase money, to execute and deliver to said E. G., in behalf of the aforesaid C. D., and his heirs at law, a deed in fee simple for the real estate hereinbefore described. A. B., Guardian,

[*or, H. G., attorney for plaintiff.*

The State of Ohio, —— county, *ss.*

A. B., being sworn, says [*and conclude in all respects as in paragraph* 12, *page* 228].

53–54. *Journal entry, ordering guardian to make deed, and give bond, when required.*

A. B., guardian of C. D., ⎫
     vs.   ⎬ *Petiton to complete contract.*
  E. G. and others. ⎭

[If there are minor defendants, first enter the appointment of a guardian *ad litem.* See par. 15, chap. 23.]

The said defendants having been all legally notified of the pendency of said petition, this cause now comes on for hearing upon said petition, the answer of the guardian *ad litem*, and the testimony. And the court being fully advised in the premises, finds that said C. D., on the —— day of —— A. D., 18—, being then of sound mind and under no legal disability, entered into a contract in writing with E. G., for the sale of the premises, in the petition described; that said E. G. paid the first, second, and third installments of the purchase money to said C. D., before his insanity, and has since paid to the petitioner the fourth installment of the same; and the said E. G. is ready and willing to comply with so much of said contract as remains unfulfilled by him, so soon as a valid deed for said premises can be made to him. It is therefore ordered, that upon payment of the residue of said purchase money, said A. B., guardian for and on behalf of the said C. D. and his heirs at law, execute and deliver to said E. G. a deed in fee simple for said premises, according to the statute in such case made and provided [*add, when so,*], and that said guardian gave an additional bond in the sum of —— dollars for the payment to the proper persons of the money to come into his hands by reason of the completing of said contract.

55–57. Form of additional bond, when guardian completes real contract, and such bond is required.

Know all men by these presents, that we, A. B., as principal, and L. R. and S. T. are held and firmly bound unto the State of Ohio, in the sum of —— dollars, for the payment of which we hereby jointly and severally bind ourselves, our heirs, executors, and administrators, if default is made in the condition following:

Whereas, In a certain cause in the —— court of —— county, Ohio, wherein said A. B., as guardian of C. D., is plaintiff, and E. G. is defendant, [*or,* E. G. and others are defendants,) the said A. B. has been ordered by said court to complete the real contract described in the petition in said cause.

Now, if the said A. B. shall account for and pay over to the persons entitled thereto, all the money that shall come into his hands by reason of the completing of said contract, then this obligation will be void; otherwise it will be and remain in full force and effect.

Signed and sealed by us, at ——, this — day of —— A. D. 18—.

Executed in presence of   A. B. [SEAL.]

                         L. R. [SEAL.]

                         S. T. [SEAL.]

58–59. Deed of guardian in preceding case.

Know all men by these presents, that, whereas, on the —— day of —— A. D. 18—, A. B., guardian of C. D., an insane person, filed his petition in the probate court within and for the county of —— and State of Ohio, against E. G. and others, heirs at law of said C. D., for authority to make a deed to E. G., on behalf of the said C. D., and of his heirs at law, for the following described real estate, situate in said county of ——, and State of Ohio, to-wit: [*describe the property,*] in compliance with the terms of a contract in writing entered into on the —— day of ——, A. D. 18—, between the said C. D., then of sound mind, and said E. G. And, whereas, such proceedings were had that the said A. B. was ordered by said court as guardian as aforesaid, and for and on be-

16

half of the said C. D. and his heirs, to execute and deliver to the said E. G. a deed in fee simple for said premises, upon payment of the purchase money remaining unpaid, which order is in words as follows, to-wit: [*here copy the order in full, inclosing it in quotation marks*], all of which will more fully appear by the records of said court, to which reference is here made: and the said E. G. having paid the residue of said purchase money; now, therefore, I, the said A. B., guardian of said C. D., by virtue of the powers in me vested by law and the order of said court, for and on behalf of the said C. D. and his heirs, do hereby give, grant, bargain, sell, and convey unto the said E. G. the premises hereinbefore described, with all and singular the appurtenances, to have and to hold the same unto him, the said E. G., and unto his heirs and assigns forever.

Signed, sealed, and acknowledged   A. B.,
     in our presence.   as guardian as aforesaid.

This deed must be acknowledged just as shown in par. 190, of chapter 6.

60. *Insolvency of lunatic.*—If the estate of the idiot, imbecile, or lunatic, is insolvent, or will probably be insolvent, such estate must be settled by the guardian in like manner, and like proceedings may be had as is or may be required by law for the settlement of the insolvent estate of a deceased person.[1]

61. *Foreign guardian of foreign idiot, imbecile, or lunatic may dispose of property belonging to his ward.*—The foreign guardian (conservator, trustee, or other person having power similar to those of guardians in this State), of a foreign idiot, imbecile, or lunatic, appointed in any other State of the United States, or any territory thereof, may possess, manage, or dispose of the real and personal estate of his ward, situate in this State, in like manner and with like authority as guardians of idiots, imbeciles, or lunatics appointed by the courts of this State, after complying with the following requirements: First—An authenticated copy of the foreign commission of idiocy or lunacy proved, allowed, and recorded in the probate court of the county, or one of the counties, in which such estate is situate, in like manner as is or may be provided by law for the admission to record of an au-

---

[1] § 6314. See Raff's Guide, chapter 9.

thenticated[1] copy of a will made in any other of the United States. Second—Evidence satisfactory to the court here, before which such foreign commission is approved, that such idiocy or lunacy still continues. Third—The foreign guardian, conservator, trustee, or other person, having powers similar to those of guardians in this State, must file his bond, with sureties, residing in this State or elsewhere, to the acceptance of the court, conditioned for the faithful administration of his guardianship.[2]

62. *Termination of guardianship; settlement.*—Whenever the probate judge shall be satisfied that an idiot, imbecile, or lunatic, or a person as to whom guardianship has been granted as such, is restored to reason, or that letters of guardianship have been improperly issued, he must make an entry upon the journal that said guardianship terminate; and the guardianship thereupon ceases, and the accounts of the guardian must be settled by the court.[3]

---

[1] "Authenticated copies of wills, executed and proved according to the laws of any state or territory of the United States, relative to any property in the State of Ohio, may be admitted to record in the probate court of any county in this state, where any part of such property may be situated; and such authenticated copies, so recorded, shall have the same validity in law as wills made in this state, in conformity with the laws thereof, are declared to have: provided, that where any such will, or authenticated copy has been or shall hereafter be admitted to record, in the probate court of any county in this state, where any part of such property may be situated, a copy of such recorded will, with the copy of the order to record the same, annexed thereto, certified by the probate judge, under the seal of his court, may be filed and recorded in the office of the probate judge of any other county in this state, where any part of such property is situated, and it will be as effectual, in all cases, as the authenticated copy of said will would be if proved and admitted to record by the court." §5937.

[2] §6315. The "First" and "Second" are incomplete sentences, mean what? Copied from the statutes.

[3] §6316.

"No more precise limit can be assigned to the authority of guardians over insane persons and spendthrifts, than that of the ward's necessities. When he becomes restored to reason or is otherwise fit to control his own person and estate, this guardianship ceases; for the purposes of the trust are felt no longer. But a period so difficult to fix should be judiciously determined; for which cause a formal discharge from guardianship is to be sought and obtained; and, meantime, the guardian's authority will continue." Schouler's Dom. Rel. 424 (Citing Dyce Sombre's case, 1 Phil. Ch. 437; Hovey v. Har-

63. *Petition to discharge land of dower of insane woman.*—A person owning real estate in this State, incumbered by the contingent or vested right of dower of an insane woman, may apply, by petition, to the court of common pleas of the county in which the real estate, or any part of it, is situate, making defendants thereto such insane woman, and also her husband and guardian, if she has either or both, for leave to sell all or any part of such real estate, discharged and unincumbered of such contingent or vested right. This petition must set forth the insanity of the woman, together with a description of the land proposed to be sold; the court must thereupon appoint a committee of six competent men, of whom at least three are physicians, who must, under oath, inquire into the fact of the insanity of such woman, and must hear testimony to be produced by her husband or guardian, or, if there is no such guardian, by her guardian ad litem,[1] to be appointed by the court in the action; and the committee must, at any term of such court, make a report in writing of the result of their investigation, signed by all the members of the committee.[2]

64. *Inquest of lunacy.*—If the committee report unanimously that such woman is, in their opinion, permanently insane, the court must appoint three judicious freeholders to appraise the real estate mentioned in the petition, whether the same is in one or several counties, who must report in writing the value of each tract.[3]

65. *Proceedings on report of such fact to court.*—Upon the filing of such report the court may direct such petitioner to convey, by good and sufficient deed of conveyance, to the insane woman, to be by her held in fee, such proportion of the real estate set forth in the petition as shall seem just and proper to the court, or the court may assign to such insane woman, to be by her held during life, after the death of her husband, if she has a husband, such proportion of the real estate set forth in the petition, as seems right and proper to the court, for her support; or the court may order the petitioner to invest an amount, to be fixed

mon, 49 Me. 269; Wendell's case, 1 Johns. Ch. 600; Kimball *v.* Fiske, 39 N. H. 110; Chase *v.* Hathaway, 14 Mass. 222).

To similar effect, 3 Redf. on Wills, 458–9.

[1] See chapter 23.   [2] § 5722.   [3] § 5723

by court, in the stock of a company, or stocks created by the laws of this State, as may be designated by the court, the profits and dividends arising from such investment to be applied to the support and maintenance of the insane woman after the death of her husband, if she has a husband; and the petitioner may, upon his compliance with the order of the court, sell all the real property he is possessed of, described in his petition, free and unincumbered of the contingent or vested right of dower of such insane woman.[1]

66. *How dower of insane womon may be barred.*—When the husband of an insane woman conveys any real estate in this State, owned by him, in which such insane woman has a contingent or vested right of dower, by virtue of such ownership of her husband, or otherwise, and she does not join her husband in such conveyance, he may apply by petition to the court of common pleas of the county in which she resides, or, if she resides out of the State, then in which the real estate is situate, for leave to have any part or all of such real estate so conveyed, released and disincumbered of her dower right therein, which petition must set forth the insanity of the wife, and a description of the land proposed to be affected ; to which petition the insane wife, her guardian, if she has one, and all persons in interest, must be made defendants, and the petition must be proceeded in, in all respects, in the manner prescribed in the three preceding paragraphs, except that instead of ordering the petitioner to sell the real estate, or to convey or assign to such insane woman any part thereof, the court must direct the petitioner to make such investment as provided in said paragraphs, or may require the petitioner to secure the amount to the use of the insane woman by the mortgage to her of unincumbered real estate of at least double the value thereof; and upon compliance by the petitioner with the order of the court, the court must enter a judgment releasing and discharging the real estate from the incumbrance of such contingent or vested right of dower. and must adjudge the holder of the legal title, or other party liable to pay to the petitioner any sum withheld or retained as indemnity against such dower right.[2]

---

[1] § 5724.   [2] § 5725.

67. *How wife of insane husband may convey her lands.*—When the wife of an idiot, lunatic, or insane person, who has been declared to be such by inquest according to law, is the legal or equitable owner of real estate in this state which she desires to sell, convey, or mortgage, during the disability of her husband, she may apply by petition to the court of common pleas of the county in which the real estate is situate for leave to sell, by contract or conveyance, or to mortgage, all or any part of such real estate. Such petition must set forth the insanity, idiocy, or lunacy of the husband, as the case may be, together with a description of the land which she desires to sell, convey, or mortgage.[1]

68. *Proceedings for such purpose. Guardian's duties, etc.*—The guardian of such husband must be made a party to the action, and be required to state any reason he may know why the petition should not be granted. Upon satisfactory proof that the sale or mortgage of such land will be for the benefit of such married woman, the court must authorize her to sell, mortgage, or convey the premises in the petition described, upon such terms, and upon such conditions as to the disposition of the money arising therefrom, as the court may direct. Such sale, conveyance, or mortgage will have the same force and effect as though made by a feme sole; and all right, title, and interest of such husband in such lands and tenements will be forever thereafter barred.[2]

69. *Apartments for lunatics, etc., in county infirmary.*—The commissioners of every county in which there now is, or may hereafter be, established a county infirmary, must provide separate apartments, in or adjoining such infirmary, for the safe keeping and treatment of lunatics and idiots, residents in such county, and who have not been and can not be received into either of the lunatic asylums, or who have been discharged therefrom.[3]

70. *Who admitted, and how provided for.*—The directors of the county infirmary, as soon as apartments are provided, as mentioned above, must admit therein all lunatics and idiots who are or may become a charge upon their county, and provide for their safe keeping, support and treatment, in such manner as they now

---

[1] § 4130.　　　　　[2] § 4131.　　　　　[3] § 970.

do for the poor under their care, and also must receive and provide for the safe keeping, support, and treatment of such lunatics and idiots, in their county, who, by their guardians or friends, may apply for admission, as pay patients, under such rules and regulations as the directors prescribe.[1]

71. *Real estate of insane and other paupers; how disposed of.*— When a person is admitted into the infirmary as a pauper, whether insane or otherwise, and such person is possessed of, or is the owner of real estate, or has an interest in reversion, or is in any manner legally entitled to any gift, legacy, or bequest in real estate, the directors must take possession of all such property or other interest such pauper is entitled to, and when they deem advisable and to the best interest of such pauper, must proceed to sell the same; and they must file a petition for that purpose in the court of common pleas, or probate court, in the county where such property is situated; and the proceedings therefor, sale, confirmation of sale and execution of deed by said directors, must be conducted, in all respects, in conformity to the practice and statutory provisions for the sale of real estate by guardians;[2] and the net proceeds arising from such sale must be applied, under the special direction of the directors, in such manner as they think best, to the maintenance of such person during his continuance as a pauper in the infirmary; but if the guardian, husband, wife, heirs, or persons who are entitled to the residuary interest in the property of said pauper, give bond to the directors of the infirmary, to their satisfaction, and pay into the hands of the clerk of the board of directors, at such times as the directors require, an amount sufficient to support said pauper while he remains in the infirmary, the directors can not take charge of said property.[3]

72. *Certain duties of assessors as to guardians of insane, etc.*— Each assessor, at the time of taking a list of property for taxation in the year 1882, and every fourth year thereafter, must take an enumeration of all deaf and dumb, blind, insane, and idiotic persons, whose usual place of residence is in any family, jail, or infirmary in his township or precinct, on the day preceding the second Monday of April, together with their names in

---

[1] § 971.[2] See chap. 6.[3] § 972.

full, their age, and the duration of their muteness, blindness, insanity, or idiocy; and he must make out a list of said deaf and dumb, blind, insane, and idiotic persons, designating those of each class, and the names of their parents or guardians, and post-office address; and he must return the same to the county auditor on or before the third Monday of May in the same year.[1]

73. *How boundary of land of idiot or insane person may be fixed by written instrument.*—See paragraph 73, chap. 19.

---

[1] § 1526.

CHAPTER 20.

GUARDIANSHIP OF DRUNKARDS.

1. *When guardian to be appointed for drunkard.*—The probate court, upon satisfactory proof that any person resident of the county wherein the application may be made, is incapable of taking care of and preserving his or her property, by reason of intemperance or habitual drunkenness, must forthwith appoint a guardian of the property of such person.[1]

2. *Will be guardian of drunkard's minor children, unless.*—Such guardian will, by virtue of such appointment, be guardian also of the minor child or children of his ward, in case no other be appointed.[1]

3. *What laws applicable to.*—All laws relating to guardians for lunatics, idiots, and imbeciles, and their wards, and all laws pointing out the qualifications, duties, rights, and liabilities of such guardians, and their sureties, in force for the time being, are applicable to the guardians contemplated by this chapter.[1]

4. *Notice to be served on party, etc.*—At least five, but not more than ten, days before the time when the application for the appointment of the guardian authorized by paragraph 1, above, is made, a notice, in writing, setting forth the time and place of the hearing of the application, must be served upon the person for whose property such appointment may be sought.[2]

---

[1] § 6317.

For forms of application, appointment, etc., readily adapted to such cases, see preceding chapters.

[2] § 6318.

5. *No jury allowed.*—The person for whose property such appointment is sought is not entitled to a jury trial on the hearing of such application.[1]

6-7. *Form of notice.*—The following form of notice would be sufficient:

To G. W.

You are hereby notified that on (*name the day of the week*) the — day of —— A. D. 18—, at — o'clock —. M., an application for the appointment of a guardian of your property will be for hearing in the probate court of —— county, Ohio, in its court-room, in said county, on the ground that, by reason of your intemperance or habitual drunkenness, you are incapable of taking care of or preserving your property.

[Signed]   A. B.

8. *How served.*—This notice may be served in any way the probate judge may direct.[2]   If served by any person other than the sheriff, or other officer in his official capacity, its service should be verified the same as the notice on page 107.

---

[1] The defendant, in the case of Hageny *v.* Cohen, tried in the Hamilton county district court, made an application in the court below for the appointment of a guardian of Hageny, upon the allegation that he was a man, who, by reason of his habitual drunkenness, was incapable of taking care of his property. The guardian was appointed. At the hearing of the case the defendant below demanded a trial by jury, which was refused. The refusal to grant a jury was the ground of error.

Judge Burnet decided the case. He remarked that the counsel for the plaintiff in error had cited the court to a statute existing during the territorial organization of Ohio, by which a jury was allowed, in inquests of lunacy, to determine the question whether the person who was alleged to be a lunatic, was a lunatic in fact. The first constitution contained the same clause that is now contained in the present constitution, that the right of trial by jury shall be held inviolate. Nevertheless, under the practice of the State of Ohio, during the time the first constitution existed, a trial by jury was not given in cases of the appointment of guardians, either for minors or lunatics. The appointment of a guardian to assume control of the property of inebriates was not known in Ohio until the recent statute of 1871. But the right of a trial by jury was not recognized in the hearing of any application for the appointment of a guardian under either the first or the present constitution. The court has no doubt upon the question. It

[2] See par 37, chap. 6.

9. *Subsequent conveyance invalid.* From the time of the service of such notice until the hearing, or the day thereof, as to all persons having notice of such proceeding, no sale, gift, conveyance, or incumbrance, of the property of such intemperate person or habitual drunkard, will be valid.[1]

10. *When guardianship shall terminate.* The court, upon reasonable notice to such guardian, and to the person or persons on

---

was not a matter to which the article of the constitution referred to the plaintiff in error was applicable.

But it was claimed that the court of common pleas had no jurisdiction under the constitution to appoint a guardian, but that this jurisdiction was conferred solely upon the probate court by article 4, section 8, and that it can not be conferred by the legislature on any other court. It was a rule of interpretation of the provisions of the constitution that they should be interpreted with reference to the institution and laws that had previously existed. The only guardians known to the law of Ohio previous to the adoption of this constitution, were the guardians of infants and lunatics. Under the former law such guardians were invested with the control of both the person and estate of their wards. This article of the constitution must be properly understood as applying to that portion of the judicial power which had existed in the state up to the time of the adoption of this constitution, and that it was intended to give to the probate court that jurisdiction which was recognized ordinarily as the probate jurisdiction of the courts of Ohio, and which previously existed in the common pleas courts. This law gives no control over the person of an inebriate, but simply gives to the guardian appointed the right to control his property for his benefit. This court would hesitate to pronounce a law of the legislature unconstitutional, being itself a subordinate court, and, unless the case were very clear, would not feel authorized to render such a decision. In the present case the court thought that the better judgment was that the law was constitutional in this matter therefore the court below had not erred.

It was claimed, however, that the judgment rendered and the findings were contrary to law. At the time the court appointed the guardian, the inebriate was engaged in business, and the court, in addition to appointing the guardian, found that it was for the inebriate's advantage that his business should be continued, and that his wife was a proper person to continue it, and that therefore she should continue it. In this the court erred. The guardian was the proper person under the statute to be invested with the control of the property, and that should have been the order of the court: and if, in his judgment, it was desirable to continue the business, and the wife was the proper person to do it, he would have authority to employ her to conduct the business. 1 Cin. Law Bulletin, 104.

[1] § 6318.

whose application the appointment was made, and satisfactory proof that the necessity for such guardian no longer exists, must order that the relation of guardian and ward terminate, and that the ward be restored to the full control of his property, as before the appointment.[1]

---

[1] § 6319.

CHAPTER 21.

TRUSTEES GENERALLY, AND THEIR ACCOUNTING.

1. *All trustees must render biennial accounts, same as executors, etc.*—Any trustee of any non-resident idiot, imbecile, or lunatic, appointed as in chap. 22, and any trustee heretofore or hereafter created by any last will or deed, or appointed by any competent authority, to execute any trust created by any such last will or deed, must, as often as once each two years, render an account of the execution of his said trust to the probate court of the

county in which he was appointed, or in which such last will or deed may be recorded, in the manner provided by law for the settlement of the accounts of executors and administrators.[1]

2. *Exceptions to above.*—The provisions in the preceding paragraph do not apply in any case in which the will or deed creating such trust designates any other tribunal for the settlement of the trust, or in which any other tribunal shall have acquired jurisdiction.[1]

3. *Manner of settling executors' and administrators' accounts.*—The only provisions of law relating to the *manner* of settling such accounts are in effect as given in the next three paragraphs.

4. Every executor or administrator must, within eighteen months after having given bond for the discharge of his trust, render his account of his administration upon oath, and he must, in like manner, render such further accounts of his administration, from time to time, and every twelve months thereafter; and also at such other times as may be required by the court until the estate shall be wholly settled; and he may be examined on oath upon any matter relating to his accounts, the payments therein mentioned, and also touching any property or effects of the deceased which have come to his hands.[2]

5. *Account must be sworn to.*—Before filing the account, the executor or administrator must make oath before the probate judge, or some other person authorized to administer oaths generally, that the same is, in all respects, correct, a certificate of which oath must be written upon or attached to such account, and signed by the affiant.[3] When an account is rendered by two or more executors or administrators, the court may, in its discretion, allow it, upon the oath of one, or may require that it be sworn to by all.

6. *Vouchers must be filed.*—In rendering such account, every executor or administrator must produce vouchers for all debts and legacies paid, and for all funeral charges and just and necessary expenses, which vouchers must be filed with the account; and they, together with the account, must be deposited and remain in the probate court.[4]

7–16. *Form of trustee's account, etc.*—The form of such accounts, oaths thereto, etc., may be substantially the same as those

---

given for guardians of minors, on pages 156–7; or the following form of account may be used:

First[1] [or, Second or, Final, etc.] account of A. B., trustee of C. D., a non-resident minor [or, idiot, etc.]

Accountant charges himself as follows:

Amount of sale bill.. $——
    "   received of G. H. on note—Principal...... $——
                                          Interest........ ——   ——
    "   "   " L. S. " book account................. ——
    "   "   " T. C. " note (not inventoried)...... ——
    "   "   for one stove (not inventoried) sold at private sale.............................. ——
    "   "   of R. P. on real estate sold him........... ——
    "   of interest received on sale notes.............. ——
    "   received of the administrator of the estate of H. B., deceased, the father of A. B., deceased. ——
          Etc.,   Etc.

And accountant claims credit for the following payments, made in behalf of said estate:

Paid M. N., appraiser.....................Voucher No. 1...... $——
  " R. S., auctioneer.......................   "   " 2...... ——
  " C. T., for threshing grain..........   "   " 3...... ——
  " C. C., for coffin for deceased.......   "   " 4...... ——
  " Y. B., widow's allowance...........   "   " 5...... ——
  " T. R., physician's bill, last sickness,   "   " 6...... ——
  " L. S., in full of note..................   "   " 7...... ——
  " J. R., " " account.............   "   " 8...... ——
  " S. C., legacy in full..............,.....   "   " 9...... ——
          Etc.   Etc.

Accountant claims the ordinary legal compensation for his services.

And asks that he may be allowed, as compensation for extra services performed, the additional sum of $90.00, for the reasons following:

Accountant says that G. H., from whom he collected the sum

---

[1] See remarks about account, on pages 155, 158.

Where several accounts are filed, it is a good practice to entitle them: "First account," "second account," "final account of," etc.

of —— dollars, resides in ——, state of ——, and that he was compelled to make several trips to that place, in order to secure to the estate the payment of said claim. His necessary expenses were —— dollars, and the time employed —— days. For these, he thinks an extra allowance of $90.00 to be but reasonable.

The notes against T. U., V. W., and R. S., mentioned in the inventory, were not collected, on account of the insolvency of said debtors.

The book account against X. Y., mentioned in the inventory, was paid in the lifetime of the decedent, as appears by his receipt, exhibited to me by said X. Y.

A. B., Trustee, as aforesaid.

17–18. *Affidavit to Partial or Final Account.*

The State of Ohio, —— county, ss.

A. B., trustee of C. D., a non-resident minor [*or*, idiot, *etc.*], being sworn, says that the foregoing account is in all respects just and correct, as he verily believes [*if any of the property was sold at private sale by order of court, here add*], and that the private sale of the property therein mentioned as made by order of court, was made after diligent endeavor to obtain the best price for the same, and that the sale reported is for the highest price that could be obtained for said property.   A. B.

Sworn to and subscribed before me, this —— day of ——, 18—.   A. C., Probate Judge.

19. *Citations and notices.*—The probate court must issue and have served in the same manner as is or may be provided by law, in the case of the settlement of executors and administrators, the necessary citations or notices by publication or otherwise, requiring all persons interested to attend such settlement and make objections thereto, if they have any.[1]

20. *Notice of filing accounts to be published.*—It is the duty of the probate judge to cause notice to be published in some newspaper of the county, of the filing of any accounts by trustees, etc., specifying the time when such accounts will be heard, which must not be less than three weeks after the publication of such notice ; at which time it will be competent for said pro-

---

[1] § 6329.

bate judge, for cause, to allow further time to file exceptions to said accounts.[1]

21. *Costs of notice—how paid.*—The costs of such notice must be paid, if more than one account be specified in the same notice, in equal proportions by the executors, administrators, guardians, trustees, etc., respectively.[1]

22–3. *Form of notice.*—The notice mentioned in the preceding paragraphs may be as follows :

Notice of Trustee's Settlement.

Notice is hereby given that the [*state which*] account of A. B., as trustee of C. D., has been filed in the probate court of —— county, Ohio, for settlement, and that said account will be for hearing on the —— day of ——, 18—, at — o'clock, — M.   All persons interested are required to attend at such settlement, and make known their objections thereto, if any they have.

A. C., Probate Judge.

24. *Examination of accountants under oath.*—The probate judge has full power and authority to examine under oath, all trustees, etc., touching their accounts; and if he thinks proper to do so, he may reduce such examination to writing, and require such trustee to sign the same; and such examination must be filed with the papers in the case.[2]

25. *Probate court to determine as to execution of trust.*—The said court has full power to hear and determine all matters relative to the manner in which the trustee has executed his said trust, and as to the correctness of his accounts rendered as aforesaid.[3]

26. *Court must require final account.*—The probate court has the power to also require any trustee, created as aforesaid within said county, on the determination of his trust, or on the removal or resignation of such trustee, or in case of the death of the trustee, to require his executor or administrator, to render a final account of the manner in which he has executed his said trust, and to hear and determine all matters relating thereto, in the same manner as the accounts of executors and administrators are required by law to be settled,[3] which is as follows.

27. *How executor, etc., compelled to file account.*—Should an ex-

---

[1] § 6402.   [2] § 6403.   [3] § 6330.

17

ecutor or administrator fail to file an account of his administration at such times as the law or the probate court may require, it is the duty of the probate judge of the county, upon the application of any person interested in the estate, to issue an order requiring the person so in default, within some short period named in the writ, to file his account according to law, or to appear and show cause why an attachment should not issue against him for his default.[1]

28. *How order to file account served; judge's duty, if not obeyed.*— The order may be served by a sheriff, constable, or any other person; and upon return being made that the executor or administrator was served by delivering him a correct copy of such writ, and upon his failing to file his account within the time limited by the writ, or to appear and show good reason for such failure, the probate judge is directed by law to issue an attachment against him, and to commit him to the jail of the county until he returns such account, or is discharged by the order of the probate judge.[2]

29. If the executor or administrator should abscond or secrete himself, so that personal service of an order can not be made upon him; or if, after being committed to prison, he should fail to return an account within thirty days, the probate court may revoke his letters, and grant administration to the person next entitled thereto after such delinquent executor or administrator, as in cases of original administration.[3]

30. *Effect of revoking letters.*—By the revocation of his letters such executor or administrator is deprived of all power and control over the estate of the decedent; and suit may be brought upon his bond to recover for any injury sustained by the estate by reason of his default or wrongful acts, and to the full value of all the property received by him belonging to the estate of the decedent and not duly administered.[4]

31. *If trustee imprisoned, how discharged.*—If an executor or administrator be committed to jail for default in filing an account, the probate court may discharge him from custody upon his delivering, on oath, all the property of the deceased under his control to such person as the court may authorize to receive the same.[5]

---

[1] §§ 6178, 6047.   [2] §§ 6048, 6178.   [3] §§ 6049, 6178.
[4] §§ 6050, 6051, 6178.   [5] §§ 6052, 6178.

32. *Trustee may be attached, etc.*—The same proceedings may be had to attach and discharge a trustee, and the same power is vested in the probate judge to revoke his letters in case of his failing to render an account within thirty days after being committed, or of his absconding or concealing himself for the purpose of avoiding the service of an order upon him ; and the same power to grant new letters, and with like effect, as in the case of an executor or administrator.[1]

33. *As to forms.*—The following are the forms alluded to in the preceding paragraphs :

34. *The form* of application for writ of citation against trustee for failing to file his account, may be as follows :

The State of Ohio, —— county, ss.   Probate court.

The State of Ohio, on application
   of H. S.,
        vs.   } *Motion for writ of citation.*

   A. B., Trustee of C. D.

H. B., one of the heirs at law [*or*, widow; *or*, creditor, etc.] of said C. D., respectfully represents that more than [*state how long*] have elapsed since said trust of said A. B. has terminated, and that said A. B. has neglected to file an account of said trust, as by law he is required to do.   The relator therefore moves the court for a writ of citation against the said A. B., and that such proceedings may be had to enforce the filing of such account as may be authorized by law.   **H. B.**

35. *Form of Citation.*

   The State of Ohio, —— county, *ss.*

To A. B., trustee of C. D.

   You are hereby required, on or before the —— day of ——, A. D. 18—, to file an account of your trust of said C. D.'s estate, in the probate court of said county, according to law, or then and there to appear and show cause why an attachment should not issue against you for your default.

   Witness my signature and the seal of said probate court, at ——, this —— day of ——, A. D. 18—.

   [L. S.]   **A. C., Probate Judge.**

---

[1] §§ 6330, 6333, 6178.

36. *Form of Journal Entry of Order of Attachment.*

The State of Ohio. on application of, etc., }
         vs.   *Citation.*
A. B., Trustee of the estate of C. D.

The writ of citation having been returned served, and said defendant having failed to file an account of his trust of the estate of said C. D. within the time limited in that behalf, or to show cause why an attachment should not issue against him for his default, it is ordered that a writ of attachment issue to the sheriff of —— county, to bring the body of said A. B. into this court forthwith, to abide such order as the court may make concerning him in this behalf.

37–8. *Form of Writ of Attachment against Trustee.*

The State of Ohio, —— county, *ss.*

To the sheriff of said county, *greeting:*

Whereas. A. B., trustee of the estate of C. D., was, by the order of the probate court of said county, required to file an account of his trust of said estate, on or before the —— day of ——, A. D. 18—, or to show cause why an attachment should not issue against him for his default; and the said A. B., having failed to comply with the order aforesaid, you are therefore commanded to take the said A. B., and have his body forthwith before said court, to abide such order as may be made concerning him in this behalf. Hereof fail not; and bring this writ with you.

Witness my signature, and the seal of said probate court, at ——, this —— day of ——, A. D. 18—.

[L. S.]   A. C., Probate Judge.

39. *Form of Revocation of the Letters of Trustee.*

A. B., trustee of the estate of C. D., having failed to file an account of his trust of said estate, according to law [*or,* to give an additional bond; *or,* to execute a bond of indemnity to his sureties, etc., *as the cause may be*], although specially required to do so by this court, his letters of trusteeship are hereby revoked and annulled, and he is divested of all power, authority, and control over the estate of said C. D.

40. *Appeal from determination of probate court.*—The determination of the probate court of any settlement of a trustee's account, whether final or intermediate, may be appealed from in the manner provided for an appeal from said court on the settlement of the accounts of executors and administrators, and the like proceedings must be had on such appeal, and the result of such proceedings on appeal certified back to the probate court.[1]

41. *How appeal taken.*—The manner of taking such appeal is stated in chapter 24, of this volume.

42. *Force and effect of the determination.*—The determination of the probate court on any such settlement will have the same force and effect as the like determination as to the account of an administrator or executor;[2] and when an account is settled in

---

[1] ? 6331.

[2] Where the administrators had filed partial accounts, which had been settled by a competent court, and had thereafter made no further or final settlement with the court, but had settled all demands of creditors, and thereupon, at the request of the heirs, made a full and final settlement with the heirs in writing and under seal of all matters of administration, and thereupon surrendered to the heirs the remaining assets: *Held*, that as to all matters that would have been embraced in a final account by such administrators with the court, such settlement by the parties is final and conclusive, unless impeached; that as to all errors or mistakes in settling said partial accounts in court, which had been a matter of record for over twenty years, and must have been known to the heirs, such settlement is final and conclusive, unless impeached.   Piatt *v.* Longworth's Devisees, 27 Ohio St. 159.

That where the names of infants are signed to such final settlement, without lawful authority, they may, on coming of age, if not otherwise debarred, disaffirm the same, and compel the administrators to make final settlement in the proper court. Such infants have a plain, adequate, and complete remedy at law, as to all matters of account, and can not invoke the aid of a court of equity to correct errors or mistakes in such partial or final settlements until they have exhausted their legal remedy. *Ib.*

In an agreement between executors and heirs in lieu of a final account in court, where specified pieces of property are turned over by the executors to the heirs, and claims mutually relinquished, and it is expressed that this is a "full and complete settlement" of all matters that have been administered on, this language is not broad enough to cover a claim for a breach of trust, outside the line of the executors, and not then known to the heirs. *Ib.*

An account rendered by an executor or administrator, and settled by the probate court, is not final, so as to bar further inquiry in regard to the assets of the estate in the hands of the executor or administrator, not accounted for or passed on.   McAfee *v.* Phillips, 25 Ohio St. 374.

the absence of any person adversely interested, and without actual notice to him, the account may be opened on his filing exceptions to the account, at any time within eight months thereafter; and upon any settlement of an account by a trustee, all his former accounts may be so far opened as to correct any mistake or error therein, excepting that any matter of dispute between two parties, which had been previously heard and determined by the court, can not be again brought in question by either of the same parties without leave of the court.[1]

The settlement of an account of an executor or administrator by the probate court is conclusive, as against parties with actual notice of the settlement, of all matters set out and specified therein, and as to such matters the party rendering the account can not be required to account a second time, unless the same is impeached for fraud or manifest error. *Ib.*

Where such an account has been rendered and settled, the probate court may, at any time within the time limited by the statute, compel the executor or administrator to render a further account of any assets of the estate in his hands not settled in a former account. *Ib.*

Under section 169 of the administration act (1 S. & C. 599), the filing of exceptions to an account of an executor or administrator in the settlement of an estate, raises a matter of dispute between the exceptor and such executor or administrator as to the items of said account excepted. Stayner's case, 33 Ohio St. 481.

When such matter in dispute has been duly heard and determined by the court, it can not again be called in question by either of the same parties on the hearing of a subsequent account, without leave of the court. *Ib.*

Exceptions are filed to items of a partial account, which are heard and determined by the probate court. On appeal to the common pleas, the matter in dispute is again fully heard and determined: *Held,* That the hearing and determination of the matters involved in the exceptions by the common pleas is final and conclusive in the probate court between the same parties, on the hearing of all subsequent accounts. In such case, the probate court has no power to open up or disregard the order, a judgment, of the court of common pleas in the settlement of the disputed items in the former account. *Ib.*

The provision of said section 169, which authorizes the opening up of all former accounts for the correction of errors or mistakes therein, upon the filing of subsequent accounts, does not authorize the probate court to open up or vacate, at the instance of either of the parties thereto, a former order by the court of common pleas on appeal, in the settlement of a former account. *Ib.*

[1] § 6332.

43. *Allowance of compensation.*—The probate court has power to make such allowance as compensation to trustees for their services and expenses in executing their trusts, as the court may deem just and equitable, not exceeding the compensation allowed to guardians for like services ;[1] and said judge is entitled to the same fees as in the settlements of administrators and executors.[2]

44. *When the court may accept resignation of trustee, or remove him.*—The probate court may accept the resignation of any trustee accounting therein or who has accounted therein, or who has been appointed thereby, or may remove any such trustee for any cause for which the guardian of a minor may be removed, or because the interests of the trust require his removal.[3]

45. *Form of resignation.*

To the Hon., the Judge of the Probate Court of ——— County, Ohio :

The undersigned, trustee of [*state what*], hereby tenders his resignation of said trust, and prays that it may be accepted.

A. B., Trustee.

46. *Form of journal entry of acceptance of resignation.*

A. B., trustee of ———, having tendered his resignation of said trust, the same is, for a good cause, accepted.

47. *Form of removal of trustee.*—[See paragraph 39, this chapter.]

---

[1] See pars. 27–34, chapter 6.   [2] § 6333.   [3] § 6334.

CHAPTER 22.

TRUSTEES FOR NON-RESIDENTS.

1. *How trustees are appointed for non-residents.*—When any minor, idiot, lunatic, or imbecile, residing out of this state, has any real estate, goods, chattels, rights, credits, moneys, or effects in this state, the probate court of the county where such property or any part of it may be situate, has power, whenever it considers it necessary, to appoint a trustee of such minor, idiot, lunatic, or imbecile, to manage, collect, lease, and take care of such property.[1]

2. *How appointment brought about.*—The probate court can make such appointment without waiting for any action on the part of any third person; yet the facts which make apparent the necessity of such action will generally be brought to the knowledge of the court by some friend or relative of such non-resident; and in conformity to the usual practice in that court, the best way to proceed would be for such friend to see that some proper person, whether himself or some one else, make a written statement to the court, and an application for such appointment.

---

[1] § 6320

3–6. *Form of application, etc., for appointment.*

To the Honorable, the Judge of the probate court, of —— county, Ohio :

Your petitioner represents that C. D. is a minor [*or, idiot, etc.*], aged ——, residing at ——, in the state of ——; that said C. D. is the owner of the following described property, situate in said county of ——Ohio [*or if not all in one county, say* in the state, and part thereof in this county], to-wit:

1. An 80-acre tract of land, in —— township, in this county, known as the " D—— Farm," probable value $6,000 00
2. Lot No. —, in the village of ——, —— county, improved, probable value......... .... 1,000 00
3. Farming utensils on said tract........................... 150 00

      [*Etc., etc. See list on pages* 41, 42.

Your petitioner makes this, his application, to be appointed trustee of said C. D., and offers E. M. residing at ——, and F. N., residing at ——, freeholders, as sureties.

      Petitioner's postoffice address, ...
      His place of residence, ...
      His place of business, ...,...
      His attorneys, ...
      Their office, ...

(*Signed.*)   A. B.

The State of Ohio, —— county, *ss.*

A. B., being duly sworn, says that the foregoing statements are in all respects true and correct, to the best of his knowledge and belief.   A. B.

Sworn to and subscribed before me, this —— day of —— 18—.   A. C., Probate Judge, [*etc*].

7. *Journal entry of appointment*—A proper journal entry of the appointment can readily be adapted from the form on page 43.

8. *Jurisdiction of court.*—The appointment of a trustee, first lawfully made, will extend to all the property and effects of the minor, idiot, lunatic, or imbecile in this state, and will exclude the jurisdiction of the propate court of any other county.[1]

9. *Bond of trustee.* The trustee must give bond, payable to the

---

[1] §6321.

state of Ohio, with such sureties and in such sum as shall be approved by the court, not less than double the value of all the property that will probably come into his hands.[1]

10–12. *Form of trustee's bond.*

Know all men by these presents, That we, A. B., residing at ——, as principal, and E. M., residing at ——, and F. N., residing at ——, as sureties, are held and firmly bound unto the State of Ohio, in the just and full sum of —— dollars, for the payment whereof well and truly to be made, we jointly and severally bind ourselves, our heirs, executors and administrators, and each of them, firmly by these presents. Sealed with our seals, and signed by us at Cincinnati, this —— day of ——, A. D. eighteen hundred and ——.

Whereas, the Honorable the judge of the probate court of said county, on the —— day of A. D., 18—, appointed the said A. B., trustee of C. D., a minor [or, *idiot, etc, as the case may be*], aged —— years, and residing at ——, in the State of ——, but owning property in the State of Ohio. Now, therefore,

The condition of the above obligation is such, that if the said trustee shall well and truly do, perform and discharge with fidelity all and singular the duties, which he, as said trustee, ought to do, perform, and discharge, and act in all things as required by law, then the above obligation shall be void and of no effect, otherwise it shall remain in full force and virtue.

A. B.   [SEAL.]
E. M.   [SEAL.]
F. N.   [SEAL.]

13. *Duties of trustee.*—Such trustee must take upon himself the care and management of the estate and property of such minor, idiot, lunatic, or imbecile, situate in his state, and the collection of debts and other demands due such minor, idiot, lunatic, or imbecile, from persons residing or being in this state, and must settle with the court, and be liable to suit or removal for neglect or misconduct in the performance of his duties, in like manner as is or may be provided by law in respect to guardians

---

[1] 6322.

of minors, and as is, or may be provided by law for the settlement of the accounts of trustees.[1]

14. *May lease or sell real estate as guardian of minor appointed in this state.*—The trustee may lease or sell the real estate of such minor, idiot, lunatic, or imbecile, under the same rules and limitations as are now, or may be provided by law, for the [lease and] sale of real estate by guardians of minors in this state.[2]

15. *How long trustee to hold his office.*—The said trustee must, unless removed by the court, hold his appointment until such minor arrives at the age of majority, whether such minor be under twelve or fourteen years of age or not, at the time of such appointment, or until the disability of such idiot, lunatic, or imbecile, shall be removed, or the minor, idiot, imbecile, or lunatic die.[3]

16. *When and to whom trustee must pay over moneys.*—All moneys due to such minor, idiot, lunatic, or imbecile, in the hands of such trustee, must, during the minority of such minor, or during the disability of such idiot, lunatic, or imbecile, be paid over to the foreign guardian of such minor, idiot, lunatic, or imbecile, so far as necessary or proper for his support and maintenance; or in case of the decease of such minor, or of such idiot, lunatic, or imbecile, to the administrator or other legal representative of such minor, idiot, lunatic, or imbecile : provided, that the court which appointed such trustee must have satisfactory proof, as hereinafter provided, of the authority of such guardian, or administrator, or other legal representative, to receive the moneys or estates of such minor, idiot, lunatic, or

---

[1] § 6322.

[2] § 6323.

These words "lease and" are not in the statutes, but are so evidently necessary to its meaning, that they are here inserted in brackets. The original section, in vol. 72, page 162, is as follows: "The said trustee may sell the real estate of such minor, idiot, lunatic, or imbecile, under the same rules and limitations as are now or may be provided by law for the sale of real estate by guardians of minors in this state."

It would seem that when the words "lease or" were inserted in the first line of the paragraph, the insertion of their corresponding words in the third line was overlooked. This section should be amended.

[3] § 6324.

imbecile, and that the security given by such guardian or administrator, or other legal representative, is sufficient to protect the interest of such minor, idiot, lunatic, or imbecile, or his or her estate, and must, moreover, deem it best for the minor, idiot, lunatic, or imbecile, or his or her estate.[1]

17. *How foreign guardian, etc., may collect money.*—When any foreign guardian, administrator, or other legal representative of such minor, idiot, lunatic, or imbecile, shall apply to have all or any of the moneys or property in the hands of such trustee paid or delivered over to him, he must file his petition, or motion, to that effect, in the court by which such trustee was appointed, giving such trustee thirty days' notice of the time of hearing thereon; and he must also produce an exemplification from under the seal of the office (if there be a seal) of the proper court of the state of his residence, containing all the entries on record in relation to his appointment, giving bond, etc., and authenticated as required by the act of congress in such cases; and upon the hearing thereof, the court must make such order, as, under all the circumstances, it shall deem for the best interests of such minor, idiot, lunatic, or imbecile, or his or her estate.[2]

18–23. *Form of application.*—The application mentioned in the preceding paragraph may be in the following form:

State of Ohio, —— county, ss., Probate Court.

F. G., guardian [*or, admin'r..etc., as may be, of, etc.*]. plaintiff,
  vs.
A. B., trustee of C. D., C. D., [*etc.. naming all who are adversly interested.*   } *Petition to have property paid over.*

Said F. G. represents that he is the guardian of said C. D. [*or, administrator, etc., as may be*], duly appointed by the [*name it*] court of —— county, in the State of ——; that as such guardian [*or, administrator, etc.,*] he has given sufficient and proper bond, and has in all other respects complied with the law, as will further appear from the duly authenticated transcripts of the records of said court, filed herewith, and from further evidence to be produced to this court, on the hearing hereof.

Said F. G., as said foreign guardian, hereby makes application

---

[1] § 6325.   [2] § 6326.

to this court for an order to said A. B., resident trustee of said
C. D., directing him to pay and deliver over to said F. G., guardian, all the moneys and other property of the said C. D., now
in the keeping and control of said A. B., trustee.

F. G.,
Guardian [etc.].

State of ——, county of ——, ss.

F. G., being duly sworn, says that he is the guardian [or otherwise, as may be] mentioned in the foregoing petition, and that
the various matters therein set forth are true, as he verily believes.   F. G.

Sworn to before me, and signed in my presence, on this ——
day of ——, A. D. 18—.   RICHARD ROE,

Notary public in and for said county.

24. Trustee may loan money in certain case.—When any money
of such minor, idiot, lunatic, or imbecile may be in the hands
of such trustee, and not likely to be needed for the support and
education of such minor, idiot, lunatic, or imbecile, said trustee
must loan the same in the same manner as guardians by the laws
of this state are required to loan the moneys of their wards (see
pages 66, 68).

CHAPTER 23.

GUARDIANS AD LITEM.

1. *Definition of.*—A guardian *ad litem*, or, expressed in English, a guardian *for the suit*, is a person appointed by the court to take care of the interests of a minor in a civil action or proceeding.[1]

---

[1] No such guardian is appointed in a criminal suit against a minor, the court there acting as such. Reeve's Dom. Rel. 318; Ward's case, 3 Leigh (Va.), 743.

He is considered an officer of the court, rather than a party to the suit.[1]

2. *Defense by; who appoints.*—Our statutes governing procedure in common pleas, superior, and district courts on appeal, specially provide, that the defense[2] of an infant must be by a guardian for the suit, who may be appointed by the court in which the action is prosecuted, or by a judge thereof, or by a probate judge;[3] and this provision is also made applicable to probate courts.[4]

3. *When appointment must be made.*—The appointment of a guardian *ad litem* can not be made until after service of summons, or publication.[5]

4. *Effect of appointment, if made sooner.*—The appointment of such guardian for minor defendants, who have not been served with process or notice, as the law requires, does not effect an appearance for them, nor give the court jurisdiction over them.[6]

----

[1] Duckett *v.* Stackwell, 12 Mees. & Wels. R. 779; Sinclair *v.* Sinclair, 13 do. 640, 646; Brown *v.* Hull, 16 Vt. 673; Bryant *v.* Livermore, 20 Minn. 313, 342.

[2] If an infant comes of age pending the suit, he can assert his rights at once, for himself; and if he does not, he can not, generally, complain of the acts of his guardian *ad litem.* Mitchell *v.* Berry, 1 Metc. (Ky.) 602.

[3] ¿ 5003. In bastardy proceedings, the death of the mother will not abate the prosecution, if the child is living, but a suggestion of the fact must be made, and the name of the child substituted upon the record for that of the mother, and a guardian ad litem appointed, who will not be liable for costs. ¿ 5628.

The power of courts to appoint guardians ad litem is wholly discretionary, and the acts of inferior courts in this regard will not be reversed. Smith *v.* Taylor, 34 Tex. 589.

The acts of such guardians, when not impeached for fraud, are binding on the infant. Ib.

[4] See paragraphs 30, 31, chapter 6.

A probate court appoints a guardian *ad litem* for an infant solely because of his infancy, the law regarding him as incapable of taking care of himself. Fleming *v.* Johnson, 26 Ark. 421.

[5] ¿ 5004. See, also, cases cited in next note.

[6] Moore *v.* Starks, 1 O. S. 369; Linnville *v.* Darby, 57 Tenn. 306; Graham *v.* Sublett, 6 J. J. Marsh (Ky.) 44; Jones *v.* McGinty, 3 Dana (Ky.) 423; Stanton *v.* Pollard, 24 Miss. 154; Prewett *v.* Ladd, 36 *Ib.* 493; Crippen *v.* Crippen, 1 Head (Tenn.) 128.

To the contrary, Banta *v.* Marsh, 2 A. K. Marsh (Ky.) 166.

5. *Who may be appointed.*—The general rule is that no person interested in the suit, in any way, should be appointed guardian *ad litem.*[1]

6. *How appointed, on whose application.*—The appointment may be made upon the application of the infant, if, being of the age of fourteen years, he apply within twenty days after the return of the summons, or service by publication; and in case of his being under said age, or of his neglect so to apply, the appoint-

———

It was error, on a bill of revivor, to decree against infant defendants, until a guardian *ad litem* had been appointed, St. Clair *v.* Smith, 3 O. 355; Rucker *v.* Moore, 1 Heisk. (Tenn.) 726.

Where a person is sued with certain minor defendants in chancery, as their guardian, and he appears, answers and defends in that capacity, and procures a reversal of the decree against the minors, a second decree against the minors will be reversed, because the record shows no appointment of a guardian *ad litem,* or proof that such person was in fact guardian. Tuttle *v.* Garrett, 74 Ill. 444.

Where an action is commenced against a minor, and judgment against him rendered without the appointment of a guardian *ad litem,* and without his appearance at the trial, and thereafter, on his becoming of age, upon his petition, the judgment is vacated and set aside, and the case set down for trial, it is error then to appoint a guardian *ad litem,* and permit such guardian to take charge of and control the defense; and judgment rendered on such trial against him by his next friend and guardian *ad litem* will be reversed. Patton *v.* Furthmier, 16 Kan. 29.

[1] Parker *v.* Lincoln, 12 Mass. 16; Walker *v.* Crowder, 2 Ired. (N. C.) Eq. 478; Walker *v.* Hallett, 1 Ala. 379; Grant *v.* Van Shoonhoven, 9 Paige (N. Y.) 255; Humes *v.* Shillington, 22 Md. 316; Elrod *v.* Lancaster, 2 Head (Tenn.), 571.

The plaintiff's husband, although father and guardian of infant defendants should not be appointed their guardian *ad litem.* Bicknell *v.* Bicknell, 111 Mass. 265.

To some extent *contra,* see McGuire *v.* McGowan, 4 Desau. (S. C.) 486.

The irregularity of appointing one who was himself not of full age, guardian *ad litem* for an infant plaintiff, *held,* not to be waived by defendants answering to the merits, where he had no knowledge, at the time of answering, of the guardian's nonage. Wolford *v.* Oakley, 43 How. (N. Y.) Pr. 118.

ment may be made on the application of the plaintiff, or a friend of the infant.[1]

7–10. *Form of Application for appointment of Guardian ad litem.*

Give the title of the case, as for instance:

The State of Ohio, —— county, ss., Probate Court.

A. B., guardian of C. D., a minor, plaintiff,   *Application for ap-*
           vs.   *pointment of guard-*
     Said C. D., defendant.   *ian ad litem.*

The said C. D., a minor over fourteen years of age [*or*, A. B., plaintiff, *or*, L. D., a relative, *or*, S. T., a friend of said C. D., *etc.*], hereby applies for the appointment of a guardian *ad litem* for the said C. D., in this cause, and suggests that R. H. be appointed said guardian.

(*Signed*)   —— ——.

—— ——, 18—.

11. *Notice to appointee, and acceptance by him, necessary.*—The guardian *ad litem* must have notice of his appointment, and must do something to signify his acceptance.[2]

12. *How notice given and office accepted.*—The guardian may be notified in any way the court may direct or sanction; but the rule, prevalent in many tribunals, that the guardian *ad litem* must appear in person in open court, and accept the office, is one worthy of universal adoption. An acceptance in writing, in substantially the following form, should be handed to the court by the person accepting, and this should be approved by the judge, and entered on the record.

---

[1] § 5004.

The appointment of a guardian *ad litem* to an infant not a party to the suit, is a nullity; but where made after such infant became a party defendant, no matter how irregular it may have been, it is not void, but voidable merely; and not being reversed or set aside, the appointment of another is void. Bondurant *v.* Sibley, 1 Ala. Sel. Cas. 489; 37 Ala. 565.

[2] Ewing *v.* Higby, 7 O. 1st pt. 203; St. Clair *v.* Smith, 3 O. 355, 364.

The court will not appoint any person guardian *ad litem* without his written consent. McVicker *v.* Constable, Hupk. (N. Y.) 102.

18

13–14. *Form of Acceptance.*

[*Give title of case, as in pars. 7–10, on page* 273, *or otherwise, as the facts require, and then add*]:

And now comes the said A. L., heretofore appointed guardian *ad litem* of said C. D., a minor defendant [*or, if guardian ad litem of more than one, name them all*], and in open court accepts said appointment.

(*Signed*)　　　　　　　　　　　　　　　　　　　A. L.

15. *Form of Journal Entry Appointing Guardian ad litem.*

[*Give the usual caption.*]

On application of A. B., [*or other person, as may be*], A. L. was this day appointed guardian *ad litem* for C. D., minor defendant to s[illegible] petition; and thereupon said A. L. appeared in open court, and accepted said appointment.

16. *Guardian ad litem can not waive notice or service of summons.* —Section 6144 provides that "no guardian ad litem shall have authority to waive notice or service of summons."[1]　Though

---

[1] To same effect, see Robbins *v.* Robbins, 2 Ind. 74; Gibson *v.* Chouteau, 39 Mo. 536.

Previous to the act of March 23, 1840, there was no such provision of the statute law, and the practice of the courts as to the manner of service upon minors varied throughout the state, and acceptance of service by guardian *ad litem* for infant defendants in some cases, and his appearing and answering for them in others, was held by the supreme court to be sufficient, especially in view of the fact that to hold otherwise would disturb the title to millions of dollars worth of property, though such practice was admitted to be loose and irregular. (See 8 O. S. 617.) "The statute of 1840, for the first time, made the proof of proper notice to the defendants a condition precedent to any action of the court in such a case, and prohibited the waiver of notice by a guardian *ad litem* in behalf of his wards. The statute having been until that time silent on the subject, a previous practice to the contrary, in these particulars, would seem to have been thereby recognized and prohibited in the future. Personal service of process was thus made a condition indispensable to the exercise of jurisdiction, and the practice was made uniform throughout the state." (8 O. S. 618.) See Ewing *v.* Higbee, 7 O. pt. 1, 198; Ewing *v.* Hollister, same, pt. 2, 138; Robb *v.* Irwin, 15 O. 689; Lewis *v.* Lewis, same, 715; Snevely *v.* Lowe, 18 O. 378; Morgan *v.* Burnett, do. 535; Moore *v.* Starks, 1 O. S. 369; Sheldon *v.* Newton, 3 O. S. 494; Benson *v.* Cilley, 8 O. S. 604.

The provision of the act of 1840, above alluded to, is nearly the same as

this section is in the chapter relating to executors and administrators, and this section itself relates to sales of lands by such officers, yet its language is general as to such guardians, and no doubt applies to all cases.

17. *His answer irregular if filed before service.*—An answer by a guardian *ad litem* for infant defendants, when they have not been served with process or otherwise notified according to law, is irregular, as they are not before the court;[1] and such answer will not make them parties.[2]

18. *Effect of his admissions, etc.*—A guardian *ad litem* can not bind his ward by his admissions against such ward;[3] nor can he waive any of such ward's rights, even by his neglect or omission.[4] No decree can be made against an infant upon the admissions of such guardian in his answer.[5]

19. *General duties of guardian ad litem.*—In deciding the ably conducted and important case of Long *v.* Mulford,[6] WHITE, J. used the following language: "The appointment of a guardian *ad litem* is not a mere matter of form. A suit against an infant can not be prosecuted without such guardian; and the object of

---

§ 6144, being in words as follows: "Sec. CXXVII. It shall not be necessary, unless the petition is contested, to appoint guardians *ad litem* for infant defendants; and no such guardian shall have authority to waive notice or service of subpœna." See 38 O. L. 146; S. & C. 590 (125).

[1] Steele *v.* Taylor, 4 Dana (Ky.), 445; Shropshire *v.* Reno, 5 Dana, 583; Ivey *v.* Ingram, 4 Caldw. (Tenn.), 129; see also note 1, above.

[2] Ivey *v.* Ingram, 4 Caldw. (Tenn.), 129; see also note I, above.

[3] Walton *v.* Coulson, 1 McLean, 120; Cooper *v.* Mayhew, 40 Mich. 528; Turner *v.* Jenkins, 79 Ill. 228; Tucker *v.* Bean, 65 Me. 352; Fisher *v.* Fisher, 54 Ill. 231; Crabtree *v.* Niblett, 17 Humph. (Tenn.), 488; Reddick *v.* Bank, 27 Ill. 145; Hitt *v.* Ormsbee, 12 Ill. 166; Tuttle *v.* Garrett, 16 Ill. 354; Masterson *v.* Wiswould, 18 Ill. 48; Carr *v.* Fielden, do. 77; Taylor *v.* Parker, 1 Smith (Ind.), 225; Crain *v.* Parker, do. 374; Benson *v.* Wright, 4 Md. Ch. 278; Revely *v.* Skinner, 33 Mo. 98; Torrey *v.* Black, 65 Barb. (N. Y.), 417.

[4] Cartwright *v.* Wise, 14 Ill. 417; Quigley *v.* Roberts, 44 Ill. 503; Pugh *v.* Pugh, 9 Ind. 132; Walker *v.* Ferrin, 4 Vt. 523; Isaacs *v.* Boyd, 5 Port. (Ala.), 388; Smith *v.* Redus, 9 Ala. 99; Lenox *v.* Notrebe, Hempst. (U. S.), 251; Chandler *v.* McKinney, 6 Mich. 217.

[5] James *v.* James, 4 Paige (N. Y.), 115; Thayer *v.* Lane, Walk. (Mich), 200; Eaton *v.* Tillinghast, 4 R. I. 276.

[6] 17 O. S. 484, 503–4.

the requirement is to secure to the infant a proper defense. 'It is the duty of a guardian *ad litem* to ascertain from the infant and his friends, or from other sources of information, what are the legal and equitable rights of his ward. And it is the special duty of the guardian to bring those rights directly under the consideration of the court for decision.' Dow *v.* Jewell, 1 Foster (N. H.), 486: Sconce *et al. v.* Whitney, 12 Ill. 150; Knickerbocker *v.* De Frost, 2 Paige (N. Y.), 304; 1 Daniels Ch. Pr. Tit. Infants. His authority is to protect; and the court will not suffer his ward to be prejudiced either by his admissions or his laches. Bing. on Inf. 135. And 'where the answer of the guardion admits the bill to be true, the complainant must prove its allegations with the same strictness as if the answer had interposed a direct and positive denial.' Enos *v.* Capps, 12 Ill. 257; 8 Ohio, 377; 4 Gill. 370."[1]

20. *In executor's, etc., sale of real estate; good rule to appoint generally.*—The statutes provide that, in these proceedings, it will not be necessary, unless the prayer of the petition for a sale is contested, to appoint guardians ad litem for infant heirs or devisees or other persons having the next estate of inheritance from the deceased who are defendants.[2] Yet it will be observed that such appointment is not forbidden in any case; and it is a good rule[3] of practice to appoint such a guardian in every case in which minors are defendants. In such cases, the guardian *ad litem* should satisfy himself that such a sale is necessary or judicious under the circumstances, and if so satisfied, should file such

---

[1] Ceasing to make his remarks general, and applying them to the case under consideration, the judge continues: " It is plain there was no defense by a guardian *ad litem*. The only evidence of the appointment of a guardian is a formal answer, the body of which, like all the other pleadings in the cause, is in the handwriting of the counsel of the brothers [they being the parties adverse to the minors.—ED.], and this answer was only filed at the time of the filing of the decree. It was evidently treated as a mere formal matter. No attention was paid to the interests of the infants, and the suit throughout was conducted as though it were an amicable or *ex parte* proceeding, involving no subject of real controversy. The counsel of the brothers alone appeared in and had the management of the case, and his acts or omissions are chargeable as theirs."

[2] § 6144.

[3] See pars. 64, 65, chap. 6.

an answer as given in paragraphs 22–23, and his duties will then be sufficiently performed. He should in no case offer merely captious opposition.

21. *Answer of such guardian.*—The guardian of an infant, or of a person of unsound mind, must deny in the answer all material allegations of the petition prejudicial to such defendant.[1]

22–23. *Form of answer of guardian ad litem.*

State of Ohio, —— county, ss., Probate Court.

A. B., guardian of C. D.,
     vs. } *Answer of minor defendant.*
Said C. D., his ward.

Now comes the said C. D., minor defendant, by A. L., his duly appointed guardian for this suit, and for answer to the petition in this cause, denies all the allegations therein contained in any way prejudicial to said minor defendant; and further says that he is of tender years, and not acquainted with the law in such cases, and therefore asks the court to protect his rights in this cause, and for such relief as may be just.   C. D.,

          By A. L., his guardian *ad litem.*

24. *Verification not needed.*—The answer of a guardian *ad litem* need not be verified on oath.[2]

---

[1] § 5078.

The answer of a guardian *ad litem* must not be his personal answer, but the answer of the infant by the guardian. Johnson *v.* McCabe, 42 Miss. 255.

Where the answer does not in express terms deny the allegations of the petition, but the record shows that it was so regarded by the court, and the plaintiff was required to prove the allegations of the petition, a judgment rendered against such defendant can not be reversed on error for want of such express denial. Randall *v.* Turner, 17 O. S. 262.

The answer of the guardian *ad litem* alleging his ignorance of the matters contained in the petition, and praying that the rights of his wards may be protected, has the effect of a general denial, and requires proof of all the material averments of the petition. Wood *v.* Butler, 23 O. S. 520.

Where the answer of the guardian admits the bill to be true, the complainant must prove its allegations with the same strictness as if the answer had interposed a direct and positive denial. Long *v.* Mulford, 17 O. S. 484, 503; Massie *v.* Donaldson, 8 O. 377.

Under the act of 1855 (55 v. 54), the guardian could appear and defend for his ward as effectually as if he were appointed guardian *ad litem.* Rankin *v.* Kemp, 21 O. S. 651. See paragraph 15, chapter 19; note 1, p. 233.

[2] § 5103.

25. *Decree under such answer impeachable.*—A decree against minor defendants, rendered upon the answer of their guardian *ad litem*, may be impeached and reversed for fraud.[1]

26. *In proceedings for vacating streets.*—In such proceedings in court as directed by law, such court must appoint, when necessary, a guardian *ad litem* for all minors and insane persons who may be interested in the matter.[2]

27. *Appropriation of property for public use; guardians therein.* The law prescribes how property may be appropriated for public uses by municipal corporations, and provides how application therefor must be made to the common pleas or probate court, what proceedings must be had, etc.,[3] and that if, at the time of such application, it appear that any of the owners of the property sought to be appropriated are infants, or insane, and that they have no guardian, a guardian ad litem must be appointed to act in their behalf.[4]

28. *His expenses incurred should be paid.*—A guardian *ad litem* for an infant defendant, who properly defends and preserves the rights of his ward, and in so doing incurs expense in the employment of counsel, or otherwise, should be reimbursed all reasonable charges paid by him.[5]

29. *Should receive reasonable compensation.*—Such guardians are entitled to reasonable compensation for the services they render, which should be taxed as a part of the costs of the case.[6] The amount of this compensation should of course depend on the amount, character and value of the services rendered, to be determined by the court.

30. *In suits before magistrates.*—When a guardian to the suit

---

[1] Massie *v.* Matthews, 12 O. 351.   [2] § 2656.

[3] § 2656.   [4] § 2213.

[5] Smith *v.* do. 69 Ill. (1873) 308; see also Waring *v.* Crane 2 Paige (N. Y.) 79, 81; Whitaker *v.* Marlan, 1 Cox's Cas. (Eng.) 285; Taner *v.* Ivie, 2 Ves. Jun. (Eng.) R. 466.

The taxing of charges in favor of a guardian *ad litem* must be in the original suit, and while it is still pending, and can not be made after the case is disposed of and gone from the docket. A petition for such taxation, while the cause is pending, will be regarded but a continuance of the original cause. Smith *v.* Smith, 69 Ill. 308 (1873).

[6] Walker *v.* Hallett, 1 Ala. 379. See par. 17, chap. 19

before a justice of the peace, or mayor, is necessary, he must be appointed by the magistrate, as follows: 1. If the infant be plaintiff, the appointment must be made before the summons is issued, upon the application of the infant, if he be of the age of fourteen years, or upward; if under that age, upon the application of some friend; the consent in writing of the guardian to be appointed, and to be responsible for costs, if he fail in the action, must be filed with the justice. 2. If the infant be defendant, the guardian must be appointed before trial; it is the right of the infant to nominate his own gardian, if the infant be over fourteen years of age, and the proposed guardian be present, and consent in writing to be appointed; otherwise the justice may appoint any suitable person who gives such consent.[1]

31. *Form of Consent to be Appointed in Such Cases.*

<table>
<tr><td>A. B., an infant, by C. D., his guardian to the suit, plaintiff,
   vs.
E. M., defendant.</td><td>Before H. M., J. P.,
—— township,
—— county.</td></tr>
</table>

I consent to be appointed guardian in the above suit of A. B., and agree to be responsible for costs, if said A. B. fail in said action.　　　　　　　　　　　　　　　C. D.

——, 18—.

32. The docket entry may be thus on the infant's application: "The said A. B., being an infant upward of the age of fourteen years, on his application, I appoint C. D. his guardian to this suit. The said C. D. appeared and filed his consent thereto in writing, and that he would be responsible for costs."

33. Or, as follows, on the application of the infant's friend: "The said A. B., being an infant under the age of fourteen, on application of his friend C. D., I appointed him guardian to this suit, who filed his consent thereto in writing, and that he would be responsible for costs."

34. *In proceedings relating to lunatics, etc.*—The appointment and special duties of guardians *ad litem* in such matters have already been fully stated, and need not be repeated here.[2]

---

[1] §§ 6474, 1744.　　　　　[2] See pars. 15–17, chap. 19.

CHAPTER 24.

APPEALS.

1. *When appeals may be taken from probate court to court of common pleas.*—In addition to cases specially provided for, appeals may be taken to the court of common pleas, from any order, decision, or judgment of the probate court in settling the accounts of an executor, administrator, guardian, and trustees, and assignees, trustees and commissioners of insolvents; in proceedings for the sale of real estate for the payment of debts; in cases where the probate court has increased or diminished the allowance made by appraisers of any estate to any widow, or minor child or children, for their support for one year; in proceedings against persons suspected of having concealed, embezzled or conveyed away the property of deceased persons; in cases for the completion of real contracts, from any order or decision in the administration of insolvents' estates by assignees, trustees or commissioners; and in proceedings to appoint guardians or trustees for lunatics, idiots imbeciles, or drunkards, by any person against whom such order, decision, or decree shall be made, or may be affected thereby; and the cause so appealed must be tried, heard, and decided in the court of common pleas,

in the same manner as though the said court of common pleas had original jurisdiction thereof.[1]

2. *Appeal bond generally required.*—The person desiring to take an appeal, as provided in the preceding paragraph, must, within twenty days after the making of the order, decision, or decree from which he desires to appeal, give a written undertaking, executed on the part of the person appealing, to the adverse party, with one or more sufficient sureties, to be approved by the probate judge, and conditioned that the party appealing shall abide and perform the order, judgment, or decree of the appellate court, and pay all moneys, costs, and damages, which may be required of or awarded against said party, by such court; when the order, decision, or decree, from which the appeal is taken, directs the payment of money, the undertaking must be in double the amount thereof, and in other cases, in such amount as the probate court prescribes.[2]

3. *Transcript, when to be filed.*—The probate judge must, upon the giving of the undertaking, or notice, as aforesaid, make out an authenticated transcript of the docket or journal entries, and of the order, decision, or decree appealed from, which must be filed with the clerk of the court of common pleas, on or before the second day of the term of said court, next after an undertaking or notice is given, as hereinbefore provided, by the person appealing, and the appeal must thereupon be considered perfected; the original papers pertaining to the cause may be used upon the trial or hearing in the court of common pleas.[3]

4. *Proceeding in common pleas, and certifying same back.*—Upon the decision of any cause, appealed to the court of common pleas, the clerk of said court must make out an authenticated transcript of the order, judgment, and proceedings of said court therein, and must file the same with the probate judge, who must

---

[1] § 6407.

Semble, that the parties have not a right to a trial by jury on an appeal from a judgment of the probate court. 1866. Shroyer *v.* Richmond. 16 O. S. 455, 467.

Quære, whether in proceedings on bonds of executors, guardians, etc., in the probate court, under the act of April 17, 1857, either party has a right to demand a jury. *Ib.*

[2] § 6408   [3] § 6409.

record the same, and the proceedings thereafter must be the same as if such order, judgment, and proceedings had been had in the probate court.[1]

5. *When appeal bond not required of a guardian, etc.*—When the person appealing from any judgment or order, in any court, or before any tribunal, is a party in a fiduciary capacity, in which he has given bond within the state, for the faithful discharge of his duties, and appeals in the interest of the trust, he will not be required to give bond, but must be allowed the appeal by giving written notice to the court of his intention to appeal within the time limited for giving bond.[2] This is also the rule in appeals to the district court.[3]

6. This is also the rule in appeals in matters relating to the appropriation of private property for public use;[4] relating to laying out, vacating, etc., public roads.[5]

---

[1] § 6410.

[2] § 6408. Executors or administrators, whether appointed in this state or elsewhere, who have not given bond in this state, with sureties, agreeably to law, and who were original parties to the action, are not authorized to prosecute an appeal without giving an appeal bond. Dennison *v.* Talmage, 29 O. S. 433; Roberts *v.* Wheeler, W. 697. [No doubt true of guardians also]

Where the law requires the appellant to give such bond, the court from which the appeal is taken has no power, by its order or otherwise, to dispense with the execution of the bond, or to relieve the appellant from the obligation to give it, the court's power in that respect being limited to fixing the amount of the bond, and designating the party to whom it shall be payable. Dennison *v.* Talmage, 29 O. S. 433.

Where the appellant, in a case where such appeal bond is required, neglects to give the same within the time limited for that purpose, the fact that the court below made an order to the effect that no bond was required, does not authorize the appellant to perfect his appeal by afterward giving such bond in the higher court. *Ib.* See Emerick *v.* Armstrong, 1 O. 513; Work *v.* Massie, 6 O. 503.

Such an undertaking, signed by sufficient sureties, is good without the signature of the appellant thereto; and where it is defective in omitting, by mistake, some of the conditions required, the court of common pleas has power to allow an amendment of the undertaking. Johnson *v.* Johnson's Ex'r., 31 O. S. 137,

[3] § 5228. See note 2, this page.   [4] § 2256.

[5] § 4689. See par. 3, chap. 17.

7. *As to bond in error, by guardian.*—The law provides for the giving of bond, among other things, in proceedings to reverse, vacate, or modify a decree in the probate, common pleas, superior, or district court,[1] but it also provides, that guardians who have given bond in this state, with surety, according to law, need not give such bond.[2]

8. *Appeal from probate court; and from common pleas. Bills of exceptions.*—"Appeals shall be allowed from any final order, judgment, or decree of the probate court to the court of common pleas, by any person against whom any such order, judgment, or decree may be made, or who may be affected thereby, in the same manner as is provided for appeals from the probate court to the common pleas in other cases; appeals shall also be allowed from any order or judgment of the court of common pleas, in like manner, to the district court, in proceedings under the sections herein relating to the enforcement of orders of distribution, by any person against whom any such judgment or order may be rendered, or who may be affected thereby, to the same extent and in the same manner as is provided for appeals from the common pleas in other cases; and bills of exceptions may be taken and allowed upon any decision of the probate court, court of common pleas, or district court, in proceedings in this behalf, as in other cases."[3]

9. The foregoing paragraph is from the chapter of the Revised Statutes, relating to executors and administrators; but its language is so general that it is believed to apply to guardians also; the section preceding it in' that chapter is so applicable by its express terms. The section last mentioned is given as paragraph 34 of chapter 5.

10. *Appeals to district court.*—A guardian desiring to appeal his cause to the *district court*, must, at the term in which the judgment or order is rendered, enter on the records notice of such intention; and within thirty days[4] after the rising of the

[1] § 6718.

[2] § 5228.   See note 2, page 282.

[3] § 6203.

[4] As to construction of when this time begins and expires, see Steinberger v. Steinberger, 19 O. 106; Morgan v. Stittigan, 10 W. L. J. 74; Harris v. Gest, 4 O. S. 469; Hoagland v. Schnorr, 17 O. S. 30.

court, give an undertaking with sufficient surety, to be approved by the clerk of the court, or a judge thereof,[1] *unless* he has already given bond, as specified above.

11. In such cases, the clerk, at the expiration of thirty days from the rising of the court, must, if not otherwise directed, make a transcript, which, together with the papers and pleadings filed in the cause, he must transmit to the clerk of the district court, as in other cases of appeal.[2]

12. *Appeals from magistrate's courts.*—Cases tried before a mayor or justice of the peace, and in which a guardian is a party, may, of course, be appealed as other cases in such courts;[3] and guardians would, no doubt, be liable for any loss occasioned to the ward because of his negligence in such appeals.

---

[1] § 5227. [2] § 5228. [3] §§ 1752, 6562, 6563, 6570, 6583–6591.

CHAPTER 25.

MISCELLANEOUS MATTERS.

1. *Foreign minors and guardians; their rights in this state, etc.*—Minors living out of this state, and owning lands within the same, are entitled to the benefit of the laws relating to resident wards; and guardians of minors residing out of this state, who have been appointed according to the laws of the state or territory where they reside, have the right to bring and maintain actions, and enforce the collection of judgments, rendered

in such cases in their favor, in the same manner and to the same
extent that they could do if they had been appointed under the
laws of this state, upon giving security for the costs which may
accrue in such actions, in the same way other non-residents are
obliged to do under the laws of this state.[1]

2. As to sale of lands of such minors, see pages 135–7.

3. *Adjoining owners may fix corner or line by written instrument.*—When the owners of adjoining tracts of land, or of lots
in a municipal corporation, agree upon or fix, in a written instrument, the site of any corner or line, common to such tracts
or lots, containing a pertinent description of such corner or line,
either with or without a plat, executed, acknowledged, and recorded, as is prescribed with respect to deeds, such corner or line
will thenceforth be deemed fixed and established as between the
parties to such agreement, and all persons subsequently deriving
title from them.[2]

4. *Record of such instrument; guardians duties as to, etc.*—Such
agreement must be recorded by the recorder in the book in his
office in which surveys are recorded; and the original agreement, after being so recorded, or a duly certified copy thereof
from the record aforesaid, will be competent evidence in any
court in this state against any party to such agreement or person in privity with him. No such agreement can be executed
by any minor, idiot, lunatic, or insane person; but the same
may be made, executed, and delivered for record, on his behalf,
by his guardian; and when so made, executed, acknowledged,
delivered for record and recorded, will be as effectual against
such minor, idiot, lunatic, or insane person, as if he had been
under no disability, and had performed said acts himself.[3]

5. *Rights, etc., of guardians and wards as to the acts of the State
Board of Public Works.*—The laws provide how the state Board
of Public Works may purchase or appropriate private property
for the use of the state;[4] as these are very extensive and important powers, the law carefully guards the rights of the property-
owners, and designates the mode of proceeding when guardians
and wards, as well as others, are interested. But as the number

---

[1] § 6290.   [2] § 4127.   [3] § 4128.
[4] §§ 7691–7707; see especially 7693.

of guardians and wards whom these proceedings can concern are comparatively few, and to state these proceedings fully would occupy much space, it may be sufficient here to allude to them only, and to state that guardians have as full power to act for their wards in these matters, as their wards themselves would have, were they of full age, and capable of acting for themselves.[1]

6. *Adopted child; rights of and as to.*—The statutes provide, in effect, that when any child is adopted, or heir at law is designated, such child or person becomes the child of the person so adopting him, to all legal intents and purposes, and as such, is the legal child and heir of the adopter, entitled to all the rights and privileges, and subject to all the obligations, of a child of the adopter, born in lawful wedlock; therefore, it follows that the person so adopting a child, or designating an heir, has the right, while such child or person is a minor, of appointing by will a guardian for such minor, who will be governed by the rules relating to any other testamentary guardian; and also has all the rights as natural guardian that he would have were he the actual parent.[2]

7. *Justice of the peace incompetent in certain cases.*—No justice of the peace is permitted by law to try a case in which he is related to either party to the suit, as either guardian or ward.[3]

8. *When guardian liable for militia fines or dues.*—For a fine assessed, or dues levied against a minor, by authority of the laws governing the militia of the state, in case such minor enlisted with the consent of his guardian, the guardian will be liable jointly and severally with his ward, for the amount of his ward's funds in his hands; and all property held in common by any [militia] society or organization, the rules or tenets of which require a community of property, will be liable and bound for all fines assessed, or dues levied, under the provisions of these militia laws against any member of such society or organization.[4]

9. *Survival of actions; revivor of judgments.*—Actions for libel, slander,[5] malicious prosecution, assault, or assault and battery,

---

[1] § 7699.   [2] §§ 3137–3140.   [3] § 584.   [4] § 3066.

[5] In Dial's Adm'r v. Holter, 6 Ohio St. 228, it was held that where the defendant, in an action for libel and slander, died after verdict, but before

for nuisance, and against a justice of the peace for misconduct in office, abate upon the death of either party.[1] In other actions as for *mesne* profits, for an injury to real or personal property for fraud or deceit, for money due, for the recovery of personal property, and many others,[2] the action survives the death of either party, and it may be necessary for the guardian to cause himself to be made plaintiff or defendant, as the case may be. It may also be necessary to revive a judgment which has become dormant.[3] As either case will involve the necessity for employing an attorney, it is not necessary here to give the details of such proceedings.

10. *Certain sureties may require creditors to sue.*—A person bound as surety in a written instrument for the payment of money, or other valuable thing, may, if a right of action accrue thereon, require his creditor, by notice in writing, to commence an action on such instrument forthwith, against the principal debtor; and unless the creditor commence such action within a reasonable time thereafter, and proceed with due diligence, in the ordinary course of law, to recover judgment against the principal debtor for the money or other valuable thing due thereby, and to make, by execution, the amount thereof, the creditor, or the assignee of such instrument, so failing to comply with the requisition of such surety, will thereby forfeit the right which he would otherwise have to demand and receive of such surety the amount due thereon.[4]

---

judgment, the action did not abate, but judgment upon the verdict could be entered after his death.

[1] § 5144.

[2] §§ 4975, 5012, 5145, 5147, 6323, 5675, 5679, 5687, 5628, 5629, 4517.

[3] §§ 5146–5161.

[4] § 5833.

Under a statute similar to this section it was held that when the surety gave notice to the creditor to sue, it was not a compliance with the statute to sue the surety alone.   Starling *v.* Buttles, 2 O. 303.

A surety who has given notice in writing to the creditor to proceed against the principal debtor, must set forth the facts in his answer; he can not otherwise avail himself of it as a defense at the trial.   Headington *v.* Neff, 7 O. pt. 229.

The notice is of no validity unless in writing.   Jenkins *v.* Clarkson, 7 O. 1 pt. 72.

And it must contain an unconditional requirement to commence an action

11. *How guardian may become liable in such case.*—As a guardian may have received such instrument as a part of the ward's estate, he may receive such notice to act, from a surety thereon ; and in such case, he would become personally liable if he neglected to proceed as directed in the preceding paragraph.

12. *Not applicable to guardian's bond, etc.*—The provisions of paragraph 10, above, are not applicable to bonds of guardians, nor to any bond or undertaking required by law to be given in an action or legal proceeding, in any court of this state.[1]

13. *Guardian's power in proceedings to sell entailed estates.*— The statutes provide how entailed estates or other qualified conditional or determinable interests, etc., may be sold, when satisfied that such sale would be for the benefit of the first holder, and do no substantial injury to the heirs in tail, expectancy, reversion, succession, or remainder ; *except* estates in dower or curtesy.[2]

---

forthwith; a notice that the surety "wishes" the creditor "to proceed against the principal debtor," and collect " the claim, or have it arranged in some way," and that the surety does " not wish to remain bail any longer," is not sufficient.   Baker *v.* Kellogg, 29 O. S. 663.

[1] § 5835.

[2] § 5803.   The act of April 4, 1859 (56 *v.* 154), and the acts supplemental thereto, passed March 30, 1864 (61 *v.* 80), and April 13, 1865 (62 *v.* 184), include as well estates created before as after their passage, but as to estates created before their passage they are in conflict with section 19, article 1, and section 28, article 2, of the constitution, and inoperative, Gilpin *v.* Williams, 25 O. S. 283 ; but not as to estates created after their passage.   Nimmons *v.* Westfall, 33 O. S. 213 ; Oyler *v.* Scanlan, 33 O. S. 308.

The act of April 13, 1865, extends and applies the acts of April 4, 1859, and March 3, 1864, to all estates tail or for life with remainder over to any other person or persons, and to all determinable estates which may be created by will, etc., after its passage.   Nimmons *v.* Westfall, *supra.*

Under the act of April 4, 1859, and said supplemental acts, the owner of a life estate in possession created by will subsequent to April 13, 1865, may institute proceedings for the sale of both the life estate and the estate in remainder ; and this may be done notwithstanding the testator provided in the will for the disposition of the land and the determination of the life estate. *Ib.*

A tenant for life who held the remainder in an undivided half of the estate, asked under this section for a sale of an undivided half in fee, and the owners of the other undivided half in remainder objected that such sale would injure them, and the tenant for life having consented to the sale of

19

14. *Sale by consent of guardian, etc.*—All parties in interest may appear voluntarily, and consent in writing to such sale; and testamentary guardians, and guardians appointed by the court of probate, may assent, in the place of their wards, to the sale.[1]

As guardians may be responsible for the proceeds of such sales belonging to their wards, the provisions of law concerning such proceeds will be given below.

15. *How proceeds of sale disposed of.*—All money arising from such sales must, for purposes of descent, succession, reversion, or remainder, have the same character, and be governed by the same principles, as the estate sold, and must pass according to the terms of the deed, will, or other instrument creating the estate.[2]

16. *How proceeds may be invested.*—Money arising from such sales must, under the direction and approval of the court, be invested in the certificates of the funded debt of this state or of the United States, or in bonds secured by mortgage on unincumbered real estate situate in the proper county of double the value of the money secured thereby, exclusive of buildings and other improvements, and of timber, mines, and minerals; or the court may order the same to be reinvested in other real estate within this state, under such restrictions as it may prescribe, which investment must be reported to the court, and subject to its approval and confirmation; the real estate in which the money is re-invested, must, for purposes of descent, succession, reversion, or remainder, have the same character, and be governed by the same principles, as the estate sold, and must pass according to the terms of the deed, will, or other instrument creating the estate sold: the court must appoint competent trustees to invest the money, and manage the same, who must, from time to time, report to the court their proceedings, and the condition of the fund; and the court must require of such trustees security for the faithful discharge of their duty; may, from time to time, require additional security; may remove such trustee for cause,

---

the whole property, and the court having found that such sale would not injure the remaindermen, decreed a sale: Held that there was no error in this decree.   Oyler *v.* Scanlan, 33 Ohio 308.

[1] § 5806.   [2] § 5808.

or reasonable apprehension thereof; and may accept the resignation of a trustee, and fill a vacancy by a new appointment.[1]

17. *Who to receive income, and pay taxes and expenses.*—The net income accruing from such sales must be paid to the person or persons who would be entitled to the use or income of the estate were the same unsold; and all taxes, and the expenses of the investment and management of the fund must be paid by the person or persons entitled to the income thereof.[2]

18. *Such estates may be leased.*—Upon like proceedings the court may direct that such estates be leased for a term of years, renewable or otherwise, as may appear most beneficial, and upon such terms as appear just and equitable; and the rents and profits must be paid to the person or persons who might otherwise be entitled to the use and occupancy of the estate, or the income thereof.[3]

19. *Privileged communications; evidence.*—A person who, if a party, would be restricted in his evidence under the next following paragraph, can, where the property or thing is sold or transferred by an executor, administrator, guardian, trustee, heir, devisee, or legatee, be restricted in the same manner in any action or proceeding concerning such property or thing.[4]

20. *When a party shall not testify.*—A party can not testify where the adverse party is the guardian or trustee of either a deaf and dumb or an insane person, or of a child of a deceased person, or is an executor or administrator, or claims or defends as heir, grantee, assignee, devisee, or legatee, of a deceased person, except: *First.* To facts which occurred subsequent to the appointment of the guardian or trustee of an insane person, and, in the other cases, subsequent to the time the decedent, grantor, assignor, or testator died. *Second.* When the action or proceeding relates to a contract made through an agent, by a person since deceased, and the agent testifies, a party may testify on the same subject. *Third.* If a party, or one having a direct interest, testify to transactions or conversations with another party, the latter may testify as to the same transactions or conversations. *Fourth.* If a party offer evidence of conversations or admissions of the opposite party, the latter may testify con-

---

[1] § 5809.   [2] § 5810.   [3] § 5811.   [4] § 5241.

cerning the same conversations or admissions. *Fifth.* In an action or proceeding by or against a partner or joint contractor, the adverse party can not testify to transactions with, or admissions by a partner or joint contractor since deceased, unless the same were made in the presence of the surviving partner or joint contractor; and this rule can be applied without regard to the character in which the parties sue or are sued. *Sixth.* If the claim or defense is founded on a book account, a party may testify that the book is his account book, that it is a book of original entries, that the entries therein were made by himself, a person since deceased, or a disinterested person non-resident of the county; whereupon the book must be considered to be competent evidence; and such book may be admitted in evidence in any case, without regard to the parties, upon like proof by any competent witness. *Seventh.* If a party, after testifying orally, die, the evidence may be proved, by either party, on a further trial of the case; whereupon the opposite party may testify as to the same matters. *Eighth.* If a party die, and his deposition be offered in evidence, the opposite party may testify as to all competent matters therein. Nothing contained in this paragraph applies to actions for causing death, or actions or proceedings involving the validity of a deed, will, or codicil; and when a case is plainly within the reason and spirit of this and the preceding paragraph, though not within the strict letter, their principles shall be applied.[1]

WARD'S REGISTERED GOVERNMENT BONDS.

21. *How guardian may collect interest of.*—The First Comptroller in the Department of the Treasury of the United

---

[1] § 5242.

This section was eleven times amended from its adoption in the code of 1853 until the adoption of the Revised Statutes. For decisions construing it in its different phases, see A. & G. W. R. Co. *v.* Campbell. 4 O. S. 583; Myres *v.* Walker, 9 O. S. 558; Hoover *v.* Jennings, 11 O. S. 624; Bomberger *v.* Turner, 13 O. S. 263; Stevens *v.* Hartley, 13 O. S. 525; St. Clair *v.* Orr, 16 O. S. 220; Raab's Est., 16 O. S. 273; Bell *v.* Wilson, 17 O. S. 640; Thompson *v.* Thompson, 18 O. S. 73; Doughman *v.* Doughman, 21 O. S. 658; Hubbell *v.* Hubbell, 22 O. S. 208; Baxter *v.* Leith, 28 O. S. 84; McNicol *v.* Johnson, 29 O. S. 85; Baker *v.* Kellogg, 29 O. S. 663; Wolf *v.* Powner, 30 O. S. 472; Mosher *v.* Butler, 31 O. S. 188; Elliott *v.* Shaw, 32 O. S. 431; Black *v.* Hoyt, 33 O. S. 203.

States has recently decided, as is shown in the four next succeeding paragraphs, concerning government bonds registered in the
names of minors, that,

22. *First.* When government bonds are registered in the names
of infants, interest-checks issued in payment of interest thereon
will be delivered and paid only to the proper guardian of such
infants when the secretary of the treasury has been notified of
such infancy.

23. *Second.* Neither the father nor mother of an infant has
the right, as a general rule, to indorse or collect such interest-
checks.

24. *Third.* The guardian of an infant, in order to indorse and
collect interest-checks in favor of his ward, is required to file
with the first auditor, evidence (1) of guardianship, (2) of his
authority being in force, and (3) of the identity of his ward as
the payee in the bonds.

25. *Fourth.* The government is not liable to refund to an infant,
on his arriving at the age of majority, money paid to him on
his indorsement of interest-checks during minority, when the
secretary of the treasury had not been notified of the fact of
infancy.[1]

26. In explanation of the matter in paragraph 24 above, the
First Comptroller of the Department mentioned states as follows:[2]

27. *What will be considered satisfactory proof of guardianship.*
(1) A duly certified copy of the letters of guardianship will be evidence of guardianship. In those states in which no letters issue,
a certified copy of the appointment by the proper court, showing
that the guardian gave bond, and accepted the trust, will be suf-

---

[1] Infant's Case, 2 Lawrence Comptroller's Decisions, 26.

[2] An allusion to the foregoing decision having been seen before its publication, a copy of it was, on request, promptly furnished for use in this book,
then already in press, by the Hon. William Lawrence, the comptroller mentioned. It being also desired to furnish therewith such forms of proof as
would be satisfactory to the treasury department, concerning the points
mentioned in paragraph 24 above, and as nobody except the proper officials
of that department could assume to declare what proof would be so, another
request was sent for such forms; and in answer to this request, the matter
found in paragraphs 27–37, below, was very courteously supplied. These
forms are, therefore, entirely reliable.

ficient. If the appointment does not show acceptance, this may be proved by the affidavit of the guardian or the certificate of the proper court.

28. *Of guardian's authority being in force.*—(2) It will be sufficient evidence that the authority of the guardian is in force if the proper court shall certify the age of the infant as shown in the record, and that the authority of the guardian is in force, with a reference to the statute showing the duration of the office of a guardian; or this may be shown by affidavit, as follows:

29–31. *Form of affidavit, as to guardian's authority.*—

State of Ohio, Logan county, ss.

I, James Smith, being duly sworn, do on oath say, that I am a resident citizen of said county and state: that I am the identical person who is the duly appointed, qualified, and acting guardian of Leila L. Finley, who resides at No. 17 High street, in the city of Bellefontaine, in said county; that she was aged 15 years June 1, 1880, and that my authority as such guardian is in force. The duration of my office of guardian is prescribed by sections 6257, 6258 of the Revised Statutes of Ohio.

JAMES SMITH.

Sworn to by said James Smith before me, and by him subscribed in my presence. this day. at my office in Bellefontaine aforesaid. And I certify that said James Smith is personally well known to me to be the identical person who is said guardian above named. and that he is a credible person.

In witness whereof, I hereto subscribe my name and affix my Notarial Seal, at my office in Bellefontaine aforesaid, April 20, 1881.

[NOTARIAL SEAL]   JOHN M. LAWRENCE,
                    Notary Public in and for said county.

32. *As to form of certificate.*—The form of a certificate may readily be prepared by reference to the foregoing form of affidavit.

33. *How identity of ward shown.*—The identity of the ward as the payee in a bond may be shown by affidavit thus:—

34–37. *Form of Affidavit as to Identity.*

State of Ohio, Logan county, ss.

Personally appeared before me, John M. Lawrence, a notary public in and for said county and state, at my office therein, James Smith, who being by me duly sworn according to law, deposes and says that he is the duly appointed, qualified, and acting guardian of Leila L. Finley, who resides at No. 17 High street, in the city of Bellefontaine, in said county; that his authority as said guardian is in force, and that said Leila L. Finley is the identical person who is the owner of registered bond known as one of the consols of 1907 of the United States, No. 960, for $1,000, issued under the acts of Congress, of July 14, 1870, and January 20, 1871, registered in her name on the books of the register's office, in the department of the treasury of the United States, and that she is still the owner of said bond.

JAMES SMITH.

Sworn to by said James Smith, before me, and by him subscribed in my presence, this day, at my office, in Bellefontaine aforesaid.

And I certify that said James Smith is personally well known to me to be the identical person who is said guardian above named, and that he is a credible person.

In witness whereof, I hereto subscribe my name and affix my notarial seal, at my office, in Bellefontaine aforesaid, April 20, 1881.

JOHN M. LAWRENCE,

[NOTARIAL SEAL.]   *Notary Public in and for said county.*

APPENDIX.

CAN A MARRIED WOMAN BE A GUARDIAN?
(See paragraphs 35, 36, chapter 3.)

1. As the question whether a married woman[1] can properly be appointed guardian in Ohio is an important one, undecided by the courts, and about which there is some difference of opinion, it is deemed best to examine it as briefly as possible with any degree of thoroughness, the intention being to give all authorities found, for and against the writer's opinion in the matter.

CERTAIN GENERAL PRINCIPLES STATED.

2. It is perfectly well established that the common law of England, in so far as its principles are not inconsistent with the genius and spirit of our institutions, our circumstances, state of society, and form of government, not opposed to the settled habits, customs, and policy of the people of this State, is in full force in Ohio.[2]

3. The principles of the common law which determine and prescribe the status of a married woman, are among those which have been adopted in Ohio, and by them her legal condition is fixed here now, *except* in so far as this condition has been expressly modified by our statutes. Where these statutes are silent in this respect, the common law governs. This idea so completely pervades our elementary and standard treatises of law, and our judicial decisions, is so generally accepted as a matter of course both in these and elsewhere, and is so thoroughly interwoven with the entire fabric of our jurisprudence, that it may be called an elementary principle of our theory of the legal structure of society.[3] It is not to *establish* this principle; it is to

---

(1) The unprofessional reader should remember that a widow *has been*, but *is not*, a married woman.

(2) Lindsley *v.* Coats, 1 O. 243, 245; Kerwhacker *v.* R. R., 3 O. 172, 178; King *v.* Beck, 15 O. 559, 563; Bloom *v.* Richards, 2 O. S. 387; R. R. *v.* Keary, 3 O. S. 201, 205.

(3) "We have few statutory provisions on the subject, but, for the most part, the law of husband and wife is common law, and you will find that it savors of its origin in all its leadings features." Walker's American Law, § 101.

"The legal effects of marriage are generally deducible from the common law, by which the husband and wife are regarded as one person, and her legal existence and authority in a degree lost or suspended, during the continuance of the matrimonial union." 2 Kent's Com. 129.

See also: Chitty on Contracts, 11th Am. ed. 231, n. k; Wells on Separate Property Mar. Wom. 83, and below, in note 1, next page; Reeve's Dom. Rel., subject "Baron and Feme.

determine the effect of departures from it by the legislature, that legal decisions have chiefly been necessary.[1]

4. It is considered, at common law, that the legal existence of a married woman is suspended during coverture, or merged in that of her husband;[2] that she is under his control, and so presumably acting under his coercion;[3] and that therefore she is incapable of acting for herself, and that her contracts, in general, are absolutely void.[4]

5. From these general principles alone, the inference would seem to be unavoidable and conclusive that if a married woman can not manage her own separate property and business affairs, except as specially enabled to do so by statute, she certainly can not, unless likewise authorized, manage the affairs and control the property of those whose interests are so jealously guarded as are those of minor wards, and that, in view of the prevalence of these principles, the practice of the courts, referred to on page 30 is well founded.

6. But it may be said that, in equity, if not also at common law, both in England and in the United States, a married woman may be a trustee, and therefore a guardian, though there are no decisions to that effect in Ohio.

7. The following citations and extracts will show that, while a married woman's right to be a trustee, under important restrictions, is generally conceded, yet the weight of authority, to say nothing of the force of our statutes (see paragraphs 64–72, below), is clearly against her right to be a guardian, though this view is not without support, outside of this state.

WHAT STANDARD LAW WRITERS SAY.

8. Perry, in his thorough and quite recent work on Trusts, §§ 49–51, says: "In equity, the absolute interest in the trust fund is

[1] See, among others, Rice v. Railroad, 32 O. S. 380; Alexander v. Morgan, 31 O. S. 546; Levi v. Earl, 30 O. S. 147; Phillips v. Graves, 20 O. S. 371.

Wells, in his lately issued treatise on "Separate Property of Married Women" (1878) says, p. 73: "The statutes we are now considering [*i. e.* statutes as to property, ED.] do not intend to regulate, or modify, or restrain, the principles of the common law in this regard, but to supersede these *to the precise scope and extent of the provisions therein enacted.*"

(2) Swazy v. Antram, 21 O. S. 87; Needles v. do., 7 O. S. 432; Alexander v. Morgan, 31 O. S. 446, 448; Coke Litt. 112 a; Metc. on Cont. 82, 83; 2 Kent Com. 129, 132; 1 Black. Com. 442; 2 Story, Eq. Jur., § 1376; Schouler's Dom. Rel. 10; Bell v. Bell, 36 Ala. 466; s. c. 37 Ala. 536; Burleigh v. Coffin, 28 N. H. 118; Davis v. Burnham, 27 Vt. 568; Cartwright v. Hollis, 5 Tex. 155; note 2, preceding page.

(3) Reeve's Dom. Rel., 98 *et seq.*; Schouler's Dom. Rel. 52; 1 Bish. Mar. Women, §§ 35, 39; Bing. on Inf. and Cov. *182; Scarborough v. Watkins, 9 B. Mon. 545; Phelps v. Phelps, 20 Pick. 559.

(4) 1 Parson's on Contracts, 345, 3 do. 413, and cases cited; Smith on Contracts, 307–9, and cases cited. See also, paragraphs 8, 10, 11, 16, 25, 31, 37, 39, below.

vested in the *cestui que trust*, the trustee is a mere instrument, and any power or authority in the trustee must have the character of a power simply collateral;[1] therefore there is nothing, as respects legal capacity, to prevent a married woman from administering a discretionary trust.[2] . . . "At the same time a husband must always have a large influence over a *feme covert* trustee; indeed, as he would be answerable for her acts, and liable for her breaches of trust, he must, for his own protection, look to the manner in which she administers the fund. And she must join her husband in suits in relation to the trust property.[3] . . . Another inconvenience arises in probate and other trusts, where trustees may be required to give bonds for the faithful administration of the trust. A court of equity may require the trustee to give security for the property, even though the trust arises by operation of law.[4] A married woman can enter into contracts only in relation to her sole and separate estate; and how far she can bind herself, or her estate, by a bond to execute a trust in property, the beneficial interests of which belong to another, would always be a perplexing question, although the sureties on such a bond might be liable.

9. "Subject to these inconveniences, a married woman can always be a trustee; and she may even be a trustee for her husband,[5] as well as her husband for her,[6] and the courts will find means to enforce the trusts; *but they will not appoint married women to such offices, nor will they appoint them to be guardians of minors.*[7] A woman, on the contrary, will be removed from the office, if she is appointed while *sole* and afterward marries."[8]

10. Redfield's Law of Wills (3d vol. p. 569–70, published in 1877) contains matter of similar tenor, of which the following is the essential part: "There seems to be no invincible obstacle against a *feme covert* being made a trustee;[9] but, there being more inconvenience in

(1) Citing Smith *v.* Smith, 21 Beav. 385; Drummond *v.* Tracy, 1 Johns. (N. Y.) 608; Kingham *v.* Lee, 15 Sim. 401; People *v.* Webster, 10 Wend. (N. Y.) 551.

(2) Same cases.

(3) Still *v.* Ruby, 35 Penn. St. 373.

(4) Clark *v.* Saxon, 1 Hill Ch. 69.

(5) Livingston *v.* Livingston, 2 Johns. Ch. 541.

(6) Bennett *v.* Davis, 2 P. Wms. 316; Shirley *v.* do, 9 Paige 363; Jamison *v.* Brady, 6 S. & R. 467 (*et al.*)

(7) *Re* Kaye, L. R. Ch. 387.

(8) Lake *v.* De Lambert, 4 Ves. 595. The trustee in this case had married a foreigner, but Lord Chancellor Loughborough simply remarked that ' it was very inconvenient for a married woman to be a trustee.' "

(9) Citing, at close of paragraph, to same proposition. *Re* Campbell's Trusts, 31 Beav. 176.

calling them to account before the proper tribunals, there will always be more or less objection against the selection of married women for the office of trustee. . . . And as the husband is, from the very necessity of the relation, always responsible for the acts of his wife, even for her breaches of trust, he will naturally exercise a considerable control over her acts; and indeed he must, for the protection of his own interests, constantly exercise a watchful care over her conduct of the trust. This will, of necessity, to a certain extent, combine the agency of another with that of the trustee, whenever the office is devolved upon a married woman. (Citing Kingham v. Lee, 15 Sim. 396, 401; Smith v. Smith, 21 Beav. 385; Drummond v. Tracy, Johns. Eng. Ch. 608.) In short, it seems to be settled, that whenever the wife holds the office of trustee, the husband must act jointly with her. The money or property, constituting the trust fund, can' only properly be delivered upon the joint receipt of the trustee and her husband.[1] . . . So that we must conclude that although there is no positive incapacity in the case of a married woman for becoming trustee, there are, under the present economy of the law of trusts and its administration in the courts of equity, numerous inconveniences which induce the courts to prefer that the administration of trusts should not be embarrassed by any such needless hindrances."

11. Hill, in his treatise on Trustees, page 48, says: "Thus *femes covert*, infants, idiots, and lunatics, and other persons who are *non sui juris*, may become trustees, subject of course to their legal incapacity to deal with the estate vested in them; wherever that incapacity has not been relieved by the legislature for that purpose."[2] But on page 41 he says that he uses the word trustee, in that treatise, as excluding guardians and other fiduciary officers there mentioned.

12. Bishop, in his treatise on Marriage and Divorce, § 527, indefinitely says: "The father is, at common law, in some sense, the guardian of his minor children, though in precisely what sense the books do not seem to be agreed.[3] When he dies the guardianship devolves, not to its full extent, on the mother;[4] but partly so, and what-

---

(1) Drummond v. Tracy, Johns. Eng. Ch., 611.

(2) Citing. Clarke v. Saxon, 1 Hill, ch. 69; Bradish v. Gibbs, 3 J. C. R. 523; Livingstone v. Livingstone, 2 J. C. R. 541; Dundas v. Biddle, 2 Barr, 160; Eyrick v. Hetrick, 1 Harris (Penn.), 494; or, one found an habitual drunkard, Webb v. Deitrich, 7 W. & S. 401. So a *nun* may be a trustee in Maryland, Smith v. Young, 5 Gill. 197.

(3) Macpherson on Infants, 51–62; Miles v. Boyden, 3 Pick. 213; Kenningham v. McLaughlin, 3 T. B. Mon., 30; Forsyth v. Kreakbaum, 7 T. B. Mon. 93; Isaacs v. Boyd, 5 Port., 388; Wilson v. Wright, Dudley (Ga.), 102; Griffing v. Hopkins, Walk (Mich.), 49; Jackson v. Combs, 7 Cow. 36.

(4) Macpherson on Infants, 60–65; Eyre v. Shaftsbury, 2 P. Wms. 103, 116; Roach v. Garvan, 1 Ves. sen. 157, 158; Mendes v. Mendes, 3 Atk. 619, 624, 1 Ves. 91; Dedham v. Natich, 16 Mass. 135, 140; Whipple v. Dow, 2 Mass. 415; Heyward v. Cuthbert, 4

ever guardianship is hers, it has been held, perhaps not justly, continues in her, though she is married a second time.[1] Concerning the latter point, a difficulty arises from the fact, well settled in law, that the second husband is not under obligation to support the wife's children by a former husband, while also he is entitled neither to their services nor their society. And indeed other authority recognizes the doctrine that the second marriage deprives, to some extent at least, the mother of her right of custody over her children by the former marriage."[2]

13. Also, in vol. 2, § 527, Married Women: "'On the marriage of a *feme* guardian, the court of chancery will refer it to a master to appoint a guardian, not for the purpose of removing her, but to ascertain what ought to be done under the altered state of circumstances.'[3] In our own country, a statute sometimes provides that the guardianship shall end on the marriage,[4] but otherwise this does not terminate the guardianship;[5] at least, not in all the States, perhaps it does in some."[6]

14. In McPherson on Infancy, 111, and Reeve's Domestic Relations, 121, both works now quite old, it is stated that a married woman may be guardian; each of these writers citing only Wallis *v.* Campbell, 13 Ves., 517. But an examination of this case (see pars. 27–30) will show that it is an exceptional one, the ward being an illegitimate child;[7] and that for other reasons it is not a sufficient basis for so general and important a principle as that derived from it; and this is especially so in view of the opposing decision and general practice given in paragraph 23.

15. In 4 Bacon's Abridgment, 548, it is stated that "Fixed habits of intemperance constitute a sufficient reason for the removal of a guardian." Also, that it "is improper that the wife of a man addicted to such habits should be guardian, she being subject to his control." (Citing no authorities of any kind.)

16. Tyler on Infancy and Coverture, 257, states that "On the marriage of the mother or other female who has been appointed guardian

<hr>

Des. 445; Tilton *v.* Russell, 11 Ala. 497; Jones *v.* Tevis, 4 Litt. 25; Osborn *v.* Allen, 2 Dutcher, 388; Curtis *v.* Curtis, 5 Gray, 535.

(1) Citing Villareal *v.* Mellish, 2 Swanst. 533; Mellish *v.* De Costa, 2 Atk. 14; Armstrong *v.* Stone, 9 Grat. 102; State *v.* Scott, 10 Fost. (N. H.), 274.

(2) Citing State *v.* Scott, 10 Fost. (N. H.), 274.

(3) 1 Bright Hus. & W. 17, referring to Jones *v.* Powell, 9 Beav. 345; *In re* Gornall, 1 Beav. 347.

(4) Field *v.* Torrey, 7 Vt. 372.

(5) Martin *v.* Foster, 38 Ala. 368.

(6) See 2 Kent Com. 225, 226, and notes.

(7) Illegitimate children are not the subjects of tutelage at common law. 2 Stephen's Com. 320.

to an infant, it is a matter of course to appoint a new guardian, for she is no longer *sui juris*, and has become liable to be controlled by her husband; but she is at liberty to go before the court and propose herself as guardian." (Citing Anonymous, 8 Sim. R. 346; Lee *v.* Gowalt, 1 Bra. R. 347.[1])

17. Kent's Commentaries, vol. 2, p. 226, contains only the following note on this question: "When a *feme sole*, appointed guardian to her infant, married, the court directed an inquiry whether she had not thereby deprived herself of the guardianship, as she was no longer *sui juris*; though it seems she might be reappointed under new sureties." *Re* Gornall, 1 Beav. 347." (See pars. 24–26.)

18. See also note 1, page 24, *ante*.

19. Schouler's standard and quite recent work on "Domestic Relations," (1st Ed., 1870; 2d Ed., 1874) contains the following as to this question:

20. "As concerns the right of a married woman to be appointed guardian there is doubt and uncertainty. The *dicta* are apt to go one way and the decision another; doubtless out of judicial deference to the sex. Some hold that married women are at common law capable of becoming guardians; but they draw their conclusions rather from the analogies of administration than from positive authority in their favor. When it is considered that chancery and probate guardians are a modern creation, the ancient cases, from such species of guardianship as are now extinct, are hardly worth looking after. It is true there are several cases which sustain the acts of married women while acting as guardians, or rather *quasi* guardians; at the same time clear precedents for their actual appointment are wanting.[2] It is lately held in the English Chancery Court, that, while a woman may be co-guardian with a man, her sole appointment is improper.[3] In spite of the liberal tendency of the age, we conclude that while such guardianship would not be deemed absolutely void, and is in fact sometimes sanctioned without investigation, public policy is decidedly against the appointment. Not the least important objection is the

---

(1) This case of Lee *v.* Gowalt was diligently searched for in every series of reports, English and American, but could not be found. This citation is believed to be a typographical error for "*In re* Gornall, 1 Bea. (Beavan) 347." See par. 24–26; For 8 Sim. R. 346, see par. 23.—*Ed.*

(2) (Wallis *v.* Campbell, 13 Ves. 517. This was the case of an illegitimate child. As cited in Macphers. Inf. 111, it might be considered authority for the appointment of married women as guardians.)

(3) (*In Re* Kaye, L. R. 1 Ch. 387.

[Macphers. Inf. 111; Anon., 8 Sim. 346; Gornall's case, 1 Beav. 347; Jarrett *v.* State. 5 Gill & Johns. 27; Palmer *v.* Oakley, 2 Doug. 433; Farrer *v.* Clarke, 29 Miss. 195; Holley *v.* Chamberlain, 1 Redf. 333; Kettletas *v.* Gardner, 1 Paige, 488; *Ex parte* Maxwell, 19 Ind. 88, are also referred to. See these cases below.—*Ed.*]

inability of married women to furnish proper recognizance, and to manage trust property without constantly encountering legal obstacles, all the more troublesome from the present uncertainty of the law of husband and wife. Hence the English rule has been, on the marriage of a female guardian, to choose another in her stead, on the ground that she is no longer *sui juris*, and has become liable to the control of her husband; while she is said to be still at liberty to go before the master to propose herself as her own successor." (Citations not given.)

CASES EXAMINED.

21. References to the following English and American cases, bearing directly on the matter under consideration, have been found, and an examination of them will show, among other things, (1.) That the disinclination of the courts to deprive a mother of the custody of her child is a strong inducement in the minds of the judges to make them construe the law, when possible, in favor of the mother. (2.) That the statutes, in some states, either directly authorize[1] the appointment of a married woman as guardian, or do not, either by implication or otherwise, forbid it: but (3.) That even in these states generally, and by the chancery laws of England, if she can act in that capacity at all, her husband must be joined with her, if a fit person, thereby virtually making him the guardian; and that if *he* is not a fit person to so act, *she* can not be appointed. (4.) That such appointments, even in most cases where permitted, are generally rather excused than sanctioned as proper, and that they are voidable, rather than void. (5.) That generally they are contrary to the policy of the law, and should not be made.

22. If we consider these points with reference to Ohio, we may say (1.) That the custody of the person and the control of the education of a child can not be taken from its mother, if she be a suitable person and the father be dead;[2] and that, therefore, in view of the further fact that there may here be one guardian for the estate only, and a different one for the person,[3] the inducement mentioned above does not exist here; (2.) That, since the husband would really be the guardian, he might very well, if a suitable person, be appointed directly, instead of indirectly. (3.) That our statutes not only do not authorize, but by implication forbid, a married woman's appointment to that trust.[4]

---

(1) See paragraph 65, and references there found.

(2) See paragraph 2, chapter 5.

(3) See paragraphs 17–18, chapter 3.
It should be borne in mind that this is not the case in all states, and that generally the guardian's office entitles him to the control of both the person and the estate of the ward, to the exclusion of all other persons.

(4) See paragraph 64, below, *et seq.*

It must also be borne in mind that the entire system of chancery guardianship in England has sprung up and been matured there by the courts since the founding of the colonies, through which we have inherited the common law, and largely so since the independence of these colonies was declared; and that, therefore, it is a matter of some doubt to what extent the rules of English chancery guardianship would apply to Ohio, even if our statutes cast no light on the question under consideration.[1]

23. In Wickley v. Whaley (reported in 8 Simmons, 346, as *anonymous*), the vice-chancellor held that it was quite of course, where a lady who had been appointed a guardian married, to appoint a new guardian.

24. *In Re* Gornall, 1 Beavan, 347. In 1830, Elizabeth Gornall, an unmarried woman, was appointed guardian of her minor child during his minority, or till further order of court. In 1832, the mother married, and a petition was presented in behalf of the infant, then twelve years old, praying for a reference to a master to approve of a proper person to be his guardian, and a proper amount of maintenance.

25. As against the petition, it was argued that the reference was unnecessary, the mother being already guardian; that a mother has a right to the custody of the person of her children,[2] of which she should not be deprived; that the recognizances were still subsisting, and that it would save expense not to disturb them. *Held*, "I conceive that it is the usual practice to make such a reference on the marriage of a female guardian; it is not, as has been suggested in argument, that this lady, by reason of her marriage, is to be deprived of her child. If the order was to that effect, I should here take a long time before I should make it. Here is an unmarried lady appointed by the court to be the guardian of her child: she is made so under the circumstances under which she is then placed—being a person *sui juris*, acting for herself in every way according to her own judgment and discretion. In that state of things she marries, and thereby loses that independent judgment and discretion, and becomes liable to be controlled by her husband. Is it not fit that the matter should be investigated and inquired into? I think the usual form of doing it is by referring it to a master to approve of a guardian: under the order the mother will be at liberty to propose herself, and it is to be hoped that her application will be successful; it may happen that she and her husband will be found to be the most proper persons to have the

---

(1) See Schouler's Dom. Rel. 395–300. As to statutes, see pars. 64–71, below.
"But the proceeding now under consideration [*i. e.* an administrator's sale of land to pay debts—ED.] is not a chancery proceeding. It is a proceeding in a court of probate, under the statute law of the state. . . ." Robb v. Irwin, 15 O. 689, 700.

(2) Citing Villareal v. Mellish, 2 Swanst. 536.

care and custody of the infant, and that she may be appointed guardian. I can not, however, interfere in that, as it will be a matter for the consideration of the master. I believe this to be the usual order; and I take it to be according to the ordinary rules of practice of this court, under the circumstances which have occurred here, to make such a reference. An inquiry is necessary, for the purpose of ascertaining whether, by the act of marriage, the guardian has not placed herself in circumstances which may not permit her to exercise that proper discretion which ought to be exercised for the benefit of the child The next friend of the child has performed an act of duty to this court in informing it of the guardian's marriage.

26. "As to the recognizances, I can make no other order than that which I understand to be the ordinary and usual order to be made in such cases. It does not follow that the persons who have entered into the recognizances for the mother of the infant would be willing to be sureties for the husband."

27. Wallis *v.* Campbell, 13 Vesey, 517 (Apr. 16, 1807). This entire case as reported, including syllabus, statement of facts, chancellor's decisions, and all, is as follows:

28. [Syllabus] "A married woman appointed guardian of an illegitimate child; and payment ordered to her upon her separate receipt."

29. [Statement of facts] "A married woman being under the Master's Report, appointed the guardian of an illegitimate child; a difficulty arose in the Register's office as to drawing up an order for payment of money to her, without joining her husband. It was therefore mentioned to the Court by Mr. Bell."

30. [Decision] "The Lord Chancellor [Eldon] made an order for payment to her, upon her separate receipt, for the purposes of the order."[1]

31. Kettletas *v.* Gardner, 1 Paige (N. Y. 1829) 488. In January, 1818, James and C. G., his wife, were appointed guardians of M. and John G., two minors. J. G. was removed on account of his intemperance, on complaint being made against him. The other pertinent facts sufficiently appear in the decision of the Chancellor, who says: "The opinion of the master, that the guardian who has become so intemperate as to be occasionally insane, is unfit for a guardian without evidence of a thorough reformation of his habits, is perfectly correct. . . . He was himself a proper subject for guardianship, and continues so, unless he abandoned those habits. The court has no assurance that there is in him any permanent reformation. He has therefore forfeited the guardianship, and must be removed. If it is improper for him to have the management of the estate, it is equally improper for his wife, who is subject to his control.

---

(1) See par. 14, p. 301.

20

The guardianship of the person of one of the infants belongs to the husband, and Mrs. G, is not a proper guardian of the person of the other. The whole guardianship must therefore be changed."

32. Halley *v.* Chamberlain, 1 Redf. (N. Y. 1860) 333. The second and last paragraph of the syllabus in this case is that "The policy of the law is against the appointment of married women as guardians of the estates of minors. And where the mother of the minor is living with a second husband, though otherwise competent, she will not be appointed guardian of his estate."[1]

33. In deciding this case, the surrogate holds that, as the statute (3 N. Y. Rev. Stat. 159, § 32) forbids the granting of letters of *administration* to a married woman, the same reasoning would forbid appointing her guardian of the estate *of* a minor. Also, that as the law gives the Surrogate the power to revoke the letters[2] of a woman who marries, it means that, in connection with other provisions, although she is not incompetent for other reason, yet marriage is of itself a reason for removal. . . . He also says: "Almost all cases reported are where there was a contest for the guardianship of the *person* of the child. The question is but little discussed as to the guardianship of the estate."

34. People *v.* Webster, 10 Wend. 554. Under a general provision of the N. Y. Rev. Stat. 600, §§ 9, 10, declaring that the directors or managers of any corporation whose charter expires or is dissolved, shall become trustees of the creditors and stockholders of said corporation. An incorporated society for the relief of indigent women and children expired. Some of its directors, at this time, were married women. It was held that *such* trustees can not be admitted to defend an action of ejectment in the place of a tenant, without their husbands being joined

35. Delamater *v.* Walmsley, 15 Abb. Pr. (N. Y.; O. S.) 323. "Section 9 of chapter 157 of Laws of 1860 (repealed by the Laws of 1862, ch. 172), which constituted every married woman joint guardian of her children with her husband, related to married women only; and they became, not the sole guardians, but only jointly with their husbands. To such as had no husbands the act did not apply."

36. Swortwont *v.* Swortwont, 2 Redfield (N. Y. 1871), 52. The surrogate's decision is almost all quoted, because, from it the pertinent facts and statutes can be sufficiently learned.

37. "At common law, an unmarried female, otherwise competent, may make as valid contract as a male, and could in like manner be

____

(1) When it is remembered that in N. Y. in the absence of appointment by the surrogate, a mother was, at that time, entitled to manage the estate of her child as guardian in socage, a right she does not have in Ohio, the reasons for holding that, in this state, a married woman can not be guardian of the estate of a minor, are much stronger than in N. Y.

(2) But compare paragraph 70, below, with this.

guardian of minors, because she was free to act as a male, but upon her marriage she ceased to be the free agent she was before; and she in law could make no contract whatever, without the consent or sanction of her husband—she was under his control. This rule was in time somewhat modified, so that, after marriage, with the consent of her husband, she might be appointed administratrix, and her husband was liable for her acts: but this rule was never made applicable to guardians. (Woodruff *v.* Cox, 2 Bradf. 153; Bunce *v.* Vander Grift, 8 Paige, 37.)

38. "Therefore, when even a mother was guardian of her children, and re-married, her guardianship ceased, because she was no longer competent to make a contract, and was under the influence of her new husband, and perhaps another reason may be added—that of the probability of other children, and the partiality that might be shown by the stepfather. There are other reasons, no doubt, within the observation of all, why the guardian in such new relation should be removed. (Lee *v.* Gowatt, 1 Bradf. 346;[1] 2 Bradf. 155; Newhouse *v.* Gale, 1 Redfield, 217.)

39. "Whatever may have been formerly the power of this Court to remove for this cause (marriage), the statute of 1837 invested it with such power (Laws of 1837, p. 530, § 34).

40. "There is no application before me for the appointment of a new guardian in this matter, but it is strenuously insisted by counsel for the guardian, that the laws of 1867 authorize her to be continued as guardian, or rather does continue her such guardian.

41. "I do not agree with the counsel. The statute authorizes the surrogate to appoint a married woman executrix, administratrix, and guardian, and married women are declared therein to be capable to act as such, as though they were single women, and their bonds given on the granting of such letters are to have the same force and effect as though they were not married (2 Laws 1867, p. 783, § 2).

42. "This act is one simply permissive; it makes a married woman competent. It removes her common law disability, and declares her capable to act. She may give a bond the same as if she were sole, which shall be legal and valid as if single; but the statute does not continue the trustee, and the question involved in this matter is untouched. . . .

43. "Let an order be entered removing H. E. S., formerly S., as guardian of her children, by H. B. S., deceased, upon the appointment of a new guardian for said children, and let her account to such new guardian." (Order accordingly.)

44. Newhouse *v.* Gale, 1 Redfield (N. Y., 1853), 217. (Part of syllabus.) "The policy of the statute is against the appointment of married

---

(1) See note 1, par. 16.

women as administratrices or guardians, and of their continuation in office after their marriage subsequent to the issuing of the letters."

45. Field *v.* Torrey, 7 Vt. 372. This case discusses at considerable length the common doctrines and the Vermont statutes relating to the question; but it is only necessary to say that a part of its brief syllabus is to the effect that when an unmarried woman guardian marries, such marriage extinguishes her right under such appointment.

46. *Ex parte* Maxwell, 19 Ind. 88. A married woman applied to the lower court to be appointed guardian of her two minor children by a former marriage, but that court refused to appoint her.

47. On appeal to the supreme court, *Perkins, J.,* held that "by the common law, as administered by the chancery and ecclesiastical courts, a married woman is not disabled to be an executrix, administratrix, or guardian.[1] . . . Our statute touching the capacity of a married woman to act as executrix is simply declaratory of the common law.[2] Touching guardianship, our statute specifies no disabilities. Does it not, then, by the ordinary rules of construction, leave the question of competency to the common law? That law requires, in the judgment of the court, a suitable person. It will occasionally happen, as in this case, that the mother, a married woman, will not only be a suitable, but will, in fact, be peculiarly a proper person to be the guardian of her own children. But she should not be appointed, unless her husband is also a suitable person to act as guardian; because he may be expected to control, in a great measure, the action of his wife. . . ." (See last two paragraphs of note 1, this page.)

48. In Hardin *v.* Helton, 50 Ind. 319, this being a suit on a promissory note, it was incidentally held, citing the case last above, that upon the marriage of a female guardian, it is not necessary that her husband should file in court his written consent to her continuing such guardian, as in the case of the marriage of an executrix or administratrix. . . ."

---

(1) Citing, to sustain this, 2 Story's Eq., §§ 1337-9; 2 Shars.-Black Com. 503, and note 15; Reeve's Dom. Rel. 122; New Am. Encyclopedia, art. Guardian; 1 Williams on Ex. 360.

But an examination of these citations shows that none of them sustain this proposition as to guardians, except Reeve's Dom. Rel., p. 121 (concerning which, see paragraph 14 of this appendix), and the Encyclopedia, which is not a legal authority, and which does not pretend to sustain its position by any citations whatever. What weight, outside of its own state, should be given to this decision, resting on such a foundation, each reader may estimate for himself.

It might also be remarked, that *chancery* and *ecclesiastical* courts do not administer common law.

(2) This statute is to the effect that no married woman shall be entitled to letters testamentary, unless her husband file his consent thereto in writing with the proper clerk, which consent shall make him, jointly with her, responsible for her acts in the premises. 2 R. S. 1876, 491, § 2.

49. Parmer *v.* Oakley, 2 Doug. (Mich.) 433. This case was ably presented to the court, and was fully considered. Though it involved matters not pertinent to the question here under consideration, the following paragraphs of its syllabus are pertinent.

50. "It is not necessary that the guardianship bond, required by R. S., 1827, p. 59, § 5, should be *executed* by the guardian; it is sufficient if a bond, with sufficient securities, be given.

51. "*It seems* that where a married woman, appointed guardian unites with her sureties in the guardianship bond, the bond will be good, notwithstanding her incompetency to execute it.

52. "*It seems* that the decree of a probate court, appointing a *feme covert* guardian, who was incompetent to execute the trust on account of coverture, would bind until reversed; and the acts of such a guardian would be valid.

53. "Both at the common law, and under the statute of 1827 (R. S. 1827, p. 57), a married woman is competent to be a guardian, with the assent of her husband; but not without such assent.

54. "*It seems* that letters of guardianship granted to a wife, without the husband's assent, would be *voidable* merely, not *void*.

55. "The husband's assent may be presumed from his joining his wife in the bond which R. S. 1827, p. 88, § 2 requires a guardian to give before sale of the ward's real estate."

56. Jarrett *v.* State, 5 Gill and Johnson (Md.), 27. This case was also ably presented and considered. It appears from its examination that the Maryland statute imposed upon natural guardians duties similar to the usual duties of other guardians, and the necessity of giving bond. A mother, while unmarried, refused to act as the natural guardian of her child, and another person was appointed. Afterward the mother married, and the guardian died. She was then appointed "natural guardian," accepted, and gave bond. Suit was afterward brought on this bond, she not being made a party defendant. The statute was silent as to whether a married woman could be so appointed, and the validity of her appointment, and consequently of the bond, was attacked. The court decided that the sureties on the bond were liable, and her appointment lawful.

57. Farrar *v.* Clark, 29 Miss. 195. This case occupies only about one page in the report, and contains almost no citations or authorities of any kind. In it, the court held that, as the statute of Mississippi directs that preference shall be given in all cases to the natural guardian or next of kin, unless such person is manifestly unsuitable, Mrs. F. (a married woman) being next of kin and not unsuitable, coverture was not an impediment, and that she was entitled to the guardianship.

58. Spaun *v.* Collins, 18 Miss. 624, and Wood *v.* Stafford, 50 Miss. 370.

The husband of a guardian, by virtue of his wife's appointment, may exercise the powers of a guardian.

59. Cook *v.* Bybee, 24 Tex. 278. "Under the Texas statutes, a mother may be the guardian of her child." (Syllabus.)

An examination of this case shows it to have been a contest between a person claiming to have been appointed testamentary guardian, and the mother, who claimed her right under the statute which (quoting from the decision) provides that "the mother, under certain circumstances, shall be entitled to the guardianship of her minor children, and shall have the custody of their persons, education and estates."

60. Carlisle *v.* Tuttle, 30 Ala. 613, 624; Martin *v.* Foster, 38 Ala. 688. The marriage of a female guardian has the effect of joining the husband in the guardianship.

61. Keene *v.* Guier, 27 La. Ann. 332. In Louisiana,[1] where the mother being the natural tutrix of her minor children, contracts a second marriage, she is required, previous to the marriage, to cause a family meeting to be convened for the purpose of determining whether she shall remain tutrix after the marriage. If she fails in this duty, she loses the tutorship *ipso facto*.

62. *Re* Dagget, 3 Pick. 280. This case is sometimes cited, though erroneously, to sustain the right of a married woman to be guardian. It was an application, by *next friend*, to sell real estate of an infant *feme covert*; but it does not appear whether the next friend was married or single.

63. Graham's Appeal, 1 Dallas (Pa. 1785) decides that the court may appoint as guardian whomever it pleases, subject to its legal discretion, which confines it to persons of the same religious persuasion, of good repute, and approved by the orphan. But there is nothing indicating that the judges had in mind the appointment of a married woman, or any other person not *sui juris*.

IN THE LIGHT OF THE STATUTES.

64. It is of course to be borne in mind that, in such matters, the statutes of the state enacting them are supreme throughout its limits, and that before them all principles of common law and equity must fully give way, no matter how well established in other states or countries.

65. Some states, by statute, expressly empower married women to act as guardians. For instance, in Massachusetts, it is provided that a married woman may be an executrix, administratrix, guardian, or trustee, and bind herself and the estate she represents, without her husband joining in any conveyance or instrument whatever, and be

---

(1) In which the *civil* law prevails; see chap. 1, par. 18.

bound in the same manner and with the same effect in all respects as if she was sole. Stat. 1874, chap. 184; see also Stat. chap. 409, Acts of 1869. And, as may be seen from some of the preceding paragraphs,[1] the laws of several of the other states favor, in greater or less degree, the same policy. We should therefore expect the *decisions* of these states, during the time such laws are in force, to be *of course* favorable to a married woman's right to be a guardian.

66. But the statutes of Ohio provide as follows: "SEC. 6292. When any unmarried woman, who has been or may be appointed guardian of any minor, shall marry, *such marriage shall of itself determine the guardianship* of such woman; and the probate court of the proper county shall appoint another guardian for such minor, to which last-named guardian all the estate of such minor shall, on demand, be delivered up by such former guardian; and she shall forthwith render her guardianship account for *final* settlement."[2]

67. "SEC. 6303. When any person having a wife shall be declared to be an idiot, imbecile, or lunatic, *it shall be lawful* for the probate judge to appoint the wife of such person his guardian, if it be made to appear, to the satisfaction of the judge, that she is competent to discharge the duties of such appointment; and any married woman, appointed such guardian shall, in her said capacity, have power to enter into official bonds, and she and her sureties thereon shall be liable in the same manner, and to the same extent, as though said bond was executed by a feme sole."

68. The inference, from these sections of the statutes, that the law does not allow a married woman to be a guardian, unless expressly authorized, seems to be irresistible and conclusive.

69. But it has been said that the law thus provides for the termination of guardianship by marriage, because the woman's relations are altered by marriage, but that had she been originally appointed after such marriage, as might have been lawfully done, the court and her sureties would have fully understood her situation and relations, and her removal would not have been necessary.

70. Had that been the view of the law, how easily it could have provided that, in case of such marriage, such guardian must give new, or additional bond, or must take out new letters? But it gives no such

---

(1) See paragraphs 41, 42, 47 and notes thereto, 53, 56, 57, 59.

(2) There is a similar provision as to an unmarried woman appointed executrix or administratrix, who afterward marries, the law being so explicit as to provide that marriage shall have the same effect as her death would have had. § 6022. Compare with paragraphs 32, 33, above.

It has been held in England that a *feme covert* might be an administratrix, but that was before 22 and 23 Car. II., which required administrators to give bond. 1 Com. Dig. Tit. Adm'r, B. 6 o, p. 487.

permission. It does not even leave it to the discretion of the judge to remove her, as for other cause, but makes the very act terminate the guardianship, and makes necessary her final settlement.

71. Suppose that we apply this reasoning to other causes of removal: that a guardian's removal from the state determines the guardianship because of changed relations, but that a non-resident of the state might have been originally appointed, and that this removed guardian might consequently be at once re-appointed, as this would necessarily follow. Or that a guardian may be removed because he has *become* a habitual drunkard, but that such a man might have been originally appointed! In these cases, certainly, such reasoning needs no refutation; and the lawmakers have never deemed it necessary to provide against it. But they *did carefully* provide how, in one certain case only, "it shall be lawful" for a married woman to be a guardian, and how she can, in that case, give a good bond.

72. The matter in the preceding paragraphs is, on general principles, as applicable to the other trustees whose duties are treated of in this volume as it is to guardians, with this difference, however, that the provisions of paragraphs 66 and 67 do not, in terms, apply to such trustees. But the other objection to a married woman's being in control of trust property are much the same, whether she be a guardian, executrix, administratrix, or other trustee.

INDEX.

ABSTRACT OF TITLE—
    must be given by guardian to court, when, 31, 39.

ACCEPTANCE—
    of guardianship, 42, 43.
    of guardianship *ad litem*, 273.

ACCOUNTS, FINAL AND OTHER. See GUARDIAN'S ACCOUNT.
    settlement of, in probate court, 7, 12, 26, 50, 150, 163, 243.
    must be recorded, 11, 152, 161.
    can not be made for guardian by judge, clerk, etc., 11, 12.
    must be settled in common pleas court, when, 12.
    mode of keeping, with ward's estate, 47, 152-9.
    when female guardian marries, account must be rendered, 50.
    when ward dies, 51, 88.
    when guardian dies, who must render, 51.
    filing of must be enforced by court, 53, 63, 161, 256-8.
    must be rendered by guardian and trustee, at what times, 26, 50, 63, 150, 253, 257.
    who may compel rendering of, and how, 63, 256-7.
    of money on deposit, how must be kept, 74, 75.
    guardian must pay costs of suit to compel filing of, 86 n.
        and costs caused by his neglect, incompetence, etc., 86 n.
    object of the account, and how made, 151, 152, 153 n., 154-9.
    should be clear and easily understood, why, 152.
    of each ward should be separate, 152.
    form of, 156-9, 254-6.
    final must show, what, 158.
    must be sworn to, how, 159, 254, 256, 257.
    notice of filing must be published, how, etc., 161, 256.
        cost of this, how paid, 161.
    exceptions to, may be filed by whom, etc., 161, 162, 255-6.
        hearing of exceptions 161-2, 255-6.
    settlement of, between guardian and ward, 163.
    guardian must exercise good faith as to, 163 n.
    is only an *ex parte* statement, when, 164 n.
    is a settlement within meaning of the law, when, 165 n.
    journal entry as to filing of, 159.
    journal entries confirming or rejecting, 164-5.
    settlement of, must be in probate court, 162 n. 166 n.
    settlement of, is final when, 165, 166 n.

21

DAMAGES—*Continued.*
    in cases of contested ownership of land, 198.
    caused by intoxicating liquors, to guardian, ward, etc., 221–225.
        must be paid by whom, 221, 224.
        to whom, 221, 223, 225.
        how collected, 224.

DAY—
    of attaining full age, 2

DEATH—
   of guardian.
    does not end surety's liability, 33 n., except, 178. *
    new guardian must be appointed, on, 232.
   of ward.
    terminates guardianship, 51, 88.
        and certain trustee's authority, 267.
    terminates lease, 140, 235.
    other effects of, 51, 88, 267.
   of trustee.
    effect of, 257.
   of party to suit.
    effect of, 287–8.

DEBTOR—
    must be sued when, if surety on a note requires it, 288.

DEBTS. See Debts; Settlement.
   of surety.
    questions as to, by judge, 33, 34.
   due ward.
    guardian can not release, 61 n., 86.
        but may compound, 64.
    bad, how to enter in account, why, 154, 159.
    should sometimes be reduced to judgment, 154, 155.
    trustee must collect, 266.
   of minor ward.
    property of, must be sold to pay, when, 95, 233.
    must be accounted for, 153, 154.
    to guardian, must be settled how, 162, 166 n.
   of insane, etc., ward.
    property of, must be sold to pay, when, how, etc., 233–235.

DECREE. See Judgment; Journal Entry.

DEMURRER. See Pleadings.

DECISIONS—
    of courts of other states, force and effect of, here, 51.
    principles derived from, stated, 73, 74, 73–90.
    concerning married women's rights, 298.

DEED—
    of ward's lands sold, ordered by court, 131.
    form of guardian's, 132.
    guardian must give, when, 235.
    must be given by sheriff, for land sold in partition, 192, 194.

 22

LETTERS OF GUARDIANSHIP. See GUARDIAN, *Appointment of.*
force and effect of, 17 n., 46 n.
how issued, etc., when more wards than one, 32.
    fees in such cases, 32.
issued before bond given, are void, 45 n.
if improperly issued, what to do, in certain case, 243.
certified copy of, must be sent to Washington, to enable guardian to
    collect interest on registered U. S. bonds, 293.

LIABILITY. See NEGLIGENCE; LOSS; DAMAGE; GUARDIAN.
of sureties. See SURETIES; BOND.
of guardian. See GUARDIAN.
of sheriff and his sureties, in partition proceedings, 193.
of guardian, parent, etc., as to apprenticed ward, 211.
of guardian, etc., as to traffic in intoxicating liquors, 221–225.
of guardian, as to militia fines of ware, 287.
of married woman as guardian, 230.

LICENSE—
must be obtained, in case of ward's marriage, 71.
damages for wrongful issuing of, 71 n.

LIENS—
on ward's real estate, paid how, if necessary, 95, 148.
must be described in petition for sale of ward's land, 98, 99.
must be paid out of proceeds of sale, 132.
may sometimes be paid by long lease 140.
as to adjusting, in proceedings to lease ward's real estate, 140.
tenant has, for improvements on ward's leased land, 143.
guardian has, for taxes paid on ward's property, 146.
tax title little better than, 148–9.
fines, etc., for sale of liquors on ward's premises, etc., are, on premises,
    224.
by drunkard on his land, invalid when, 251

LIBEL—
as to suits for, 287–8.

LINE—
of ward's real estate fixed by guardian, how, **286.**

LIQUORS. See INTOXICATING LIQUORS.

LITIGATION. See SUITS.
costs of, who must pay. See COSTS.

LISTING—
ward's property for taxation, 145–147.

LOSS. See NEGLIGENCE; DAMAGES; LIABILITY.
as to guardian's and trustee's liability for **76,** 74, 75, 60–61 n., **66 n.,**
    67 n., 74–76 n., 78.
LOTS, TOWN. See REAL ESTATE.
ward's land may be divided into, for sale, when, 98.
as to description of, in petition, 98 n.
guardian must pay taxes on ward's, 144, 145.
sold for taxes, may be redeemed, when, 148, 149.
land divided into what, in partition matters, 190.
corner or line of, may be fixed, how, 286.

23

NAMES—
of certain guardians must be reported by assessor, 248.

NEGLECT—
parent and guardian must protect bound minor from, 209.

NEGLIGENCE—
guardian liable for, when, 60–61 n., 66 n., 158 n., 178, 289.
who may sue for guardians, 178.

NEWSPAPER. See NOTICE.
notice must be published in, how long, etc., 107, 108, 125, 161, 181, 201, 256.
copies of, containing notice, must be mailed to defendants, 107.
affidavits as to publication in, 109, 129.
if none published in the county, what to do, 129.

NON-RESIDENT. See RESIDENCE; WARD; TRUSTEE.
minor land-owner, rights of, 17. 285.
rules for determining who is, 19.
can not be guardian, 23, 28, 29, 51.
nor sureties on his bond, 30.
may be served with notice by publication, 181, 107–110, 201.

NON-RESIDENT GUARDIAN, TRUSTEE, ETC. See FOREIGN GUARDIAN, TRUSTEE, ETC.

NOTARY PUBLIC—
may administer oaths required in probate matters, 10, 42.

NOTE—
for balance purchase money for ward's land, how received, 120.
to whom given, 134.
how accounted for by guardian, 152.
his liability on, in certain case, 67, 152 n.
sureties on, may require creditor to do what, 288.
sureties on, how released, etc., 288–9.
guardian's duty, etc., as to this, 289.

NOTICE—
of proposed removal of guardian, must be given him, 53, 54.
forms of, 55, 56.
of proposed selection of guardian by ward, 58.
of petition to sell ward's land, must be given, how, 102, 104, 105,
how served, 102 n., 102–5, 106.
if record shows that "due notice" was served, effect of, 103 n.
want of, makes sale void, 103 n.
but merely defective notice will not, 103 n.
how must be served upon minors. 104, 105.
how served, generally, in probate court, when law is silent, 105.
form of journal entry as to, 105.
form of notice, 106, of return to, 106.
form of affidavit as to service of, 107.
service of, by publication, 107–110, 181, 184.
affidavit to authorize service of, by publication, 107, 108.
of sale of ward's land, 125.
proof of publication of, as to sale of ward's lands, 128, 129.

REAL ESTATE—*Continued*.
    proceeds from sale of, how accounted for, 153.
    how rights of adverse claimants to, decided, etc., 196–199.
    widow's dower in, how assigned,

   sale of. See SALE.
    when guardian or trustee may sell, how and why, 66, 95–97, 233–235, 267.
    petition for, must contain what, 97–99.
       form of petition, 99–102.
    may be sold free of insane woman's dower, when, 245.
    wife of insane man may sell her own, when and how, 246.
    for support of lunatic or idiot owner, 247.
    conveyance or encumbrance of, by drunkard, invalid when, 251.
    sold for taxes, redeemable when, 148, 149, 197.
    management of, by trustee, 264, 267.
    appeal from sale of, may be had, 280.
    boundaries of ward's, how fixed by guardian, 286.
    how may be appropriated for public use, 201–4, 286–7.

   dower in. See DOWER.

   lease of. See LEASE.

   taxes on. See TAXES.

   partition of. See PARTITION.
    what is subject to, 188.
    contracts as to, by ward's ancestor, rights under, etc., 226–228.

RECEIPT—
    guardian should take, from ward, when, 163, 165.
    effect of, in such cases, 163, 164 n., 166 n.
    "in full of all demands," from ward to guardian, not conclusive, **164 n.**
    for payments made in partition matters, 193.
    concerning estate of lunatic, idiot, etc., deemed void, when, 231.

RECORD—
    final must be kept by probate court, and how, 10.
    of accounts must be kept by probate court, and how, 11.
    of bonds, do., 11.
    effect of recitals in, 22.
    of mortgage security must be made, 31.
    authenticated copy of, required when, 52.
    showing that due notice was served, effect of, 103 n.
    of indenture of child's apprenticeship, must be made, 209.
       failure to, releases child, 209.
    of guardian *ad litem's* acceptance should be made, 273.

REDEMPTION—
    of land sold for taxes, etc., 147–149.

REFORM SCHOOL—
    ward may be sent to, when, 214.

REGISTERED GOVERNMENT BONDS—
    how interest of ward's collected, 292–5.

RELATIVE—
    should be appointed guardian, when, 24 n., **30.**
    wishes of, as to ward, when to be consulted, **90 n.**
    24